Many tales have been told of Krynn. Tales of warfare and ambition, darkness and light, and magic and danger. But these tales are only half of the world's story. For Ansalon, the land of Solamnic Knights and Dragon Highlords, draconians, kender, and gully dwarves, is but one part of Krynn, one small continent on a much larger planet.

There are other lands besides Ansalon.

A place known only in legend and rumor, Taladas boasts its own unique geography, history, and culture. It lies on the far side of Krynn, thousands of leagues from Ansalon's shores. Here warlike barbarians ride over endless plains, armies of men and minotaurs battle the hordes of the undead, and elves who lost their homes long ago fight to keep their new holdings safe.

Here an ancient evil, slumbering for centuries, has begun to stir again.

Legend and rumor . . . until now.

Presenting the first Dragonlance tale to be told in Taladas, written by Chris Pierson, the author of previous best-selling novels set in the fantasy world of Krynn, including Spirit of the Wind, Dezra's Quest, and, most recently, the Kingpriest Trilogy.

TALADAS TRILOGY

Novels by Chris Pierson

Bridges of Time series
Spirit of the Wind
Dezra's Quest

Kingpriest Trilogy
Chosen of the Gods
Divine Hammer
Sacred Fire

The Taladas Chronicles
Blades of the Tiger

DRAGONLANCE

BLADES OF THE TIGER

TALADAS TRILOGY

VOLUME ONE

CHRIS PIERSON

BLADES OF THE TIGER

©2005 Wizards of the Coast, Inc.

All characters in this book are fictitious. Any resemblance to actual persons, living or dead, is purely coincidental.

This book is protected under the copyright laws of the United States of America. Any reproduction or unauthorized use of the material or artwork contained herein is prohibited without the express written permission of Wizards of the Coast, Inc.

Distributed in the United States by Holtzbrinck Publishing. Distributed in Canada by Fenn Ltd.

Distributed to the hobby, toy, and comic trade in the United States and Canada by regional distributors.

Distributed worldwide by Wizards of the Coast, Inc. and regional distributors.

DRAGONLANCE, WIZARDS OF THE COAST, and their respective logos are trademarks of Wizards of the Coast, Inc., in the U.S.A. and other countries.

All Wizards of the Coast characters, character names, and the distinctive likenesses thereof are property of Wizards of the Coast, Inc.

Printed in the U.S.A.

The sale of this book without its cover has not been authorized by the publisher. If you purchased this book without a cover, you should be aware that neither the author nor the publisher has received payment for this "stripped book."

Cover art by Matt Stawicki
Map by Dennis Kauth
First Printing: April 2005
Library of Congress Catalog Card Number: 2004098086

9 8 7 6 5 4 3 2 1

ISBN-10: 0-7869-3569-3
ISBN-13: 978-0-7869-3569-7
620-17626-001-EN

U.S., CANADA,	EUROPEAN HEADQUARTERS
ASIA, PACIFIC, & LATIN AMERICA	Wizards of the Coast, Belgium
Wizards of the Coast, Inc.	T Hofveld 6d
P.O. Box 707	1702 Groot-Bijgaarden
Renton, WA 98057-0707	Belgium
+1-800-324-6496	+322 467 3360

Visit our web site at www.wizards.com

For Rebekah. Yay!

The Continent of Taladas

Prologue

From the Archives of Nightlund, Volume XIX
Penned by the Red Robe Pelander

My dreams grow more vivid every night. I wake cold and damp with sweat while darkness still rules the sky and the moons ride high. The moons sing to me while I sleep, for they have seen much in their new time looking down upon Krynn. They know this world better than any man, elf or dragon could. They see all.

There has been talk, particularly in the glory days at the ends of the Third and Fourth Ages, of lands beyond this continent of Ansalon—lands that know not of Solamnic Knights, nor Highlords, nor the War of Souls. Lands of fire and death, of bloodthirsty barbarians and shattered ruins. Lands where man, elf, dwarf, and minotaur have forged empires that no one on Ansalon has seen with his own eyes.

Scholars have long debated the existence of such places, most vigorously when my mentor, Bezok of Austas, proclaimed not only that such lands existed but that, with good enough ships and brave enough men, an expedition could actually *reach* them. I regret that the Second Cataclysm and the subsequent (and thankfully temporary) loss of magic in the world stopped the fulfillment of his ambition—just as the First Cataclysm aborted the ambitions of those explorers who hoped to set forth for lands far from poor, doomed Istar. Since Bezok's unfortunate disappearance some seventeen winters ago, talk of these far lands has been silenced.

Let the silence now end. For I now share Bezok's dream. I have seen the far lands, borne to me upon the song of the moons. I have seen the shores on Krynn's far side, where all is different and lore and language are strange. I have walked among its people, invisible, and seen their troubles and trials. And this is no mere phantasm as many—within my Order and without—will be wont to claim. For the land is much changed since Bezok first wrote of it, and changes still.

I speak, and dream, of Taladas.

The tale that follows is of this land, but before we begin, you should know something of the place and its people. For while it is much the same as Ansalon, it is also as different as the red moon from the silver. Or the black.

Consider Krynn—an orb of blue, a sapphire globe, set upon black velvet. See Ansalon, resting upon its southern half. Now take it in your hand and turn, turn, until the lands you know face away. See the markings of green and brown—and burning red—in the north? This is Taladas. Here, just as Istar once ruled over Ansalon, a great empire once held the continent in its grip. Its name was Aurim, a realm of great sorcery ruled by emperor-mages, not all of them kind. But like Istar, Aurim is no more. Its glory ended on the same day—or rather, night, as it was on the world's far side when the First Cataclysm struck. This the folk of Taladas call the Great Destruction, and it did even worse to their lands than the burning mountain did to ours. They have names for many things that seem strange. The moons are Solis, Lunis, Nuvis; the Age of Mortals is known as the Godless Night; and the Summer of Chaos is called the Dread Winter. Even the gods themselves go by different names, their aspects hidden by forms alien to us.

In the Great Destruction, a great hail of fire fell upon

BLADES OF THE TIGER

Aurim, smashing the empire and splitting the earth itself wide open. Rather than sinking beneath the sea, the Old Empire was swallowed by molten rock from below in a great cauldron of flame more than a hundred leagues across. The heat of this fire burned the lands around it to ash and shining glass, and spewed poisonous steam that killed men and dragons alike by the thousands.

Yet some endured. On the far-flung Rainward Isles, refugees of the Destruction built new kingdoms away from the ruins of Aurim. In the southern jungles of Neron and the northern snow-fields of Panak, tribes of savages dwell side by side with unspeakable creatures, the names of which I do not know: tentacled horrors and dead but still moving monsters the likes of which I know only from nightmare. Tinker-gnomes—the scourge that no part of Krynn seems able to escape—ply the Burning Sea in ships of steel and dwell on its shores beneath great columns of black stone.

The tale I must tell may visit these places before it is done, but it does not begin there. It starts in the great realms of Hosk, home to the nations on Taladas' more peaceable western shores. Here, in the south of Hosk, is Thenol: a dark kingdom ruled by priests of fell gods. Here they raise the dead to serve them and to fight their wars. Such a war is ending, even now, in defeat for the Thenolites. Their great temple burns, their mad bishop lies slain, and the conquering armies are marching back north, following grim tidings home.

These armies are of men and minotaurs, fighting side by side for the glory of the Imperial League. The only true empire Taladas has known since the death of Aurim, the Imperial League has covered all the inhabitable parts of Southern Hosk, save for battered, bleeding Thenol and the forbidden woods of Armach, where the elves dwell. Ruled by minotaurs, the League has even spread its influence into the savage lands to the north, across the dangerous Tiderun Strait. But something terrible has now stricken this empire's heart, and the coming months may bring civil war.

Look now across the Tiderun, to the plains known as the Tamire—seas of grassland and steppe, where tribes of men and elves ride wild for league upon league, and where barbarians follow herds of goat and antelope with the changing of the seasons. Here live many peoples, but none so strong as the Uigan, a nation of many horse-riding clans under a great prince, a Boyla, who leads them in war against their rival tribes. The man who rules them now is called Krogan, and he is old and wise, but his reign will soon fail. Winds are blowing upon the grasslands and they, too, speak of war.

I can wait no longer. Already, my dreams begin to fade. I must set them down on this paper, lest they vanish from my mind forever. And that would be a terrible thing—for Taladas has few histories of its own and much that has happened has been lost to the ages already.

This tale begins in the League, at night, in a quiet village known as Blood Eye. A ship now stands in her harbor. . . .

Chapter 1

BLOOD EYE, THE IMPERIAL LEAGUE

The town of Blood Eye lived off of the sea. Spread out around the rim of a broad inlet with a wall of high cliffs behind it that provided shelter from storm and surf, it consisted of little more than a harbor with seemingly endless docks, storehouses, smoke rooms, and taverns. Indeed, nearly half its people didn't even dwell on land, living instead on the boats whose forest of masts bobbed and rocked with the ceaseless waves. The Eye-folk were fishers, hauling in fat nets of tuna, salmon, and speartooth off the banks just beyond the coast. Every morning as dawn gathered behind the bluffs, the wharf blossomed with colorful sails as the ships set out. Every afternoon, the marketplaces thrived. There were treasures to be found among the day's catch: blue lobsters and spike-shell crabs, scallops and giant oysters, shark fins and—on lucky days—gigantic, sweet-fleshed dragon turtles.

At night, Blood Eye slept. Not long after sunset, the markets emptied and all the harbor turned dark—even the rowdy ale-houses snuffed their lamps and shut their spigots soon after dusk: early risers caught the most fish, after all. The only sign of life after darkness fell came from the tower above, which gave the town its name.

It was a high spire of dark stone, with sheer sides

and a crown of spikes atop it, and in the midst of the slender spire glowed a fire of unnatural, crimson flame. A wide wall surrounded the spire, penning in lush gardens of plants unknown to that part of the world. The plants were brought from all over Taladas: the jungles of Neron, the Ghostwood far to the north, and the Black Forest beyond the Burning Sea. Strange night-birds called from among the trees, and now and then a fearsome growl cut through the night. Though they were grateful for Blood Eye Tower—its eldritch fire made a fine lighthouse—the Eye-folk did not go up there. Even the brashest young men refused to enter its grounds. Though few had ever seen him, all knew it to be the home of Ruskal Eight-Fingers. And all knew Ruskal did not like to be disturbed.

The bells atop the town's main temple had just tolled the midnight watch when a shadow appeared at the rail of the *Horn of Silver* and gazed up at the spire high above. A galley that had put into port just yesterday evening, the *Horn* had come down from the capital of Kristophan, half-a-hundred leagues up the coast, carrying slave oarsmen and bolts of sailcloth—both precious goods for the Eye-folk shipowners. It would move on again two days hence, its hold filled with smoked fish and pearls—delicacies and riches for the minotaurs who ruled the League. Unbeknownst to its captain and crew, however, the *Horn* had carried something else on its voyage, and with a glance at the cloud-scattered sky, that something slipped over the side of the ship and arrowed down into the sea, striking the water with neither splash nor sound.

A short while later, Shedara of Thelis climbed, still shadow-silent, up over the edge of the town's boardwalk and pressed herself flat against the nearest cover. It was a statue of a huge, fierce minotaur, a bull-headed giant holding a barbed trident. It could have been an emperor, a hero, or one of the bull-men's gods—Shedara wasn't sure. Nor did she much care. One minotaur was as good as another in her eyes. Or as bad.

Shedara had spent half her life in the shadows, it seemed, keeping out of sight of the minotaurs and the humans they ruled—like the people of Blood Eye. Had she ventured out in the open, she would have stuck out like a rose in a dungheap: her almond eyes, delicate features, and sharp-pointed ears were impossible to disguise. While elves were not wholly unwelcome in the League, they did not go unnoticed.

And being noticed was the last thing a moon-thief wanted.

She had boarded the *Horn* a week ago in secret, while it sat at anchor in Kristophan. Since then she'd concealed herself in its holds. It was not the first time she'd gone to such lengths for a job, and she was being paid well enough to make it worthwhile. She didn't know what her task was yet, only that it was to take place here. Her orders were sealed. She would read them only when she arrived at the job. That was how she worked, and her discretion had made her a favorite among her people when they had need of such talents as she possessed.

Carefully, Shedara checked her gear. She wore a simple, dark-brown suit of sharkskin, both form-fitting and waterproof, and her short, copper-hued hair was hidden beneath a cap of the same. Her gloves and boots were oiled leather, and her face was stained dark with nightberry juice. Over her shoulders was slung a bundle of oiled canvas. After satisfying herself that it was still secure, she leaned out from the statue and glanced around.

She stood at the edge of a plaza. From the stink of the place, they sold shellfish there during the day. The cobbles were mostly clean, but here and there glowflies buzzed around heaps of offal. A rat near one pile eyed her for a moment, then returned to its meal. A few street-lamps still glimmered, but of the guardsmen who kept them lit there was no sign. Nor were there any lights in the shops and houses that loomed, close packed, around the plaza—the only light was high above, atop the tower.

All clear.

First, she had to find better cover. Her careful eye spotted something at once: an alley about twenty paces away. She would be out in the open for a few heartbeats, but there was no one around to see her, and it was plenty dark even if there were. With a deep breath, she tensed to run . . .

Then stopped, swallowing a curse. She flattened herself against the statue's plinth once more. The clouds had shifted—the moons were out.

It wasn't as bright as it might be. Solis, the silver moon, was only half-full and waning, while Lunis, its crimson sister, was waxing gibbous. A rosy glow washed over Blood Eye, making the cobbles and whitewashed buildings glisten. Shedara crouched lower, glaring at the sky. This sort of thing had been easier a few years ago, during the Godless Night. Then, there had only been one moon in the sky, a pale mockery of these, Krynn's real moons. That lone moon had reigned supreme for more than thirty years following the gods' disappearance, after the Second Destruction. It had been a good time to be a thief, those years. Even when that moon was full, it was pale.

However, the gods had come back to Taladas, and with them came Solis and Lunis—as well as Nuvis, their black cousin whom only astronomers and wizards tracked. That made Shedara's life more complicated.

She couldn't resent the moons entirely, however. No moon-thief could. Their return was as much blessing for her as curse. Moon-thieves were magic-users, and her power came mostly from Lunis, though she drew from all three. She could feel the red moon burning in her now as she glanced up at its staring eye. For the whole of the Godless Night she had been deprived of that power, as had all true mages. Now, though, it was strong as ever. In many ways, that made up for the inconvenience.

BLADES OF THE TIGER

The clouds moved on and the glow dimmed as they devoured first Solis, then Lunis. The wind was blowing hard off the sea, smelling of salt. In the distance, lightning flared—too far off for thunder. The storm would not make landfall for hours. Still, it thickened the gloom, which was welcome. With any luck, there would be no more holes in the clouds for the moons to peer through. Taking another breath, Shedara darted for the alley.

Only the rat, still feasting, saw her run.

There were more vermin in the alley, both rodents and large scuttling beetles with glowing spots on their backs. They scattered before her, and she kicked a pile of garbage to make sure there wasn't a drunk sleeping under it. Alone, she unslung the canvas bundle and opened it on the ground. It held her supplies, kept dry for the swim from the *Horn*. She took them, one by one, and secured them on her person. A pair of flat throwing knives, strapped to each forearm. Two fighting daggers, on her hips. A set of thirty different lockpicks of all shapes and sizes, tucked into a sleeve on her left boot. A bag of spell components, in her right. And last, a leather scroll-tube, which she opened and shook out.

Two sheets of papyrus emerged. She selected the first, which was a map of the town, and quickly found her location. A moment later, she picked out the best route to her target. The tower, of course—she hadn't known till now, but she'd been reasonably certain. She hadn't come here to steal haddock.

It wasn't far to go, so she put the map away again and peered at the second page. It was a message, in Elvish, written in precise, elegant script.

You will enter the tower of Ruskal Eight-Fingers. His home is said to be well-guarded, and possibly trapped as well. We know little more than that. Within, he keeps a collection of fine artworks from all parts of Taladas. Our agents report that one of these is a portrait of Silvanos, First Speaker of the old kingdom. If this is true, it does not belong to him, but to our people. Acquire it and return it to us.

All methods are at your disposal. Blood shall be forgiven.

Beneath was a simple seal: the Elvish rune for *th*, ringed with seven-pointed stars, and stamped in green wax. Shedara's eyebrows rose as she studied it. This was the royal seal of Armach. Princess Thalaniya, the Voice of the Stars, had sent her on this mission. She hadn't known that.

So, she thought. *The reward's bound to be good.*

Carefully, she pulled out one last object from the bundle: a small, stone flask. Unstopping it, she poured its contents over the papyrus. It held wine, which dissolved the fragile pages in an instant. No matter what happened, there would be no evidence. There never was.

Shedara dropped the sodden mass that had been the map and her orders, then raised the flask to her lips. There was wine enough left for one swallow. Smiling, she tossed the bottle, the canvas, and the scroll-case onto the garbage heap and started down the alley.

Tonight was going to be interesting.

Ruskal woke with a start, sitting up in his silk-heaped bed. This was nothing strange. He seldom slept through any night. He was old, and a veteran of both the gladiatorial fights of the Imperial Arena and the wars of the legions. Forty years with a sword in his hand had earned him a fortune to retire on and a personal legend that would endure well beyond his death. It had also earned him many scars, which ached more and more as the years went on. This time it was an old arrow-wound in his thigh that had woken him, burning as if the offending shaft were still lodged there. He groaned, rubbing the aching limb, but the throbbing got no better. He would not sleep again that night.

His bedchamber was dark. The wind had blown out the candles by his bedside. With another groan, the old man heaved himself to his feet, relit a half-melted taper, and walked to the balcony overlooking the town below. Blood Eye Tower stood at the top of the cliffs on a pinnacle that could only be reached by a long, winding road. A tall wall of black marble ringed the gardens. Several white tylors—small, wingless dragons brought from the snowfields of Panak—prowled the gardens, guarding against intruders. He watched one stalk out of the wooded garden into a clearing, pause briefly by a fountain, then slip away again among the trees. All seemed still, save for a storm flashing over the sea, many miles away.

Ruskal sighed, shaking his head. Emperor Ambeoutin himself had granted him this fief, as a reward for long and loyal service. But after only two years' retirement, the old warrior had grown bored and restless. Blood Eye was too quiet for one bred to battle, particularly one who had neither married nor sired any children. Not for the first time, Ruskal wished he hadn't lived so long. Better to die with a sword in one's hand, he thought ruefully, than forgotten and alone in a bewitched tower. He glanced up at the red flame blazing high above. The fire, like the tower, was a remnant of ancient empires long since vanished from the world. Not even the wisest sages in the League knew why it burned.

Wine, he thought. I must have wine.

He was just about to turn and leave the balcony when something caught his eye. He held his breath, leaning forward to see. For an instant, he'd been sure he'd seen a shadow move, down in the garden. One of the tylors? No, it hadn't looked right—not dragonlike.

It had been mannish.

Old instincts took over. The last vestiges of sleep left him and his ears twitched, straining to pick up sounds. A less battle-honed man might have put the shadow aside as a trick of the eye, but Ruskal knew better. Someone was down there, and while his home was well-defended—besides the tylors he had a minotaur bodyguard, Kesh, who stayed on the lower floor at night—he felt the old thrill all the same. His senses told him blood would be spilled that night. Ruskal Eight-Fingers wanted to be the one to spill it.

He'd kept his old sword, which hung above his bedchamber's vast hearth, oiled and sharp. A hand-and-a-half blade, which most people found funny since he was missing two fingers on his left hand. He didn't see the humor. He pulled it down and hefted it, grunting. It seemed heavier than he remembered, but he could still lift it all right. At sixty-three summers, he wasn't so far past his prime. Not yet. Sweeping his thinning gray hair out of his eyes, he strode to the door and pushed it open.

Ruskal's home was a museum of sorts. Late in life, he'd taken a keen interest in art and had used much of his fortune to purchase objects of beauty from across Taladas. Everywhere one looked, there was something precious—tapestries from Old Styrllia, stone-paintings of the Fianawar dwarves, glass sculptures from the Shining Lands, broken idols from the ruins of Old Aurim. Striding past these, he made his way down the rich-carpeted hall to the grand staircase. The steps led down into the manor's great, central gallery, where paintings and statues and ancient clay urns stood tastefully arranged.

At the foot of the stair was a crystal lamp—an oddity made by the Pillar Gnomes, lit not by flame but by a metal wire, heated until it glowed white. It cast the only pool of light in the room. Ruskal crept toward it, sword held ready behind him. His heart pounded, blood roaring in his ears—the old war-lust, not forgotten. He moved in silence despite his bulk—he had always been muscular, and though the quiet life had turned some of his brawn to fat, he was still an imposing figure. He strained to see past the lamplight into the gloom of the gallery. He'd had rivals in the imperial courts, even a few enemies. But would any of them have sent assassins for him now, after so long? Why would they bother?

He was six steps from the bottom of the stairs when a figure stepped suddenly into view. Ruskal gasped, bringing his great, notched blade around to defend himself—then stopped, seeing who stood there.

"Damn it, Kesh!" he swore. "I might have gutted you like a deer!"

Kesh Ak-Chorr was an old friend, a minotaur slave who had served Ruskal faithfully since his days in the imperial legions. He was one of the most fearless fighters Ruskal had ever known, and had once waded into battle alone against thirty Thenoli Death Warriors, emerging from the fight missing a horn and half his ear, but otherwise intact. Anyone who wished harm upon Ruskal would have to climb over Kesh's corpse to do it. He waved Ruskal back, baring a muzzle full of pointed teeth. In his hand was a huge, iron cudgel that had crushed hundreds of skulls in its day.

"Return to your chambers, sir," he bade, his voice low and growling. "It is not safe."

Ruskal hefted his sword. "I know that."

Kesh scowled, but said nothing more. He knew better.

"Where are they?" Ruskal whispered. "How many?"

"I don't know," Kesh replied, turning back to peer into the dark. "I only saw—"

He stopped, stiffening. The mace fell from his hands, which went to his throat. He made a low, gargling sound.

"Kesh?" Ruskal asked, his voice rising.

The minotaur did not reply. He was already dead as he crumpled to the floor, a slender blade lodged in his throat. No blood poured from the wound—some part of Ruskal noted that, found it odd.

"*Khot!*" Ruskal swore in the minotaur tongue. Any moment, he expected another knife to flash out of the dark. He edged back from the lamp's glare. "Who is there?"

No answer came. Ruskal felt the sting of fear, but fought it back as he'd always done in battle. His foe was out there, somewhere, and had the advantage. The enemy must be cunning to have stolen past the tylors in the garden—and to fell one like Kesh with a single, unseen throw of a dagger. The injustice of how easily his admirable slave had died gnawed at Ruskal.

He was in deep trouble. His only hope was to draw the enemy out, engage him hand to hand.

"Show yourself, cowards!" he bellowed. "Come taste steel!"

A crash behind him made him jump. Flattening himself against a wooden baluster, he turned to look back up the stairs. From the sound, someone had knocked over one of his glassworks, sending it shattering on the floor. Was there one upstairs? How many intruders were in his home? He turned to glance back at the gallery—

—and gave a startled yell. A dark figure was bolting up the stairs at him, a blade in each hand. Wildly, he swung his sword, but the shadow twisted away and the stroke found only air before slamming into the wall. Splinters flew.

Ruskal had no time for a second swing. His attacker was on him, blades flashing. One pierced his wrist, sliding painfully between the bones and making his sword hand go instantly numb. The blade clattered to the floor as the dark-clothed figure's second knife drove into his thigh— right where the arrow had pierced him, long ago.

Again, he noticed there was no blood. But there *was* pain. With a howl, Ruskal fell.

※————※————※

Shedara was not quite to the top of the cliff when she heard the shout. She froze, her mouth dry, clinging to the sheer stone face like a spider. Magic bound her to the rock, a simple spell that let her climb without rope. She shifted her weight, glancing up above her. The noise had come from the tower: a bellow of pain, perhaps a death cry. No mistake about that. She had heard the sound many times, sometimes on the end of her own knife.

What had just happened up there?

She waited a precious minute, hearing nothing else. Whatever was going on, she still had work to do. Princess Thalaniya would get her painting. Shedara had never abandoned a job before, and she wasn't about to start with a royal mission.

She felt the magic pulse in her veins and knew the magic would only last so long. She had to move, so up she went, pressing her hands and feet against the rock. As she made progress, she rehearsed the other spells she had studied: incantations for deadening noise, sensing the presence of enchanted traps, opening doors with a word, and paralyzing whomever she touched—standard moon-thief fare. She probably wouldn't need them all, but they were a comfort nonetheless. During the Godless Night, when magic was stilled, she hadn't had any of them. That had been hard.

The cliff ran out, giving way to the garden's encircling wall. The climbing-spell worked just as well on cut stone as on rough. As she neared the top of the wall, she readied another spell, one that sent forth a beam of silver light that would stun anyone it touched. A handy one for unexpected guards.

The top of the wall sharpened to a razor point. She avoided touching it, carefully climbing over, then dropping down into the garden below. She landed in a crouch and stared around, one hand on a dagger. The garden was watched, according to all she'd heard, though what watched it varied from tale to tale. Whatever it was, Shedara preferred not to meet it. She could hold her own in most fights, but *not* fighting was always the best option.

There was no sound but the creak of branches in the wind. She was in a grove of Neroni snakeboughs, their scale-barked limbs slowly writhing and twisting, making a tangle of the shadows. Keeping low, she crept through the copse toward the tower. It was only thirty paces away, its marble walls dim in the starless gloom. Halfway there, the trees ended in a broad, green sward, cut in two by a path of crushed white stone. On the path crouched a shadow.

Being an elf, Shedara could see in the dark. Her elvensight did not make out the details, but could tell a hot body from cool stone. The thing on the path was still slightly warm, but grew cooler by the moment. Dead, then.

Biting her lip, she moved to the edge of the copse and eyed the dead thing warily. It was a long, serpentine shape armored in milky scales—like a dragon, but not quite. She shrugged. Some of the tales had named Ruskal's guardians as tylors.

One glance confirmed it no longer breathed. A long wound gaped in its underside, from chin to bowels. Something had cut the beast open, as precise as a butcher, yet there was no blood. Not a drop, on wound or ground, when there should have been great pools. Shedara guessed it wasn't the only one of the tower's guardians to be lying dead in the gardens. Whoever had killed the tylor would not have left its mates alive.

What in the Abyss was going on?

There were two doors into the tower: the great entrance at the front, and a smaller door in the rear. Both were shut. Shedara ignored them both, searched for a window, and climbed up to it, the spider-spell still lingering. An iron grate protected the window, but another word of magic turned the iron to rust, which flaked away to nothing when she rapped her dagger on it. Clenching the blade between her teeth, she hoisted herself up over the sill and into the room beyond.

It was a small chamber—some sort of study from what little she could see. Scanning the floor for tripwires and oddly shaped tiles—sure signs of a trap—she stole to the door and pushed it open a crack, then caught her breath. Beyond was a huge hall, mounted with a bewildering array of artwork. It had to be worth a dozen fortunes in all. Looking around, she knew the painting she sought had to be somewhere on those walls. She just had to be patient, and careful, and. . . .

She stopped, swallowing. Something warm was moving across the floor.

It took her a moment to make it out, but once it crawled closer she noted its human shape and knew it must be Ruskal. He was trying to rise, his breath coming in wheezing gasps.

Sweet Lunis, Shedara thought. Every bit of common sense told her to leave him be, to wait until he died—from the look of him, it wouldn't take long—then to go about her business, keeping an eye open for whoever had murdered him. Some deeper intuition, however, told her otherwise. Carefully, she eased the door open, slipped through, and made her way across the gallery to where he was flopping around, still fighting to get up.

His eyes widened when he saw her coming, and he tried to crawl away, but his strength failed him. By the time Shedara reached the dying man's side, all he could do was lie still, clutching a horrid gash across his stomach. Looking down at him, she could see entrails bulging through his flesh. There were other wounds too, all over his body. Someone had carved Ruskal One-Eye like a venison haunch. But nowhere on his body was there any blood.

He looked up at her blearily, his eyes rolling white. "Kesh? My . . . friend?" he hissed. "Is that you?"

He thinks I'm someone else, Shedara thought. I should just put a knife in his heart and end his suffering. But she couldn't yet. She needed to know what had happened here.

"Who did this?" she asked. "Who did this to you, Ruskal?"

He shrugged, wincing at the pain. "Never saw . . . his

face. His servants . . . cut me, but he . . . stayed in the shadows. Only asked. . . ." He stopped, coughing. Foam frothed on his lips.

"Asked for what?" Shedara pressed.

"Hoo—" Ruskal began, then stopped to draw a ragged breath. "H-Hooded One. But he's . . . not here any more, is he Kesh?" He choked a laugh, which became a groan. "No, I sent him away."

Shedara's brow furrowed. The Hooded One? She had no idea what—who?—this poor dying fool was talking about. "Sent him where?"

"Oh, no," Ruskal breathed, and shook his head. "Won't tell . . . not even you, my . . . friend. He is safe. From . . . *him*."

He was almost gone, already growing cold.

"K-Kesh?" he whispered, afraid.

"What is it, my friend?" she asked softly.

"My . . . sword," he replied. "Will you . . . bring. . . ."

"Where?" she asked.

He pointed behind him. There were stairs back there. At their feet lay a broken lamp, next to the cold corpse of a minotaur. Kesh, she thought as she glanced at the corpse—then her gaze drifted up the steps. A heavy sword lay on one of the steps, as though forgotten. She went to it, picked it up, and cradled it in her arms as she carried it back to Ruskal.

His eyes flickered, and he managed a ghastly smile. He tried to raise a hand, but no longer had the strength, so Shedara bent down, placed the hilt in his hand, and gently closed his fingers.

"Thank. . . ." he breathed, and it was done.

Shedara stood over the body, frowning. True, she herself would have killed this man had he tried to stop her from taking the painting—but someone had killed him in grotesque fashion just before her arrival—then immediately left the premises. Why? And who was the Hooded One?

A moment later, she came back to her senses. She was in the home of a murdered man who had made a terrible outcry when he was struck down. How long before guardsmen came to investigate? She had a job to finish, fast.

Chapter 2

HILL OF LOST VOICES, THE TAMIRE

A lone hawk circled high above the plains, riding the dawn breeze as it searched for prey. The Tamire grasslands made for rich hunting, and before long the hawk dived, tucking in its wings and flashing downward like a spear. There was a soft squeal, then the bird was flapping up again, the limp form of a young hare clasped in its beak. It wheeled once and soared away toward a thicket of ash trees.

"A good omen," said Chovuk Tegin, shading his eyes against the light. The sun was just cresting the eastern horizon, bloodying the distant Ilquar Mountains behind him. "May our own hunt go as well as Mother Hawk's, *tenach*."

Standing just downhill of Chovuk—who, as chief of his tribe, deserved the higher ground—Hult, son of Holar, nodded. He had learned early in life that it was best not to speak unless there was something to say. That was one of the first lessons a boy of the Uigan people learned, even before he mounted his first horse. Standing with the Tegin, he stared across the plains until the bird was out of sight.

Chovuk and Hult looked enough alike to be brothers. Both were tall for their people, with the lean, stone-hard frames of men who spend much of their waking lives in the saddle. Yet Chovuk was approaching old age, already past forty, while Hult, at nineteen, had only become a man five summers ago. Still, their brown faces were both weathered, and they sported identical thin, black beards, untouched by gray. They shaved their heads in the manner of their people, leaving only one long braid to hang down their backs, and both sported blue tattoos on their cheeks, markings that identified them as members of the White Sky clan. Only in their clothing did they differ especially. Chovuk's leather vest was dyed crimson, the bright color denoting his rank, while Hult's was plain brown. The chief wore bracers of steel, plundered by his ancestors long ago, while the younger man's were hammered bronze. Both sported the same necklace, however: strings of white scales, talons, and fangs, taken from the bodies of dragons they had slain as part of their initiation into adulthood. Chovuk toyed with his, turning a claw between his fingers as he gazed across the plains.

In truth, they were not even kin—at least, not by blood. Hult was *tenach* to Chovuk, an honored position for one so young. In the Uigan tongue, the word meant many things: protector, enforcer, and friend. Hult had sworn an oath, more than a year ago, to serve the Tegin with every drop of his blood, even if it meant his own death. A *tenach* did not question; a *tenach* only acted. In return, he shared the chief's yurt, and second choice of everything else—meat, loot, horses—after Chovuk himself. Everything except women, for the *tenach* did not marry, nor take anyone to his bed. That was hard, but it was a good life, even if for most *tenachai* it was a short one as well.

"The Boyla comes," said Chovuk, laying a hand on the hilt of his *shuk*, the long, curved saber favored by the Uigan. "He rides with the wind, down from the north. Go, *tenach*. Climb, and keep watch."

He pointed to his left, where wind and rain had

stripped the soil from the hill's crown. There was an outcropping of ruddy stone, carved by time and the hands of men to resemble an inhuman face: a long, gaunt-cheeked visage with empty eyes and a mouth that gaped wide and deep into the rock, a ghastly rendering of a scream. There were seven of these things carved into the flanks of the Hill of Lost Voices, by whom and for what purpose not even the old ones could say. When the wind blew into those hideously yawning maws, it made a sort of music—a low, mournful keening that Uigan tradition claimed were the cries of those who had been betrayed unto death. Hult tried not to shudder at the thought.

"I will be at camp," Chovuk said. "Call when you see his horses."

Hult bowed, pressing the knuckles of his right hand to his lips. "As you bid, Tegin," he said, then walked up the slope.

It was thirty steps from the base of the stone face to the top. Hult climbed with ease, his callused fingers skilled at finding cracks and ridges. The elders had named him *Jasho*—"Monkey"—when he was a boy, for he had always loved to climb. That name was gone now that he was an adult, but he still enjoyed the thrill of pulling himself up trees or cliffs with nothing but air beneath.

The wind was strong up high, whipping grit into his eyes. It was cold still, for this was only the first day of spring. The grass of the Tamire, stretching out for miles upon miles all around him, was ghost-pale from winter's frost, with patches of green where the streams ran. The hill—the White Sky's wintering ground—was the highest ground between here and the Ilquar peaks to the west, three days' ride away. There was no better vantage from which to watch for their guest's approach.

A thrill ran through Hult at the thought that Krogan Boyla would soon be there. He had never seen the man, who ruled all the tribes of the Uigan people, but he had heard many tales. Krogan had fought in the great battles of the Godless Night, when the elven clans had come down from the north to make war on men. Legend had it he'd slain a hundred of the vile creatures in one terrible day, and that the elves had retreated, greatly terrified. That had been thirty years ago, when Hult's own father (dead before Hult's birth and dwelling in the halls of the god Jijin with his ancestors) was but a boy, but the old ones still spoke of it like it were yesterday. That Krogan still lived, let alone ruled, was a testament to both his ferocity and the love of his people.

By tradition, the Boyla visited a different tribe every spring to lead the First Hunt. There were many tribes on the Tamire, however, and it had been nearly a century since a Boyla had hunted beneath the banners of White Sky. Though his face remained calm and blank, as a warrior's must, inside, Hult rejoiced that he would soon ride out with the legendary Krogan, bending his bow alongside the lord of the plains.

He glanced back the way he'd come. Chovuk was already gone, descending to the cluster of skin yurts that were his people's home during the fallow months. Ringed by a fence of pointed stakes, fire-hardened to ward off enemy riders, the village of Undermouth huddled about a pool at the foot of a waterfall, fed by a spring within the hill's rock. Fires smoldered among the tents where old women cooked the morning meal for the rest of the tribe: red tea, flavored with salt and butter, and cakes made from millet flour, mixed with wild snowberries gathered the day before by the children. Strips of antelope meat were drying around smokefires nearby. Hult watched as one of the camp dogs, a scrawny yellow beast with a brown patch over one ear, stole a cake from a griddle, narrowly escaping the foot of a cursing old crone before it skulked away with its prize. He allowed himself a snort of laughter at the crafty animal, though one day it would likely end up in the stewpot for its thieving.

Beyond the camp, he spied movement amidst the sea

of swaying grass, and he straightened, his eyes narrowing as he tried to focus. A *tenach* needed perfect vision, and Chovuk bragged to all who would hear that Hult could see a snake move through tall grass a league away. An exaggeration, yes, but Hult could still see farther than nearly any other man of the White Sky. Half his fellow riders wouldn't have even noticed the indistinct shapes, moving several miles away across the plains.

There were too many for it to be Krogan. The Boyla traveled with a small band, again by tradition—seven of the mightiest warriors in all the Tamire, recruited from the tribes as his personal bodyguard. The mass Hult saw was perhaps five times that many. He held his breath, worried it might be enemies. The elves hadn't come south of the Turgan Oasis, some twenty days from the Hill, since the Godless Night ended, and the goblins of the Ilquars almost never came down to the plains, but there were other enemies who dwelled on the plains. The Kazar, the Uigan's ancient foe, lived only five days' ride away. But there did not appear to be any riders on the backs of the animals Hult saw—nor did the animals seem to be horses.

Ajaghai, he thought, making them out at last. He felt a momentary thrill. The *ajaghai* were a type of large antelope, hunted by the Uigan since the first riders took saddle on the plains. Their meat was rich, and their hides made matchless tents. They were also quite rare—Chovuk would be glad for the news that a herd had strayed so close to the village. So would Krogan, when he came. The Tegin had been right: it was a good hunting-day.

So intent was Hult's gaze upon the *ajaghai* he nearly missed what else moved across the plains. Less than two miles from Undermouth, a lone rider traveled at a reckless gallop. A rider moving that fast should have thrown up a plume of dust, but winter's memory was fresh, and the first rains of the year had kept the ground soft and muddy.

BLADES OF THE TIGER

Watching the lone rider, Hult felt like an adder had crawled into his stomach. The man was too far away to make out his face, but on his head was a helm crowned with spiral horns. Hult recognized those at once: only the Boyla's retinue wore such helmets. Where there should have been eight horsemen, however, there was only one, and the one carried himself oddly, listing to one side and leaning forward against his bay stallion's neck. Where were the Boyla and his other men?

The answer came a moment later, when the rider reached to his saddle and pulled out a staff. Raising it high, he let a long banner unfurl to stream behind him: a flapping pennant of blood-red silk. Seeing it, Hult took a step back in shock.

Then he clambered as quickly as he could down the rock, shouting as loud as he could, *"Aki! Aki bo tumagi!"*

Woe! Woe and great pain!

He jumped down the last few paces, landed in a crouch, then sprang up and ran on down toward the camp, yelling all the way. Behind him, the howling faces stared out at the distance, uncaring, their groans rising with the morning breeze.

※————※※————※

Chovuk was already in the saddle when Hult reached the village and was waving his *shuk* above his head, calling to his warriors. Looking past the stake-fence, Hult could see the Boyla's sentinel crest the nearest swelling of the plains. By now he had dropped the banner, which writhed across the grasslands like a crimson serpent, and was sagging farther and farther sideways in the saddle. Hult called his mount to him—Nightsedge was a fine black stallion with white fetlocks, second among the tribe's herds only to Chovuk's own gray, Dragonbone. The animal came, without tack or harness. He didn't care, vaulting up and digging his heels into its flanks. A Uigan rider learned to handle a horse bareback before his eighth summer, if he wanted to avoid shame.

At last, the Boyla's man stopped. He tried to look up, but his strength was gone, and he toppled from the saddle.

"*Tenach*, with me!" Chovuk yelled, gesturing to the crowd of riders that had gathered around him. He had slammed a steel helm, crowned with a red horsetail, onto his head, but wore no other armor. "The rest of you, watch the surround. This could be a trick. If the Kazar dogs appear, feather their breasts."

Casting jealous eyes at Hult, the other men reached for their bows. Some nocked arrows, while others yelled for the women and children to hide in their yurts. Undermouth hadn't been attacked for a long time, but they were still ready. *The unprotected throat cries to be cut*, the old ones said.

A boy of twelve summers ran to the gate without being asked and hauled it open. A breath later Chovuk galloped out, with Hult at his right hand, sending clods of damp earth flying. Both men held their sabers, wary for signs of ambush. There was no one there, though. Even the *ajaghai* had bolted from the commotion and were vanishing in the distance.

The warrior lay on his side, groaning in pain. His horse remained nearby, cropping grass. Chovuk hauled on his reins and sheathed his saber. "Be my eyes, *tenach*," he bade.

"And your shield, Tegin," Hult replied.

It was the ritual promise he'd made when Chovuk chose him. He would safeguard his chief, even if it meant throwing himself onto an enemy's lance. He stayed on his horse, *shuk* gleaming in the morning light as he looked around for trouble.

The chief, meanwhile, jumped down from his saddle and knelt beside the fallen warrior. A curse pushed past his lips. Risking a quick glance, Hult saw the man had two arrows in him—one in the meat of his shoulder and another in his hip. Neither wound looked mortal, but he'd lost a lot of blood. How far had he ridden with these wounds?

"Kazar," Chovuk said. "Those dogs must have ambushed the Boyla."

Hult looked closer. Rather than feathers, the Kazar tribes used strips of leather, stiffened with slivers of bone, to fletch their arrows. That was what quivered in the man's flesh with every shaky breath. He wondered if the shafts were poisoned too.

The Tegin wasted no more time, hoisting the warrior up and throwing him back across his horse's saddle. The warrior grunted with pain, then went limp. Senseless or dead, Hult couldn't tell.

Chovuk swung up to his saddle again. "Ride!" he barked, handing Hult the fallen rider's reins. "We don't have much time if we want to find Krogan."

He galloped back toward Undermouth, yelling for the gate to open. His heart thundering, Hult followed, the injured warrior jostling behind him.

Healers among the Uigan belonged to no particular tribe. Those who practiced the mysteries of the goddess Mislaxa were wanderers, moving from one camp to the next, dwelling on the fringes and living off the charity of the riders. Sometimes, a month or more might pass when a clan had no one to tend its sick and wounded, for though the Godless Night was well past, there were still too few servants of the gods in the Tamire.

There was a Mislaxan in Undermouth that day, though—a small, frail woman who never spoke and could have been thirty or sixty summers old. She was waiting in the middle of the camp when Chovuk and Hult returned, standing in her plain brown robes by the communal fire, where the men gathered at night to drink fermented mare's milk and boast about battles and women.

She gave the Tegin a disapproving glance as he dismounted. He glared back, laying a hand on his *shuk*.

"If he dies," Chovuk said, "you will live but one breath longer."

Most of the White Sky had gathered round. They murmured to one another at the open threat. Mislaxans traveled the Tamire freely, for the tribes knew that if they harmed a healer, the whole order would revoke their gifts for three generations. It had happened before, though not in most folk's memory. Chovuk swept his people with a furious glower, showing his threat was serious.

The healer shrugged as if none of it mattered, and set to work. "Water," she spoke, kneeling beside the warrior—her first word since coming to Undermouth, two weeks before. Then she spoke a second. "Cloth."

Someone ran to fetch them as she inspected the warrior's wounds, clucking her tongue against the roof of her mouth. When her supplies came, she handed them to Hult without a word. Feeling awkward, he bent down beside her. Some feared the Mislaxans, but Hult did not. His sister had left home to join the order when he was just a boy. He had not seen her since, but hoped one day she would come to Undermouth—or Three Brooks, the tribe's encampment during the warmer months.

The healer nodded to herself, reaching with thin fingers to touch one of the arrows. The Boyla's man groaned, but did not wake. The healer nodded again. Then, without pause, she seized the shaft and pulled it out.

A great deal of blood poured forth, and the tribesfolk cried out at the sight of it. Chovuk even half-drew his *shuk*, but the healer didn't flinch. Instead, she yanked free the second arrow, then held out a hand to Hult. He offered her the waterskin, but she made a sour face, so he gave her the cloth instead. She pressed it over the wounds. It soaked through, turning bright red.

"Difficult," she said, lifting the blood-drenched cloth away.

"What are you doing, woman?" Chovuk demanded. "He's going to bleed to death!"

It was true, as anyone could see, but the healer seemed preoccupied. She rose from the dying man's side and, pushing past the chief, walked to the fire and began to chant. The sound made Hult's skin prickle—her low singing seemed to come from the earth beneath her. As she raised the cloth, her voice split in two. A second, whistling sound rose above the main chant, almost too high to hear. He watched in awe as she sang, then stopped and threw the bloody cloth into the fire.

At once the flames changed, leaping high and taking on the color of blood. Ruddy smoke billowed skyward. Hult stumbled to his knees, amazed, as the tribesfolk edged back. Usually the Mislaxans performed their magic in secret, away from the eyes and ears of common folk—and ordinarily, it wasn't magic at all, but herb-lore and simple medicine. Few in the camp had ever seen a proper healing rite. The flames leaped higher, carrying the iron tang of blood and beneath it, a deep, fetid stink. The stink of death, Hult thought, biting the heel of his hand to ward off evil. *She is sacrificing the man's blood to keep death at bay.*

The Mislaxan stood before the flames, cackling—a shrill noise, not at all like the booming song she had sung to bring forth her goddess's power. She threw back her hood, letting her long, white hair blow in the wind. Black smoke billowed high. Then, with a shout, she stepped right into the middle of the blaze.

Hult leaped forward, expecting the *whoosh* of flames catching cloth and the sweet smell of burning flesh. But none of it happened. The Mislaxan stopped in the middle of the scarlet fire and stayed there, immersed but unharmed. Not even her hair was singed. She was still laughing several breaths later, when she emerged again without a single smudge of soot on the hem of her robes.

When the unnatural fire died back to its normal, golden color, someone cried out and pointed. The White Sky People stared at the Boyla's warrior in amazement. His wounds were gone, and his face—which had been nearly as pale as a southerner's—had adopted a healthy tan.

The healer smiled to herself, bowed, turned, and walked away.

Chovuk watched her go, then bent down by the healed rider and motioned to Hult. "The water," he said.

Hult brought it, and Chovuk splashed some on the unconscious warrior's face. The man moaned, then his eyes opened. Hult could tell he still felt great pain and was confused as well. Chovuk held the waterskin to the man's lips and let him drink. Even after he'd quenched himself, his voice came only as a croak.

"Where is this?" he asked.

"Undermouth," Chovuk said, his eyes burning like stars. He pointed to the carven faces, moaning above. "You found us. Now tell us . . . what happened to your master?"

They rode off almost right away, Hult with a saddle now between him and his horse, and with two dozen other men following him and Chovuk across the plains. The Boyla's man stayed behind, still too weak from his ordeal to make the ride. But he had spoken clearly enough for all the White Sky to know what had befallen Krogan, Lord of the Tamire.

A canyon. Three leagues east of here. They fell on us like jackals.

Who? Who attacked you?

Kazar.

Hult's skin burned at the name. Like all Uigan, he

hated the Kazar—though they were also human and looked like his people, the tribes of the eastern Tamire were true savages. Their men grew their hair long, rather than shaving their heads. They did not mark their faces when they came of age. They wore the skins of bears, a sacred animal, and drank millet beer instead of mare's milk. Hult gripped his bow tightly, hoping for the chance to put arrows in Kazar hearts.

Seven miles from Undermouth, the grassy ground grew rocky, giving way to steppes as it rose toward the Ilquars. The riders' eyes went to the tops of the craggy cliffs, to clumps of grimbarb bushes . . . to anywhere an archer might hide. There was nothing—only blood on the stones and here and there a broken arrow.

Chovuk dismounted and plucked a shaft from the rocky ground. This one was intact; its leather vanes gave its former owner away. He spat in the dust, then got back into his saddle, the arrow still clutched in his hand. They rode on, and a mile later found the first body.

It was a Kazar—the filthy hair gave it away. He had been cut from left shoulder to right hip, a horrible wound around which flies gathered. Hult stared at the dead man as they rode by, loathing darkening his heart. The second corpse, a short way farther on, was Kazar too, but the third was different. Lying faceup, a leather-fletched arrow lodged in his eye, was a man in a horned helmet. One of the Boyla's. He still held his *shuk*: a true warrior, he had fallen with his sword in hand.

They found more and more remains, most Kazar, but here and there a Uigan as well. Surveying the carnage, Hult could see how the ambush had played out. A quick strike from cover, then the enemy had closed in to fight, picking off Krogan's men one by one—all but one rider, who had escaped and ridden to Undermouth to sound the alarm.

"We are too late," Chovuk said. "It is over. The dogs have already gone, and left the Boyla for the crows."

The other riders looked down, agreeing. So did Hult. The Kazar must have retreated right after the fight, or they would not have left their slain fellows. The people of the Tamire revered the dead, particularly those who fell in battle. Later, Chovuk would cut up the dead Kazar and feed the pieces to the dogs.

"What shall we do, Tegin?" asked a man.

Chovuk waved his arm. "Gather the bodies. Do them honor," he replied. "Everyone—except you, *tenach*. You will come help me find Krogan."

They left the rest behind, winding on into the steppes, following the trail of blood. There were horses too, though not many—the thieving Kazar had stolen those that still lived. The canyon grew deeper, until its rusty walls towered overhead, drenching them in shadow. The day was young, and this place only saw light when the sun was high. Hult put away his bow and drew his *shuk*—then stopped, bringing the blade up.

"Something's there," he said, pointing with the blade. Ahead, a dark form stood out against the gloom.

Chovuk nodded. "It is him."

Hult's eyes adjusted to the darkness. A spur of rock like a crooked finger jutted from the canyon wall. Sprawled against it, propped up, lay Krogan Boyla. He had an arrow lodged in his side and a gash across his face that had ruined one eye and laid bare his cheekbone. Another cut ran across his left knee, splitting the cap and crippling him. Despite the ghastly wounds, he retained the regal air of a great lord. At nearly seventy he was ancient for a Uigan, and his braid and beard were the color of snow. He wore a knee-length coat of chainmail interspersed with bronze plates sculpted to look like dragon scales. The antlers of an *ajagh* crowned his helm. The tattoos on his face were the most elaborate Hult had ever seen, blue and black and vivid green, telling the tales of battles uncounted. He still held his *shuk*, wet to the hilt with the blood of his foes. He did not move, made no sound.

Chovuk stared at the Boyla, who lay perfectly still. His voice was soft, but Hult knew his master well enough to sense his rage. "O, my lord," he said. "If you could see what they have done to you."

"I still have one eye."

Tegin and *tenach* both fell back in shock. The body on the rock wasn't dead, though it had every right to be. The Boyla sat up, a ghastly, red-toothed smile lighting his face. Hult thought of evil magic and fought back the urge to bite his hand. This was Krogan, he reminded himself. There was no tougher old wolf beneath the sun.

"Chovuk," rasped the Boyla. "My man found you?"

Hult's master shook his head. "You should be dead."

"Maybe," Krogan said, chuckling. "But the gods know better than to let some Kazar dog slay me! I hope you have an extra horse, my friend. I seem to have lost mine." He reached out, offering a dragon-gauntleted hand.

Chovuk stared at the old Boyla and did not move.

Hult looked from one to the other, his brow furrowing. What was the Tegin waiting for?

He was just about to step in and help Krogan up when Chovuk finally responded—by raising his bow. The Boyla's eyes narrowed, then understanding lit his face. Hult followed his gaze to Chovuk's arrow. It was the one he'd picked up, back down the canyon.

Fletched with leather.

"Wait—" Krogan began.

"I'm sorry," Chovuk replied, and loosed.

Chapter 3

KRISTOPHAN, THE IMPERIAL LEAGUE

There should have been singing, should have been bright banners and horns blaring as the Sixth Legion wended the last miles of its march back to the capital. They had fought a hard war, spent three years in fearsome lands surrounded by enemies who took no prisoners, and they had won. But the soldiers chanted no hymns of victory and the only color the standard-bearers flew was deep violet, the color of raw wine. The color of mourning.

Ambeoutin XII, Emperor of the League, Lord of the Conquered Lands, High Captain of the Horned Race, was dead.

Barreth Forlo, marshal of the Sixth, shook his head at the thought. Such a calamity hadn't befallen the League—or any realm—since the Destruction sundered Old Aurim four hundred years ago. To have it happen now, on the heels of victory—it was unthinkable. One moment he'd been looking forward to returning in triumph to kneel before the emperor's feet, and the next a message had come telling him that Ambeoutin would not be waiting for him. There would be no glory; only grieving.

He sighed, glancing back at the long, snaking column of his soldiers: seven hundred men and minotaurs in blue-

and-crimson colors. The legion had been two thousand strong when they set out for the dark realm of Thenol, an ancient foe, ruled by dark clerics, who had ferociously attacked the League soon after the Godless Night ended. The Sixth had been the first legion to answer the call to battle, and had fought more than thirty battles from the start of the war to the finish. Forlo—a rare human among the minotaur marshals who dominated the imperial armies—had pushed them hard and buried more than half his troops in foreign soil. But that was war. His men knew it as well as he did, and they accepted his leadership. He had wept with them, bled with them, and killed with them. Even against the undead hordes the Thenolites commanded into battle, he had shown no fear. And in the end, he had been at the fore when the League's armies converged on Hawkbluff, the last stronghold of Thenol, site of their greatest temple.

The temple was gone now, burned and pulled down. Ashes and broken stone. The gruesome idols and bloodstained altars pounded to dust by vengeful minotaurs with sledges. Hawkbluff was a ruin, and it would be years before Thenol recovered. If it ever did.

There should have been singing.

That wasn't even the worst part, he thought, turning back to gaze up the road ahead. The wide, stone-paved highway wound between hills covered with vineyards and orchards, and was flanked by tall statues of minotaur heroes—horned warlords bearing tridents and spiked maces and swords like butcher-blades—not a human among them. Ahead, through the drizzle that had seemed to dog the legion the whole way back, he could make out the haze of Kristophan—the city itself still hidden behind the rolling ground. The worst part was that they had been forced to leave their work unfinished.

Ordinarily, the Sixth would have remained in Thenol as conquerors, occupying the fallen realm and making sure the peace was kept until an imperial governor arrived to assume control. There would have been insurgents to behead, taxes to collect, and more churches to raze. The laws of the League, however, dictated that all soldiers must return at once to the capitol upon the death of an emperor. It was foolish, for the men of Thenol were vipers, and the priests of Hith Bone-lord would already be regathering their power. Without the legions to pacify it, the League's enemy would rise again. Someone would ascend to take the place of Bishop Ondelos, who had died, howling curses, in the fall of Hawkbluff. There might even need to be another war.

My best chance at glory, Forlo thought bitterly. Glory, and a name in the histories. Now I will be a footnote—and more men will die for no good reason.

"Have you heard the latest word?" asked a gray-furred minotaur beside him, a brawny behemoth with a deep, fresh scar on his muzzle and a flicker in his yellow eyes. Grath Horuth-Bok hefted a massive axe onto his shoulder as he peered up at Forlo. Unlike men, the minotaurs did not ride. Horses were for the weak, in the bull-folk's eyes. "They're saying over in the Third that old Ambo was in bed when it happened. And if you believe he was sleeping . . ."

"Good way to go," Forlo responded, summoning a humorless chuckle. He looked back at the minotaur, his second in command through the campaign and the best friend a warrior could ask for. "Did Trondal tell you that?"

"Aye," Grath said with a wink.

"Tell him his lies stink worse than last night's latrines."

The minotaur boomed with laughter. Forlo turned his eyes back to the road ahead. The messages the armies received had not said anything of the circumstances of Ambeoutin's death, and there had been all sorts of rumors about how he'd met his end. Fighting in the Arena was one popular tale, for that had been one of the emperor's favorite pastimes. Others said one of his courtiers had poisoned him. A few claimed, more quietly, that he'd gotten drunk and fallen from his balcony in the imperial palace. All quite possible, Forlo knew. He and the emperor had been—well, not friends, but as close as one could get with such a powerful lord.

"I wonder who's in charge now," said Grath. "Probably Ambo's son, eh? Emperor Khultam IV . . . good sound to it."

"Although he's a bit young," Forlo said. "The senate may have chosen one of the other lords."

"Well, we'll see soon enough."

There was a furlong to go before they reached the top of Sedron's Ridge, a crest strewn with shards of broken stone that stretched up and up before them. Once they cleared the ridge, they would begin their descent into the cove where the capitol stood: Kristophan, a jewel of pearl and lapis on the shores of the Western Ocean. Despite everything, it was good to be back in the League, away from the black towns and demon-carved fanes of Thenol. Whoever ruled now, it didn't matter. Forlo had secured a promise from Ambeoutin not long before the war. After his next campaign, he would be allowed to retire. After twenty-five years, first as a soldier, then an officer, then the last six as a marshal . . . after all that time, he could lay down his sword.

The minotaurs, whose lives revolved around battle, and who never lost the taste for blood, even in old age, thought he was mad. Grath did, and so had the emperor. But Ambeoutin had granted his wish, and whoever sat upon the Sea Throne—a seat carved of a single block of turquoise to resemble foam-cresting waves—was bound to honor Ambeoutin's word, even after death. And then . . . then he could go *home*.

Essana, he thought wistfully of the wife he'd left behind—a wife who'd been waiting for so long. *I'll see you soon.*

"At least we've still got our prize," Grath chimed in, trying to be cheerful in spite of everything. He patted a leather bag, which swung from his belt. It held a round, heavy object. "I've half a mind to toss it over the wall when we reach the gates. A hundred silver says I can clear the battlements. Eh, my friend? What say—"

As they topped the rise, the minotaur's chatter choked off in a grunt of surprise. He stood blinking for a long, stunned moment, then clenched his fist, threw back his head and roared with anguish. Beside him, Forlo reined in, staring in utter disbelief.

"*Khot*," he swore.

Half the city was gone.

Kristophan had stood for over three hundred years, after being founded in the first hard winters after the Destruction by the few ragged humans who had escaped Old Aurim and the great fires that had killed that ancient realm. The minotaurs had come soon after, from across the sea. Mariners for thousands of years, they had lived in servitude in the faraway empire of Istar, on the other side of Krynn. The Destruction had wrecked that realm, too, and the newly freed bull-men had set sail for other shores. They had come to Taladas and forged a new empire on its shores. The humans proved easy conquests, and in a handful of years the minotaurs' realm had grown to stretch from the Western Ocean to the poison-shrouded Steamwall Mountains, from the shores of the Tiderun Straight in the north down to the foulness of Thenol. Kristophan, which had been little more than a dirty town of thatch hovels when they found it, had grown into a metropolis of thousands, man and minotaur living side by side among white marble halls roofed with blue stone, soaring towers and broad agoras, and surrounded by sixty-foot walls whose gates not even a dragon could sunder. It was the greatest city in Taladas.

Or had been.

There had been troubles all across the League, ever since the Godless Night ended. Something strange had happened to the land which made natural disasters more common than they were even in the months after the Second Destruction. Rivers flooded and wildfires burned on the plains. The hot springs at the pleasure-city of Thera had grown more active, opening geysers in the bathhouses there. Mudslides afflicted the highlands, burying entire villages. A small volcano had appeared in a field near Trilloman, rising from a tiny smoldering pustule to a huge cone in a single afternoon. And all over the empire, there had been earthquakes—at least one a month, mostly in and around the mountains.

In Kristophan, the emperor's advisors had assured him that no such troubles would afflict them. They were safe.

The emperor's advisers hadn't known about the fault line that ran under the great city. Not even the handful of dwarves who dwelt in the capitol had guessed. And so, when the first rumblings stirred beneath Kristophan, scarcely anyone took notice. It wasn't until the first big tremor caused the Street of Glass Pillars to erupt into a storm of flying shards that people began to fret. The quake that followed less than a minute later was even worse, collapsing roofs across the city's northern quarter and causing a segment of the east wall to crumble. Great cracks ran through the agoras and made arches and pillars topple in heaps, crushing those beneath. Finally, a roar like a hundred thunderstorms split the air and a rift opened beneath the imperial palace itself. That great castle, with its central spire that resembled a mainmast and silken banners that spoke of sails, had been home to the League's sovereigns ever since Eragas the Brutish first declared himself emperor. It had vanished in an instant, toppling into the void. With it went not just Ambeoutin, but all his sons, daughters, and wives.

The Forum of the Senate fell into the abyss as well, and one by one the keeps of the high lords followed.

Even the stoutest-walled fortresses turned to rubble as they tumbled down the sides of the chasm, the screams of the dying lost amid the crashes and rumbles of the devastation. The chasm grew wider and wider, while the minotaurs fled through the streets in panic, certain their whole city would soon plummet down deep into the bowels of the world. In the end, though, only the northern part vanished. The southern districts, including the Imperial Arena and the walled hilltop known as the Old City, survived, though many homes, shops and temples crumbled there, too. The last to be swallowed were the city wharves. Then the sea rushed in, filling the rift and drowning those few who yet lived amid the wreckage at its bottom. Great clouds of steam and dust billowed high into the air. Then, eerily, all grew still.

The toll was terrible. Thousands died, and twice as many were left homeless. The empire had no ruler. It barely had anyone left to claim the crown, which now lay beneath tons of stone and even more seawater. A five-mile-long cleft filled with brine was all that remained of the castle where the rulers of the Imperial League had dwelt. The city of Kristophan lived still, but it would bear the scars forever. And a new emperor had yet to be found.

"Keep your eyes open," Forlo said as he and Grath walked down the road toward the city's remains.

The minotaur laughed, though his eyes were grim. He shifted his axe from one shoulder to the other. "You don't have to tell me."

Forlo had ordered his officers to take the Sixth off the road and make camp. They would await word from him before coming any farther. There was no telling what chaos might erupt if an entire imperial legion marched through the gates. With just Grath and another soldier—a minotaur so young his horns hadn't fully come in yet, who carried the leather sack with its hidden prize—he had set out for the shattered capitol.

The gates bristled with guards. He could feel them sighting down their crossbows at him as he came closer, holding his hands up to show they were empty. "*Atta, Kristophan!*" he shouted. "We seek to enter!"

For a breath, he had the horrible feeling that one of the sentries would make a mistake. They were nervous. It would take only one twitchy finger to end his life's journey. But then a head poked over the battlements, a grizzled, gray bearded human who brought half a smile to Forlo's lips.

"Barreth?" the old man asked. "That you?"

"No, it's the king of the gnomes, you blind fool," he called back. "How are you, Tyrel?"

The man made a sour face. "Oh, very well. The city fell down, but elsewise it's been a lovely spring." He waved to the guards. "Let 'em in, lads. Anyone who troubles this one finds out what drawing and quartering feels like. Well, the drawing, anyway."

There was the sound of a portcullis rising, then the creak of a winch. The great stone gates, carved with the imperial sigil of horns and a war galleon, rumbled outward. On the other side, more crossbowmen stood ready, keeping their weapons cradled. Forlo waited until the old man came down to him. Tyrel Morr had been one of his officers until two years ago, when a Thenolite blade took his sword arm off above the elbow. He wore no hook or wooden limb, but bore the stump with pride. He grabbed it in salute, and Forlo returned the gesture, clasping his right fist in his left hand.

"So," Tyrel said. He offered a skin of wine.

Forlo drank, then handed the wine on to Grath. "So."

"Suppose you're wondering who's in charge now."

"You'd be right."

"Well, don't ask me," the old man said. "It changes with

the direction of the wind."

Grath rolled his eyes. "Can you not talk plain, old man?"

"And *hai* to you, too, Grath," Tyrel replied, then turned back to Forlo. "Charming as ever, isn't he?"

"It's been a long way home," Forlo said. "And not a welcome sight at the end. Come on, Tyrel. Who's running things?"

"Oh, *running things*," the old warrior said. "That's easier than who's in charge. There are about six of Ambeotin's kin still trying to claim the crown. Cousins, mostly. But they haven't even made a new crown yet, so it's going a bit slow. For now, Duke Rekhaz is keeping the peace. He'll be glad to see you, I'll warrant."

Grath made a quiet sound. Forlo looked at him, saw the thought behind the minotaur's eyes, and shared it. Rekhaz. Of all the people to survive....

"Tell me where he is," he said.

"In the Arena. Where else?" Tyrel said. "Most defensible place left, anyway. Watch yourselves, though—his men are jumpier than mine."

Forlo nodded. "I'll see you again, old man. There's more wine to be drunk."

"You know where to find me," the guardsman replied, then grinned. "Long as my gates don't drop into the sea."

The streets of Kristophan were eerily quiet. There were signs everywhere of recent trouble—broken windows, refuse in the gutters, rusty spatters of dry blood on white walls—but the people were subdued now, and drew back into doorways and alleys as the leaders of the Sixth walked down the Shoreward Road, toward the Arena. Grath and Forlo exchanged looks. Both knew what must have happened here, just weeks ago. There would have been mass panic in the wake of the noble quarter's collapse. Order had been imposed, and many people had died. And there surely hadn't been any mercy shown—not with Duke Rekhaz governing Kristophan.

Rekhaz An-Thurn was a legend in the empire, a warrior who had once slain sixteen gladiators single-handedly on the Arena sands. He was also a tactical genius. There were few finer generals in the League, which was why Ambeoutin had named him the head of both the imperial army and the navy. He had never lost a fight in his life, it was said.

Forlo hated him. Not out of envy—he had never coveted Rekhaz's position—but because the Duke might just be the cruelest minotaur alive. He never left a prisoner alive and had been known to execute subordinates who dared question his judgment. When Forlo saw the bodies of five humans—and two minotaurs—hanging by their necks from a covered walkway off a side street, the only surprise was that there weren't more.

Ukot Ghuranal, the Plaza of Champions, was empty save for a single huddled body near the far end, riddled with crossbow bolts. More corpses dangled from the huge statues that stood around its edges, depicting the legendary heroes of minotaur history. At the far end, the tall, broad Arena where the gladiators fought had been turned into a keep, with all but one of its many entrances blocked with rubble, and with ballistae mounted on the roof. The closer Forlo got, the smaller he felt. He kept his empty hands out the whole way—as did his companions.

The minotaurs standing guard at the Arena's sole remaining entrance were less cheerful than Tyrel had been. Once he identified himself and surrendered his weapons—as if he, or any sane man, would draw sword here!—they sent him in. "He is on the sands," their captain said. "Training."

"Where else?" Grath muttered.

They went through an arched gate, passing through the shadowed galleries where the minotaurs thronged on fighting-days, then down a long tunnel back toward daylight. The sands of the Arena were a hundred paces across and gleaming white except for a few ominous darker patches. The stands, which could seat twenty thousand and hold twice that number standing, stood empty above. Violet banners flew atop the walls, archers patrolling between them. The memories came back in a rush. Like many human officers in the legions, Forlo had earned his rank on the sands, fighting for his life. He had stayed away from the Arena for almost a decade, trying to forget the sights and sounds of the place.

His discomfort must have shown, for Grath gave him a long look. He shook his head, waving the minotaur off.

"Let's get this over with," he said.

There, in the middle of the sands, was Rekhaz. Tall even for a minotaur, he stood nearly nine feet from hoof to horn. His coat was white—a rarity—and his long, black mane was gathered in thick braids. He was fighting barechested, with a kilt of mail about his loins. He wielded two huge clubs, one in each hand. And facing him . . .

"Sargas's spit," said Grath. "Is he fighting three at once?"

He was. Forlo shook his head, watching as a trio of minotaur soldiers closed in on Rekhaz, their own cudgels at the ready. He could already guess how this would turn out. Rekhaz's opponents were hesitant, watching one another to see who would move first. The duke, on the other hand, waited calmly, taut as a drawn bowstring. Forlo raised a hand, and his companions stopped with him to watch.

The minotaur on the left moved first, but Rekhaz leaped at him before he could take two steps, parrying with one club and snapping the other around and down. A sickening crunch rang off the stands, and the soldier dropped to his knees, clutching his broken snout and bellowing in pain. The other two came on at once, and Rekhaz stumbled back, seemingly caught off-guard—but it was a ruse, one Forlo recognized easily. The soldiers were caught unaware, though, and when the duke reversed direction and charged them, the surprise on their faces was almost comical. Then they were down, laid out on the sand with two economical swings of Rekhaz's clubs. One tried to get up, and the duke kicked him in the head. Then it was over.

It had taken less than a minute.

Forlo clapped. "Well fought, Your Grace."

Rekhaz looked up, squinting in the sunlight. "Forlo?"

"Of course."

"You got the message, then," the duke said. "Good. How went the war in Thenol?"

Forlo shrugged. "Show him."

The young bull-man who had come with them opened the sack. A head dropped out, slick with tar. The man who once possessed it had been fat and old, with piggy eyes and an ulcerous growth on his cheek. Long strands of thinning white hair spilled out around it on the sands. Flies buzzed. The stink was eye-watering.

"May I present Bishop Ondelos, lately of Thenol," Forlo declared.

Duke Rekhaz stared at the head, his face unreadable. Then, slowly, he walked across the Arena, planted his foot atop the grisly trophy, and crushed it beneath his heel. Pulp oozed across the sand.

"Victory," he said, eyes gleaming.

"But Thenol isn't pacified," Forlo replied evenly. "If we could have stayed—"

"Yes, yes. But the law is the law, even with no emperor to issue decrees," Rekhaz replied, waving his hand. He walked away from the ruined mess of tar and brains. The others trailed him. "And with no clear heir, things are going rough. I've held the peace this far, but it hasn't been easy. Factions are forming. I need men to keep the rabble down, or we'll have civil war."

"The Sixth is yours," Forlo said. "The other legions

are soon behind us. They will be at the city by tomorrow night."

The duke nodded. "Good . . . but not good enough. I need men to lead them."

A sour taste filled Forlo's mouth. He'd been half-expecting the conversation to take this turn. Clenching his fists, he made himself stop walking. "I am to retire, Your Grace. Grath can lead the Sixth just as well as I could."

Rekhaz stopped, then turned around with a baleful glare. Forlo had seen hard men, men who had faced the worst war had to offer, cringe before that glowering, red-eyed stare. He almost quailed himself, but gritted his teeth and kept his composure, meeting the fire in the duke's eyes with ice in his own.

"I am not asking for Grath, Lord Forlo," Rekhaz growled. "You owe me your fealty."

"Your pardon, Grace," Forlo replied, "but I owe you nothing."

Rekhaz's eyes flashed, but before he could do anything Forlo reached to his belt and produced a sheet of vellum. He had been ready for this. He'd been ready for some time. Slowly, he unfurled it to reveal the horns-and-ship seal of the imperial court, then he handed the vellum to the duke.

"A severing writ," he declared. "Signed by Ambeoutin himself. When the campaign in Thenol is over, I am relieved of all duties to the League."

The duke read the message, his brow furrowing. "This must be the only copy," he said when he was done. "All others would have perished when the nobles' quarter fell."

"Perhaps," Forlo replied. "But it bears the imperial seal, making it law."

"And the law is the law," Grath added, smiling.

Rekhaz's lip curled, but he said nothing more.

"I am done," Forlo said. "For three years I have fought

in the south, and seen neither home nor wife. Now it's over. I have fought my last battle."

For a moment, there was tension and silence.

"Last battle?" the duke finally barked. "A warrior *has* no last battle, except the one that kills him!" With a sneer, he threw the writ back at Forlo. "Remember that, marshal," he said. Then, turning, he stalked away.

Forlo watched him go. So, it was over—he was free. The damned bull-men could squabble over the throne, they could all kill one another. Thenol could rise anew.

Forlo didn't care. He was going home.

But as he watched the duke stride angrily across the Arena floor, a cold feeling settled inside him. He realized he had made an enemy today—and foes didn't come any deadlier than Rekhaz An-Thurn.

Chapter 4

THE BORDERWOLD, ARMACH-NESTI

There was no boundary, no monument or wall, not even a milestone declaring the border of the elf-realm. No roads led into it; only thick woods of spruce and poplar clinging to every inch of soil that touched the rocky hills. The air was clean and crisp with the last vestiges of winter, and did not smell of fish, sweat, or offal—a welcome relief from the stenches of the cities. Birdsong went on without end, and in the distance a wolf voiced its low, mournful howl. Through the branches came tantalizing glimpses of water, sparkling in the morning light. This was a land of brooks and splashing waterfalls, cold and clean and pure, lined with banks of willows, sweet-scented grass, and riots of wildflowers.

Home. . . .

Had she been human, Shedara knew, she would already be dead. The rim-watchers had been tracking her for a league, arrows on their strings, waiting. She hadn't seen any sign of them, nor would she without the aid of magic. The elves who ranged their kingdom's boundaries were masters of the forest, capable of vanishing completely among the trees so that not even the animals marked their passing. But they were there all the same. No one came to Armach-nesti without being watched. And only elves were allowed to live.

It had been this way for twenty generations of her people—about two thousand years. Like the minotaurs of the League, they had not always lived in Taladas, though they had dwelt there much longer than the horned folk. Indeed, in the long-lost days they had lived close to the minotaur lands, on the continent of Ansalon. Their home had been a realm called Silvanesti, the eldest elf-home of that land, and they had left it by choice—not to come here, but to follow the great lord Kith-Kanan to found a new land, Qualinesti. As their armada sailed north around Ansalon, however, a storm had arisen and blown some of the ships off course. These vessels wandered the seas for many weeks, first trying to find home, then looking for land of any kind, and they had come at last to these shores. They dubbed this land Armach-nesti, which meant "dry land" in their tongue, took the name Silvanaes, and settled down, driving out the human barbarians who had lived there before. They sent ships to seek a passage back to their lost home, but none ever returned, and so they lost hope of ever seeing their kin again.

One of the first things the Silvanaes did after settling in Taladas was to establish the laws of their new land, the First Edicts that would guarantee the purity of their realm and their blood. Since that time, if a single human, dwarf, minotaur or other *heerikil*—those not of elven descent—had seen these lands and lived, it was not recorded in history or memory.

Despite the arrows surely trained on her, ready to pierce her heart should she prove not to be what she appeared, Shedara felt safe. For the first time since that night in Blood Eye, she did not look over her shoulder, or imagine the footfalls of unseen beings creeping up behind her. She had no reason to believe the things that had murdered Ruskal Eight-Fingers knew of her, but still she felt cold whenever she passed a deep shadow or heard a stone fall in the stillness. Only now did she walk without a hand on her dagger. It was a good feeling.

She walked past thickets and brush, over moss-bearded logs sunk deep into the soil, and through brakes of ferns glistening with the morning's dew. In these lands, a human would quickly become lost, but Shedara had passed through this forest many times in her hundred and thirty years. Every tree, stock, and stone was familiar to her. At last, she came to a break in the foliage, a meadow of clover riddled with tiny blue flowers. Fat bees hummed from bloom to bloom, and not ten paces away a doe and two fawns stood watching her. They did not bolt, did not fear her as they might a human hunter—only stared as she paused briefly in the trees' shade. At the glade's far side was a pool girdled with tall stones, rough-hewn slabs arranged in a ring and carved with crude spiral patterns, nearly lost under cloaks of ivy. The stones predated the Silvanaes, harkening back to the tribes who had lived on the land before the elves came. It had been a place of sacrifice, the histories said. A hallowed place where they had spilled the blood of captured enemies, to pray for a bountiful hunt. A waterfall fed the pond, tumbling noisily down from cliffs that loomed above.

She and the deer were not alone. Another elf sat on a stone by the pool, reed-thin, with hair the gold of young willow-bark tumbling over his shoulders. Glittering, silvery mail peeked past his green-dyed hunting leathers, and he had a gray cloak flung over his shoulder, revealing a long, slender blade on his hip. Slung over his back, unstrung, was a bow as long as he was tall—and he stood nearly six and a half feet—with a quiver of white-fletched arrows. He rose, feathery eyebrows lifting, as Shedara stepped out of the woods.

"You," he declared, "are late."

"Don't you have duties to attend to, *Shalindi*?" she replied.

The elflord shrugged. "Only when you are here, sister. Otherwise I bide, awaiting your return."

Despite herself, Shedara laughed. "You don't need that blade, Quivris," she said. "Your tongue's sharp enough."

He came forward, embracing her. Their foreheads touched, then their lips, in greeting. When they parted again, Shedara sensed that her unseen watchers were gone. No sound, no motion to signal it—just a feeling of no longer being watched. Quivris was the Lord-Protector of the realm. If he welcomed her, they needed no more reassurance.

"Has all been well, my brother?" she asked.

"Well enough," he said, spreading his hands. The answer had to be more complicated than that, but not in any important way. "Your task? Did you succeed?"

"I did." Shedara tried to keep her face calm, but her eyes must have darkened, for a thin line appeared in her brother's brow. "There was trouble. Lord Ruskal is dead."

"By your hand?"

She shook her head. "I must say no more, until I am in the presence of the Voice."

"Ah." Quivris eyed her a moment longer, then gestured behind him. "Let us waste no more time, then."

At his signal, a pair of creatures appeared atop the cliff, near the waterfall's source. They were strange mixes of animals, with the heads, foreclaws, and wings of golden eagles, and the hindquarters of horses—one sorrel, the other white. Hippogriffs, humans called them—the Silvanaes preferred the name *sky-steeds*. Both wore saddles, leather chased with gold and silver in patterns reminiscent of twining vines. One raised its head and skirled, the sound ripping through the silence. Unfurling their wings, they leaped from the precipice and glided down to alight beside the pool.

"Falasta," Shedara said, holding out a hand. The white hippogriff came forward and nuzzled it with its head. The feathers were soft to the touch, the movements surprisingly gentle. "I missed you too, Lady."

Quivris had already climbed into his saddle. The hippogriffs had no reins. Proud beasts, they would not wear bridles. Fortunately, they were smart too, and could be trained in the elven tongue. The Silvanesti had done the same thing, with griffins, back in the homeland.

"Come on," Quivris said. "Her Highness awaits."

Stroking the hippogriff's neck, Shedara swung herself lightly onto its back. As soon as she was settled in, the beast let out a cry, then vaulted into the air, spreading its wings to catch the wind. Quivris rose beside her, and in moments the meadow and the waterfall had dropped away. The two of them wheeled, then swept away north.

The forest skimmed by beneath them, a carpet of green and gold laced with threads of silver. It seemed to go on without end, stretching from horizon on her right to the rocky seashore on her left, with no sign of the cities of man and minotaur in any direction. From above, Armach-nesti looked almost completely wild. The only signs that anyone inhabited it were the spires of New Silvanost, almost lost in the haze to the west. The fluted needles of white stone glittered in the sunlight, with gossamer arches of silver threading from one to the next. The elves had built the spires with hopes of recapturing the glory of their old homeland across the sea. The memories had brought them grief rather than joy, however, and the city had stood empty for centuries, slowly being reclaimed by the forest. Beneath the treetops, the towers' foundations were long lost among shrub and creeper and drifting leaves. The Silvanaes dwelt elsewhere now, hidden from all eyes save their own.

They flew for nearly an hour, and at first Shedara delighted in the tug of the wind. She had been riding sky-steeds for longer than many humans or minotaurs had lived, and the experience was beyond compare, a thrill that seemed greater each time she did it. Eventually, though, her feeling of freedom began to yield to foreboding. She had come home, but ill news had come with her.

At last the hippogriffs began to descend, swinging

about in lazy arcs until they came down on a promontory overlooking a broad valley, down the middle of which a river foamed through gorges of stone. Several servants, in robes of gray silk, hurried forward to see to the steeds. Quivris and Shedara left them behind and followed a narrow path that wended its way down from the height.

The trail leading down into the forest was narrow and treacherous to anyone who didn't possess wood-craft. It leveled off, at last, upon reaching the valley floor. Statues of polished green jade flanked the path here, half-overgrown with vines. These were the Voices, seventeen in all, who had ruled Armach-nesti since its birth. The eighteenth pedestal was empty, representing the current Voice. The Silvanaes did not paint or sculpt living elves.

The path ended at the edge of the ravine, at a dais of living rock overlooking the raging rapids. Atop this platform, perched to view the river, was a hazelwood tree, sculpted to look like the petals of an orchid. In the midst of this bloom sat a small, ancient figure.

Lady Thalaniya had been Voice of the Stars for more than two hundred years, and she was one of the oldest elves in the realm. Her hair, once shimmering gold, had turned to silver, and lines of care were etched around her mouth. Her eyes, however, remained clear and sharp, the hue of amethysts. Nor did her movements betray her age as she rose from the throne and strode across the dais to greet Shedara. Her ivory-white robes billowed as she walked. Her crown, a circlet of silver set with pearls and green dragon teeth, glistened in the sun.

"Highness," said Shedara, touching foreheads with the queen of Armach-nesti. "It is good to see you again."

"And you, child," Thalaniya replied. "Oft have I thought of you, these past weeks. So too has the Lord Protector. When the scouts reported you had returned, he barely remembered to ask my leave before he rushed to meet you."

Quivris flushed, and the Voice laughed. Shedara

smiled, but again she couldn't keep the worry from her eyes. Thalaniya's brow furrowed.

"Something is wrong. What is it?" the Voice asked. "Did you not gain the painting?"

Shedara shook her head, reaching beneath her cloak to produce a tube of nightwood. Within was a canvas bearing the image of Silvanos, the first king of her people, father to Kith-Kanan himself. "I have it, Highness," she said. "But there was trouble."

"How, trouble? Tell me." Thalaniya raised a hand, staying Shedara before she could speak. "No, you must do more, child. You must show me."

※━━━━━※━━━━━※

Shedara lay back wearily and plucked a violet from a bowl of candied flowers. She placed it on her tongue and let it melt there, the fragile flavor of the bloom dancing in her mouth. Then, from a blue crystal goblet, she took a sip of golden wine. Its sweet warmth suffused her, restoring some of her strength as she looked out across the Voice's vale. The forests were shadowed now, the sky above burning red with twilight. The roar of the river soothed her as the first stars kindled among the clouds. Solis peered over the horizon, a sliver from full and on the wax.

It had been a trial, road-weary as she was, showing Thalaniya what had happened in Blood Eye. At the Voice's bidding, they had gone to the Seeing-pool, a spring-fed pond from which a stream spilled down to the rushing water below, and there they had used magic to conjure images upon its waters. Together, she and Thalaniya had drawn in the silver moon's power, shaped it with their will, and released it into the water. The pool, a perfectly round bowl of stone that manifested no reflections on its surface, had burst into sudden, heatless white flame. Those tongues of misty fire had spread across its surface, flickering high, then slowly coalescing as the Voice urged Shedara to open her mind and memory.

Shedara had relived that night, from her arrival at the wharf to her flight from Ruskal's bloodstained tower. When the dying man breathed his final words, Thalaniya's eyes had widened, her alabaster skin turning ashen. After the spell ended, the Voice had stood silent for a time, still staring at the water while the flames dimmed, then died.

"I must consider this," the old elf murmured. "We will meet again this eve."

Then she had withdrawn to walk the paths of the forest as she often did when thinking. Shedara had remained for a long moment, then wandered down a trail and a hill and sat down on a bench carved from the rock of the ravine. There was nothing around her but forest, no sign that anyone lived there. She knew better—there were hundreds of elves in that part of the forest, the most thickly populated area of Armach-nesti. The Silvanaes disguised their homes so well, they seemed to vanish among the trees only a few paces away.

Shedara sighed, nursing her wine. She didn't look forward to working the magic again, even less to discovering what troubled Thalaniya so. But if the Voice willed it, she had no choice.

Quivris leaned against the trunk of an old larch, nibbling a golden pear. He had no wizardly training, but had intently watched the scrying. "I have the feeling," he said, "that you won't be long in Armach-nesti, sister."

I never am, Shedara thought. Her jobs sent her all over—to the League, the dark realm of Thenol, the Marak Valleys where the kender lived . . . even across the Tiderun Straight to the northern grasslands where barbarians still ruled. Whenever she returned home, another mission was always already awaiting her. There was always someone in need of a moon-thief's skills. Once she had counted, and she guessed that of the sixty years that had passed since she came of age she had spent a total of eight at home. It would have tormented most elves, to be away from their beloved woods for so long, but Shedara longed to see the wide world. It made coming home all the sweeter.

Still, she had *hoped* to spend a few weeks in Armachnesti this time, rather than leaving at once. She knew Quivris was right, though. Something in Thalaniya's eyes when they parted had told her she would not be staying for very long.

They sat in silence a while longer. She ate rose-petals and finished her wine, and was about to call for a servant to bring her more when a boy, tall and slight, appeared out of the trees and beckoned to her. "Her Highness awaits, *Shalindi*," he declared.

With a look at her brother, Shedara rose from the bench, and with another sigh followed the boy up a flight of stairs carved into the hillside. Quivris pitched the core of his pear over the cliff and followed.

The stairs led to a trail, and the trail back to the pool. The Seeing-pool was half a dozen paces across, its surface dark and still except for faint ripples, painted silver by Solis's rising light. Thalaniya stood on the far side, staring into the depths. She was still pale, the lines around her mouth had deepened. In her hands was a violet orchid, each petal marked with a flash of orange. A tall, dark-haired elflord stood beside her, clad in white robes: a pure wizard, who still dressed as his forebears had when the Silvanaes dwelt across the sea, following the tenets of High Sorcery. His name was Nalaran, and he was the greatest mage in Taladas.

Shedara raised an eyebrow. "*He* wasn't here before," she murmured to her brother.

"That," the Voice replied, looking up, "is because we need stronger magic than before. We must look further back, and the River of Time flows strong."

"How far back?" Quivris asked, concern deepening his voice. "The last spell was hard on Shedara."

"On both of us," Thalaniya said.

"I will bear most of the burden," said Nalaran, lacing his fingers before him. He spoke softly, his eyes glinting in the moonlight. "Her Highness wishes to know more about this Hooded One. She fears—"

The Voice held up a hand. "Never mind what I fear," she said, and the wizard fell silent, his cheeks reddening. "We shall see it for ourselves."

Bending down, she laid the orchid upon the pool's surface and pushed it away. It spun slowly, moving out to the midst of the water. Already Shedara felt the pool's power begin to grow, a faint but insistent tingling in her scalp. She took a deep breath and slowly let it out.

Nalaran began the spell. His hands traced complicated patterns through the air and, in a strong, clear voice, he spoke spidery words that seemed to slip through Shedara's mind, devoid of meaning and eluding her memory. With each movement and sound he drew in more of the silver moon's power, until the air seemed to shine around him, making his eyes gleam like mirrors. At the end, he held his hands out over the pool, and white flames poured down, skimming across the water until it was all a ghostly blaze again. The orchid vanished in a tongue of purple fire, and sorcery thickened the air, making it warm and sultry.

"Show us," the Voice bade, waving a slender hand. "Show us what we seek. Show us the Hooded One."

Nalaran moved his hands, and the flames parted, clearing a window in the pool's midst. The water was bright with light, though the moon was low in the sky. Slowly, like molten wax cooling, an image began to form: a vast city of golden-hued stone straddling a river that snaked among sandy hills. Green fields surrounded it, and mighty walls girded it, tipped with spikes of iron. Spires and domes of silver gleamed in the red light of dusk, as if stained with blood. A rocky pinnacle rose on the city's north side, looking down upon it, and at its peak was a sprawling palace, with blue pennants fluttering on its rooftops. One could see for a hundred miles and more from its tallest balconies, out to blue mountains in the north and the glistening arc of the sea to the south.

Shedara bit her lip. She knew this place, though it had vanished from the world before even the Voice had been born: Old Aurim, the City of Songs, center of the greatest empire Taladas had ever seen. It had been obliterated in the Destruction, when the gods' fist had come thundering down and shattered the land. That empire was long dead, killed by fire, plague, and war. A boiling sea of lava was all that remained, according to the tales. Shedara had never seen this place, nor did she want to. She shuddered at the vision.

A lone figure stood atop the palace's central tower, looking down upon the city. At Nalaran's command the view shifted, focusing on this man—a human, robed and cloaked in blue satin and cloth-of-gold—great, draping sheets of it, shimmering as it ruffled in the wind. A deep hood covered the man's head, obscuring all within in shadow. Shedara's skin prickled at the sight of him, though she didn't know why. Across the pool Thalaniya's hands clenched into fists.

"It is as I feared," the Voice murmured. "It is him."

"Who?" asked Quivris. "Who is it?"

No one answered. Again the images shifted, and now the pool showed a dark chamber, filled with ranks upon ranks of gray stone statues—soldiers, clad in the antique, banded armor of the Aurish regiments. At their head loomed an icon of black rock, which seemed to swallow what little light there was in the cavern. The statue was hooded and cloaked, as the man on the tower had been—then the same man entered the vault and walked up to his stony likeness, raising his head to stare at it. As he did, the hood fell back, slipping off his head.

Shedara screamed, and the world grew dim around her. She heard Quivris call out in surprise, and felt him catch her as her knees buckled. She shut her eyes and collapsed against him.

When the sun crested the mountains the next morning, it found Shedara on her sky-steed's back, soaring once more over the treetops of Armach-nesti. With her she bore all she had taken with her to Thalaniya's court, except for the painting—but she also carried two objects that were new to her: a message, which she hadn't yet read, scribed on a sealed roll of vellum; and a silver necklace whose central charm was a large, white pearl. It lay heavy against her breast, pulsing with a warmth she knew well. Magic . . .

"Take it with you," the Voice had bidden at dawn, when Shedara prepared to climb astride her steed. "I will need to speak with you more about what we have seen. Look to the pearl."

Maddeningly, she had not said anything more about the horrible sight they had beheld in the Seeing-pool. Instead, Thalaniya insisted the message would tell all there was to know. She had departed, and Shedara and Quivris had taken to the sky. He had flown with her for an hour, then reached across to touch her arm in farewell before turning back for home.

Once more, she was alone. As she flew, heading back toward the border of Armach-nesti, Shedara wondered. She would read the message when she was safely on the ground, beyond Armach-nesti. Perhaps then she would understand better what she had seen in the waters. For now, though, all she could think of was the last image that had flickered in the pool before weariness and dread had robbed her of her senses. In her mind, she saw the hooded man, staring at the statue that was his likeness. She saw the hood slide back and drop, and felt a fresh spike of horror at the memory of what lay beneath.

The thing in the hood hadn't had a face.

Chapter 5

MOURNING-STONE, THE TAMIRE

The Mourning-stone was a blade of red rock, resembling the tip of a lance, more than two hundred feet from base to jagged tip. It stood tall at the head of the Vale of Princes, a steep-walled gorge that cut through the foothills of the Ilquar mountains, where oaks and ferns grew around a narrow, clay-banked stream—a sacred site to the Uigan and a place feared by all the other peoples of the Tamire.

Word of Krogan's death had gone out across the plains soon after Chovuk and Hult brought him back to Undermouth, borne by young riders bearing dead crows on long staffs—the traditional sign that Uigan had lost their lord. It spread quickly, as tidings often did on the Tamire, and the tribes had begun to gather in the Stone's shadow a few days after. They had massed in the valley over the course of a fortnight, until the last riders from the land's farthest reaches straggled in, caked with dust, their horses frothing and half-blown from the ride. Ninety-three Tegins had come, the lords of all the clans that had survived the Godless Night. They had spent days hunting and telling boastful tales about the old Boyla's battles in Krogan's honor. At night they drank *kumiss* and sang songs or sparred with blunted *shuks* until they passed out.

When they heard the Kazar had killed Krogan, they spat in the dirt and swore vengeance upon their ancient foes. None of them questioned Chovuk's word. Hult said nothing—after all, hadn't the beer-drinking dogs of the east meant to slay the Boyla? Did they not deserve slaughter for that, even if they had failed?

At last, the day of hanging came. Krogan was given over to the *Yemuna*, the Ghost-Widows, a band of old women who had remained unmarried and virginal all their lives. Clanless, they dwelt always near the Mourningstone, keeping watch over it. The Ghost-Widows prepared Krogan's corpse for the funeral, carrying out secret rites that no man could see to preserve his flesh and make safe his passage into the after-world. This was the way among the Uigan—only the elderly and husbandless could handle the dead—with the Boylas receiving the care of the *Yemuna*. Now, their mysteries done, the stooped, yellow-robed crones brought his body down from their caves beneath the Stone, bearing him on a litter to sit, as though alive, before the gathered Tegins. The killing arrow was gone from his eye, and his face, though pale and sunken, showed no signs of rot. Strips of cloth, dyed with saffron, covered his wounds.

"The Boyla is dead," said Groaning Wind, the eldest of the Widows. The other women wore shrouds that obscured their faces, but hers was bare, skin and hair dusted with powdered bone to whiten them. She had to be ninety winters old, at least, but her power was unmistakable. The lords of the plains feared to look directly at her. "For fifty-three summers he ruled our people, in war and in peace. Because of him, we survived the troubles of the Dread Winter, the raids of the elves and ogres, the terror of the Second Destruction. He saw us through the Night, and lived to sing beneath the red moon once more. He was a great prince."

"A great prince," the Tegins murmured, hard men all, their voices soft and low.

"But even the summer sun must set, and the joyful song must have its ending," Groaning Wind went on. "The Boyla is dead."

"Let the Kazar be next!" shouted one of the younger lords. A rumble of agreement rose among the gathering, but Groaning Wind flashed them a fierce look.

"Still your cries for blood!" the Widow shouted. "His corpse is not yet hung, and already you speak of slaughter!"

Obediently, the men fell silent. At a sign from Groaning Wind, another of the old women raised a mallet and struck a large, bronze gong. Its shuddering sound filled the valley as two more *Yemuna* came forward and tied long, jute ropes to Krogan's armor. Still others hauled on the other ends of the ropes, and the Boyla rose from his litter, then from the ground. Pulleys hoisted him higher and higher up the face of the Mourning-stone, up to a ledge where two more Widows awaited. They had driven spikes into the rock face, and now they used bowstrings to lash Krogan to the rock. This was how the Uigan honored their dead lords. Not by burying them in earth or rock, or giving them to fire, as savages like the Kazar did, but by hanging them from the Stone. Above Krogan, scores of bodies dangled—Boylas past, from his predecessor Yakinf, his mummified face leathery but still recognizable to the eldest Tegins, to the bodies of men who had ruled the Tamire in ages scarcely remembered, now nothing but bones and hair, rattling in the wind. It was said, though only by the shamans and the mad, that should the Uigan ever need their aid, the bodies of the old Boylas would return to life and ride to fight for their people. For now, though, they twisted and swung upon the stone.

Now Krogan was one of them. The Widows left him, and Groaning Wind turned to stare up at the slain prince, dangling fifty feet above the ground, one of more than a hundred who had ruled the plains since the first Uigan mounted horses in the youth of the world. The rest of the riders followed her lead, all staring at the man who had, only a few weeks ago, been their prince.

"*Acha*, lord of the grasslands, master of many herds," she intoned, speaking the ritual farewell. "Jijin see you to your rest among your fathers in the fields beyond. The gods tell your tale now."

"*Acha*, Krogan," spoke the Tegins.

When it was done, the gong sounded again, and the lords stood silent for an hour beneath Krogan's sightless face. Then, without another word, they left the Stone and returned to their camps, their *kumiss*, and their women. They would rest during the day—for that night, they had a solemn task before them. By sunrise the next day, a new Boyla would rule the Tamire.

The drumming began down below in the valley. Hult caught his breath, then looked over his shoulder at the closed flap of Chovuk's yurt. The Tegin had been in there some time since Krogan Boyla's funeral. That had been in the morning. Now the sun was setting, the clouds shining like plundered gold as the steppes grew dim. Yet despite the growing shadows, no light shone within the chieftain's tent. It wasn't Hult's place to wonder about this, but he couldn't help it. Squatting in his customary place, just outside the yurt, his *shuk* lying naked across his knees, he found himself fretting about Chovuk. With the thunder and chanting rising below, he worried. Was his lord well? Did he know the hour?

He looked this way and that across the camp. The White Sky People had come en masse to the Mourningstone, as befitted the tribe the Boyla had been with when he died. There was no longer anyone there, though—only a lone camp dog nosing through the ashes of a fire. They were all down in the valley with the riders the other tribes had sent—waiting. The rite would not, *could* not start without Chovuk. Legs aching, Hult rose and walked back to the yurt.

He saw at once he had been wrong to think it was dark inside. As he grew closer, he could see a glimmer from beneath the flap. It was not the familiar, warm light of tallow-lamps, but a strange sheen of silvery blue. Magic, he thought with a shiver. The Uigan had had sorcerers in the old days before the Godless Night, but they had never fully trusted them. When the moons vanished, taking the magic with them, the riders had stoned the powerless wizards. As the moons were back, there was talk that magic had returned as well—but Chovuk? The Tegin was no mage, Hult was certain.

Hult was still staring when the blue light vanished, as quickly as snuffing a candle. He reacted at once, scrambling back to his place. If Chovuk suspected he had been spying, he would beat Hult with a cudgel for it. A *tenach* did not intrude on his lord unless something was urgent. Hult had just squatted back down when he heard the rustle of the flap being thrown back.

"Master," he declared, standing. He kept his eyes downcast. "The ritual has begun."

"I hear it," replied Chovuk. He was smiling. "We are late, but that is good. Let the other chiefs look for my coming."

Hult looked up at his master and fought to keep his eyes from widening. There was a strange glint in Chovuk's eyes, the gleam a man got when he had a killing fever. Sweat beaded the Tegin's brow. Hult instinctively knew this was because of the magic he'd felt—but why? And where had the light gone? He could not ask these questions. It was against custom, a sign of disrespect.

Another: *why did you kill the Boyla?*

"*Tenach*? Does something trouble you?"

Hult started, realizing he'd been staring at the tent. "N-no, Master," he murmured. "We should go."

"You must trust me," Chovuk said, smiling again. "All will be well."

"I trust you always, Master."

The Tegin clapped his arm. "Good," he said, walking toward the sound of the drums. "Let us go down to them, then. The time of choosing has come."

"I don't understand," Hult said, in that horrible, still moment after Chovuk shot the Boyla. He couldn't take his eyes off the body of Krogan, the man's mouth wide with shock, his remaining eye a ruin, pierced by the Kazar arrow. "He would have lived. He needed no pity-slaying."

Chovuk stood still, his face inscrutable as he slowly lowered the bow. He did not answer.

"Tegin?"

The chieftain turned and looked at Hult without recognition. After a moment he blinked and came back to himself, like a shaman of Jijin roused from a sweat-dream. He smiled.

"You must trust me, tenach," he said. "The world has changed, but Krogan would not. This needed doing, and I was not the only Tegin to think so. Most of us did, though no other would dare act upon it."

Hult stared at his master for a long moment, then frowned and looked back at the Boyla.

"You will not speak of this," Chovuk pressed. "Krogan died in the ambush, with his men. The Kazar dogs killed him. There will be a mourning time, then we will hang his body and choose a new Boyla. None can know."

Hult took a deep breath, then let it out slowly. "I trust you, Master. May I lose my tongue if I lie."

Chovuk studied him, then smiled. "Good. Now go back and find the others. Tell them Krogan Boyla is dead."

When Hult and Chovuk came down into the valley, a great fire was burning at the foot of the Mourning-stone.

Around it, on stools of fine wood and horn, sat the Tegins. They were all different, from men who had reached the ancient age of seventy summers to youths who had only just come of age. Some were hugely muscled, others thin and wiry, and a few fat and shining with sweat. Many bore prominent scars, or were missing fingers, hands, even entire arms. All wore tattoos on their cheeks, denoting their standing among the Uigan. Behind each stood poles bearing their tribal standards—a silken flag, a bear's skull, a black horsetail farther along. Squatting at each lord's right hand was his *tenach*, saber at the ready to defend his master should trouble strike.

Chovuk was indeed the last to arrive. All eyes watched as he strode into the circle of firelight, Hult carrying stool and standard behind him. The Tegins fell silent as Chovuk sat in the place of honor, closest to the Stone. The White Sky were one of four tribes that could lay claim to the rank of Boyla, for Chovuk could trace his ancestry back to Ajal, the first man to rule all the Uigan. The other three royal lords, Sugai of Raven Eye, Torug of Ten Arrows, and Hoch of Wolf Moon—Krogan's eldest living son—watched with dark eyes as he took his place by the fire.

"Chovuk Tegin," growled Torug, a long-bearded mountain of a man who wore the pelt of a griffin as a cloak over his mail-coat. "We are honored that you finally join us."

Some of the Tegins laughed at that, but most kept quiet. Chovuk and Torug held no love for each other: this was well known. Squatting at his master's side, Hult watched the towering lord's *tenach*, a pale-skinned mute known only as Fox. The warrior stared back, his black eyes full of disdain.

"I am just as pleased," Chovuk replied. "To see you sober is a rare pleasure, Torug Tegin."

There was more laughter, louder this time. Torug's lip curled. In the past, Tegin-circles had sometimes degenerated from councils into brawls that left dozens of great lords dead. Hult wondered if this might be one of those meetings. He tightened his grip on his *shuk*. If Fox took so much as a step toward Chovuk, he would put the blade through the man's throat.

"Stop your yapping, you pups," snapped Sugai, at sixty the eldest of the four royal Tegins. His braid and beard were the color of snow, as Krogan's had been. "We have business here this night, and it is not to gripe at one another."

"Show respect," Hoch added. He was only fifteen, with few hairs on his chin. "My father is newly hung above us."

"And how lucky for Chovuk that he found Krogan's body!" leered Torug. "How fortunate it gives him the right of first claim, by our laws."

Chovuk's face could have been carved from stone. "Speak straight, Torug—if you can. What is it you imply?"

Hult bit the inside of his cheek, forced himself to remain calm. Betray nothing, he told himself. Show no sign you know the truth. He kept his eyes on Fox, who glowered back.

"I imply nothing," Torug replied, grinning to show several missing teeth. "You are merely a lucky man."

Growling, Chovuk leaned forward. Torug met his gaze, a wolf's smile tightening his mouth. Fox licked his lips.

"I said *enough*!" thundered Sugai, rising from his stool. He drew his sword. "Whoever makes the next taunt, I answer him with steel."

The lesser lords murmured at this. Sugai was well respected among the Tegins, though for his wisdom, not his prowess at arms. Once he had been a fine warrior, but all knew age had stiffened his joints. That he offered to keep the peace here showed how important peace was. Torug and Chovuk didn't seem to hear him, however. They continued to glare at each other for a long while before, finally, Chovuk broke the contest with a shrug, as if the other man wasn't worth the bother. He looked to Sugai, who still held his *shuk* ready.

"You will judge this, then?" he asked. "You make no claim to rule?"

"I do not," said Sugai. "I am old and soon to die. Let a man with life ahead of him be Boyla."

"But not so young a man as I," said Hoch. "I will rule my father's tribe, but not the Tamire. Not yet."

"Then it is between us," Torug said, his eyes gleaming in the firelight. "Or will you withdraw your claim, Chovuk?"

"I will not," Chovuk replied, standing and clapping a hand to his mailed chest. "I am the rightful Boyla. I lay first claim."

Noise erupted within the valley. The lesser Tegins shouted encouragement for Chovuk. Torug's face darkened, for it was clear Chovuk had most of their support. Hult was not surprised. Torug was a brute, and his tribe a quarrelsome one, killers and horse thieves. There hadn't been a Boyla from Ten Arrows since before the First Destruction.

Nonetheless, Torug rose from his stool and spoke vehemently. "And I challenge," he declared. "Let a warrior lead our people and bring death to the dogs who slew Krogan!"

A chorus of lusty shouts answered him—fewer than had yelled for Chovuk, but more than Hult had expected. By playing on the Tegins' yearning for blood, he had won some support away from his rival.

Chovuk was undeterred. "Of course you would bring death to the Kazar," he said, gesturing at the faces around the fire. "Who here would not? But you have no vision beyond, Torug. Some men behold a thunderstorm and see the power of the gods. You would call it pretty lights in the sky."

Laughter at this, and a warning look from Sugai. Torug's face twisted in mute fury; it could have belonged to one of the prince-corpses swinging from the Mourningstone.

"And what is your vision, Chovuk?" he growled.

"War. Not just raiding, but war. Yes, let the Kazar bleed for their wrongs, but we have other foes as well. And none greater than those who cling to our southern lands."

The Tegins murmured, raising their eyebrows as they looked at one another. Hult glanced up at his lord, startled. Fox flexed his arms, his eyes bare slits. All knew what Chovuk meant, the minotaurs of the Imperial League, once separated from the Tamire by the waters of the Tiderun. Nearly ten generations ago, they had built their first colonies on the Run's northern shore, in lands the Uigan had held for thousands of years. The bull-men had not negotiated with the riders, but had simply pushed them out—with sword and spear when necessary. There had been much strife in those days, but in the end the League's legions had proven too strong to overcome, so the Uigan had left.

But they had never forgotten.

"What say you, Chovuk Tegin?" asked Sugai. "Do you speak of the bull-men? Would you challenge the League?"

"I would do more," Chovuk answered. "I would make open war on them and drive them from their cities of stone, back across the Tiderun! Send them out of our lands forever!"

Some of the Tegins roared and stomped their feet, but most of the lords did not know how to react, and Hult couldn't blame them. Part of him reveled at the thought of making war on the League, for the bull-men's colonies pushed farther into the Uigan lands every year, particularly now that the Godless Night was over. But the bull-men were strong, and their warriors had won every battle they had fought against the folk of the Tamire. The Uigan raided their caravan lines sometimes, but they hadn't openly challenged the League in more than two centuries.

"A fine dream," Torug scoffed, folding his arms across

his chest. "But greater men than you have chased this phantom and died for it! You would lead our people to a fruitless doom!"

Chovuk spat into the fire. "Long have I known you a fool, Torug, but not before today would I have called you coward."

Sugai, who had raised his hand to intervene again, now stepped back, shaking his head. It had gone too far, even for his wisdom to mend. When one Tegin called another coward, only one thing could follow. Immediately Torug yanked an iron hammer from his belt and brandished it at Chovuk. Flecks of spit flew from his lips as he spoke.

"Coward, is it?" he roared. "You shall regret that—but not for long!"

Fox moved like a striking serpent, leaping to his feet and pointing his blade at Hult. Hult rose as well, returning the gesture. The two *tenachai* moved to stand protectively before their lords, even as Chovuk slid his *shuk* from its scabbard. Sugai, Hoch, and the other nearby Tegins moved away, clearing a ring of bare earth by the fire. Now there would be a blood-duel. Four men would fight, lords and protectors together. At least two would not leave the Vale of Princes alive.

"Come on, then," said Chovuk. "You will like the taste of my steel."

For a long moment no one moved. The only sounds were the crackle of the fire and the creak of the Boylas' corpses, swaying above. Hult studied Fox, guessing how the attack would come. It was up to a *tenach* to make the first move. Most duels ended in a few breaths, and more often than not, it was the attacker who made the first mistake. Besides, Fox was known to be impatient, impulsive.

And now, he attacked. He was horribly fast, his blade almost disappearing with the speed of its arc. Hult leaned back, felt the saber's tip blow by his face, then spun aside, bringing his own *shuk* about and thrusting for his opponent's bowels. Fox twisted, avoiding the blow, but the edge still scored his side, cutting through his leather vest to leave a bloody gash in his skin. With bared teeth, he reversed his swing, jerking his sword hilt-first toward Hult's jaw. It struck home, and Hult reeled back, tasting blood and probing a loose tooth with the tip of his swelling tongue.

Fox parried the next blow, then shoved Hult back, almost making him stumble. Hult blocked a backhand slash at his knees, then turned aside a following stab.

Torug was laughing, cheering on his *tenach*. Fox sneered, sensing the kill. Steel rang against steel, again and again, as Hult tired.

Just then, a knot in a huge log on the fire burst, sending up a shower of cinders with a loud bang. Hult blinked, surprised by the noise—but Fox did worse. He *flinched*, his eyes flicking toward the blaze—then widening as he realized his mistake.

Hult leaped, feinting for Fox's side, then spinning around him and flicking his *shuk* at the back of the man's knee. The blade bit deep, cutting through flesh and tendon, and Fox stumbled. The tip of his saber drove into the ground as he tried to steady himself, and the look of shock on his face gave way to resignation—then burst into agony as Hult's sword slid between his ribs. With a gasp, Fox collapsed and lay wheezing, sliding quickly toward death.

Hardly believing his luck, Hult jerked his *shuk* free—then suddenly he was on the ground, stars exploding in his head amid the clanging of enormous bells. Blood washed down the side of his face, and the world swam around him, blackness scrabbling at the edges.

At first, he didn't understand what had happened. But then he saw Torug, standing over him with his warhammer, and he knew. He'd devoted all his thought to Fox, forgetting that Fox was only a *tenach*. It was a wonder Torug hadn't killed him outright, hadn't smashed his brains into the dirt. Now all he could do was lie stunned as the Tegin raised his hammer.

A strange thing happened next. He heard Chovuk speaking, but the words were not those of the Uigan tongue. Indeed, they were something he had never heard in his life: strange, skittering sounds he could never have mimicked, no matter how hard he tried. Hult could almost grasp their meaning, but the words eluded him, like heat-shimmer over the plains in summertime. He felt a surge around him, making him think of the air before a thunderstorm—and then Torug fell back, his eyes wide with horror. The Tegin turned, tried to run. . . .

With a bloodthirsty roar, a huge, striped form struck Torug from behind. Through the haze of his dimming vision, Hult saw long, ripping claws and even longer teeth like sword-blades. *Steppe-tiger*, he thought, watching it slam Torug to the ground. The hammer went flying.

But that made no sense. There hadn't been a steppe-tiger in that part of the Tamire for a thousand years. The Uigan had hunted the beasts out, making the land safe for horse and man.

Torug flailed, trying to get up, but his legs wouldn't obey. His back was broken. He could only fumble at his belt for a knife as the tiger gazed down on him with piercing black eyes. It held a massive paw above Torug's stomach, then, almost gently, drove a single claw in. A scream of pain burst from the Tegin's mouth, followed by blood.

The tiger did a strange thing, then—something it should not have been capable of doing. Looking down on its dying prey, it smiled, the lips curling in a grin of cruel glee. A look completely alien on the face of an animal. It even seemed to laugh, massive shoulders heaving up and down. Torug gurgled, helpless, his eyes pits of stark terror. Jaws open wide, the tiger stooped over him . . .

. . . and the world swam away from Hult at last. The last things he heard, before all went black, were Torug's dying shriek, and the crunch of teeth through bone.

Hult lay beneath a heap of blankets in the dark warmth of a yurt. Chovuk's yurt. His head hummed like it was full of bees, and when he tried to sit up they all stung at once. Moaning, he sank back down, his vision blurring behind tears of pain.

"Be still," said an old woman's voice. A dark shape bent over him. He saw brown robes: a healer. "You're lucky you didn't end up a smear on Torug's hammer last night."

Last night? Hult thought. What is the hour? He tried to ask her, but the words became a long, slurred mumble. It was dark in the yurt.

"I said be still!" the healer repeated, then looked back as the tent flap opened behind her. Bright daylight poured in. "My lord," she said. "He is just awake."

Another figure strode up beside her. Hult willed his vision to clear—and slowly, it did. Standing over him was Chovuk. He no longer wore his chieftain's leathers, but instead had on a coat of mail fashioned in the shape of dragon scales.

Chovuk Tegin was now Chovuk Boyla, prince of all the Uigan.

"Rest, *tenach*," he said. "You will mend, but you need a few days. That wretch almost killed you."

Hult sucked in a breath, made himself speak clearly. "T-tiger," he said. "Where. . . ?"

"Later," Chovuk said. "All will be clear, when you have rested. Don't worry, *tenach*. You did well."

He smiled, and Hult gasped in awe. He knew that grin. It had been the last thing Torug Tegin saw.

Chapter 6

HAWKVALE, THENOL

Something flashed by Barreth Forlo's eye, making him blink and jerk back. He heard a hiss, then a thud as the object struck a blackwood tree behind him. He glanced over his shoulder, putting a hand to his face, and saw an arrow quivering in the tree's trunk. Slivers of bark fell to the ground.

Khot, he swore silently. That was meant for me. Another half an inch, and I'd be dead.

"Treason!" cried a voice to his left. "Betrayers! Foes in the—"

The shout choked off into a pained grunt. The man beside him crumpled, a feathered shaft in his heart. More arrows were flying, bodies were falling. All around, men and minotaurs went down... some dying, most dead. *His* men and minotaurs. It was a slaughter.

I am dreaming, some part of him thought. This is a battle I have already fought. It took place on the last march, to Hawkbluff. We were camped, waiting for the muster to attack. I survived then. I am in no danger now.

Thinking and believing were different things, however. The fear took over, the same terror that had driven him then—that he, like so many of his men, would end up buried in the accursed earth of Thenol. That he would not return home. That Essana, his wife, would still be waiting for him when the emperor's messengers brought her his broken sword, a traditional gift to wives whose mates were slain in battle.

His sword shrieked as he jerked it from its scabbard. The blade clipped another arrow, sending it spinning away as his heart lurched. Twice, he'd missed death by sheer luck.

He cast about, trying to see what was going on. His men were camped in a clearing, surrounded on all sides by trees. The distant shadows of mountains rose to the south. Above, the red moon shone, its glow lost to the fires that flickered among the orderly rows of tents. There was little order now, however. Men were running and shouting everywhere. Some of the tents had collapsed. On the camp's far side, a storm of golden embers rose into the sky. Bellows of rage and confusion filled the air.

There. His eyes focused on the trees, and in the fire-glow he saw what he was looking for: an archer crouching low, thinking he was out of sight. He was garbed and cloaked in black, little more than a shadow, and beneath his hood was a hideous mask, painted to look like a leering skull. His bow was small, made of horn and bone, and the arrow he pulled from his quiver was tipped with bone as well.

Thenolite, Forlo thought. Damn the slime.

He moved quickly, running not toward the man but slightly to the left, forcing his gaze away. It worked. The archer didn't move, convinced he was invisible in the shadows. He nocked the arrow and raised the bow, beginning to draw back the string—then stopped, crying out as Forlo suddenly turned toward him. Taken by surprise, the archer let fly, and his arrow flashed uselessly away into the night. He rose to flee, but Forlo was quicker, his sword lashing out in a precise, lethal arc. A fan of dark blood spattered the ferns, and the archer collapsed, the top of his head sheared off.

Forlo spun before the man hit the ground. "The trees!" he yelled. "Look to the trees!"

His men didn't need to be told twice. The humans and minotaurs of the Sixth Imperial Legion were well trained, and the initial disarray of the sneak attack was already wearing off. With a chorus of shouts, the soldiers charged the woods, swords and axes flashing. A handful died, killed by one last round of arrows. Then the air filled with a sound Forlo knew well, the hacking of steel into flesh that he recalled from scores of battles over more years than he wanted to count.

There was something different about the din of battle tonight, though: no clash of steel against steel, no cries from the Thenolites as the Sixth Legion tore through them. They died quietly, not fighting back. Indeed, the next archer Forlo found all but leaped onto his sword. The eyes beneath the man's skull-mask rolled white with madness before dulling forever.

Fanatics, Forlo thought, and spat on the body as it slid off his blade. Curse this country and the madmen who live in it.

It was over as suddenly as it began, the sounds of killing fading away, leaving only the groans of the injured. Forlo turned and looked back over the camp. His men were already falling to duty, again without his prompting—aiding the wounded who could be saved and cutting the throats of those who couldn't. Others combed the brush around the camp, searching for archers still in hiding. Forlo nodded in approval, then made his way back to where he'd been standing when the attack began. He found a rag and wiped the blood from his sword, then stopped, staring at the first arrow the fanatics had shot, the one that had nearly hit him in the face. It had driven more than an inch deep into the blackwood, its point strengthened by unholy magic and twisted runes smoking along its length. They were already fading, and he could no longer read them.

Meant for me, he thought.

He was still regarding the arrow when a hulking figure loomed up beside him: a gray-furred minotaur with a double-bladed waraxe. Blood caked the blade, and matted the fur on his forearms.

"Grath," Forlo said. "What word?"

The minotaur shrugged, snorting in disgust. "We got them all," he said. "No prisoners, though. It was like they all wanted to die."

They did want to die, Forlo thought. It was bred into the Thenolites from birth as a part of their faith. To die hurting one's foes was a noble end, a sure way to earn their gods' favor in the afterlife. He shook his head at the thought. Surely that wasn't so. Even the minotaurs, whose god was not a friendly one, believed the Thenolite fanatics damned. They must be rotting in the Abyss, even now.

He glanced at the arrow again, burning with dark magic, green flames leaping up off it. He'd come so close to the same fate tonight. . . .

"Have the men build a pyre. We will burn our dead tonight," he commanded. "Stake the Thenolites' heads, and give their bodies to the dogs. And have whoever was supposed to be on watch tonight flogged. I won't stand for—"

He stopped, smelling something foul, like brimstone but more sour—and beneath it, was that the stink of roasting meat? He glanced around, puzzled. That was when the pain finally hit him. A burning blaze in his leg, in the meat of his left thigh, just below the buttock. It was as though someone had cut him open and forced nettles into the wound. Jolts like lightning pulsed from the wound with every beat of his heart.

With a yell, he collapsed. Then he saw: not all the Thenolite arrows had missed him. One had hit, though nowhere vital, and not deep. The fury of battle had blotted out the pain. The bone-tipped arrow was ablaze with green fire, like its mate in the tree, whatever

Sargas-be-damned spells the fanatics had put on it taking hold.

Shot in the arse, he thought, as he had on that day . . . what a stupid way to die. He groaned, fumbling for the shaft. Gods, how it *burned*. . . .

Grath saw it too, and swore. He knelt down, calling for a cleric, a mage, *anyone* . . . then, without thought for himself, he grabbed the arrow. The venomous flames enveloped his hand, charring the flesh, adding a new stink. Baring his pointed teeth, the minotaur planted a foot next to the wound and leaned back, pulling with all his might. The arrow fought him: it was *alive*, somehow, didn't want to come out.

They both screamed. . . .

Fog, fresh air, a gray glow in the east. Forlo gasped, the echo of a yelp ringing in his ears. His own voice. Where was he?

The pain in his leg had decreased to a dull, throbbing ache. He put a hand to his thigh, where the arrow had been in the dream. There was a knot-like scar there now, which the Mislaxans had told him would hurt whenever the weather turned wet. He remembered the rest of that night, how close the arrow's spell had come to killing him. The clerics had worked through much of the night to save his life. Elsewhere, he would find later, similar bands of assassins had killed three other marshals in the night.

But he had survived, and he'd cut off Bishop Ondelos's head. That should have been satisfaction enough—but the nightmares still came. He'd never had them before, not in all the years he'd fought for the League. Ever since he'd retired, though, they rode him hard. He lay back, safe in a rocky gorge near a row of old, cracked pillars, and shuddered. Would the nightmares continue for the rest of his life? Would he ever sleep soundly again?

"Dreaming again?"

He snorted, his head snapping up again, and saw the horned shadow nearby, crouched in the glow of his campfire's embers. Grath leaned forward, his face strangely gentle in the ruddy light.

He saved my life, Forlo thought. I would have died that night, if he hadn't called for help. That was the way with soldiers, though—they muddle through because of each other. He had beaten back death for Grath, as well.

"The night the Thenolites waylaid us in the Hawkvale," he said. "When I got shot."

Grath nodded, looking down at his hand. Forlo couldn't see in the dark, but he knew what he was looking at. The burning arrow had scarred him, too.

"It's all right," the minotaur said. "You're safe now. Soon, home."

Forlo nodded. "You're sure you've never had any dreams?"

"No." Grath made a sour face, looking like he meant to say more, then shook his head. "None."

Sighing, Forlo lay back again. "I wish I knew why *I* do."

"Don't look to me to explain how your mind works," the bull-man said, and snorted. "You humans are weird creatures. I've always said it, and now's the proof."

Forlo chuckled, then yawned. Sleep was coming back to him. He hoped it would be peaceful this time. "Thank you, my friend. For saving me."

"You were my commander."

It was all the answer Grath gave. All he had ever given. It was enough. Sighing, Forlo shut his eyes and drifted off again.

"I couldn't tell you this before," Grath said the next day, leagues from the ravine where they'd slept. He leaned on his shield, which was planted in the ground before him. Its face was emblazoned with the crimson and azure of the Sixth, with crossed axes over it in gold: a marshal's sigil. "But now that I'm in command, I'll say it. I think you're a damned fool."

Forlo nodded, accepting the rebuke. One made allowances with minotaurs—not least because the bull-men could break a human's neck with one hand. No minotaur would do what he'd done, give up his rank and command after all his years with the legion. Their whole civilization was built on the ideal of honorable combat. It was in their blood. Grath thought he was mad. So did half the humans in the Sixth, for that matter.

"You may be right," he said. "I might have agreed with you, before Thenol. But I've done enough. The emperor agreed, or he wouldn't have given me his leave."

They stared out together across a long, shallow valley that wound among the ridges of the League's northern provinces. Down below, gathered in orderly ranks, their red cloaks blowing in the wind, were the Sixth. The survivors of the Thenol Campaign. They had come north with him as a courtesy, to the borders of the fief of Coldhope, but now the time had come to part. They were needed to the east, in the hills of Okami. Bandits were raiding the towns there, taking advantage of the confusion of the interregnum to score some easy plunder. Duke Rekhaz had sent the Sixth to show the brigands that the League still took its laws seriously.

They had come as far as they could. It was time to part.

"You'll miss it soon enough," Grath said. "Your ears will start itching for the sound of war-horns. You know where we are if they do."

Forlo might have argued, might have told Grath of how heavy his heart grew when he thought of war. Instead, he turned and clasped his longtime second's arm. "Take care of the men," he said. "You'll make the Sixth even prouder than before."

The minotaur grinned and returned the gesture. Then he turned and called out across the vale. *"Tamar khai!"*

At his command, the soldiers raised their spears, the steel heads flashing white in the sunlight. A thickness settled in Forlo's throat. He felt a surge of regret that those spears were no longer his.

Eyes stinging, he drew his sword and lifted it in reply. The men and minotaurs of the Sixth cheered.

"I will see you again," said Grath, saluting. "Until then, fair winds at your back, my friend."

"And a full mug before you," Forlo replied: the old warrior's farewell. He returned the salute, then clasped the minotaur's arms. Both warriors' eyes were glistening when they separated again. Smiling sadly, Forlo turned his back on the Sixth and started down the ridge, toward home.

Coldhope was a large holding, though scarcely populated, which lay on the League's northern coast overlooking the Tiderun Straight. A hundred miles to the west stood proud Thera, the minotaurs' pleasure city. A hundred to the east was Faroen, a gray, rain-soaked town of little cheer. Coldhope itself boasted only a handful of villages among its farmlands, where peasants raised crops of barley and longroot, or tended herds of stubborn sheep and goats. It was a five-day walk from the fief's edge to the main town and its keep, both of which shared the region's name.

For most of those days, Forlo saw hardly anybody, and spoke to no one. That suited him well enough. He had no dearth of thoughts to wear on him. He wondered what would become of Grath and the legion. Would someone rise in the Thenolite Church to take Ondelos's place? And could the League survive the struggles among Ambeoutin's would-be heirs? Who would rule, when the dust settled?

Each day, however, these troubles faded. The deeper into the fief he went, the more his thoughts turned to what lay ahead. Coldhope Keep beckoned. Ancestrally owned by his wife's family, the keep had been his home since the day he'd married. That had been fourteen years ago, but he'd only spent a few months within its walls, all told. Well, that would soon change. He would live off the taxes of his peons for the rest of his days—not a vast amount, but enough to dwarf the pittance the army paid him on his retirement. It would do.

The nightmares continued, every night a different battle echoing through his mind. He began to grow used to waking in the dark, cold with sweat, and that thought troubled him more than the dreams themselves. Would he ever again have peace from dusk to dawn?

On the last night, camped in a hillside hollow, a coney roasting over his fire, the dread came over him at last. It was a familiar feeling, one that had haunted him every time he returned home from battle. What if something had gone wrong in his absence? What if his home was gone?

It was totally irrational, of course. He'd been gone three years, true, but news traveled quickly within the League's armies. He would have heard if anything was amiss at Coldhope. In his heart, he knew all was surely well. Even so, that didn't stop Forlo's mind from roving. He imagined himself coming over the last rise to see the keep nothing more than a burnt-out shell, or emptied by plague, or burst asunder by dragonbreath. Perhaps the peasants had risen up and stormed the place, slaughtering all within. Or—and here was one he hadn't thought of before the disaster at Kristophan—maybe the rock on which it stood had crumbled, casting all into the sea.

With a snarl, he leaped up from the fireside, took two paces to the north—then stopped, trying to convince himself it was all right. Coldhope would be there in the morning. He hesitated for a long moment, torn between charging ahead or returning to his fire, then his wits returned and he turned back, laughing at himself. He would not come home at night, like a wolf or a thief.

Sleep came fitfully, haunted by steel and shouting. He woke in the dawn light more tired than when he'd laid his head down. Gathering the last scraps of the coney—hung from a tree to keep it from foxes—he wolfed the meat down and chased it with the dregs from his wineskin. The stuff was sour, burning all the way down. Soldier's grape was one thing he wouldn't miss about the legions. There were better vintages in Coldhope's cellars.

The road stretched on as it had for the past four days, over hills dotted with hazel and down through grassy dells where clear streams ran. Something had changed this morning, however: the sea was near. He could smell the tang of salt on the breeze as it blew in his face. Gulls wheeled overhead, blown inland and squalling as they fought their way back toward the sea. He imagined he could hear the distant rush of the waves, but it was still too far away. It was only his ears playing with him. He knew this part of the fief well, had crossed it many times. He knew how close Coldhope lay.

The images that had worried him the night before came back strong when he climbed Axeman's Tor, a gray, treeless hill that formed the last barrier before the road reached its destination. He focused on its peak, felt his pace slowing as it drew near. He half-feared what sight lay beyond, and the last few steps up the tor's shoulder were as hard as any he'd taken. Holding his breath, he clambered up over the stones . . .

Beyond, the ground dropped slowly down toward the water. The strait was narrow here, muddy from low tide. Beyond, dim and almost lost in the mist, was the dark line of the far shore, where the plains of the Tamire began. Closer, on this side of the channel, lay the village—thatch-roofed cottages of limestone in a haze of cookfire-smoke, jumbled about a small marketplace at the foot of another tor, where an armless statue of a minotaur stood crusted with bird dung. Docks reached out into the water, their long piles exposed, the fishing and trading vessels at moor there stranded until the tides rose again.

His eyes flicked back to the bluffs and traveled up to the fortress perched on their highest point. It was hewn of white rock and surrounded by a thick crenellated wall: a tall five-pointed keep with copper roofs all green with age. Watchfires burned on the battlements, and a beacon shone white atop the tall, middle spire. Gold banners stirred listlessly on the feeble wind, and stained-glass windows sparkled in the sun. A long spur of rock extended out toward the water, like a finger pointing at the far shore. A balcony was carved into its top, surrounded by a low balustrade, with pots of bloodblossoms dotting the top. The Northwatch, it was called, one of the best vantages along the empire's north shore.

Forlo smiled: Coldhope Keep was whole.

Going down the tor was far easier than climbing it. He had new thoughts to occupy him as he went. He would go straight to the keep, try to get to the manor before the servants raised a stir. With the help of Voss, the chamberlain, he would find out where *she* was, then he would sneak up. . . .

Then he stopped, his mind emptying as he saw the figure on the castle wall, looking out at him. Tall, slender as a willow-wand even as she neared her fortieth summer, long black hair piled and pinned atop her head, and a gown of red and golden silk gathered about her. He was too far away still to make out her face, but he knew it anyway, knew the way the light danced in her ice-blue eyes, the knowing rise at the corners of her mouth. She never could hide her smiles.

So Barreth Forlo saw Essana, his wife, for the first time in three years.

The last mile was a blur he never remembered. Before he knew it he was through the gates, guards and footmen scattering out of his way. She waited on the wall, her smile blooming full as he took the stairs three at a time—then he stopped at the top, blood pounding in his ears. She stood ten feet from him, almost unchanged. There was a bit of gray in her hair now, and deeper crinkles around her laughing eyes, but she was every bit as beautiful as when he'd left on the long road to Thenol. Maybe more.

"Starlight," he breathed, his name for her. It was all he could manage.

A tear dropped from her lashes, and broke his heart. The scent of honeybloom hung about her, heady as Theran pipe-smoke. Below, the keep's servants and guards gathered, watching in respectful silence as lord and lady faced each other.

"You came back," she said.

Then he was on her, grabbing her in his arms and pressing her against his armored chest, his lips crushed against hers, laughter and tears all coming at once, and he didn't care about anything else in all of Krynn.

Forlo sat up, the world coming back to him. He was groggy, and tired, and his head hurt. But he was also in a real bed, with warm, bare skin pressed against his. He couldn't count how long since he'd felt either—unlike many soldiers, he didn't dally with camp followers.

The nightmares had come again. He'd hoped being back with her would make them go away. He lay there, memories of men on fire hanging before his eyes, and shivered in the cold. Something gnawed at him, down deep.

The room—his bedchamber, which he hadn't seen in years—was dark, lit only by the banked fire upon the hearth. Rich carpets, woven by artisans on the great looms of Rudil, covered the floor and a fresco of a clear, summer sky covered the ceiling. When the room was lit, it looked open, like a courtyard. There was a couch, chairs, a table, all made—like the broad, fur-heaped bed—of white ghostwood. The shutters were closed and the candles were doused. Bits of clothing and armor were scattered everywhere. He stared bemusedly at one of his pauldrons, dangling from a bedpost.

Forlo lay back, wiped his eyes, then turned over to look at the woman who slept at his side. He'd wondered, over the long journey back to Coldhope, how Essana might have changed. He knew he had—more scars on his body, less hair on his head, a beard he hadn't had before. To his surprise, she was almost exactly as she had been. Everything about her was familiar. He could spend hours admiring the curve of her naked back, glowing amber in the firelight. He'd done just that, in his youth. He reached over and brushed her long hair—unbound now, long and gleaming—from her shoulders. Then he kissed the place he'd uncovered.

"Mmmm," she said, shifted, then lay still again.

Starlight. He'd first met her when he was a young officer in the Sixth, twenty years ago. Half his life. He'd been in Kristophan, enjoying the city after a hard-fought campaign against hobgoblins in the eastern marches. She'd come to the city with her father, Lord Varyan, Baron of Coldhope. He'd stolen a dance with her at the Festival of Masks, half-drunk on Hulder-wine. At dawn they'd kissed in front of a lute-shop, and from then on he'd known he would marry her. The Baron had disapproved, but they'd kept their tryst, and after a year of wooing he wore Lord Varyan down and won Essana's hand. Two years later, the Baron had died of a burst heart, and she inherited his lands.

Gods, what a long time ago—during the Godless Night, beneath the pale moon. They'd made a home here, in the keep, and had tried to have a family. Despite their best efforts, though, they couldn't sire any children. Then the war had come, and he had left to fight in Thenol. It seemed he'd been away a thousand years, and at the same time it was as if he'd never left their bed.

An ache in his bladder snapped him out of his reverie. Wincing, he bent over to kiss her again, then swung his legs out of bed. The evening air was freezing and the floor was made of ice. He shivered as he dragged a robe over his naked body. She'd had the servants bring a bottle of Hulder-wine for them to share, and they'd drank and made love until they'd fallen asleep. Hours.

When he came out of his robe again, she had rolled over to lie in the middle of the bed. He sighed at the sight—she'd grown accustomed to sleeping alone—then went to the door and out, down the curving stair to the keep's great hall. It was empty, hung with swords and shields and tapestries depicting Lord Varyan and the barons before him. Another fire burned low at the near wall, in a hearth whose gray mantel was carved to resemble two intertwined dragons. He walked past the great feasting-table, a board long enough to seat forty men, then down a narrow flight of steps to the kitchens. A few servants were there, washing pots and gossiping. They fell silent, bowing as he entered.

He waved them away when they offered to help. Even when he wasn't in the field, Forlo liked to cook for himself. He put a skillet over the fire and got to work on a dish of peppers, mushrooms, and duck eggs. There was half a kettle of tarbean tea left, too, so he poured himself a mug, then took it, the skillet, and a spoon back up to the great hall, and out yet another door to the Northwatch. It was twilight. The rose of sunset faded to violet and the moons were low over the eastern horizon, hiding behind rags of cloud. The waters were rising again, and surf beat against the rocks below, sending plumes of spray into the air. Reorx, the red planet the dwarves revered, hung low before him. Beneath, on the far shore, glowed the lights of Malton, one of the League's colonies, where traders brought furs, oil, and good horses from the tribes of the plains.

He didn't know how long he leaned against the balustrade, staring at nothing while he ate. When he heard her stealing up behind him, though, both eggs and tea were gone and the sky was dark. He pretended not to hear her and started when she slid her arms around him. She laughed, laying her head upon his back. They stood like that for a while.

"I woke and you were gone," she murmured. "I thought you'd left again, till I saw your armor."

He turned, embracing her. "I'm not going anywhere, Starlight. I'm done—released from service."

"Done?" she asked. "With the troubles in the capital, they still let you go?"

"Well, Rekhaz didn't like it, but he couldn't do anything." He kissed her hair. "It's over. No more war for me."

She pulled back, her eyes narrowing as she looked up at him. "What will you do?"

"Love you," he said, shrugging. "Live here. Help you run the fief. Hunt, sail, deal with any problems that might happen. I thought we might try for children again."

Essana bowed her head. "I'd feared you'd say that," she said. "It won't happen, Barreth. My womb—"

"We'll get a healer to help. The Mislaxans have their power back now," Forlo said. He touched her chin, raised it so she looked at him. The look in her eyes made him crumble a little: hope and fear at war. "I don't expect anything, Starlight. But we can try. All right?"

She held his gaze for a long moment, then laughed, blotting tears from her eyes. "I'm sorry. None of this seems real. When I saw you come over the tor, I thought I'd gone mad. I'm still not sure what's happening."

"I know," he said. "Come on. Let's go inside. I'll make you something to eat."

He put his arm around her shoulders; she slid hers around his waist. "I'd like that," she said, smiling as they walked back into the keep.

Chapter 7

ULD, THE STEAMWALL MOUNTAINS

Shedara had traveled from one end of Southern Hosk to the other, and up into the plains to the north. She had witnessed the great necropolises of Thenol, where tombs and mausoleums stretched from horizon to horizon. She had watched a black dragon pulled apart by blood-vines in the dank dark of the Blackwater swamps. She had spied on the dark knights of New Jelek, who had come across the sea not long before the Godless Night and who claimed to worship a goddess named Takhisis—a demon-deity unknown in Taladas. Despite this, she had never been anywhere that made her so uncomfortable as the Steamwalls.

Traveling overland—the hippogriff had taken her only to the edge of Armach—it had taken her three weeks to reach the jagged, smoke-wreathed mountains that dominated Hosk's east coast. Here was where the earth's wounds began, the outer edge of the great ring of fire that still boiled at Taladas's heart, where stone and flame had fallen from the heavens and smashed Old Aurim to oblivion. There were no lakes of magma here, as there were farther in, on the far side of the Boiling Sea, but the land here was still dreadful. The air stank of brimstone and hot metal, making tears sting her eyes despite the perfumed scarf she had tied around her nose and mouth. The air was hot and damp, and great waves of ash blew among the peaks like ghosts, leaving everything caked in gray. After a day, the cinders had mixed with the sweat that plastered her clothing to her skin, making a paste that seemed to cover every inch of her body. It felt like it would take years to get clean again.

The mountains themselves were just as forbidding. The Steamwalls had been thrown up in a day, the result of a massive number of volcanic eruptions in the wake of the Destruction. They were black, jagged things, threatening the skies like bony claws, all sharp obsidian and crumbling pumice, alive with steam vents and geysers that sent plumes of noxious steam billowing high into the air. In the distance, several peaks burned as new eruptions arose. Black smoke curled west on the wind and huge fountains of molten rock sprayed bombs that cooled in the air, then exploded when they hit ground again, spattering death everywhere. There had been no trees for days. Nothing but a hardy, rust-colored moss that made food for white, sickly lizards, which in turn made food for things far worse. Ahead, there were clouds of steam rising from the Boiling Sea—and the fires of Hitehkel, the great flaming wound where Aurim had been—reached miles into the air, painting the sky a sickly yellow.

Shedara hadn't seen anything green in over a week. Threading her way among the tangled passes through the Steamwalls, she thought, to her horror, that she was beginning to forget what the color looked like. Was there anything in the world but sulfur and soot and dark, rippling rock?

She still didn't know where she was going, but each day the path grew clearer. She felt close. Another day, maybe a little more, and she would find the spot where Ruskal had sent the Hooded One. If only the possibilities didn't seem to decrease with every league she walked.

Dwarves, she thought, making a sour face behind her

scarf. Why must it be dwarves? The mountain-people weren't as bad as hobgoblins, or the death-lovers of Thenol, in that they did not torture captives before killing them. Still, they had never been friends to the elves. The Silvanaes revered nature. The dwarves destroyed it, ripping open the bones of mountains to prize jewels from the rock and clear-cutting woods to fuel their forges. In the old days, in the faraway lands of her ancestors, wars had been fought between elf and dwarf. Shedara had the suspicion that only two things kept the same from happening here: the distance between their lands, and how few there were of either race in Taladas. In her many years of wandering, she had seen only a handful of the wretched mountain-folk, gods be praised.

There was a rumbling, and the ground trembled beneath her feet. She stopped, putting a hand against the mountainside. The rock—black and flocked with cinders—was warm to the touch. Beneath, the molten stone was coursing. Three days ago she'd seen a volcano erupt from across a wide valley barely a mile away, had watched golden, liquid fire spill down its sides. It had been both beautiful and horrible to see, a beacon of death. If the mountain beside her decided to do the same, there would be no beauty to the sight at all. She would die here, encased forever in stone.

Be still, she bade the mountain. Leave me be, and I will not disturb your rest.

The tremor lasted another minute, then stopped. She tensed, waiting for the mountain's top to blow off, but it remained still, a black cloud covering it like a crown.

The hour was late, so as she crossed a narrow saddleback ridge to the next mountain she studied the face above her, looking for a cave where she could shelter for the night. It got cold in the Steamwalls after sunset, and the constant pall that hung in the air blocked the light of moon and star. With the heat of the volcanoes foiling her elvensight, she was doubly blind. Traversing the passes in the dark was asking to break an ankle, or to step over a cliff and plunge screaming into some chasm.

Half a league on, she found what she was searching for. Fifty feet above her, a cleft opened in the stone. She stopped, watching it for a while to make sure no steam was coming out that might cook her alive in the middle of the night. It remained dark and quiet, though, so she started climbing, grabbing cracks in the rock and stepping on tiny ledges. She didn't need her magic to help her with this. Though steep, the slope was rough enough to let her handle it with her own muscles.

The cave mouth was an overhang, which made the last part of the climb more difficult. She eyed it carefully, looking for the right purchase, then found it and pulled herself over. Gritting her teeth, she got hold of the stone lip, then kicked away from the cliff, leaving her legs to dangle over two hundred feet of nothing. She glanced down at the tangle of broken volcanic glass far, far below, grimacing.

Then, with a determined grunt, she began to swing, side to side, legs churning the air, each time her feet windmilling a little higher, left, right, then left . . . until her heel dug into the ledge beside her, bringing her to a stop. She paused for a breath and, clinging to the rock, pulled herself up the ledge and rolled over onto the floor of the cave. She lay panting for a moment, then reached down, drew a dagger, and peered inside.

The opening was shallow, and there was some old, dried guano on its floor, but nothing seemed to dwell within the cave. It would be enough shelter for one night, though her bones ached for the comfort of pine needles and soft earth. She cleared the floor of rock shards, then spoke a quick word of magic and passed her hands over the bare rock. A low fire sprang up, burning bright and warm despite the lack of fuel. That done, she took a blanket from her pack and used her throwing knives to pin it over the cave's entrance. The magical fire gave off no smoke and she sat down beside it, took a drink from her water-flask, and stared into the dancing flames. As she did, her mind cast back, as it did every evening, to the third night after she left Armach-nesti.

That night, the pearl medallion had grown heavy and warm against her breast, and began to shimmer with pinkish light, as if both Solis and Lunis were trapped inside. The moment she reached for it, a strange feeling had struck her, as though there were another mind in her head. Fighting off the urge to let go of the amulet, she had focused all her thoughts upon the other presence within her brain.

When the presence finally spoke, she hadn't been surprised. "I have tidings for you, Shedara," the voice of Thalaniya had said. "I have spent these days in study, reading books of ancient lore, written in the time of my grandmother's grandmother, when Old Aurim was strong and ruled Taladas. Now I must tell you what I have learned."

"About the Hooded One," Shedara had said—thinking the words, not speaking them aloud.

"Yes."

"In its youth, Aurim was a bright realm, the center of human civilization in Taladas: a land of art and magic, philosophers and heroes, that warred against dragons and ogres to forge civilization in the wilderness. Squabbling city-states and ancestor-worshipping barbarians came together, forming the only great empire this continent has ever known. Unlike long-lost Ansalon, where Ergoth gave birth to Solamnia, which birthed Istar in turn, there had only been Aurim, mighty and unchallenged, covering more than half of Taladas at its height.

"As the centuries passed and its power continued to grow, however, the golden realm's emperors grew degenerate, no longer caring about those who dwelt beyond the walls of their lofty, rose-shaped palace. They studied the arts of Nuvis, the black moon, and sought the secrets of the wild-wizards of old, in the days before the taming of magic. For seven generations, each fouler than the last, this dynasty of dark sorcerers and its disciples enforced a reign of terror across the empire and beyond.

"The last and worst of these was Maladar an-Desh, called Maladar the Faceless in his later years. The histories did not tell how he lost his face, though every sage had theories—a conjured demon from the Abyss had turned on him, or a horrible spell had gone wrong, or he had ruined his own face deliberately, to gain some unusual power—but all agreed he was hideous. His eyes, ears, and nose were mere black pits; the bones of his cheeks were laid bare and surrounded by black, puckered flesh; and his lower jaw was gone completely, so that all that remained of his lipless mouth were his upper teeth and the stump of his tongue, jutting from a ghastly hole at the top of his throat. To hide his hideousness, Maladar kept his face hidden beneath a hood, revealing it only when he wished to strike terror into those nearby. His magic allowed him to see, hear, and speak from within the cowl's shadows.

"Though he only ruled Aurim for a brief time, the list of atrocities Maladar and his followers committed while he sat the throne was sickeningly long. Among the worst of these was the Great Impalement, when—following a failed attempt by the nobility to overthrow him—he ordered the second son of every lord in the empire brought to the Square of Spears, which stood before the imperial palace. There, as Maladar watched from the highest tower, his followers skewered every one of the young men on stakes of barbed iron. The streets of Aurim echoed with the cries of dying men and boys for two days and nights. It was said that he gathered their blood and bathed in it, then had the bodies fed to giant crocodiles in the rivers outside the city.

"Even worse was the fate of Am Durn. A beautiful city, whose walls were sheathed in silver and whose towers gleamed green with malachite, Am Durn had been the third-greatest citadel in all the empire. It was a city of song, and art, and peace. But when the sultanate of Olm, Aurim's southernmost province, rose in rebellion against the throne, Am Durn's prince refused to send an army to aid Maladar in suppressing the uprising. In reprisal, Maladar called upon the sea itself to rise up and take revenge for him, and the sea obeyed: a thousand-foot-high wall of water descended on the city, smashing its academies and amphitheaters, then drowning the pieces. When the waters receded, nothing remained of Am Durn but kelp-choked rubble and broken bodies, swarming with crustaceans. Maladar's wrath had wiped it from the face of Krynn.

"All accounts agreed that Maladar deserved his singular ending. After nine years wearing the emperor's golden helm, after killing countless thousands of his subjects and torturing many more, he fell, in the end, to his own cupbearer. One night, the servant, a boy of eight summers whose father and brothers had died horribly in the imperial dungeons, laced Maladar's wine with the bile of a green dragon. How a servant got such a potent venom no one knew, but Maladar died screaming in agony.

"That should have been the end of it," Thalaniya's voice had said in Shedara's mind, the image of the Faceless Emperor's thrashing body still vivid there. "Maladar was heirless, and his dynasty ended with him. Nobler emperors followed, though Aurim would never regain its old glory, and would fall into evil again in time—an evil only the Destruction would end. It was whispered, though, that Maladar was not dead at all. In case someone slew him, he had placed his soul within an object, to keep it safe from harm. This object was a statue, crafted of black stone in his likeness, cowled to hide a face the sculptor had never carved. The statue was called the Hooded One. His disciples swore to awaken the statue, their master, one day.

"There followed a grand purging—all across the

empire, every icon of Maladar was smashed, sanctified, and scattered to ward against his return. For a century, scholars believed that no statue bearing his likeness remained—but eventually rumors arose that a sect of his followers had kept the Hooded One secret and safe. Only the Destruction ended these rumors, for the statue must have been obliterated with the rest of Aurim. So the sages have believed, ever since."

Sorrow crept into Thalaniya's voice. "They were wrong, it seems. The statue remains, and fell into Ruskal Eight-Finger's unwitting possession, brought out of the ruins of Aurim by treasure-seekers. Now someone is looking for this great artifact, and will kill to find it.

"It is said that, if Maladar returns, his wrath will be beyond measure. His power is greater than any we now know. Whoever seeks to free him must be stopped . . .

"And Shedara, my child . . . for the sake of Taladas, the Hooded One must be destroyed."

Shedara woke shivering, the magical fire having gone out. She knew it was dawn—the spell that conjured the flames had disappeared when the day's first light appeared in the sky. Beyond the blanket she had set over the cave mouth appeared the sickly, brown glow of what passed for sunshine in the Steamwalls. She rose from where she lay, took a drink of fresh water from her flask—it chased the rotten-eggs-and-ashes taste from her mouth, for a while at least—then broke camp. When she was done, she crouched in the cleft, staring out at the black peaks that stretched off into the poisonous clouds that were heaped on the horizon.

Bough and branch, she swore silently, *I want out of this place.*

She shut her eyes, concentrating, as her hands began to move before her. The words of the spell scuttled through her mind and down over her tongue. Lunis was waning today, a ruddy fingernail beyond the mountains' haze, and the magic felt sluggish as it poured through her veins—but it was strong enough still to shape the spell she desired. As she concentrated she pictured the statue, as it had appeared in the Seeing-pool. When the picture was fixed in her mind, she held her right hand out, flat before her, and forced the magic out through her fingertips. A part of her went with it, and she had the disorienting sensation that she had leaped from the cave and was flying out across the void between the mountains. It was only her spirit flying, however. Her body remained where it was, sitting safely in the mouth of the cave, an empty shell awaiting her return at the spell's ending.

Even though she had cast the spell many times before, some part of her still wanted to panic, to break the enchantment and cry out in disoriented fear. Shedara was disciplined, however, and had learned well how to control both the magic and herself. She let her mind roam, questing across the Steamwalls for the Hooded One. Wreaths of toxic vapor flashed past, and she passed through the plume of a vent that sent boiling steam rushing a mile into the air. In the distance, a volcano belched ash in a long trail across the sky. Below, a noxious brown stream coursed among the peaks, its rapids foaming orange as it rushed down toward the Boiling Sea. She could see the open water, barely three leagues from where her body perched, roiling and bubbling and giving off steam that poured back down on the hither slopes as smoldering rain. There, perched improbably around the toxic stream's mouth, was a small village of stone houses, carved into the rock on terraces overlooking the valley.

The town was five hundred feet tall, built almost entirely on the vertical, showing little but doors and windows, and occasional friezes and pillars hewn from the living rock. Stairs cut into the slope led from one level to the next, zigzagging their way to the very top, Here and there, small, bearded figures moved on the paths, or stood on ledges overlooking the abyss below.

So it *is* dwarves, Shedara thought, her distaste growing. They're the ones who bought the Hooded One from Ruskal.

She was about to release the spell when she spied something else: more small figures, darker and more slender than the dwarves, climbing up the sheer slope to the town. They moved swiftly, with a sureness that even her thief-training envied, and there was something strange about their aspect. It was as if they weren't quite there, for every shadow they touched seemed to blend with them, like water-droplets running together. Looking at them for more than a few moments made her feel dizzy.

Miles away, Shedara's body leaned over the edge of the cave-mouth, lips moving, silently shouting a warning the dwarves would never hear. Her enemies had found the statue's trail, and they were a step ahead of her.

Her eyes snapped open, and in a rush of vertigo she was back in her own body, still far from the village. There was no way to reach the dwarves in time, but she jumped up anyway and scrambled down the cliff to the path below. She moved with reckless speed, heedless of how close she came to falling. She could not lose the image of those awful shadow-things, spider-climbing toward the unsuspecting dwarves. Nor did she have any illusions about what would happen when they reached the village. The slaughter would be beginning, even now.

She half-slid the last fifteen feet to the path, landing on the balls of her feet. Then, with the cries of the distant dwarves ringing in her ears, she began to run.

Uld, the place was called: an ugly name for an ugly people. She looked down at the map she had brought, at the tiny dot on the Steamwalls' eastern edge. Then she looked up, and knew the dot of Uld would be marked on maps no more.

Even from here, standing on an outcrop half a mile away, she could tell it was over. She had seen towns, even entire cities, laid waste by war and calamity, but there was something unsettling about this place that she'd observed only once before. An unmistakable stillness about the village—no ruins, no flames . . . not even smoke. Just the silence of death.

During the Godless Night, she had stumbled across a human town whose inhabitants had all died from plague. It had been weirdly tranquil, empty, the buildings intact and filled with the dead. Uld had that same feeling to it.

She made no sound as she crept down toward the village. There was no sign of the shadow-creatures, but she didn't take chances. She held a flat knife in either hand, blades pinched between her fingers, ready to throw. Ahead, heavy stone gates loomed above the path. They stood open. The dwarves hadn't known there was a threat until it was already among them. The body of one watchman hung over the battlements, his throat cut to the bone. No blood dripped from the ghastly wound, though both carotid and jugular had been severed, on either side.

Another dwarf lay in a broken heap in the middle of the road. He'd been ripped open, entrails spilling out on the stones. He hadn't bled, either. Shedara crept past the corpses, on up the trail. The trail worked its way up the cliff, switching back and forth until it reached the first row of homes. Here were more bodies, sprawled on the ground and slumped against walls. A couple held axes and hammers, and one had a sword, but most had been unarmed when they died, cut and slashed and torn. To her amazement, Shedara felt pity for the dwarves. They were an unpleasant people, but they did not deserve this butchery. No one did.

So it went, from delving to delving. She found a forge with the blacksmith slumped over his anvil, his tongs lying just beyond his unmoving fingers. A hundred yards away, an elderly couple sat at a table in their home, a barely eaten meal spread before them. They had just sat down for their morning repast when the shadow-creatures came and carved them open. Children lay in their beds, murdered as they dreamed. There must have been four hundred dwarves in Uld, and not one remained alive. Nor was there any sign of what she sought.

The Hooded One was gone.

Thalaniya listened to her report, her face white in Shedara's mind. She looked away for a moment, shook her head.

Shedara clutched the pearl medallion in her hand, waiting for instructions. To anyone watching, she might have seemed a madwoman, moving her lips soundlessly and cocking her ears, talking to no one—or, perhaps, herself. But there was no one left alive to watch.

"I must know more," Thalaniya said finally.

"What would you have me do, Highness?"

Thalaniya hesitated, reluctance in her eyes, and Shedara knew at once the terrible answer. The sense of distaste that flooded her mind told her what was required. Shedara gritted her teeth, waiting for the words to be spoken.

"It seems to me," said the Voice, "that the only ones who know the answers . . . are the dwarves."

Shedara nodded, cold inside. "If that is your wish, Highness. We will speak again after."

Thalaniya nodded. Her image flickered, then faded, leaving Shedara alone. She sat on Uld's highest ledge, the lifeless village arrayed beneath her. Carrion birds circled—mangy, ragged creatures tumor-ridden from the vapors blowing in off the sea. Dwarf-meat was tough, but the sheer number of them promised a rare feast to the scrawny vultures. Shedara watched them dive, and come back up gobbling terrible things.

"We are not so different, you and I," she told the birds. "Not with what I'm about to do."

Necromancy was a forbidden art, and had been since before the First Destruction. The elves, who revered life more than any other people, loathed it in particular. The use of magic to control the dead, like that used by the Thenolite church, was a profane thing, punishable by permanent exile. Still, moon-thieves were versed in all forms of magic—even the unspeakable ones. Sometimes, dire tactics were necessary.

Shedara had only used the dark art twice, the last time more than twenty years ago. Today would make a third. She shuddered at the thought, at the memory of how the necromancy felt. Yet it was the only way to discover what had happened here. The only way to know the Hooded One's fate.

Rising, she made her way down the winding path, back to where the bodies began. She needed a fresh one, and one still relatively intact. The dead did not cling to their shells long, particularly if those shells were despoiled.

It took her a while to find what she sought. The shadows had ruined most of the corpses, and the birds were quickly ravaging the rest. At last, though, she spotted a warrior in armor, unmarked except for a deep gash in his side, which had cloven through his lung. He had died a quick death, which was good. The ones who had suffered were harder to command.

She laid him out, flat upon the ground, and took off his helm. There were flies on his mouth; she brushed them away. His homely face was made uglier by a grimace of agony. Like every other body in Uld—like Ruskal, his minotaur bodyguard, and his pet tylors—there was no blood, not a drop anywhere. The shadows had drained it all, it seemed.

Reaching out with her magic, Shedara sought the black

moon. It was there, heavy above her, almost full. Nuvis, the source of all dark enchantments, marked in the night sky only by the stars' absences. Its presence felt like poison thorns digging into her mind. She focused on it, moving her hands and speaking profane words to draw down its power.

The spell came together, making bile rise in her throat. She cried out, forcing the magic out of herself again, and burning as it went.

Into the corpse.

Something appeared above the body: a gray smudge, a wisp of fog. It seeped out of the dead dwarf's nose and mouth, coalesced, grew, and took form. Its shape was the same as the corpse beneath it, writhing and twisting on some unseen wind. Its face was shriveled, its cheeks were sunken, and its lips pulled back to reveal long teeth. The eyes were blank, white. Hate came off the ghost in waves.

She stared at it and felt tears sting her eyes. It was hard, holding the spirit here. Pity reared inside her—and fear. The ghost would harm her if she lost control. It could kill her.

"I will free you soon," she said. "But first, I have questions."

It glared. Its teeth were sharp, like a rat's.

"Will you answer?" she asked.

"I must," the dwarf replied. "Or do you offer a choice?"

She shook her head.

The ghost's eyes flared with white fire. "Then begin."

Tears crept down Shedara's cheeks. She fought the urge to vomit. "There was a statue. . . ." she said.

Chapter 8

MOUNT XAGAL, THE ILQUARS

The mountain loomed high over the Tamire, tall and jagged, standing out behind the crumbling, dusty foothills. It stood in shadow, silhouetted against the afternoon sun, an ominous, dark monolith that already cast a long shadow, though midday was only two hours past. A few blood-needle trees, scraggly things with gnarled, thorny branches, clung to its lower slopes, among skirts of scree. Above, they gave way to banded, ruddy rock, which rose in great treacherous sheets, unassailable to any being not born with wings. Patches of snow, melting with the coming of spring, dotted the heights, breaking away here and there to slide off the mountain's side, where the wind shredded them into icy dust. And at the crown of the peak, where the lowest shreds of cloud scudded, were three spires of red rock, forming something that, from a distance, looked like a raptor's talons.

These talons gave the peak its name in the Uigan tongue: *Xagal*—the Claw. Around the Claw, smaller peaks spread away for miles in all directions, too short for both snow and for blocking out the sun just yet. Xagal was by far the highest of the Uesi Ilquar, the spine of mountains that split the northern plains in half. Few living Uigan had ever seen the Claw up close, and with good reason.

It was the home of the Wretched Ones, the last of the goblins of Hosk. Once, the stunted, bestial creatures had thrived across the land, from the Ur'musk Valley in the west to the edge of the Ghostwood that shrouded the Ring Mountains. They were already ancient when the Uigan first came here, and even predated the Elf Clans of the north. Bit by bit, they had been whittled away, forced into the mountains by the other races, and put to the sword when they resisted. Now they dwelt in the deep caves beneath the Claw and elsewhere in the Ilquars. They were a fading people, and little seen. The Uigan avoided them, considered them cursed.

A small band of riders pulled up on a stone path, which had been a streambed at the start of the year's thawing and had been reduced to nothing but a runnel and stones. The path led straight into the Ilquars, past the first stunted crags, and all the way to Xagal and the goblinhome. Hult, sitting on Chovuk's right as always, flicked a glance down the line at the others. Hoch Tegin was present, the young man's teeth bared to ward against evil. Yamad, his *tenach* and the lone survivor of Krogan's party, sat next to him with a hand on the hilt of his *shuk*. Beside them were Sugai Tegin and his protector, a lanky warrior with crow-feathers woven into his braid and a two-handed *arshuk* blade slung across his back. The elder lord pursed his lips, glancing sidelong at Chovuk Boyla. Hult studied that gaze, missing nothing. The old man was wise, of that there was no doubt. The worrying thing was that he was clever, as well. Clever men were not to be trusted.

Look at Chovuk, Hult thought wryly, regarding his master—resplendent in the gilded scale armor of Uigan royalty. He is clever, and Krogan paid for it with his life.

Hult was riding to the heart of a monstrous land, led by a man who had won his crown by slaying his own predecessor. A man who could change his skin and become a steppe tiger, who could tear an ogre apart with his teeth.

"I do not like this place," said Hoch, glaring up at the mountain's needled crown. "It is evil."

Chovuk, sitting with hands folded atop his saddle horn, did not look back. "I did not think you knew fear, Tegin."

Lord Sugai smiled, faintly. Hoch saw this, and scowled. As youngest of the horde's high lords, he had often been the butt of jokes over the long ride across the steppes, from the Mourning-stone. "I am *not* afraid," he blustered. "But the reckless rider doesn't see the gully until he falls in."

"Do not call the Boyla reckless," snapped Sugai.

The air changed as the Tegins' humor gave way to scorn. Mocking one of their own was one thing; an insult against Chovuk was something else. One did not offend the Boyla and live. Hoch fell silent, flushing with shame.

"Forgive me, lord," he murmured.

Chovuk could have taken his head, and Sugai would not have objected—at least not here. Instead, Chovuk smiled and shook his head. "It is nothing. You are right, Hoch—this might seem a rash thing to do. But I have my reasons. We must find the Wretched Ones."

It had been an eventful month, full of shouting and thundering hoofs. From the Mourning-stone, the Uigan had followed Chovuk east, then south, gathering riders at every village they passed, sending messengers to the more far-flung clans to send horsemen of their own. The horse-folk, tempted by the twin prospects of slaughtering their Kazar enemies and raiding the minotaur cities on the coast, responded with wild enthusiasm. Within the span of a few weeks, the three hundred who had gathered at the Stone for Krogan's funeral swelled to nearly five thousand, with more streaming in across the grasslands every day. There hadn't been a comparable mass of riders since before the Godless Night. Maybe since before the First Destruction.

Then, three nights ago, Chovuk had left them.

Looking out upon his thronged warriors, he had

summoned the high Tegins to him, and bidden them ride back west with him, into the dry hills. The bulk of the horde remained on the plains, where the game was plentiful and they could remain until their rulers returned. Gathering Hoch and Sugai—and each man's *tenach*—he had declared his desire to journey deep into the Uesi Ilquar.

Hoch and some of the other young Tegins had bridled at this, demanding an explanation. The Ilquars, after all, were home to awful monsters who ate the flesh of the men they killed. Why would the Boyla seek such a place?

Chovuk had not answered their questions, and Sugai—who had become Chovak's chief advisor within the horde, just as he had been Krogan's—had browbeaten the other chiefs into submission. So, not knowing why, they had followed their Boyla into the uplands, all the way to Mount Xagal, where the Wretched Ones lurked. For five days they rode ever deeper into the hills, arrows nocked and watching the cliffs for signs of ambush, but they had not yet seen a single living thing.

They rode on, deeper into the mountain's shadow. Hult's heart hammered in his breast as the path began to climb the slope's shoulder. Every now and then he sensed something strange—some movement just out of sight, or an echo that sounded wrong—but wherever he looked there was nothing. He had never seen a goblin, but the elders said they could hide among the stones even better than a tiger in the long grasses. They were all around, and had been for days—likely since the Uigan first set foot on the highland paths.

"Why do they wait?" Hult had asked the previous night, when the party camped—the fourth restless night among the strange sounds and chill air of the Ilquars.

The Boyla, drinking from a horn of *kumiss*, had glanced away into the dark and shrugged, his expression unchanging. "Because they can. They could kill us any time they wish. If we show fear, if we turn back, they will fall on us like jackals. But we go on. That makes them curious, so they let us live. For now, anyway."

Hult had shivered to hear Chovuk speak so. But the Boyla was not afraid, and that boosted his own courage. Besides, he was *tenach*: if his master rode into the pits of the Abyss, he would follow. What else was there to do?

Ahead, they spied the glint of the sun on water: a narrow mountain lake, fed by streams that trickled down from cracks in the rocks above. Along its shores stood nine tall, wooden stakes. A body hung impaled on each. Three of the bodies were human, young Uigan men from the look of their clothing. Another may have been an elf, though it was little more than bones. The rest were stunted, ugly things, abominations Hult didn't recognize, and therefore took to be goblins. Most were old husks, withered by the dry mountain air, but a couple had been killed in the past several months. Crows hopped from one to the next, seeking tasty morsels. They had already taken the eyes and cheeks, and presently squabbled over noses and ears. Bones, some with scraps of hair and skin still clinging to them, littered the stony ground.

The Boyla raised a hand, and the party halted. They stared at the gruesome sight, the sacrifices, the rusty, dried blood that caked the bases of the wooden poles. Their lips curled with disgust. Hult watched Chovuk, half-expecting a command to fight, but his master looked calm, staring past the stakes toward the lake and the high, ruddy cliff beyond.

Chovuk threw his head back and howled like a wolf. The other Tegins looked at him in surprise as he repeated the call a second time, and a third. Then, throwing wide his arms, he shouted across the water.

"*Akan tsekushu!* People of the Mountain!" he cried. "I am Chovuk Boyla, lord of all the Uigan upon the Tamire. I come to pay honor to your king."

"Honor?" murmured Hoch. "To goblins?"

He fell silent after Sugai shot him a fierce look. Hult

could tell from the old lord's eyes he was thinking the same thing, though.

For twenty breaths, nothing moved. Hult had to fight back the urge to draw his *shuk*. The other *tenachai* already gripped their blades, as did Hoch himself, but he would not bare his own saber until Chovuk bade him. The wind moaned through the valleys around Xagal, making ripples on the lake's dark water.

Finally, an answer came. A voice like a death-rattle called out, though they still could not see the one who spoke.

"We know you," the voice said, its accent and broken tongue making it barely understandable. "You not go mountain. Not friend, not see king."

Chovuk smiled. "I *am* your friend," he replied. "Here is the proof."

Slowly, he reached toward his belt. Hult held his breath, waiting for an arrow to appear in his master's breast, but the unseen goblins did not attack. Still curious, he thought as he watched the Boyla produce a leather pouch from his belt. Chovuk had carried the pouch since they came to the Ilquars, but had not spoken of it, nor shown anyone what it held. Untying the drawstring, he stepped forward and upended the pouch, spilling its contents on the ground.

Hult caught his breath when he saw what the pouch held. Out spilled silver rings, some fifty of them, each set with a large turquoise. The stone of death. Hoch's eyes widened at the sight of them.

"You know these," Chovuk shouted. "They are the jewels of Kazar warriors. Only men who have slain fifty enemies in battle may don these rings. More than a few of those fifty were likely your people. These rings were bought with the blood of your kin.

"Now is the time to avenge that blood. I offer you these rings, and the chance to fill them with Kazar fingers, if you will take me to your king."

A broad smile split Sugai Tegin's face. The others

looked at the Boyla in wonder. Hult felt a surge of pride—what *tenach* served a master more cunning than his?

Again, no answer came for quite some time. Finally a low rumble shook the ground. Beyond the lake, at the end of a narrow path leading around its edge, a crack opened in the stone of Mount Xagal. Shadows lay thick within. Still there was no sign of the Wretched Ones.

"You come," rasped the unseen voice. "You, and one other. King waits. Bring rings, you give him."

Chovuk nodded, turning to the other *Tegins*. "Wait here. We should not be gone long. Touch nothing—they will be watching you."

"Yes, lord," said Sugai, bowing his snowy-braided head.

"And if you don't return?" Hoch asked, his eyes flicking about the vale.

Chovuk shrugged, dismissing the question. Of course he would return. He handed the empty pouch to Hult, then nodded to the rings on the ground. "*Tenach*, gather those and come with me. The mountain awaits."

If the mountains had been unsettling for a warrior bred in the open land of the Tamire, the caverns of Xagal were terrifying. The stone seemed to press in around Hult, tons of it hanging above his head, waiting to fall down. The tunnel was too narrow for him and Chovuk to walk side by side, so Hult went first, a guttering torch in his hand. It shed only enough light to make the gloom seem even more oppressive. It was *black* under the mountain, darker even than a starless night. He had the feeling his fire-brand was the first to light these warrens in long centuries. Maybe ever.

The walls of the passage were crudely cut, irregular and unfinished, and the path twisted like a serpent, or the bowels of some vast, stone beast. The floor was no better, and sometimes they almost had to climb to keep going forward. Meanwhile, in the darkness, the mountain groaned, sending trickles of grit spilling out of cracks over their heads. The air was stale and dry, smelling faintly of rot.

If this way collapses, Hult thought over and over, they will never find us. We will be devoured by the stone, and our ghosts will haunt this place until the world's ending.

Chovuk seemed untroubled. Maybe he was only hiding his fears, but Hult felt certain he truly was unafraid. That made his chest swell with pride, and drove away some of his dread. His master was a great man. If his plan to make war on the bull-men succeeded, he would be remembered as one of the greatest Boylas the Tamire had ever seen.

The cave came upon them so abruptly that it nearly cost Hult his life. One moment the tunnel was snaking ahead, plunging ever deeper into the heartrock of the mountain, and the next, his foot stepped on nothing but open air. He began to fall, and only Chovuk's firm hand, grabbing the back of his vest, kept him from plummeting into the chasm. Ahead was nothing but yawning blackness, untouched by the torch-light.

"You come," said the raspy voice from the midst of the dark. "King waits."

"There," Chovuk whispered, pointing to their left. "Follow that."

There was, indeed, a path, though barely visible: a narrow ledge, maybe an arm's length wide, that wound around the wall of a cavern, carved out of undulating, milky flowstone. The wall was wet. Trickles of water ran down it, making the ledge slippery as well. Hult edged along, testing his footing. Slowly the path descended, until finally the floor—made of the same pale, glistening rock— rose to meet them. Hult stepped off the path first, then Chovuk. The trail went on into the looming darkness, marked by bladelike shards of obsidian, set into the softer rock. On either side, great stalagmite pillars rose like trees toward the unseen ceiling. The sound of dripping water was everywhere. There was movement all around them too, just out of sight. Hult could feel it, as surely as he could sense a pheasant in the grasses. He also thought he saw points of red and yellow light—*eyes*—dancing beyond the glow of his flame.

O my ancestors, he prayed. O great Jijin, watch over me in this terrible night . . .

The path ended. A flight of steps, crudely cut into the milky rock, led up onto a dais. Hult looked back at Chovuk, who nodded, and they began to climb. The shuffling of feet and the scratch of claws filled the air behind them.

"If anything goes wrong," the Boyla murmured, "stay near me."

What could go wrong? Hult thought, and nearly said aloud. He had to fight back a bubble of panicked laughter—if he let it out, he wasn't sure he would be able to stop.

They came to the top of the steps. Ahead, something huge loomed in the shadows. Chovuk put a hand on Hult's shoulder, stopping him as he reached for his *shuk*. He pointed at the pouch instead, and Hult opened it again, spilling the rings upon the dais.

"Great King," Chovuk proclaimed, raising his voice to nearly a shout. Eerily, no echoes greeted his words, for the cave devoured noise as well as light. "I bring gifts before you, and ask your alliance."

The hugeness stirred. A voice boomed out of the dim shadows, deeper and clearer than the one that had greeted them outside. "You would ally with the mountain people? Pah! We know you, who call yourselves men. You would have us as slaves to do your bidding and carry your burdens for crusts of moldy bread! Then you would cut our throats, rather than let us come back here in peace. Thus has it always been. We will not hear you."

Chovuk nodded, undeterred. "You are right to suspect us. Often have the men of the plains used you and given no reward. But this is a different day. I am not like my forebears—I shall deal plainly with you, on my life and the lives of my kindred."

Again the shadows shifted. Hult heard a worrying sound, as of a great, leathery weight sliding over stone.

"Say on," the voice rumbled. "What would you give us?"

"Blood and plunder," Chovuk said. "We make war on the Kazar, and then on the bull-men. You know they have great riches, and their flesh is sweet to your tongues. You will have your choice for the feasting, and one part in four of all we loot from their fat cities."

A horrid sound rose from the darkness behind them—a chorus of chittering and slobbering that made sweat spring from Hult's brow. He kept his eyes forward, though, upon the darkness. The huge presence stirred again, scraping the rock.

"You hear my people," the thing before them said. "They crave what you offer. But you count on this—of course you do. That is why you say these things. The words of men are poisoned honey. I do not believe you. *Tsopuk!*"

At the strange, hissing word, blazing light sprang to life. Hult gasped, turning away and shielding his stinging eyes, then made himself look again. In the harsh, blue-white glow that had blossomed before them, the cave shone like a skull, filled with fangs of rock that thrust down from the ceiling to meet the columns from the floor. Holes studded the walls, leading to other caverns deeper into the mountains. On the ledges between these, and all over the floor, the Wretched Ones had gathered: horrid, squat, yellow-skinned things with snaggle-toothed jaws and evil, catlike eyes. They carried spears of rusty iron and hatchets of sharpened stone, and wore furs and skins for armor, laced with plates made from the shells of giant beetles. There were more of the creatures than he could tally—certainly hundreds, maybe thousands—all snarling and leering and sticking out black, pointed tongues. They had lit the lights—great, stone bowls of blue fire that stood all around the cave.

Hult dropped his torch and reached for his *shuk*, knowing he couldn't possibly hope to overcome so many. He *would* kill enough to make them rue the day, though.

"*Tenach*," Chovuk murmured. "They are not the problem. Look forward."

Hult glanced at the Boyla, who looked unusually pale in the eerie light, then turned back and saw what was on the dais with them. For a breath, his wits fled. It took three more to convince himself he hadn't gone mad.

If the King of the Mountain had been a goblin once, it showed only the barest signs of that lineage. Its face had the same low-browed, glowering stupidity as the gibbering things in the cave behind them, but was bloated and colorless, with bloodshot pink eyes widely spaced on either side of its bony snout. Long, slender fangs jutted from between its lips. Below that huge, ugly head was something even worse: the body of a giant worm, white with purple veins coiled beneath the skin. It stretched six paces in length, all dripping with slime, with a hooked barb on its tail. A bead of black venom hung from the stinger, and he knew that its sting was death.

"Now you die," the worm-thing snarled. The cave filled with the cheers of the goblins.

Instinct alone saved Hult's life, for his mind was still lost in terror. He threw himself sideways, hitting the rocky floor and rolling as the fanged head darted forward. He ended up hanging halfway over the edge of the dais, and had a horrible moment when he thought he would fall. Grimacing, he heaved himself back upright, then his saber rang clear of its scabbard, the noise loud in the stillness of the cave. He saw that Chovuk had dodged the King as well, having leaped to the other side, and the Boyla had his own sword out, held before him as the abomination turned toward him. Its stinger rose off the ground and swayed back and forth, scattering drops of poison that smoked when they hit the stone.

Madly, Hult leaped at the worm, his blade flashing in a tight arc. Steel plunged into the worm's belly, and black grease sprayed from the wound, stinking of rotten fish. The creature roared, its head whipping around toward him, and he heard a whistle and ducked just in time to avoid the stinger as it flashed at his face. He stabbed the worm a second time, and the *shuk* lodged in its innards. The King thrashed, screeching, and the blade was wrenched from Hult's hand. He staggered, then the stinger plunged at him again. He caught the tail and held it, barely an inch from his face, the force of its weight bearing him down until he lay flat on the dais. The weight of the monster crushed him, made his arms burn with the effort of pushing it off him. Drops of venom fell on his cheeks, and he howled in agony as they seared his flesh. The monster laughed horribly, and the goblins shouted in encouragement.

Then the goblins' cries changed from glee to horror, and Hult heard a sound—a menacing, feline snarl. He'd heard that sound before, at the Mourning-stone. His eyes flicked sideways. In the Boyla's place, crouched low and glaring, was the huge, lithe form of a steppe-tiger.

That's not possible, said a voice inside him, for some part of his mind had refused to accept what his master had done to defeat Torug Tegin. Then the stinger twitched, dropping even closer to his face, and he had to turn his full attention back to his predicament. He could see the venom glands throbbing on either side of the tip of the beast's tail. Amid the reek of the King's blood, he smelled his own flesh burning.

Then the worm shrieked, making an unholy sound like tearing metal. The tiger answered with a roar and a leap. At once the barb tore from Hult's hands and whipped away, and he lurched to his feet, gasping. He looked, just in time to see the great cat clamp its powerful jaws around the worm's throat. Black slime gushed over both of them, and the tiger shook its head mightily, trying to break the King's neck. Dying, the worm raised its stinger one last time.

Hult moved without thinking, once again. He dove for Chovuk's *shuk*, where it had dropped after his master had changed his skin. Scooping up the blade, he spun, lashing out with a cry of rage. Steel bit into flesh, and the tip of the worm's tail sheared away, slapping into the wall behind it, then tumbling down to the cave floor. Ribbons of ichor gushed from the wound. The monster's strength flagged, and the tiger bore it to the ground. Bringing its hind claws up, the cat raked them through the worm's bowels. With an awful, choking gargle, the King of the Mountain died.

Across the cave, the goblins fell silent. Stunned, they watched as Hult and the tiger rose from the ruins of the beast that had ruled them. Hult lifted his master's dripping sword, ready for their vengeful onslaught. But they did not budge. They stared as the tiger padded forward to stand at the head of the stairs.

The air shimmered and blurred, and Hult blinked, fearing the worm's poison had blinded him. But then it stopped, and he stared in amazement—as did the Wretched Ones. The tiger was gone, and Chovuk stood in its place, battered and bloodied but whole. He glared out across the cavern, then reached behind him. Hult stepped forward, handing him his *shuk*. Blade in hand, the Boyla turned and hewed the dead King's head from its body with a single, mighty stroke. Raising the gruesome trophy high, he cast the head down the stairs to burst on the floor below. The goblins looked at one another uneasily, shying back from the dais.

"I say again!" Chovuk cried. "Plunder and blood are yours, if you join us! What is your answer, people of the mountain?"

The cave was silent. Then a large goblin with a withered arm came forward. He wore a headdress made from the carapace of a cave scorpion, the wicked tail rising up over his head. In his good hand he held a staff hung with dried ears. He stood amid the remains of the King's head, staring up at the Boyla.

"I Gharmu," he rasped, clapping his hand to his chest. Hult recognized the voice that had greeted them outside the mountain and brought them to this place. "Speak for mountain people."

"*Hai*, Gharmu," Chovuk said solemnly, raising his saber in salute. "Will you follow me?"

The deformed goblin paused, then laid his staff upon the stairs. The Wretched Ones murmured in awe. "Blood and plunder," he snarled. "We follow you . . . King."

To Hult's amazement, Gharmu knelt. The rest of the goblins followed his lead, prostrating themselves before the Boyla. Chovuk tossed his head proudly, a gesture that evoked the tiger he had been bare moments before, then smiled down upon his new subjects.

Hult couldn't help it. A grin spread across his face, and he began to laugh.

Chapter 9

HAWKBLUFF, THENOL

The rain worsened as the legions marched, turning to fine razors that drove through mail and flesh to chill the bone. The ground softened to greasy, foul-smelling muck as the trees thinned to scatterings of scrub and bracken. The soldiers' progress slowed as the ground sucked away their boots, or held fast to the butts of spears. In places, it gave way to marshland, tufted with cutting clawgrass and riddled with deceptively deep ponds covered with sheets of algae the color of dried blood.

The Hawkvale. Forlo knew the march well. This was not the first time he'd dreamt of it. The Sixth had spent an uneasy, sleepless night watching for more Thenolite ambushes and listening to strange, distant sounds that carried across the long valley. Moans and screams, mostly, but something else—something that could have been cats yowling, or babies crying. He shuddered, closing the door on that memory.

In spite of it all—the noises, the weather, the very land that seemed to fight them—the minotaurs and men of the League would not be deterred. This was it, they all knew: the fateful day, doom at long last for Thenol. Horns of brass-bound ivory and drums of polished copper sounded the advance, driving them on through sleet and muck. The regimental battle-standards hung heavy and dark, water running off their bottoms in sheets. Somewhere, miles away, thunder growled.

"This dreck could be a blessing," said Grath, marching at the center of the Sixth, at Forlo's side—where else? "It will hamper their archers more than our crossbows."

Forlo grunted, not wanting to grant that much. By his experience, foul weather never favored the attacker. He looked up through the gloom to where the lights of the temple of Hawkbluff glimmered. The temple perched on a cliff of white rock half a league away, lonely, with neither trees nor boulders around it. It was carved out of the rock itself, its fluted walls and curving towers resembling nothing so much as a giant ribcage, the remains of some long-dead giant, a slim, central tower like a spur of bone jutting up from its midst. Gargoyles perched on its heights, as well as worse things—banners made from what could only be human skin, rotting bodies dangling from every battlement and rooftop, and heaps of skulls everywhere. This was the greatest church of the dark god Hith to be found in Taladas. Looking upon it, half-lost in the gray, rainy pall, Forlo vowed silently that the Bishop's great temple would fall.

"I'm surprised we haven't seen any of their scouts yet," he said. "Ondelos is no fool. He wouldn't have left this approach unguarded."

"Maybe we've hurt him worse than we thought," Grath replied, shrugging his massive shoulders. "We certainly left the way behind us washed in enough Thenolite blood."

Forlo shook his head, troubled. It looked too easy: the word *trap* kept echoing in his head. If the Bishop had any last dice to cast, it would be here. Had to be—there was no place left for him to go.

"Send word to the other marshals," he commanded. "Double the watch on our flanks and rear—and keep eyes on the skies, too, as best we can."

"The skies?" Grath replied, and laughed. "You expecting swarms of dragons to descend on us?"

"I don't *expect* anything," Forlo snapped. "Except my men to carry out my orders."

Grath drew back slightly, looking hurt. Then, clamping his hand around his forearm in salute, he wheeled and strode off among the columns of soldiers, bawling for messengers. Forlo watched him go, regretting his tone. In all his years in the legions, he'd never had a truer sword-brother than Grath. He hoped the minotaur would understand how frayed his nerves were. With the entire army to lead, and the-emperor-knew-what lying in wait, he had good reason.

The sky darkened to the hue of slate. The thunder muttered more fervently, with flashes of violet light kindling in the clouds. The storm was not natural. It could only be Ondelos's doing, or that of some warlock working with him. Forlo considered asking the clerics who marched with the legions to call upon their gods to drive the darkness back—but doing so would be costly, and he had the feeling the priests would need their strength for more pressing matters, soon. Matters like a few thousand dead men.

He knew from what his scouts had told him that at least a few regiments of the Thenolites' corpse-soldiers remained. They formed the bulk of the fell realm's army—no one who died under the rule of Bishop Ondelos went to the grave or pyre. With Hith's power, he made their bodies—or their bones—arise anew, as mindless hulks that obeyed his commands without question or fear. They needed neither food nor sleep, and their morale never flagged. They even fought on through wounds that would cripple a living man. And their effect on living opponents was not something to be dismissed. It was one thing for a soldier to confront a foe who might put a sword through his heart. It was another to be faced with ghouls who would rend him to pieces and devour his flesh.

The Sixth slogged on, slowing with each step. Even the scraggly bushes gave way, leaving nothing but great fields of mud, churned by the passage of numerous feet. The Thenolites had been here, maybe as recently as that morning. Without the sun, it was hard for Forlo to know the hour, but he guessed it was wearing on midday. Noon would pass before they reached the Bluff.

At last, the great promontory loomed out of the fog. It was jagged, all sharp angles of pale stone, its sides curved to form figures: leering skulls, horned demons, and mad-eyed fanatics with wicked sickle-swords. A narrow path wound up its sides, leading to the temple high above. There were other ways up, Forlo knew—two they knew of, a third they suspected, and who knew how many others? There was only one true road, though. The rest led into mazes of twisting tunnels, alike enough that getting lost was far too easy.

And there, at the base of that ghostly escarpment, waited their enemy.

They are so few, Forlo thought, gazing upon Thenol's last defenders. It was difficult to get a true count, with the rain, but surely there could not have been more than two thousand men gathered there, a mile away. Less than a third of what remained of the League's legions. Most of the Thenolites were soldiers, living men in bronze armor and horned helmets, gripping bows or leaning on long-hafted waraxes. They were the hardest foes for Forlo to fight, for they were not much different from him—career soldiers, or conscripts drafted from the fields and cities to defend their realm. They were not evil men—not most, anyway.

Not like the fanatics who had ambushed the camps last night, with their foully enchanted arrows. They were easier to kill, for their minds were gone, lost when they swore their oaths to Hith. They wore no cloaks, nor anything more than loincloths and skull-masks. Many had slashed their bare chests with sickle-shaped knives, letting blood wash down and mix with the mud underfoot.

They howled in wild rage, dancing forward to taunt the disciplined legions.

"Hold!" Forlo shouted, raising an empty hand. "No one shoots until I give the signal."

At his command, the army ground to a halt. The crossbowmen cranked their weapons and stood ready, awaiting orders. They were still too far away, too far for bow or crossbow—but some of the crazed Thenolites were loosing arrows anyway, to arc high and fall well short of the mark, into the muck. The commanders of the enemy did not stop them.

We have numbers, we have discipline, Forlo thought. They have *him*.

Bishop Ondelos stood on a grassy hummock, toward the rear of his troops. He was a hugely fat man, hairless and pale save for a wine-colored birthmark that covered the left side of his face. Robes of white and red draped over his girth, and a scarlet miter covered his head. He leaned on a staff of polished onyx, its headpiece carved into a grinning skull. The carving's eyes were huge garnets, glowing with magic. Around him crowded his disciples, the lesser priests of Hith's church, armed with sickles and flails, men and women both with their heads shaved bald and dusted with powdered bone.

"What of the dead?" Grath murmured. "We know they're still around. Why wouldn't Ondelos have them here?"

"I don't know," Forlo admitted. He had been thinking the same thing. "There's trickery at work here, I think."

He took off his helm and ran a hand through his short-cropped, graying hair, trying to think. In all his days, he had never met a foe so cunningly evil as Ondelos. He didn't know how it would happen, but he was sure if he gave the order to attack, it would lead his troops to slaughter. Still, he could only hold off for so long. The minotaurs craved battle; it was in their blood. The longer he kept them from the fight, the harder it would become to control them.

What, then? What was Ondelos's advantage?

There was a craggy rock nearby, a blade of stone jutting out of the bog. Forlo turned toward it, intent on climbing to get a better view—but when he tried to take a step, the muck clung to his boots and he stumbled. Angrily—this wasn't the first time he'd gotten stuck today—he bent down and tugged his feet free. First left, then—

When his right foot pulled out, it brought something with it. Something long, hard, and pale. He stood staring, his heart lurching against his ribs as the rain washed the grime away. The thing at his feat was a human thighbone.

Grath saw it too, and bent down at once, digging with the haft of his axe. The wet earth yielded more remains: a pelvis, ribs, a skull. The minotaur's yellow eyes went wide as he straightened back up. Together, he and Forlo looked around at the League's grand army, the thousands of soldiers waiting for the battle to start.

All of them standing shin-deep in mud.

"*Khot*," Grath swore.

Forlo nodded, numb. They knew where the dead army was.

Forlo pulled the bowstring back to his cheek and held it, waiting as he sighted down the arrow's length. Beyond lay blue sky, and below, darker water. The tides were high this morning, with Solis new and Lunis a waning quarter. He wondered idly what the black moon was doing. It wasn't in the same phase as the other two, for astronomers and navigators noted such concordances. One was due in a few months, by what he'd heard.

Once, before the Destruction shattered Taladas, Northern and Southern Hosk had been one landmass, stretching uninterrupted for nearly four hundred leagues, from the frigid wastes of Panak to the hot, misty reaches of the Blackwater Glade. When the rains of fire and stone came, however, a crack had split Hosk down the middle, and the seas had rushed in to fill it. So was born the Tiderun Straight—or the Run, as most folk called it. It was not a deep body of water, and the tides affected it more than any other. This became most pronounced when the moons aligned. Then, the high water would be higher than ever, overflowing waterfronts all along either shore, and hours later, the Run would be dry, and Hosk's two halves would be one again. Such days caused a stir among the local peasants, who ventured out onto the muddy flats to haul in fish that lay gasping and dying. There were even a few places where the ground was rocky enough for a man to ride across—or walk, if he moved fast enough.

For now, though, there was water in the Run. Forlo thought he might go for a sail in the afternoon, taking out one of the smaller fishing vessels. He was a fair mariner at best, but he liked the smell of salt as he skipped over the waves. And besides, he was desperate for something to do.

He hadn't figured retirement would be like this. With Essana running the Hold, every day was a struggle to keep himself occupied. He'd already read half the books in the keep's libraries, and went hunting so often the gamekeepers were nervous about the local stock of pheasants and deer. He'd ridden to Thera twice, to catch up on news across the League: no new emperor had been crowned, though the factions vying for the throne had narrowed from seven to three. There was scant word of the Sixth, but the local lords thought it likely that Duke Rekhaz would call the army back to the capital soon. Most folk thought a battle would be fought to decide the succession before the summer was out.

Whenever talk turned to fighting, Forlo's sword hand began to itch. He thought of Grath, and of the men he'd commanded, and wondered if he'd made the right choice. Several times he'd considered riding out to seek his old legion, but then he would think of Essana, and how good it felt to hold her while they slept, and he put such thoughts aside. She was his life now, not the sword.

And she would never give him nightmares.

There was movement now, beyond his arrow: small, white shapes darting down over the waves. He held steady, then lowered his sights half an inch and loosed. The string snapped forward and the arrow streaked away. He marked its path, watched it climb, then hit one of the white shapes as it started to drop again. There was a burst of feathers, and bird and shaft spun down out of sight. He smiled, and reached to his quiver for a second arrow.

"Barreth. What are you doing?"

Forlo started. Essana was coming up the steps from the manor, her skirts hitched up above her ankles. She was beautiful, as always, her raven hair shining in the sun. She had a cross look about her, though, and when she saw the bow in his hands she rolled her eyes in disgust.

"Starlight," he began, flushing. "I—"

"You were shooting gulls again, weren't you?" she asked, striding along the catwalk to stand glaring at him. "You know the fisher-folk hate that. They say it's bad luck."

"Maybe for the gulls," he said, smiling lamely.

Essana rolled her eyes again. "I don't think I can take it if you're going to spend the rest of your days rattling around, looking for amusement. You've got to find something productive to do."

"Like what?" he snapped. "Embroidery?"

That was a mistake. Essana turned pale, saying nothing. She was alarmingly cold and brittle when she was angry.

"I didn't mean it," he said. "Starlight, listen. I've spent the last three years fighting armies of dead men and maniacs. I'm having trouble with . . . this." He waved his hand vaguely. "I'll try harder, though. Maybe learn to fish."

For a moment longer she only stared at him, and he thought he'd annoyed her even more—then a smile broke across her face, and she shook her head. "Oh, very fine," she said. "Either you're going to shoot all the gulls, or you're going to starve them."

He laughed at that, set down his bow and pulled her to him. She pretended to resist, then yielded with a sigh as their lips pressed together. That was *one* thing he'd never tire of. Seeing the look in her eyes when they came apart again, he thought of another.

"I don't have any business until after luncheon," she said, one corner of her mouth crooking upward.

He grinned, his hands running over her. "Really. How shall we pass the time?"

With that, he scooped her up in his arms. She yelped in surprise, then laughed and laid her head on his shoulder as he carried her down the steps, the bow forgotten behind them.

Chapter 10

COLDHOPE, THE IMPERIAL LEAGUE

Afterwards, they had the servants bring the midday meal to their chambers, and ate it in bed—cold venison with leeks, fresh bread and oil, and a pitcher of watered wine. They fed each other yellow grapes, still naked in the bed, then made love a second time, slower than before. Later, they dressed and went down together toward the great hall.

"You had another dream last night," she said. "I heard you."

He paused on the stairs, glancing at her, and felt his cheeks flush. "I'm sorry, Starlight."

"Don't apologize. I'm worried about you, Barreth. Not a night goes by."

"I know." He sighed, staring up at the ceiling. "I wish I could make the dreams stop, Essana. Sometimes I wonder if I will ever have a good night's sleep again."

Her fingers touched his arm, gentle. He covered her hand with his.

"Are they truly that bad?" she asked.

Forlo considered, then shrugged. "It's always something from the last few days of the war," he murmured. "Up until the last battle, at Hawkbluff. Last night I dreamed about the start of it."

"When you found the dead soldiers under the mud."

"Yes." He'd told her all about it. She shuddered. "I'll dream the rest of it tonight, I know I will. And tomorrow it'll begin again. And on and on, for the rest of my damned life!"

He slammed the heel of his fist against the wall, then stood there silently, his hand stinging, feeling foolish.

"We'll stop it, Barreth. We'll find a way."

He shrugged, his stomach clenched with nausea. He hadn't even told her the worst part. In his dreams, the battle never ended. The war had finished in the tunnels beneath Bishop Ondelos's church, when he and his men had finally chased the wicked priest down, where he had cut the man's fat head from his shoulders. But the nightmares always stopped before he got to the temple. The nightmare would stop there again, that night. Even his own memory of that last chase through the caverns of Hawkbluff had grown hazy.

Gods, he thought. What if I'm going mad?

Essana only watched him, her expression troubled. She may have guessed there was more he wasn't sharing, but she didn't speak. Instead she nodded, and managed a smile.

"Come," she said. "We can't while the whole day away, out of sights. The servants will talk."

He chuckled at that, and together they walked the rest of the way down the stairs.

Voss, Essana's elderly chamberlain, was awaiting them when they reached the great hall. He bowed as they entered, his bald pate shining in the light that streamed through the high windows. "My lady," he said, "I did not think I should disturb you while you were ... relaxing ... but there is a matter that requires your attention."

"Of course, Voss," Essana replied. She looked past him, to where a plump, well-dressed man stood, clad in a blue tunic and a mantle of green silk. Forlo didn't recognize him, though he marked him as a merchant. "Good day to you, sir," Essana said, touching her forehead in greeting. "How may—"

"It's about time!" the man huffed, striding forward. "I've been waiting nearly an hour for you to come down from your tower, while—"

He stopped, the tip of Forlo's sword a hand's breadth from his throat.

"I would ask you," Forlo said pleasantly, "not to take that tone with my wife."

"Barreth!" Essana exclaimed.

Forlo didn't back down. He stared at the merchant, who blew out his lips and backed away from the blade. With a nod, Forlo sheathed his sword again.

"May I present Sammek Thale," said Voss, seemingly unruffled by the confrontation. "A trader from Malton, across the Run. Lady Essana, Baroness of Coldhope, and her husband, Lord Barreth Forlo."

Essana touched her forehead again. Forlo smiled, but not with his eyes. The merchant blushed, pressing his fat hands together. "I apologize for my rude manners," he said. "Only something most troubling has happened, and I thought you might help, since it took place in your waters."

"Our waters?" Essana asked. She traded glances with her husband. "What sort of trouble?"

"Only pirates!" Sammek half-shouted. "My flagship, the *White Worm* . . . we were on our way home from the inland seas when we were waylaid, not ten leagues from here. The dogs ransacked our holds and locked us below. It took us three days to break free!"

Forlo looked at Essana again, then stepped forward. "How many ships? Did you see their captain, or what colors they flew?"

"A black trident, on scarlet," Sammek said. "They had only the one ship, but it was the quickest wave-cutter I've seen. The one they called boss was a minotaur with one horn, and a foul temper."

Essana sighed. "Damn it. Harlad."

"Harlad," Forlo echoed, and thought: *I can't believe He's still alive.* He leveled a stern gaze at the merchant. "Very well, Master Thale. You should know your wares are probably already gone. But we'll do what we can."

Essana looked over at him, her smile saying everything. At least he had something to do now.

Lamport was a small, dirty town, built in a tiny notch of a cove a dozen leagues west of Coldhope. Travelers seldom passed through the town, and the local lords left it alone: it was well known that nearly everyone who dwelt or stayed there was a bandit, pirate, or some other sort of scoundrel. Every few years the emperor sent a brigade to empty the place, but its denizens always seemed to find out about the raids well before they happened. The soldiers would burn the taverns and brothels, and drag a few drunks away in irons to fight in the Arenas—then a few days after they marched away again the riffraff would return, to start anew.

Forlo stood at the tiller of his boat, looking inland across the harbor. Smoke hung over the dirty town like a shroud, and not a green thing grew beneath. Wooden walkways crisscrossed streets of mud, leading from one rundown inn to another. In the midst of everything was a patch of bare ground: the plunder-market, where everything stolen on sea or land was bartered and traded. With the spring-tides running high, the market was an empty lake, and many of the streets were brown rivers. Lamplight glowed within the windows of the pubs, the only sign of warmth in the light of the damp, hazy dawn.

Eight ships stood moored along the wharf, of various sizes and styles, with not an honest captain among them. Forlo's eyes flicked from one to the next, settling at last on a narrow, knife-shaped galley with a single level of oars and three tall masts. It flew no colors at port, but painted on its side was an unmistakable sign: a black trident. On the prow was the vessel's name: *Blade of Sargas*. A lipless frown settled on Forlo's face.

"Harlad," he murmured. "You've gotten predictable in your age."

He guided his boat up to a dock, well away from the *Blade*. He climbed onto the pier, made fast the mooring lines, and tossed a gold coin at the startled harbormaster. Then, with a hand on the hilt of his sword, he strode into the town.

Harlad the Gray had been prowling the Tiderun and the inland seas for a very long time. Forlo remembered hearing tales about the grizzled pirate when he was a boy. Despite his age, the old minotaur showed no signs of slowing down. Most of the local lords, after years of fruitless attempts to catch him, had instead made agreements to pay fees to keep him out of their waters. In return, Harlad policed the other pirates as well. Coldhope had paid for this protection for the past thirty summers, and Harlad had always kept his word. Forlo wondered, as he clumped along the boardwalk, why the pirate had broken the old treaty now. Greed? Complacency? Hubris? Harlad boasted all three in abundance.

The Green Lady was named after one of the more exclusive wine-houses of Kristophan—lost now, to the quake that killed the emperor—but it was little different from the rest of the taverns in the town. Ruddy light spilled through its greasy windows, curses and rough laughter through its open doors. A huge, red furred minotaur sat on a stool outside the entrance, a spiked club at his side. Dried blood on the weapon made it clear it wasn't just for show. A few bodies lay propped against the wall beyond the bouncer, maybe drunk, maybe hurt. Forlo knew better than to check. He simply tossed another coin to the minotaur, who yawned and let him pass.

BLADES OF THE TIGER

The reek of the place—stale beer and sweat and piss—made Forlo's eyes water, but he managed to keep from retching as he looked around. Wraiths of smoke coiled around the roof-beams, glowing in the firelight. Sawdust covered the floor, crusted in places with blood and worse. The picked-over carcass of a dog turned on a spit over the fire, and sausages—the ingredients of which he didn't want to consider—hung from the rafters. In the room's midst stood a badly carved wooden figure of a naked woman, its coat of green paint worn away in all the obvious places.

It was either very early or very late for business, and the taproom was mostly empty. A few hooded dwarves huddled in one corner, singing dirge-like songs and lifting foaming tankards to each other's health, and a handful of men and minotaurs snored facedown on the tables. The bartender, a pale human with arms like tree trunks, squinted at Forlo from where he sat, picking his teeth with a knife.

"Help you?" the man muttered.

"Mug of Black-peak," Forlo replied, watching the shadowed corners as he crossed the room. "And may be a little more. I'm looking for someone."

"Ain't everyone?" the barkeep answered, going to the kegs to fill a dirty cup with dark beer. He thumped it on the bar, and Forlo paid him in silver, then added five more gold. The money disappeared. "Who d'ya want?"

Forlo took a drink, then set down the mug. The beer was as good as the tavern was awful. He glanced over his shoulder, then leaned in. "The Gray. He's here," he added, as the barkeep began to shake his head. "The *Blade*'s moored out yonder, and this hole's his favorite, gods know why. Now say you point me toward him and skip the nonsense. Aye?"

The barkeep grinned, showing three missing teeth, and nodded toward a door at the back of the tavern. "No nonsense, that's me. He took a private room. Him, three o' his mates, and a barrel and a couple bottles. Ain't seen a hair on their hides since three bells past midnight."

"Good man," Forlo said, and put another three gold coins on the bar. They vanished too as he walked to the door. Reaching out, he put a hand on the handle.

The door wrenched inward, nearly yanking him along with it. Instinct taking over, he leaped back as a heavy axe-blade whistled through the air where his neck had been a moment ago. In the doorway stood a giant minotaur, nearly nine feet tall, his shaven chest covered with tattoos. Nostrils flaring, he glared at Forlo for an instant before he charged, axe held high.

Forlo moved easily, spinning to the right and whipping his sword from its scabbard. His foot lashed out, kicking a stool into the minotaur's path. The bull-man tripped, stumbled, and went down with a crash. Without hesitating, Forlo turned and thrust his blade into the brute's thigh. The minotaur howled and blood soaked the sawdust. Forlo left him there, clutching the crippling wound, and continued into the private parlor.

"You'll have to do better than that, Harlad," he said.

There were three more bull-men waiting in the room. Two, nearly as large as the one who had attacked him, stood with weapons bared. The third was smaller and silver furred, and held no blade. His right horn was missing, shorn off in some long-forgotten battle. In all the tales Forlo had heard, Harlad the Gray was the one with the single horn. A half-empty bottle of red liquor sat on a table before the Gray.

"Sargas smite me," the pirate captain said, his tone pleasant. "You must be Barreth Forlo. I'd heard you were back from Thenol."

"I am back indeed," Forlo replied, keeping his sword in front of him. "I've given up soldiering, but I still know how to use this."

Harlad nodded. "So I see. Ease off, lads. I know this one by his commendable reputation. Rugal, go make sure poor Bek out there doesn't bleed to death on the floor. Stang, stay here—but put your cutlass away. There's a good fellow."

The bodyguards did as Harlad bade. He pushed the bottle forward. "How's your lady-wife? Still as sweet as Hulder-wine?"

Slowly, Forlo lowered his blade. "She's well, thank you. But I didn't come all this way to drink your spice-brandy, Harlad."

"So I see," the pirate said. He thought a moment, then laughed. "That puling pig Thale came to you, did he? I should have known."

"I thought we had a deal," Forlo said. "Five hundred gold a year, and you don't show your colors in Coldhope waters. I have a habit of holding men to their oaths."

"Fair enough." Harlad leaned forward, his eyes shining. "You can have your gold back, if you want. What's more, I'll double it. And I'll keep clear of you for the next five years, no payment necessary. But I keep what I got."

Forlo had opened his mouth to argue, but now he blinked. "All for one raid? What was he carrying?"

"Oh, you know," the pirate said, and winked. "Priceless riches, ancient relics, that sort of thing. Didn't he tell you? He's been trading with the dwarves, down in the Steamwalls. Had a hold full of gold and jewels, and a few other trinkets. Of course, he paid the tariff for entering your waters with foreign goods, aye?"

Forlo shook his head, suddenly annoyed with Sammek Thale. The merchant had tried to cheat him, refusing to pay for the right to pass by Coldhope. Then he'd sent him into a fight with Harlad. He'd have words with Thale when he got home again.

"If you want," Harlad added, "instead of paying you back, I'll simply make the pig disappear."

"Tempting," Forlo said. "But no. Essana and I'll handle him. Your offer's not enough, either. I want something else . . . something to show for this trouble, besides the gold I'm due."

The bodyguard, Stang, growled and reached for his sword, but Harlad hissed, raising a hand. "You were always hard on me, Forlo. And I've always respected you for it. Too many lords line up to kiss my hinder these days. Boring.

"All right, there is something valuable I stole from the pig . . . something I'd never be able to sell in this gods-forsaken town, anyway. It's yours, if it interests you."

Forlo raised his eyebrows, sheathing his blade. "I'm interested. Show me."

"Eh? Was I lying?" Harlad asked as Stang opened the door wide.

The hold of the *Blade of Sargas* was filled with riches—ingots of gold and silver, new-cut emeralds and topaz, hunks of moonstone and malachite ready for carving. It was a fortune, all of it marked with dwarf-runes. Sammek Thale had tried to smuggle it to Malton without paying the necessary tribute. Probably he'd been doing the same thing for a long while. Looking at all that wealth, Forlo couldn't help but smile. The fat merchant deserved to lose this bounty. There was a certain justice to it. At least Harlad was honest about being a criminal.

"Where's my precious memento?" Forlo asked.

"In the back. Don't worry, I'm not going to thump you on the head and dump you in the Run," Harlad added when Forlo hesitated. "If word got out that you disappeared looking for me, I'd be in trouble up to my horn with the other lords. Not to mention the army, assuming Rekhaz would spare the men to hunt an old dog like me. Come on."

With that, he led the way down the ladder into the hold. Casting a quick glance at Stang, Forlo followed. Wood creaked around him as the pirate lit a nearby lantern, spilling dim light across the hold. More gold and jewels sparkled from the dancing shadows' edges. The old minotaur grinned.

"You could retire on this," Forlo said.

"I could have retired thirty years ago," Harlad answered. "Wealth's not the point. The hunt's the thing."

They went on, into the back of the hold. There, in the shadows, something big loomed over the rest of the treasure. As they got closer, he made out details: a statue of black marble, life-size or a little bigger, of a robed man whose face was obscured by a deep hood. He stared at it, wondering.

"This is Aurish," he breathed. "It's got to be a thousand years old."

"Aye." Harlad nudged him. "Worth twice its weight in gold. But not the trouble of trying to find a buyer—one who buys from a pirate, at least. Maybe you can find a use for it."

Forlo stared at the statue, amazed. The imperial historians were always on the watch for artifacts from Old Aurim. After the interregnum was settled, he could bring the statue to Kristophan and sell it to the new emperor's court for a fortune. Until then, it could stay at Coldhope. The keep had plenty of room. He craned his neck, trying to see what lay within the hood's shadows, but the sculptor had hidden the face from view.

Harlad leaned toward him, his eyes sly. "So? We have a bargain?"

Forlo looked at the statue a long moment, then nodded. "Done."

Chapter 11

MISLAXA'S NECKLACE, THE TIDERUN

Sleep. I must sleep. So cold.

You will sleep, do not fear. But first, I must ask you some questions.

Hard to remember. It is very different here. Gray.

I know. This is not easy for me, either. But it must be done.

Can I not sleep?

Questions first.

Very well.

Do you remember a statue? It was called the Hooded One.

Statue...

Your people bought it from a man, in Blood Eye. His name was Ruskal.

Ruskal... yes. It was precious, from Old Aurim. A good bargain.

It is the reason you were killed.

It was? Ah. A bad bargain after all, then.

The ones who killed you came after it. It wasn't to be found, though, was it?

No. Sold it already. Just the day before.

Who bought it?

I... can't remember.

136

Try. Please.

Difficult... wait. Human. A merchant, from Malton-on-the-Run. Sammek Thale.

Thale. Where was he going to take it?

Don't know. Back home, perhaps.

What was his ship's name?

Name ... it is hard. I do not remember how to read the human tongue. I do not remember much.

Show me the shapes of the letters.

W-H-I-T-E W-O-R-M.

Thank you. One more question: do you know who killed you?

No. Didn't see well. Shadows only, then the blade in my body. I still feel it, entering my flesh.

I am sorry. You may sleep now. I have all I need.

I have a question for you first.

Ask.

My people? My village? Did any of them—

No. They are all dead. I will make a pyre for them.

And for me?

And for you. Now sleep. Reorx awaits you.

Sleep....

—————✦✦—————

Shedara awoke with a gasp, her heart beating fast. The cave was dark, the sounds and scent of the sea very near. Her elvensight showed crabs scuttling across the stone, nothing more. She lay back, tears springing into her eyes. The dead dwarf's voice, conjured by magic the elves reviled, still haunted her sleep. She didn't even know his name, but she feared she would dream about the dwarf for a hundred years or more.

She was tired, but made herself get up. There was pale light in the cave's mouth: dawn approaching, the tide rising. Before long, the water would creep into the cave. She needed to be gone before then. She gathered her things, pulled a bulbous, mottled green fruit—picked on an island not far from here—from her pouch, and ate it as she walked out into the morning.

The last few weeks had been hard. Tracking Sammek Thale had only been the first chore: she'd taken a small dwarf-skiff that had survived the razing of Uld and headed north. When she got to Malton, on the northern shore of the Tiderun, she'd found him gone, his people knew not where. Indeed, they were worried for him, that some storm or other peril had claimed the *White Worm*. He was a week overdue. She'd asked Thalaniya's help in tracking him, but Solis was waning and the magic was weak. It would be days before the amulet's enchantment would function again. She'd resolved to find him the old way, as she'd done things during the Godless Night. She sailed from port to port, asking after the *Worm*. And finally, after four days, she'd found him, moored thirty leagues west, and on the Run's far shore.

But not the Hooded One. Pirates had taken it, Thale told her, along with the rest of the riches he'd bought from the dwarves. The statue was long gone, and he would be lucky if his business partners didn't hang him when he got back to Malton. It would take years to recover the money he'd lost in the expedition. Sammek Thale was going home a broken man.

This was not Shedara's concern.

She had a new quarry, and Thalaniya couldn't yet help her. Solis was new, and the pearl remained dark, as though no spell at all were cast upon it. She'd set out on her own, seeking Harlad the Gray, and followed his trail to Mislaxa's Necklace: a chain of rocky, pine-dotted islets that had been hills before the First Destruction drowned them. The day before, she'd spotted his vessel, the *Blade*, anchored in a cove three leagues away. She'd held off confronting him then, choosing to wait until the morning. Many of his men would be senseless in the morning, victims of too much grog the night before. It would be safer.

Clouds blanketed the sky, and a rainy haze in the west promised a foul day. That was good—the pirates would rise later, might have even drunk more last night if they knew this was coming. The sea-lanes would be quiet, with no one to plunder.

Her skiff—sentimentally perhaps, she'd named it *Forgotten Uld*—was moored fifty paces from the shore. It had been ten paces the past night, at ebb-tide. She ate the fruit—it tasted something like a pear steeped in wine—while she looked at the blocky, square-rigged boat. The core of the fruit was mealy and sour, with tiny, black seeds. She tossed it away for scavengers. Making sure her pack was watertight, she waded out into the sea and swam. The water was warm.

A few minutes later, she was on the skiff, the sails unfurled and lines cast off. Wind caught canvas, and she was underway, a sure hand on the tiller guiding her among the rocks.

The Necklace was dangerously rock-clogged, something avoided by most larger vessels. Charts of its waters were rare, but evidently Harlad had one, for he had taken the *Blade*—no small ship, for a pirate cutter—in deep to hide. Shedara guided the *Uld* among the islets and hidden shoals, all the time watching the curtain of rain advance behind her stern. The wind was picking up, and the water was dotted with caps of white. When she saw the spire of rock she sought—a steep-walled pinnacle topped with a ring of standing stones, white with gull droppings—she tacked and put the ship in irons, waiting for the weather to come to her. The *Blade* lay on the far side of that spire, waiting.

The rain came on, fine and cold, making her shiver. It made it hard to see more than a dozen paces, and the clouds dimmed the light even more. It was time. Furling the sails, she pushed the anchor overboard and felt it clank against the rocky bottom. She checked her blades, made sure they were all where they ought to be, then took her pack and swung over the gunwale, into the water again.

The rocks on the shore were slippery, but she found handholds and hoisted herself up, startling a bird that had been intent on cracking clams. It squawked at her in annoyance, winging away. Shedara started up the slope of the island.

When she reached the top of the hill, she entered the ring of stones. Some had toppled or cracked, but most stood erect, having survived millennia and two Destructions. They were twice as tall as she was, gray and narrow, and capped with orbs of different hues—some white, some black, and some red. Weird runes were graven into their sides. It was a calendar, she guessed, for tracking the moons—and with them, the ebb and flow of magic in the world. The hulderfolk, a race of wild elves who dwelt in dark, unspoiled woods beyond the Conquered Lands, still made rings like these. She glanced around, raising an eyebrow—had these hills and valleys once belonged to that secluded people? Had forests of oak and redleaf covered these lands, instead of water? If so, the humans must have driven the hulder out, just as the Silvanaes had driven them out later, to forge Armach-nesti.

The circle, she decided, was a good enough place to work. The hulderfolk would have built it in a place where sorcery was strong. Lunis was waxing, and had enough power for simple spells, if not the great works Princess Thalaniya cast. The incantation to shrink the statue so she could carry it—should she find it—was a simple spell.

She cleared her mind, opened it to the red moon's power, and began to move. Her fingers danced on air, tracing symbols—not unlike those graven into the standing stones. The motions drew down the light of Lunis, focusing and binding it within her. It felt like the rush of lovemaking to her, and she ached at the memory of its absence during the Godless Night. Some had claimed to pull the same power from the air around them, during that time, but she had never mastered that ability. Now that the magic was back, she reveled. Eldritch words formed in her head, flaring in her memory as she spoke them, then fading into forgetfulness.

"*Teval im eosang, shai-unak poralan....*"

If the motions drew the power, the words gave it shape. With them, she wove a shell around her, like a caterpillar spinning its cocoon. When it was done, she brought her hands down. For a moment it seemed everything around her had turned as clear as glass. Then it faded back into view, and it was she who disappeared—a shimmer in the air. Smiling, she walked out of the circle and up onto a fallen stone that gave a vantage on the cove beyond.

There was the *Blade*, quiet and still, hardly anyone moving on her deck. The black trident flew atop her mast. Shedara knew Harlad by reputation: every thief in Southern Hosk did. The minotaur was a legend, the subject of a hundred chanteys sung from Rudil to the Fisheries of Syldar. She admired him, in a way. True, he had no respect for anyone or anything, including his own word, but he had fame and accomplishment. Moon-thieves worked in the shadows and did not earn such reputations as Harlad's.

All the same, she would sheathe her dagger in his heart if it won her the Hooded One.

She stood where she was for a time, letting the rain worsen. The invisibility spell would hold until she chose to let it lapse. She watched the *Blade*, working out where Harlad's cabin would be, spotting the lone guard who stood watch, and planning where she would come aboard. She must be quick and sure. She was still plotting when, in the distance, she saw something that drove a needle of fear into her gut.

Another ship.

The rain darkened everything, but there was no mistaking that it was black, narrower, faster, and more dangerous even than the *Blade*. Full sails held taut on its two masts. Even in the ragged weather, it was moving fast. There was something odd about the black ship. It took her a moment to realize that it was sailing straight into the wind. Impossible, even for the finest mariners on Taladas. It could only mean one thing.

Sorcery.

"No," she muttered, through lips grown thin. "Not again. Not this time."

Jumping down from the stone, she started to half-run, half-slide down the slope toward the *Blade*. She had to get to it fast, had to reach Harlad before the shadows did, before she lost the Hooded One again.

They didn't see her; wouldn't have, even without the spell. The few pirates who were awake stood at the portside rail, watching as the shadow-ship sliced into the cove. It moved of its own accord, not beholden to wind and current. Even the waves refused to break against its bow, instead sliding apart to let it pass. It seemed to throb with witchery, as if it were spun out of smoke and held together by will and the black moon. Perhaps this was so. Dark figures swarmed on its deck like ants. Shedara glimpsed them as she hoisted herself over the *Blade*'s starboard gunwale, up onto the deck. If the pirates had been looking, they would have seen an inexplicable shower of water as it dripped off her invisible form. Instead, she went unnoticed.

The black ship was closing in. The pirates drew cutlasses and reached for belaying pins. A few held crossbows. It wouldn't be enough. Shedara knew the crew of that dark vessel to be the same creatures that had killed both the dwarves of Uld and Ruskal Eight-Fingers. Harlad the Gray and his mates might be the most feared raiders of the Run, but they couldn't stand against such power. And neither could she. If she listened to the voice in her heart that urged her to fight beside the pirates, to add her blades to theirs, she would accomplish nothing—except to die with them.

They weren't important. The Hooded One was.

One minotaur hadn't gone with the others: the guard at Harlad's cabin. He remained at his post, presently turned around and speaking through the door, opened a crack. Describing the scene, Shedara thought. Harlad would emerge soon and join the fight.

She crossed the deck at a run, boards creaking beneath her feet, the sound unheard among rain and shouting. A glance over her shoulder showed the dark ship looming and pulling alongside the *Blade*. The shadows would board their prey soon. She could smell the coming slaughter. So could the minotaurs, who were beginning to shy back, the curses dying on their lips. Shedara shuddered at the thought of what sights might make hardened bull-men anxious. She was glad she couldn't see the black ship's crew.

Don't be too smug, she told herself. You may yet.

The guard must have heard something, for he turned, a great, red furred hulk, and squinted in her direction. A spiked cudgel came up in his hand and whistled through air where she was no longer. She rolled and sprang up with her dagger in her hand. She cut the back of the guard's knee, the knife biting deep, slicing the hamstring in two. He dropped with a grunt, too surprised to cry out. The cudgel fell from his hand. Shedara spun, dodged a massive, flailing fist, and leaped onto his chest, driving her blade into his jaw, just under his chin.

Blood poured from the wound, but the minotaur made no sound. He was already dead, his body twitching for a moment before falling still. Shedara yanked the knife free. She would be visible now. The contact of battle always broke the spell. But the pirates remained intent on the other ship, shouting to one another to keep their courage up. Greed outweighed their terror: they would not yield the loot they had pillaged, even if it threatened to cost them their lives.

Fools, Shedara thought, and slipped through the door.

Harlad's cabin was dark, the windows shuttered. For a frightening moment Shedara was blind, but then her elvensight took over, showing her shapes: a table, two stools, a foot-locker, and some random trinkets spread about—coins and jewels and a silver candlestick, unlit. No statue, though; no Hooded One. Likely it was in the hold, below.

A narrow bunk stood on the far side of the little room with a figure sitting on its edge. A minotaur with one horn. She knew him from the tales, even in the dark.

"Who's there?" growled Harlad. "Stang? Answer me, man!"

Shedara said nothing, creeping forward. She saw the bottle of brandy, empty beside the bed. Like the pirates who still slumbered, Harlad had drunk too much last night, and why not? He'd been safe, as far as he knew. He shook his head groggily, groping for the shutters.

She acted at once, a throwing knife dropping from its wrist-sheath into her hand, staying there for a breath, then flying through the darkness to pierce Harlad's reaching hand, pinning it to the wood behind.

Harlad was tough. He didn't scream, only grunted, grabbed the hilt of the knife, and started to work it free.

"Sargas's balls," he growled. "Whoever that is, you're going to get new holes to breathe through! Lads! To me!"

The shout went unheard. Shedara felt the bump of the black ship's hull against the *Blade*'s, then the bellowing of the minotaurs, first in rage, then in fear . . . then, unmistakably, pain. The attack had begun. From the enemy, the shadows pouring onto the ship, there came neither cries nor footfalls.

Harlad was almost free. She came at him from the flank, which was wise because when she got close his fist hammered through the air with force enough to break her neck. He missed her entirely, however, and she kicked him, hard, in the side, and hit the spot she meant to: his kidney. He grunted again and fell back on the bed. She drew a second blade and came down beside him with a dagger against either side of his throat. She pushed the daggers, loosing trickles of blood.

"Move, and you die," she said.

Harlad stiffened, held his breath, then began to laugh.

"*Khot*," he swore. "Bested by an elf, and a she-elf besides. I might have known it would come to this. I'll never live it down, when they hear of it back in Lamport."

You'll never see Lamport again, Shedara thought. The cries of the crew were dwindling. The fight was almost over. She was out of time.

"The statue," she said. "A man with a hood. Tell me where it is."

Harlad sneered. "You'd best pray I never find out who you are, elf. If I do, I'll wear your pointy ears as rings on my own."

She put a little more pressure on the blades, felt the veins beneath pulse, and heard the pirate catch his breath. Quiet now, on the deck. The air was growing chill, and the shadows were drawing near.

"The statue," she said.

"What of it? I don't have the thing any more, you fool!" he snapped. "I gave it away. Search if you want, stem to stern. You won't find it. You came here for nothing!"

A creak behind her, the door swinging wide. Cold like the winds of the Panak filled the cabin. No light, though. Something blocked it out. Shedara didn't look, didn't have to. She could feel the shadows draw near.

"Who?" she whispered urgently. "Who did you give it to?"

Harlad saw something behind her, standing in the doorway of the cabin. His eyes went wide. The terror came off him like a smell. She was afraid too, all her instincts telling her to get out, to leave *now*. She made herself stay, the blades firm against Harlad's throat.

"Tell me," she said. "If you do, I'll kill you quick. Don't, and I leave you to *them*."

Harlad stared at the doorway behind her, then at her, then back at the doorway. He swallowed and breathed a name.

"Thank you," Shedara said, and cut with both blades.

She whipped around at once, as the blood fanned from the twin slashes on Harlad the Gray's throat. There was something in the doorway, all right. It was smaller than she'd expected, dark, cold, and twisted. Man-shaped, though little taller than a goblin. It, too, held a blade in each hand: wicked, sickle-shaped knives. The shape came at her silently, its weapons whistling through the air. She leaped sideways, bumping into the wall, and parried each dagger with one of her own. For a horrid moment she expected the sickles to pass through her knives like smoke, but they were solid, and momentarily blocked. The creature leered, its face barely more than a skull covered in taut-stretched skin. She had never seen its like before.

Or had she? Something about it was familiar. Something . . .

Oh, gods, she thought. She knew what she faced—or what it had been, before evil magic had twisted it.

It was too strong for its size, too strong for her. It pushed, throwing her off balance, the sockets where its eyes should be blank and unreadable. Shedara brought her knee up and slammed it into the little fiend's chin. It reeled, stunned, then snapped back together, every joint tensing, its blades flicking forward like scorpion tails.

She dodged and felt one sickle score her side. The wound was numbingly cold and no blood came from it. Hoping it wasn't deep, she stepped to her right, swung behind the shadow, and planted a dagger in the back of its head.

BLADES OF THE TIGER

The blade turned freezing, and she let go with a gasp. The shadow fell, and Shedara felt a rush of relief. Whatever these things were, they could be killed. As she watched, its body unraveled and vanished like smoke, leaving behind nothing but her dagger.

She felt more cold: another shadow at the door. She knew she couldn't handle any more. She was wounded, and she'd barely beaten the first one. She reached past Harlad's hand, pinned to the wall, and opened the shuttered porthole. Gray rain-light spilled in, barely brightening the cabin. Shedara glanced over at the door with a gasp. There were three creatures there, not just one. All little and hideous, wizened and withered like mummified kings in ancient tombs. All held hooked blades, and shadowstuff clung about them like floating cloaks.

Kender, she thought with a start. Once, those things were kender.

A taller figure loomed behind them, robed and hooded. For a wild moment, Shedara thought it was Maladar, the Hooded One himself, come to life. But all the tales said the Faceless Emperor wore blue robes, and this figure wore black. He reached out a gloved hand.

"Surrender, elf," said a soft voice, sweet as honey. "Tell me where the Hooded One is, and you may live."

Shedara nearly did. The voice compelled her, the black moon's power running thick through the words. The name Harlad had told her leaped to her tongue and hung there, begging her to speak. The robed man held her transfixed for a breath . . . two . . . three. Then she shook herself, shuddering as the enchantment lifted, and threw her second knife at the figure in the doorway. Without waiting to see whether it struck, she turned, threw her arms up over her face, and leaped through the window.

The glass exploded outward, shards biting into her arms as she flew through the air. Then she was falling, and the water rose up to slam into her. She sank beneath the surface and stayed there, gazing up at the hulk of the

Blade above her, the black ship beside it. Holding her breath, she waited for the shadows to dive in after her.

But they didn't.

Her lungs burned for air. She had to do something. She summoned the strength to cast another spell, invoking Lunis's power. The water dragged at her hands, making it hard to form the necessary gestures, and the words were meaningless as they bubbled from her mouth, taking with them the last dregs of air. But the magic suffused her again, and she felt it run deep, filling her chest.

This had better work, she thought. She opened her mouth and inhaled.

Water flooded down her throat, filling her lungs. For a moment she choked at the sensation, and had to stave off the urge to panic. After that moment, though, the feeling of drowning subsided, and she smiled. She was breathing the water.

Shedara stayed there a while longer, staring up at the *Blade*. Cold leeched from its hull, down into the sea. She could sense the shadows moving beneath its decks, murdering and savaying the crew as they went. They wouldn't find the Hooded One, though. Only she knew where it had gone. For the first time, she had the advantage over her foes.

Wheeling about, she took a deep breath and swam away.

Chapter 12

GHOST HILLS, THE TAMIRE

Chovuk was talking again, alone in his yurt, in the dead of night. Hult, who had sat guard since the evening's feast—the Boyla had shot a succulent running-lizard upon the plains—roused from drowsing. There had been *kumiss* to go with the meat, made from the milk of Flying Star, Chovuk's favorite mare. Hult reflected, as his head swam, that he could have done with less drink.

He would have to find some *yarta* root to chew in the morning, to get his stamina back. If he had time before the battle.

The hum of his master's voice was too low to hear again. It always was. Hardly a night had passed in the month since they'd left the mountains of Ilquar without the Boyla speaking to his unseen companion, late at night. In all that time, Hult hadn't made out a single word of their conversation. Nor had he mentioned it to Chovuk. He had many questions, but not the station to ask them. It was not his place.

The Wretched Ones hadn't joined the horde right away. It would have made for an uneasy alliance, and the goblins were not all united. Instead, Chovuk had named Gharmu to rule in his stead, instructing the shaman to gather all the tribes scattered throughout the Uesi Ilquar and to meet him two weeks' ride northeast of Mount Xagal to take their revenge against the Kazar. Then he and the Tegins had left the mountains, bound east across the broad sweep of the Tamire.

Not all the lords liked the alliance he had forged with the goblins. Hoch, in particular, resented it. He had argued against the alliance as recently as three nights ago, at the speaking-fire where the highest Tegins gathered to confer with the Boyla.

"Peace?" Hoch had scoffed. "With the Wretched Ones? They are weak, traitorous. They are not worthy to fight alongside men. Whom will you ally with next, Chovuk? The Snow-men of Panak?"

The Tegins had laughed at that notion, and Chovuk had joined him. Then, almost casually, he had drawn his *shuk* and in a flash brought it sweeping around at Hoch's neck. It stopped in time, creasing the young lord's flesh and drawing a trickle of blood.

The laughter had died abruptly.

"If I mean to, I will tame the flame-folk of the Burning Sea," Chovuk had said, his voice soft and gentle. "I will call the gnomes out of their tunnels and the white apes down from the Ring-peaks. All the north will fight beneath my banner, if I wish it." Slowly, he lifted the saber away. "But you, Hoch Tegin, may leave this company now, if you choose. Do you?"

Hult had to fight back a smile. The Boyla had turned the question from the wisdom of his decision to Hoch's loyalty. The young Tegin had designs on leading the Uigan one day, and if he quit a war-band, the shame would rob him of that chance. His face dark, Hoch had shaken his head and not spoken a word for the rest of the meeting.

"The goblins will fight with us," Sugai Tegin had said, the old man's face pale beneath his many tattoos. "They will be the first into battle and into the teeth of our enemies' archers. Thus our people will remain strong, and fewer will die. It is no different than using dogs to hunt."

BLADES OF THE TIGER

The other Tegins had nodded. They had long respected Sugai's counsel. Still, a few had remained troubled.

"It is one thing to tell this to us," Yol Tegin, lord of the Horned Moon clan, had said. "We are learned men, all. But the common rider . . . what will he say when the goblins join us? Will there not be discontent?"

"There will not," Sugai had replied. "You will keep your men in line, Yol. All of you will."

"Any man who questions shall be flogged by my command," Chovuk had added. "Let the whip be my answer. If he complains again, or threatens to leave, then it is the sword. Stake his head so all may see."

Murmurs had greeted this. Some of the chiefs had looked troubled, but others smiled and nodded their heads. "Listen to the Boyla," they had said. "The Tiger is wise."

That, in the end, was all it took. Chovuk the Tiger, Chovuk Skin-changer . . . not since the days of the Great Boylas, days known only in song, had the lords of the Uigan had the power to take the form of beasts. After the Destruction, such magic had vanished from the Tamire. But Jijin had blessed their prince and given him the power of the steppe-tiger. Who were they to question one favored by the gods?

So there they were, on the edge of Kazar lands, awaiting the Wretched Ones. Waiting for their hunting dogs to come. There had been a few skirmishes with Kazar outriders, but no real battles yet. The Uigan horde—ten thousand lances strong—stood poised to avenge Krogan Boyla, here at the Tamire's edge, where the rocky hills wore beards of snow. They had camped here for two days, a mass of yurts and cooking fires filling three separate valleys. Then, the previous night, the scouts had reported from the west: a mass of goblins was approaching, two thousand strong, and was marching across the Tamire. Gharmu had kept his word. The next day, they would arrive. The next day, the war would begin.

In the moonless dark—it was past midnight and halfway

to morning—Hult gazed into the distance, into the lands of the Kazar, and felt the stirrings of doubt. Alone of all the warriors in the horde, he knew that the Kazar had not slain Krogan. Yes, they had tried . . . come close, even. And yes, they had been the enemies of the Uigan since time out of memory. But *Chovuk* had killed the old Boyla and made it look like the Kazar had done it. All so he could rule the Tamire, and have his war. There was nothing wrong with war, but every day it troubled Hult more that all of this, all that had happened and would happen, was based on a lie.

You are *tenach*, he told himself. Your master is all. You do not question. You only act.

He grimaced, rubbing his aching head. He could never speak out against Chovuk. No one would believe him—and even if they did, if they agreed the Tiger was not worthy to rule, what would become of Hult? His life as *tenach* would be over, and that was all he had. Besides, there was another thing: he loved his master, right or wrong. Even beyond any oaths he had sworn. How could he turn against a man he loved?

Hult wasn't sure when the murmuring within the yurt began to change, but suddenly he was aware of a new urgency in the Boyla's voice. His voice was higher and tighter—louder, too. For the first time, he could make out words, but they were not of the Uigan tongue. Instead, they seemed to crawl around his mind like ants, their meaning out of reach. He glanced over his shoulder in alarm, his hand going to the hilt of his sword, and caught his breath.

There was light within the yurt, spilling out beneath the flap. It was not the warm, golden glow of candle or oil-lamp, however. This light was pale and sickly, a putrid hue between brown and green. It brightened and dimmed as he watched, pulsing like a living thing. There was a sound, as well . . . a heartbeat thrumming so low that he sensed it in his bowels more than his ears.

Sorcery! At once he was on his feet, blade drawn, the

haze of *kumiss* gone from his head. He was forbidden from entering the yurt without permission—unless he was convinced that his master was in danger. He was through the flap without a second thought, ready to lash out at whatever was shedding that horrible glow. It stabbed at his eyes, making them water, and he threw up a hand to ward it off. The noise made his stomach lurch, nausea awakening deep inside him.

Chovuk stood in the middle of the tent, surrounded by a ring of the rancid light, which shimmered like a curtain up to the ceiling. He was nearly naked, wearing only a breechclout and his dragon-claw necklace. His arms stretched out to either side, hanging in the air as if held up by cords. His head was thrown back and his mouth twitched as it formed the words of magic.

There is someone else here.

Hult felt the presence, as he had sensed the goblins in the caverns of Xagal. The feeling made him think of the jackals that followed the shepherds of his tribe, skulking beyond the lights of the campfires and waiting for a lamb to stray from the flock. There was the same sense of patient hunger to whatever was in the yurt with them. Hult raised his *shuk*, looking for whoever had done this to the Boyla.

"Show yourself!" he shouted. "Bring yourself to my blade!"

There came a new sensation, which made him stagger: hate, a great spike of it, driving through him. He gritted his teeth, fighting to keep his feet—then, with a quaking, joyless laugh, the presence vanished from the room. The green light flared, then went out, leaving crimson ghosts dancing before Hult's eyes. He blinked, and when he could see again Chovuk had fallen to his knees. The Boyla's eyes had rolled back, showing white. Foam flecked his lips.

"Master!" Hult cried, dropping his sword and leaping forward.

He caught Chovuk as he was beginning to fall, easing

the listless weight to the floor. The Boyla was covered with sweat, but his skin was cold. For a long moment he did not breathe, and Hult cast about desperately, not sure what to do. He was just about to cry out for Sugai, or one of the other Tegins, when Chovuk sucked in a ragged, gasping lungful of air. For a few breaths he twitched and struggled, but Hult held him fast. Finally, the Boyla relaxed, his eyes fluttering. His chest rose and fell slowly. Hult spoke his name, but he didn't respond; he had fallen into deep sleep.

Calmer now, Hult lifted Chovuk from the floor. The Boyla was not a small man, but he felt strangely frail and light as Hult carried him to the mound of furs he used for a bed. Carefully, Hult laid him down and covered him with a blanket, then rose and went to fetch his sword. He looked around the yurt one last time, but there was no sign of the presence he had sensed earlier. They were alone.

With a sigh of relief, Hult went back outside and sat down again, his blade across his knees. He peered out into the gloom again, but this time he felt no fear. No, he felt doubt . . . the doubt was back, and now it was growing.

The goblins arrived shortly after dawn, beneath a cloud-sheeted sky—a huge, disorderly mass of them, abristle with tribal standards and hooked spears. They moved on foot, cowled and cloaked against the sunlight they despised, their pale red eyes gleaming. Gharmu rode at their head, resplendent in moldering robes, his scorpion-shell headdress glistening in the rusty morning light. He raised his good hand in greeting as Chovuk and Hult rode out to meet him.

Behind the Boyla, the Uigan gathered, the Tegins at the front. Archers fitted arrows to bowstrings, ready to loose if anything went wrong—but Sugai watched them, snapping at any who hastened to raise his weapon. The

Wretched Ones shifted and muttered to one another, eyeing the riders as warily as the Uigan eyed them. All it would take was one misfired arrow, and this alliance would collapse in a welter of blood.

In the silence, broken only by the hiss of wind through the grass, Chovuk dismounted and walked up to the goblins' new king. Hult followed, a hand on the hilt of his *shuk*.

"We come," grunted Gharmu, bowing his head. "Bring many tribes. Would bring more, but no time."

"It is enough," Chovuk replied. A smile tugged at the corners of his mouth. "You have brought me a mighty force. Well done, Gharmu—I am pleased."

The shaman glanced up, an almost pathetic look of pleasure in his eyes. Sugai Tegin had known better than he realized, likening the Wretched Ones to dogs. It was a hound's admiration in Gharmu's eyes. Gharmu raised his head, the gnarled stub of his nose twitching as he caught something on the breeze. It blew out of the west, swaying the few scattered birch trees that grew among the Ghost Hills.

"Smell them. Kazar dogs," croaked the shaman, his eyes narrowing to slits.

"Yes, my friend," said Chovuk. He laid a hand on the goblin's head. Hult tensed. He sensed no treachery from Gharmu, but the elders' tales were filled with dead lords whose *tenachai* had sensed no treachery until too late. "I have decided to honor you for your long journey and loyalty. You will taste first blood this day."

Gharmu looked up, awestruck. "First blood? You say true?"

"I say true." The Boyla pointed west. "Beyond our camp lies Khal, the greatest town of the Kazar. Your people will attack it first, and kill as you please. Take fingers to fill the rings I have given you. I only ask one thing of you."

"What thing? Say, and I give."

The shaman's eyes were gleaming now, the promise of slaughter giving them a feverish sheen. Nearby, other goblins—from little, stunted imps to hulking, hunchbacked brutes, no two alike—fingered their weapons and bared crooked fangs. Even those who hadn't heard Chovuk's words could sense the coming bloodshed. Hult shivered, looking at the ravening mob. For an odd moment, he felt a flash of pity for the people of Khal. There would be much grief among the Kazar today.

"When you find their chief, do not kill him," Chovuk said. "He is for my blade alone. Will you do this?"

Gharmu stared at him, long and hard. Finally he nodded. "We spare chief. Give to you."

"Good," said the Boyla. "Now go, Gharmu of Xagal. Go, and slake your thirst upon your enemies."

Khal was a quiet town, a place of tents and sod huts, surrounded by horse paddocks. Smoke hung over the town, which was sheltered from the wind by snowy hills, like a blanket. At the center of town, a large stone well sank deep into the earth. It was very old, and had been there when the Kazar first came to those lands, centuries ago. The remains of thirteen statues encircled the well; tall, beautiful figures that were neither man nor elf. Most were broken in some way, missing an arm, or a head, or sheared away at the waist. The Kazar called them *Dejal Ugai*, the First People. Their tale-singers said the Abaqua ogres, who dwelt in the thick pine forests farther east, were all that remained of them. They prayed, sometimes, to the statues, but no answer ever came.

They did not pray that day. They knew the Uigan were close, and that the statues' power—if they had ever had power—would not protect them. Not in a hundred years had their blood enemies penetrated so deeply into Kazar lands. They looked to their king, Duskblade, for guidance.

Should they flee? Seek shelter in the caves, deeper in the hills?

"To what end?" answered Duskblade. He was a tall man, nearly seven feet, as slender and taut as a whip, and clad in thick furs from head to toe. He wore his graying hair short, in the custom of his people, save for a knot bound up at the back. His moustaches were long and braided, and kept supple with rancid butter. He gestured around him with the blade of his *varun*, the cleaver-like blade his people wielded instead of the *shuk*. "Do you think we would escape them? They have come for our blood, and will not be deterred if we run. And we would be scattered then, and easier to pick off. No . . . this is our home. We will face the Uigan worms here! Let the songs of this day be ballads of glory, not dirges of defeat! Drive them back, say I—drive them back, all the way to their corpse-hung rock!"

The warriors of Khal replied with a round of raucous shouts, lifting their *varuns* into the air. It was a fine speech, and gave them courage. Then a sound rose that stole their courage away.

They had expected the thunder of hooves, the high, keening shouts of the riders as they approached. There had never been a time when Kazar and Uigan were not at war, and the warriors of the eastern tribes knew well the din of an approaching band of horsemen. But the clamor that arose beyond the hills was nothing like that. Instead of the hooves, there was the tromp of many running feet. Instead of battle-cries, there was a cacophony of bestial noises: growls, snarls, gibbering, and shrill howls that made the men grit their teeth. The men glanced at one another, confused, then at their king.

Duskblade was as puzzled as they were, though, and cast about, looking to the scout-towers west of town. The towers were crude works of lashed-together wood, rising up to platforms fifty feet above the ground. Young men stood watch atop them, with great drums to sound when danger was near. The drums had begun to roll, with a signal unheard in Khal for many generations, not since the dark times after the Destruction. This was not the low, ominous roll that warned of approaching Uigan, but a series of short, sharp thuds that grew fast, then slow, fast then slow.

The Wretched Ones had come.

"That makes no sense," Duskblade muttered, though there was no denying that the shrieks and yowls echoing among the hills were the voices of goblins. None of the outriders had said anything about the Wretched Ones. It was Chovuk Boyla and his horde they all spoke of. So what—

"Look!" someone cried. Fingers pointed. Somewhere, across the town, a woman screamed.

Duskblade turned. Figures swarmed over the western rise now, hundreds of them, running as fast as galloping horses. Vicious little creatures, yammering and waving bent and rusty weapons. Horror-struck, he watched as they broke around the guard-towers. Some started to climb, while others hewed with axes at their bases. In the end the latter won out, and the towers groaned and toppled while the goblins continued their climbing. Most of the watchmen died in the crash, but a few rose and set to with their blades, trying to keep the Wretched Ones back. None of them lasted more than a dozen breaths, however, before the sheer weight of the goblins bore them down, and they vanished in the flood.

Duskblade's mouth went dry. He'd expected to fight this day, probably to die . . . but he'd counted on his foes being men. This was different. His people would meet their end, but there would be no honor in it. There would be only suffering.

He glanced at the statues in the midst of the camp, then spat in the dirt, cursing the *Dejal Ugai* and all their works. They had proven no help at all.

The Wretched Ones poured down the hill, toward Khal. The warriors of the Kazar shifted, no longer certain what to do. Their king was also uncertain, but he would not show his vacillation before them. Would not show fear. He raised his *varun*, his lip curling in a sneer.

"Bows!" He cried. "Loose your arrows! Send these filth back to the Abyss! Kill them all!"

Emboldened, his men answered with a raucous cheer. They sheathed their swords and fit leather-fletched arrows on their bowstrings. One by one, then in waves, they pulled and released. Black shafts rose, then dived down into the midst of the charging goblins. A few fell, pierced and shattered. Not enough, though—Duskblade could see that. So could any man with eyes.

The Kazar launched a second volley, then a third. A few men managed a fourth. But that was all—a few score of the Wretched Ones were dead, and the rest were slamming into Khal's earthen ramparts with force enough to shake the whole town. Screeching for blood, they climbed up and over and into the town. Into the ranks of the warriors, drawing their *varuns*, the terror back in their eyes and never to leave them again. Men died in waves, skewered, pulled down, and torn apart. Fangs sank into flesh. Rending sounds mixed with screams of agony.

Duskblade watched, sick to his core, as the Wretched Ones swept over his men. It was already ending, over nearly before it could begin. The rear ranks, seeing the ruin that became of the front, scattered and ran. Goblins chased them down, rammed spears in their backs, tackled them and bore them to the ground. Some carried torches. The westernmost huts were burning, dark tongues of smoke licking the sky. Tears tracked down Duskblade's face. He was the king of a dead people. The singers would never utter his name.

There was only one thing left to do. With a roar of grief, he raised his blade and charged the onrushing monsters.

There wasn't much left by the time the Uigan arrived. Khal was in flames and the statues at its center had been pulled down. Dust and smoke hung in the air. Bodies and parts of bodies littered the ground, torn apart and half-devoured. Goblins chased women and children through the burning wreckage, killing with glee. The screams of the dead and dying filled the air.

Hult tasted bile as he beheld what had become of the town and its people. He'd heard tales of the destruction a marauding goblin tribe could cause, but had never seen it firsthand. As much as he hated the Kazar, he felt a twinge of pity as well. This was no way to die, not when they hadn't even killed Krogan. He fought to keep his face blank, expressionless.

There was laughter elsewhere among the riders. And why not? As far as they knew, the Kazar were Boyla-slayers. They deserved this. And the Uigan had gotten their revenge without a single man lost. Obeying the commands of their Tegins, warriors began galloping around the town to encircle it, then fanned out to ride down any Kazar who had escaped the mayhem. Hult knew there wouldn't be many, but some *shuks* would still be bloodied. And there was always the next day: there were more villages, not far away. Plenty of kills to go around, once they left Khal in blood and ashes.

Chovuk flashed a predatory smile. "Good, good," he said. "Better than I'd hoped, in fact. The bull-men will not stand long before this."

"They may, behind their walls of stone," said Hoch Tegin, who sat his horse nearby. He was enjoying the slaughter as well.

The Boyla laughed. "Do you think I forgot about the minotaurs' walls? Leave that to me, boy."

Hoch's face colored at the insult, and he opened his mouth to reply. Before he could, however, Sugai pointed back down toward the town. "Gharmu. He comes, with a burden," the old man said.

BLADES OF THE TIGER

So he did. Peering through the smoke, Hult saw the shaman leading two of his larger brutes up the slope from Khal. Between them, the big goblins bore the limp figure of a very tall man, clad in furs. One hand, missing all but one of its fingers, dangled down from the body, trailing in the dirt.

Duskblade, king of the Kazar, was still breathing when he was dumped at Chovuk Boyla's feet—but just barely. "He kill thirty of us," Gharmu explained. "Not easy to stop."

"No," Chovuk said, swinging down from his horse. "He would not be."

The Kazar's face was a ruin, covered in blood—some his own, most of it goblin. His mouth was filled with jagged, broken teeth, his nose mashed flat, and one eye was so badly swollen it could no longer open. A mallet to the face had brought him down. His good eye rolled as he looked up at Chovuk, and he tried to speak, tried to curse the Boyla. All that came out, though, was a long thread of bloody spittle.

The Boyla drew his *shuk*.

"Your kind slew our prince," he declared, and Hult tried not to flinch at the spoken lie. "You ambushed him and left him filled with arrows. You have brought this on yourselves. Know that when we are done, the Kazar will be a scattered people, dying slow among these Jijin-forsaken hills."

Duskblade shook his head. He raised his unmaimed hand, an absurd protective gesture. Tears leaked down his cheeks.

"Go to your ancestors, dog," Chovuk said, and swung his sword twice. The first blow took off the man's hand at the wrist. The second cut off his head.

All was still. Chovuk stood over Duskblade's corpse, watching the blood darken the earth around it. The Tegins did the same. No one laughed or spoke. Even Gharmu stood silently, waiting for what would happen next.

Finally, Chovuk turned to Hult. "Take that," he said, pointing at the king's head. "I will plant it on a spear before my yurt. Let all who behold it know justice is done for Krogan Boyla. The goblins can have the rest."

He turned and strode away, the Tegins trailing after. Hult watched as Gharmu ordered his brutes to take Duskblade's body. The shaman, meanwhile, picked up the severed hand and began to remove fingers, for the rings the Boyla had given him. His prizes.

His face like stone, Hult bent to pick up King Duskblade's head.

Chapter 13

HAWKBLUFF, THENOL

"*Khot!*" Grath swore again, more fiercely this time than before.

Looking out across the lifeless, muddy field spread out at the foot of Hawkbluff, beneath the grinning skulls and demons of Hith's great temple, Forlo felt his soul go cold. The men of the Sixth were arrayed all around him. Peering through the gray rain-curtains, he saw the banners of the Third Legion as well, green and gold; the Fifth, white and orange; and the Ninth, black and violet. Thousands of men awaited the order to attack the ragged force of Thenolite soldiers and fanatics who waited before them. Waiting for the horns to sound.

But others were waiting, too. He knew the bones he'd accidentally unearthed from the muck weren't just there by chance. The Thenolites had buried them there, and many more like them, skeletons and rotting corpses, concealed in water and soft earth, awaiting the necromantic spell that would awake them. An ambush so clever and ruthless that the tactician in Forlo's mind—the cold part of him that had pushed the League this close to victory—couldn't help but shake his head in admiration.

"Say nothing," he murmured. "If the men find out, they'll panic—I don't care how much training they have."

Grath nodded, keeping his face studiously blank, giving nothing away. "What, then?"

Forlo thought, wiping water from his face. "Send word to the officers. Have them tell their clerics, *and no one else*. They must be ready, and spread out among the troops. When Ondelos awakens his army, they must act quickly. Understood?"

"Aye," the minotaur said. "I'll make sure it's kept."

"You'd better."

Grath flashed a sharp-toothed grin. "This is pretty bad, eh?"

Forlo laughed, but the cold lump of horror stayed where it was, lodged in his gut. When Grath was gone, he turned back to gaze toward the Hawkbluff, and the army at its foot. Atop the hummock, Bishop Ondelos had not moved. But now, despite the rain and the distance, Forlo was sure he could see a smile on the Bishop's face.

It took too long for Forlo's orders to be carried out. Any moment, he expected someone to figure out what was going on: either his men would realize the Thenolite dead were lurking underfoot, waiting to feast on their flesh, or Ondelos would understand why he was delaying, and order the attack before the clerics were in place. He made a show of studying the opposition, all the while watching as men and minotaurs with purple priest's sashes over their armor filed silently among his troops. The rain drowned out the cries of the fanatics, and the murmur and rattle of the League's soldiers. He tried not to think of the hungry, moldering things beneath him—thousands strong, he was sure, ready to dig their way out of the sludge and to kill every living thing they found.

Wait, he told himself, keeping his hand on his sword but refusing to draw it. *Wait a bit longer....*

When Grath returned, his face was troubled. "We need

to do something now," he murmured, his yellow eyes flicking back the way he'd come. "You're not the only one who's found something."

Following the minotaur's gaze, Forlo saw his meaning. In several places, troops had pulled up bones, or even worse things. They clustered with their heads together as they tried to figure out what this meant. It wouldn't take them long. Then terror would spread like fire through dry brush. Biting his lip, Forlo slid his blade from its scabbard.

"Horns," he declared. "Sound the attack at once. Slow march."

Grath raised a massive arm, opening and closing his fist once. A chorus of long, low notes blared across the field, followed by the steady thudding of drums. First the Sixth sounded the call, then the others took it up. Soon, the entire army was moving, pikes thrust forward above walls of interlocked shields. Across the distance, the mad Thenolites cheered and came on at a full charge, gnashing their teeth and raging against their foes.

Ondelos remained atop his hillock, and Forlo imagined his laughter. He watched the Bishop speak briefly with one of his underlings, then fold his hands across his drooping belly and bow his head to pray.

Shadows gathered around the Bishop, swirling like clouds of filth in water. Blacker and blacker they grew, until they all but hid him from sight. A cold wind picked up, whipping across the field, making ripples on the brackish pools, turning the rain into stinging, icy needles. Forlo peered through the rain, shielding his eyes, and saw the fat priest raise his hands, the sleeves falling back to reveal leather bindings around his arms, interlaced with little bones. The shadows blossomed as he moved, flowing upward to form a pillar of darkness that stretched hundreds of feet into the sky. Then Ondelos's voice rose to a piercing shriek, and the whirling gloom burst, flowing outward in a terrifying, billowing ring.

The spell overtook the Thenolite soldiers first, then the charging fanatics, and poured on toward the League's army. In its wake the ground began to churn, geysers of mud erupting as the dead clawed out of their earthen prison.

They were in all states of decay, from bare, brown bones to bloated, wet horrors, to pale corpses that still showed the ragged wounds that had killed them, as recently as days ago. Most wore some sort of armor, either Thenolite or that of the League, and though most were human, there were some minotaurs as well. Dead soldiers from both sides, gathered and brought here by the Bishop's followers . . . dug up from graves, or plucked from battlefields and buried again in the Hawkvale. Their eyes burned ruddy orange, like dying suns, and their jaws gaped wide, baring yellow, jagged teeth. They snarled and groaned, shrieked and blubbered. The stink surged up Forlo's throat.

Thousands of them, and more coming.

The wave of shadow towered above, ready to crash down. The soldiers paused, quailing before the wave. It was nearly two hundred feet high and filled with things that might be faces, things that appeared suddenly out of the dark and vanished again just as quickly. Forlo felt his own throat clench and sweat sprang from the palm of his sword hand. He knew the shadows would overtake him regardless, but even so, every instinct told him to flee, to get out, for the gods' love, *run*.

Instead he raised his blade, challenging the dark, and bellowed to his men.

"At your feet!" he cried. "Look down, and use your swords!"

Once, on a youthful dare, Forlo had climbed into the Highvale Mountains in wintertime and dived into a near-frozen lake. The Bishop's spell reminded him of that feeling as it crashed down around him, driving the breath from his lungs and chilling him until warmth seemed forever beyond hope. It was all he could do to keep from

BLADES OF THE TIGER

falling to his knees and doubling over from the excruciating pain. Then the spell was past him, and moving deeper through the army.

The ground below him was beginning to roil . . .

The body of a half-naked fanatic surged up before him, half its face cut away, black slime dripping from its nose and remaining ear. Long, filthy fingers reached out for him. With a yelp of shock, he lashed out with his sword. The corpse's head fell away, and the body sank to the ground, twitching as the Bishop's magic left it. Beside him, Grath swept his axe around in a two-handed fashion, striking a leathery skeleton right in the middle. It toppled in a shower of ribs and broken bones. To his right, a soldier screamed as gnarled hands erupted from the ground, seized his ankles, and pulled him down. All around, men were shouting and minotaurs were bellowing as the dead arose. There were nearly as many of the ghoulish creatures as there were League soldiers upon the field, strewn throughout the ranks, breaking up formations and killing without hesitation.

Forlo knew Ondelos was rubbing his fat hands together with glee that his trap had been sprung. "Not so fast," Forlo said, half to himself. Turning to the nearest cleric, he raised his shield-arm as a signal.

Created by the evil of necromancy, the undead were vulnerable to divine power. At Forlo's signal, the army's priests began to pray—first a few nearby, then more at a distance, and still others all across the valley. They raised their hands to the heavens, calling on the gods for strength, and silvery light seethed around him. They gathered the light, then swept their arms down like great, chopping blades. As Forlo watched, the divine glow swept across the battlefield like a hundred exploding stars.

The bloodthirsty howls of the Thenolite dead turned into anguish as the clerics' spell first struggled against, then overcame the magic that bound their spirits to their bodies. Decaying flesh burst into white flame, peeling and falling away. Bones blackened and crumbled to ash. All that remained when the silver glow passed were charcoal smudges and heaps of white powder, soaking into the ruptured mud. The dead army had unraveled into nothing.

"Ha! Your plan seems to be working," roared Grath, chopping a ghoul in half at the waist with a great sweep of his axe.

The pieces flopped down into the mud, tried for a moment to crawl back to each other, then stopped as Grath's axe cleaved apart its skull. A moment later, the holy light washed over them and the pieces dissolved. So did the one-armed horror Forlo had just spitted upon his sword, which had been clawing mindlessly at the blade, trying to work itself free. Its mouth opened to scream, spilling out worms, then it burned away into a cloud of drifting soot.

All across the field, the horror played out. The dead tried to escape, but could not. Instead, they fell to the blades of the legions, or were annihilated by the clerics' power. In some places, they hadn't even fully freed themselves from the mud, and the ground collapsed over where they had lain, leaving charred black limbs sticking out of the soil like some unholy crop. Elsewhere, soldiers hacked and stabbed the mud itself, destroying their enemy before it could reveal itself. In minutes, what could have been a catastrophic defeat for the League became an unquestionable victory: only a few dozen soldiers perished before the fighting died down. A great cheer went up among Forlo's troops.

It took him a moment to realize they were shouting his name.

"They should stifle that," he muttered, the corners of his mouth tightening. "The battle's not done yet."

"May as well be," Grath replied. "We've got them outnumbered for real now."

Across the field, where a few straggling undead had escaped the brunt of the priests' assault, the Thenolites had fallen back on their heels. Even the fanatics looked doubtful, and some of the common fighters had thrown down their weapons to flee. Atop the hummock, Bishop Ondelos had turned as white as his raiment. Forlo couldn't help but grin at the sight of the great ruler of Thenol, reduced to desperation.

"On, before they regroup!" he shouted. "Give quarter to he who asks for it—and leave none alive who doesn't! A thousand gold galleons to whoever brings me Ondelos— two thousand if he's alive!"

The drums picked up the march again—double time now—but were barely able to keep up with the pounding of boots as the army charged. But Ondelos was no longer there. He had fled the field already. Forlo lifted his gaze to the pinnacle above, where skeletal birds slowly circled the towers of the temple of Hith, and swallowed. His quarry hid within.

Sword ready, he moved on toward the dark church.

"It unsettles me," Essana said. "It's almost as if it were. . ."

"Alive," Forlo finished when her voice trailed off.

She nodded. "I'm glad you think so, too. I was afraid you'd think I was frightened of shadows."

"Never you," he replied. "I thought the same thing when I first saw it on Harlad's ship."

The statue stood before them, in the center of the great hall, half-mantled by shadow as the afternoon lengthened. It did not move, and it did not shimmer with magic or anything so obvious. But his wife was right—something about the thing seemed wrong, somehow. As if the stone were alive.

Essana shivered. "I feel like it's watching me."

That made no sense. It didn't even have eyes. The hood hid its eyes, along with the rest of its face. Forlo wondered if the sculptor had crafted eyes anyway, hiding them from view, a secret within his craft. There was no telling, when it came to artifacts from Aurim. The art that had survived the First Destruction was prized for its subtleties, its cunning.

"It's worth an emperor's ransom," Forlo said, more to himself than to Essana. "Once the succession's sorted out, I'll find someone to buy it."

"I wish you could do it sooner," she said, and shuddered again. "I would prefer it out of my sight."

Forlo felt a flash of irritation. The statue could double their fortune and ensure their family's dominion over its holdings for generations to come. Essana shouldn't be complaining about it. In his heart, though, he had to agree with her. The thought of seeing that grim, weirdly watchful figure every day wasn't pleasant.

"I'll have it removed," he told her. "I'll have it put below, in the vaults. You won't have to worry about it then."

She considered it a long moment, frowning. "Well, perhaps you shouldn't—"

"What, then?" he snapped, his annoyance growing. "Throw it in the sea? Drag it out into the woods?"

Essana turned away, flushing, tears in her eyes. That surprised him. It wasn't like her. She'd always been willing to snap back and call him a fool when he was in an ill temper. He went to her and put a hand on her shoulder. He touched her cheek with his other hand, turning her around. There were wet tracks on her face and fear in her eyes.

"Starlight?" he asked. "What is it?"

"You could guess." The words barely rose above a whisper.

He thought, trying not to lose his patience. He could feel the statue's gaze, just like she'd said. Finally he shook his head. "I don't kn—"

Then, a breath late, it came to him.

"Oh, hang me. You're not."

BLADES OF THE TIGER

She nodded, more tears spilling, her hands moving to cover her belly. "I wasn't sure," she said. "I didn't think it was possible any more. But a Mislaxan came to the town while you were gone. I sent for her to find out the truth."

"When?" he breathed.

"It must have happened right after you returned," Essana said, smiling. "Maybe even that night. It's still early yet, and much can go wrong. But if the gods smile, in the wintertime we'll have a son."

Son. Not child. The Mislaxan had told her the child would be a boy, evidently. Some of the more skilled healers could sense such things, even early on. "Starlight," he breathed. "Our son."

"And heir," she said.

Her smile brought tears to his own eyes. He hadn't wept since he was a boy. He caught her up and held her to him, kissed her and drew back, staring into her eyes. Both their faces were wet. This day had been long in coming.

"You're pleased." She grinned.

He kissed her again. "Very nearly."

They held each other a while longer, then he felt his gaze drawn away. He glanced across the room and saw the statue standing there. Watching them. Ridiculous, but no denying it.

Looking back at Essana, he saw that she was staring at the statue too. She was pale and afraid. A strange look for her. He felt a surge of anger at the thing he'd brought back from Lamport. He thought of Harlad and of how freely the old pirate had gotten rid of it. He was beginning to understand why.

He had a son coming, though. He couldn't give the statue away, or destroy it, or whatever the small voice in his head was telling him to do. Its value might be great.

"The tunnels," he said. "Out of sight. We'll forget it's there, in time."

He half-expected her to argue, but she shrugged instead, her mouth a lipless line. "Do what you think is best," she said.

She kissed him again, on the cheek, then stepped out of his arms and away, up the stairs to their chambers. Forlo watched her go, hating himself for disappointing her. Then he glanced back at the cowled statue and felt its aspect change slightly. Not just watchful now. Something else. Pleased?

Glaring at the hooded figure, he turned on his heel and strode out of the hall, not the same way his wife had gone.

A week passed, and midsummer drew near. The days sweltered, but the needed rain never came. The nights were little better, being windless and sultry. It did no good for anyone's mood, and though he knew better, Forlo still sulked when he and Essana were together. They hardly spoke and barely touched at night, all when he should have been happier than ever in his life. She tended to the Holding, while he rode in the countryside or hunted or taught the servant boys how to wield a sword. Time crawled.

At least the statue was dealt with. Before the first night, the servants had taken it away, down into the deepest recesses beneath the keep. Forlo had only been down to the deepest vaults a few times and hadn't liked it. Coldhope Keep was built over much older ruins, whose tunnels had been dug out thousands of summers ago, by men forgotten by history, as a place to bury their dead. The statue was locked away down there in the dark, with bones for company.

He could still feel it, though, even down there. It wasn't watching any more, but it was waiting. *Skulking*, a poet might have said. Forlo didn't care for poets. But the word was apt. Whenever he was within the keep, he thought he could sense the statue, as his warrior's instincts had trained him to sense enemies lying in wait. The same sense that had told him of the dead army at Hawkbluff. At night, after the nightmares woke him, he fancied he could hear the hooded statue breathing.

Essana never spoke of it, nor did she have to. Every time she looked at him, it was there in her eyes: *get that dreadful thing out of here.*

On Sargasday, the end of the week, he was out most of the day, stalking a stag in the woods to the south. The stag eluded him in the end, but the chase was good, and he feathered three coneys on the way home. There were still a few hours left till dusk and the sun was well above the horizon—enough time for the cooks to dress his catch and roast them for supper, with parsnips and a sauce of berries and honey. He was humming an old warrior's tune, *The Sun Upon My Shield*, when he came out of the forest and started up the road for home.

The song died on his lips when he reached the gates. There was another horse there, a hulking stallion tethered in the bailey. The stableboy was giving it water to drink. Its flanks were caked with road-dust. It wore no barding or caparison, for the weather was too warm, but its harness was familiar. The leather was dyed in martial colors. Crimson and blue.

The Sixth.

Dropping the coneys, Forlo bolted up the keep's steps three at a time, shoved through the doors to the great hall—and slammed right into Grath Horuth-Bok. The minotaur let out a roar of surprise, then embraced him in a crushing hug.

"A son! I knew you'd breed one day, you old fox!"

Forlo blinked, then smiled and gave his friend a shove. "When did you get here?"

"Less than an hour ago," Grath said. "Rode hard. Gods' grief, but I'd rather march." He rubbed his backside.

"I was about to send someone for you," said Essana. He glanced at her, sitting on a chair in the shadows. He hadn't known she was there. "You saved me the trouble."

He winced at the curtness in her voice, wishing he could undo all the tension that had been piling up between them these past days. Instead he turned back to Grath, who grinned at him, oblivious.

"What brings you here?" Forlo asked. "And if you say your horse, you'll regret it."

The minotaur laughed briefly. "The war," he said. "Or the troubles, or whatever they're calling it in Kristophan. Soldiers are dying, no matter the name. It *is* getting close to an ending, but there are some hard battles ahead."

He stopped, looked at Forlo a moment, then opened his mouth to say more. And closed it again.

Forlo's good mood vanished. "Grath. What—"

"Just listen. There's someone you should talk to. He's only a few days' ride away."

"Who?" Forlo demanded. "One of the claimants to the throne?"

Grath nodded. "You don't have to say anything now," he said.

A sigh escaped Forlo's lips. He looked across the hall.

"Go," said Essana. "But come back."

He knew what she meant. Maybe a week or more apart would help. He shook his head. "All right," he said. "But your friend isn't going to like what I've got to say."

The rains came, turning the roads—unpaved in the north—to mud and leaving both Grath and Forlo sullen and quiet. They rode slowly, three days stretching to four, then five. The hills they passed were bare gray ghosts crowned with the shadows of pines. They went inland, south and west, back toward Kristophan, passing hardly anyone on the road. Travel and trade were slight this year

BLADES OF THE TIGER

in the League, with war threatening. Thunder muttered above.

Grath refused to say who awaited them at the end of their journey, and the issue preyed on Forlo's mind. There were only two minotaurs vying for the throne left, according to the tales: Shold Ar-Torath, called Woe-blade, and Count Akan of Highvale. Forlo cared for neither of them very much. Shold was a distant cousin of the late emperor and a former marshal of the Fourth Legion. He and Forlo had fought in the same battles, a decade and more ago. He was a hard one to like, dour to his peers and downright vicious to the men under his command. Once, he'd had a soldier beheaded for returning a day late from leave to visit his wife and infant son—a flogging offense under most commanders.

Akan was worse. Not related in any way to the imperial house, he had worked his way into the circles of power through guile and ruthlessness. He had been Ambeoutin's favorite, of all the regional lords. Forlo, who had always respected the emperor, doubted this was because of any friendship between the two. More likely, Akan had known some scandalous secret. Now the snake had the crown nearly in his grasp—and he had never once raised a sword in defense of the realm. For that reason, more than any other, Forlo would have favored Shold. So would Grath, he thought.

So the Woe-blade was his preference, he decided on the second night as he lay in a wooded hollow, listening to the rain on the boughs. Whatever happened, his answer would not change. Whatever he did, the League would have a bad emperor after the interregnum's end. Why should he have a hand in that?

On the fifth day, a little after noon, they came to the top of a ridge and halted. The road went on, down a switchback path carved into the slope and into a valley below, along the shores of a lake. Silvermere, it was called, for it was known to shine brightly in Solis's light. Presently, however, it was the hue of lead beneath the glooming sky. Along its rocky edge were many tents and crimson and blue banners, all hanging heavy with rain-water. The Sixth was here, at least what remained of it. They had lost maybe thirty additional soldiers in the east, chasing bandits. Now, however, they had a new leader. Surrounded by a picket of fire-hardened stakes, a broad, round pavilion marked the dwelling of the one they sought, the minotaur who had drafted Grath into his service.

Forlo stared, not believing his eyes. Even from this high vantage, it was easy to make out the blazon on the standards outside the tent. It wasn't the sign of Akan, the black star on a blue field, nor of Shold, whose colors were a gold ship on purple. Instead, it was a sign Forlo knew too well: two silver swords crossed on a black, starry sky. The emblem of Duke Rekhaz.

"*Him?*" he blurted, looking to Grath. "*He* means to win the throne?"

"He does more than mean it," Grath replied. "He will succeed. He slew Lord Shold in a duel three weeks ago, and hopes to have Count Akan's head by autumn. Then he'll go to Kristophan and name himself emperor. I mean to be at his side when he does."

Forlo stared at Rekhaz's tent a while longer, then shook his head.

"What makes you think I want anything to do with him? What makes you think I'll even *talk* to him?"

Grath shrugged. "You rode all this way."

"But why Rekhaz?" he pressed.

"He's my commander," Grath replied. "And I'd rather see Akan wear a noose than the crown."

"Fair enough," Forlo said, then shook his head with a sigh. "You're right. I came sixty leagues to see this. I'll go the last furlong." I'll hear Rekhaz out, he added silently, then I will go home.

He grimaced, following Grath down the trail. He already knew it wouldn't be that easy.

Rekhaz stared at him from across the tent. He was in a temper, fists clenching and unclenching at his sides. It made Forlo glad the sentries hadn't asked him to give up his sword. Most men wouldn't have been permitted to wear a blade into the heart of the camp. Most men hadn't led the soldiers of the Sixth to war and victory.

The duke's nostrils flared. "Well? What is your answer?"

He'd made a good case. He was more suited to rule than Count Akan. He could control the armies better and had a head start on handling the League from his service as governor at Kristophan. And the peasants didn't hate him in the way they hated the lord of Highvale. He needed help, though, in swaying the other nobles. Forlo's support, his presence in the capitol, would do much to bolster his cause. The lords thought highly of Forlo: word had spread of his doings in Thenol. Rekhaz had even offered Forlo a lordship of his own and his own fief in the south, once he had the throne.

Forlo took a deep drink of wine—good stuff, not soldier's grape, brought from the duke's own vineyards. Rekhaz kept his tent austere—just a cot, a footlocker, a stand for his armor and weapons, and a table spread with maps—but he enjoyed some comforts. Forlo had another sip, then lowered the plain pewter cup and met the duke's gaze.

"No," he said.

It grew very quiet in the tent. Grath shifted his weight, shook his shaggy head, cursed under his breath. Rekhaz blinked, amazed. Then the surprise wore off, and fire filled his eyes. Forlo could see the rage building within him. His lips curled, baring fangs. He drew a breath to reply.

Forlo held up a hand, cutting him off. "There's nothing you can say to sway me, my lord. My service to the League is honorably ended. I will not be drawn in, for land or gold. I have my home, my wife, and a son coming at last. Why would I give that up, to ride to battle again?"

"You can lose all those things," Rekhaz rumbled.

Forlo shrugged. "Perhaps. You could always find some reason to arrest me, seize Coldhope, even take my head once you're emperor. But it wouldn't do any good for your rule. I'm a hero, remember? If you win the crown I will come to your coronation, swear fealty, and send all the taxes and tributes required. I will watch over the Run, and never say a word against you. All I ask is for you to leave me alone to live my life."

Rekhaz looked as if he were about to start breathing smoke. Forlo half-expected him to reach over his shoulder and draw the massive broadsword slung across his back. He wondered what Grath would do, if things went that way. He didn't envy his friend the choice he'd have to make.

"You'll find the Sixth hard to control," Forlo said quietly, "if you do anything rash now."

The duke snorted, then turned and slapped the wine-bottle off the table. It spun across the tent, spattering red droplets and leaving a stain on the far wall. "I rode this far north, just to speak with you," the duke said.

"I'm sorry," Forlo replied. He folded his arms across his chest.

Rekhaz was still for nearly a minute, visibly calming his fury. "Very well," he growled at last. "You have made your choice. One day, you may come to regret it."

Forlo nodded, deferentially.

"Go."

Forlo held his breath and turned his back, waiting for the ring of sword leaving scabbard and ready to defend himself against being struck down from behind. If Rekhaz hadn't been his enemy before, he certainly was now. It wouldn't be easy for him, if the duke won the crown. He walked swiftly, forcing himself not to look back. Grath followed him out, the flap flying as he emerged from the tent.

"That was stupid," the minotaur muttered.

"Probably," Forlo said, not breaking pace. "But I vowed to retire, and he knows it. If he'd ever been a friend to me in the past, I might have considered helping him. But no . . . he'll have to do this without me. What of you?"

Grath glanced back at the tent. "He'll want to head south again at once. Tomorrow at dawn, I reckon. Akan's down near Vinlans, trying to build support of his own. Rekhaz will take the fight to him—the longer he waits, the more nobles will go over to Akan. He needs Highvale's head on a pike, and soon."

Forlo nodded. They came to the horses, and he looked around the camp. Men were gambling, drinking beer, telling lies: everything he remembered and missed. Not as much as he would miss Essana, though. It gave him comfort to see the soldiers carrying on their lives. The Sixth was doing fine without him, and his wife was waiting. Carrying his child.

"I'll do fine, riding back alone," he said, then leaned close, speaking so only Grath could hear. "Watch yourself. Rekhaz will play you like a piece on a *shivis* board."

Grath nodded, clapping Forlo's shoulder. "I'm sorry to see you go, my friend—but only so sorry. Good road ahead of you, Barreth."

"And you."

The minotaur turned and walked back into the camp, without looking back. Forlo could hear Rekhaz bellowing at the men, taking out his wrath on them. They would march to Vinlans, and bring war with them. Without him, thank the gods.

Forlo got on his horse and rode north, back up the ridge and away through the rain.

Chapter 14

COLDHOPE HOLDING, THE IMPERIAL LEAGUE

Solis was high and full, and Lunis was nearly so. It was a concordance, though not a great one. The aligning of all three moons was two months away—an important detail for the folk who lived along the Run, who still had time to prepare for the tidal flooding. It was not as important for Shedara. Nuvis would not affect her magic. What mattered to her were the white and red moons, and their combined phases were a blessing and a curse. The magic was strong, but the night was bright. A moon-thief had it easiest when the moons were full, but hidden behind clouds.

There were no clouds overhead that night, though something ominous was beginning to boil across the Run to the north and east: a storm, it seemed, the likes of which she had seldom seen. Anvil-shaped clouds piled atop each other over the strait's far shore, burning green and gold with swallowed lightning. It was a strange thing, to see such a violent-looking tempest when the sky above was clear, with the stars shining down. Unnatural was the thought that occurred to her. Unpleasant. The hair on her neck prickled. Watching the storm seethe—still growing, not even broken yet—she knew she wasn't the only wizard at work that night. Something was happening over there, something big. Those clouds were magic-born. She had no doubt of it.

The bright moons, the strange tempest . . . bad omens. Ordinarily, the answer would be to wait a day. Weather was volatile along the Tiderun. It could well be pouring rain by the next night. But nothing was ordinary any more. Shedara had no time to waste. She knew she was ahead of her shadowy foe. The chance to seize the Hooded One lay before her. She wouldn't squander that by dawdling.

Coldhope Keep was simple and stout-walled, with a tall inner house. There were little castles like it all over the League, particularly in the northern provinces: old human structures from the years before the minotaurs came. She knew these types of places well and had plied her trade in them before. There would be guards, but not many . . . maybe a dog or two. Certainly no tylors, like Ruskal had kept. The lord of the keep would be a warrior, too, but chances were that he was away south, on one side or another as the minotaurs squabbled over the throne. Ambeoutin's death, while unfortunate for relations between the League and Armach-nesti, had proven a boon for Shedara. There were far fewer soldiers patrolling than was normal in peacetime.

She watched the castle from the forest's edge for an hour or more, hidden among the white-barked pines and darker bentwoods. Shedara was all but invisible in the dark, dressed in blacks and browns. Her dark mask was pushed back on her head so she could see clearly. She never took her eyes off the keep as she got used to the rhythms of the men who kept watch, looking for weaknesses in their patrols and finding them: times when a length of wall went unmonitored, if only for a few minutes. Another sign the lord was away, that slackness.

She was just gathering herself to move on the keep when she felt a faint pressure at her throat, a warm pulse as though of a living heart. She put a hand up to her neck and felt the pearl medallion beneath her tunic. The magic coursing through it left her feeling exposed and vulnerable. To one skilled in the Art, she would stand out like a beacon in the shadows. She doubted any of Coldhope's sentries were skilled in magic and she couldn't ignore the amulet's call. Thalaniya wanted to talk, and one did not keep the Voice waiting.

Retreating into the shadows, she pulled out the medallion and clasped it tight in her fist, reaching with her thoughts across the miles to the elven kingdom. She spoke no words, nor did she have to. The proper spells were being worked on the other end, back in Armach-nesti. She shut her eyes for a breath, focusing inward on the strange mind-itch the amulet gave her. Thalaniya's mind brushed hers—soothing, calm yet majestic, like some vast-winged eagle. A silvery image flickered to life before her, bright in the center and dimmer around the edges. As she watched, the image grew more solid and more real. It shimmered in the moonlight. There stood the queen of the Silvanaes, radiant as ever.

"Highness," Shedara murmured. "It is well you chose to speak now. Another hundred-count and I would not have been able to reply."

"I apologize, child." Thalaniya's smile was soothing. "You have found this keep you seek?"

Shedara nodded. "I was about to enter it, with your blessing. If Solis smiles upon us, the statue will be in our possession tonight."

"Good. I have not been able to sense the shadows you fought on the pirate's ship." A thin line appeared between the Voice's brows. "I do not think they are near you. There should be no difficulty from them tonight."

"I hope not, Highness." *I hope I never see them again,* she added silently. "What of what I told you . . . what I saw when I beheld their faces?"

Thalaniya raised an eyebrow, the rest of her face deceptively mild. "That they appeared to be kender? It is possible. I have sent your brother on an errand to the Marak valleys, to see if there has been trouble there. I do not expect him back for several days."

Shedara nodded, understanding. The little kender were an innocent folk, peaceful but skittish around stronger races. They kept to their deeply wooded valleys, far to the southeast of her present location, at the feet of the Steamwall Mountains. Sometimes a few wandered free, but never more than a couple in one place at a time. Certainly nothing like the numbers she'd sensed aboard the black ship that night on the Tiderun. And never looking like the shriveled *thing* she had killed in Harlad's cabin. She shuddered at the memory of the skin like taut leather, the bony cheeks, the long yellow teeth, the staring, empty eyes. . . .

She clenched her fists, clearing her thoughts. Those eyes peered out at her from the dark, as they had every night of her journey to the keep. She told herself she was safe, that the shadow-kender would not track her to the keep so quickly. She meant it as a comfort, and it nearly worked.

"Is there anything you wish of me, before I begin?" she asked the Voice's image.

"Only that you are careful," Thalaniya answered with a smile. "I doubt I need to tell you that, though."

"No, Highness."

"The blessings of our people be upon you, then. We will speak again, when you have the Hooded One."

The image faded like mist in the morning. The pearl's pulsing stopped and the warmth faded. It became a dead thing again, inert. Shedara tucked it away, closed her collar, and moved back to the wood's edge.

Coldhope awaited, dark, silent. Shedara checked her knives and pouch, making sure everything was in place. Then, pulling down the mask to cover her face, she spoke words of magic and vanished.

Getting into the keep was as easy as she'd guessed. Inch by inch she hauled herself up the wall, finding cracks and chinks for her fingers and toes, until she reached the battlements. She thought she didn't even need the spider-spell to make it up, but she used it anyway. Why not? The moons were strong, and no risk was better than slight risk.

Soon enough she was over and in, landing in a pile of hay.

The courtyard was quiet; just a glow and a dull ringing from the far side, where the keep's smith was working late. She slid out of the hay, brushing it off her body as quickly as she could, then slunk back into the shadows, still unseen. No dogs after all. Good. They were harder to deal with than men, though not as bad as the hunting cats the richer nobles favored in the south. Or tylors. Or. . . .

She realized she was gripping the hilt of her dagger and made herself relax and put it away, temporarily at least. No need for that. In a proper job, perfectly planned and executed, steel was never bared. Jobs were so seldom perfect, though. Any thief who thought they were was asking for a quick end.

The ways into the keep—the front door, the servants' entrance, and the windows—were all quite high. She chose the front door. The kitchens would be full of scullions, working on the next day's meals, and the lady of the house—if there was one—would be asleep in her chambers, on the upper levels. At worst, the chamberlain would be in the front hall and might give her trouble. Chamberlains were easy, though—soft, and never really good at protecting themselves. It would be less of a bother . . . at worst, some quick blade-work.

She crept up the front steps and ran her hands over the carved oaken doors—there were reliefs of waves and sailing ships graven into the wood, but no traps that she could find, no odd catches or hollow places, or concealed gnomish clockwork. She tried the handle. It didn't budge. Burglars were uncommon in the north, but apparently nobles still bolted their doors. If she was lucky, it would only be a lock, and not a bar blocking from within.

A flick of her wrist, and her lockpicks dropped from a hidden sheath into her waiting right hand. She bent low, studied the lock a moment, and picked a pair, each bent in its own peculiar way. Shedara knew there was no point to this—she had spells to open locks, as did any mage worth his weight in moonlight—but she enjoyed picking by hand, the challenge of it. She was also very good. A few breaths of twisting and probing was all it took. With a soft click, the bolt sprung. She tucked the picks away, glanced around the quiet yard, and eased the door open, just wide enough to slip her slender body inside.

It was empty—no chamberlain, no boy lighting the lanterns, no maidservants up late gossiping. No one at all. She let out a sigh of relief.

She could feel the Hooded One's presence . . . near her, in the building. It might have been just her imagination, but she didn't think so. She'd been on the statue's trail for too long and come close to finding it too many times to indulge in false hopes. It was in Coldhope . . . waiting for her. Where?

The spell came to her lips with almost no bidding. Moving her hands through the air, she whispered the incantation, drew down the red moon's power, and felt it flow through her, warm as brandy. Then she forced it out through her fingertips. Eyes shut, she reached out with her mind, letting it roam the halls of the keep, searching. Her heart beat loudly in the dark, though her mind roved far away from her body.

A room. Rough-cut stone. Damp, cold. Niches with old bones. Runes she couldn't read upon the walls. Deep dark, the kind only found underground.

"Cellar," she murmured. She pulled her mind back, ending the spell.

She crept down the hall, silent as settling dust, trying to keep her excitement at bay. The door awaited her, just slightly ajar, the stone stairs curving down into the rock of the sea-cliffs. There was a glimmer of ruddy lamplight below, and the muttering voices of men, standing guard. She would have to find a way past them. Shedara drew a deep breath, held it, and let it out slowly. Then, swallowing, she pushed the door open—its hinges didn't squeak, Lunis be thanked—and crept down into the catacombs below the castle.

Two men loitered at the foot of the stairs in a little, dome-crowned room of fitted stone. They were common folk, not trained warriors, clad in simple coats of riveted leather, with a hatchet and cudgel between them, and both weapons leaning against the wall by the door on the far side of the anteroom. They had taken off their helms and were sitting on them, playing some sort of dice game. As Shedara watched, the taller of the pair won a throw and laughed as he scooped a pile of copper coins away from his scowling partner. They took turns drinking from a leather tankard—beer from the smell, and hardly the first they'd had since their watch began—then turned back to their game. It was the shorter man's turn. His brow furrowed as he shook the dice.

A knife slipped easily into her hand. Shedara knew thieves who would have knifed them in the back without a second thought. Sometimes she wished she could be so cold-blooded.

The big man was clearly the stronger of the two, but he looked slow, and was rather more drunk. She raised the knife, held it poised, then flung it at the shorter guard's head.

The spell of invisibility lifted from the knife first. To the sentry, it simply appeared in midair, hurtling toward him literally out of nowhere. He sucked in a breath, his eyes widening—then it hit him square in the forehead, pommel-first above the bridge of his nose. It made an awful cracking sound and he went down, senseless and bleeding. His partner blinked, then lurched to his feet with a roar, fumbling behind him for his club as he turned to face Shedara. She was visible now, too.

She was also fast. Even before the throwing knife hit the ground, she had begun to move. She leaped into the air and lashed out with her foot at the middle of the man's chest. He made a sound like a ruptured bellows, slammed back against the door behind him, then sat down hard. Shedara kicked him again, hooking around to strike his jaw. His head snapped back, and he fell on top of his partner and lay still.

She took their weapons—and her knife—tore strips off one man's cloak, and bound and gagged them.

The door they had been guarding gave way to a tunnel of older make, hewn into the living rock by hands long forgotten. Cold air spilled out, carrying the faint, spicy smell of old rot. Shedara shuddered. The closeness of tombs was hard to endure, and the stale air burned her lungs. And those within were not always quiet. In such places, the dead sometimes walked.

There was no movement in the tunnel, though; no sounds from within. She snuffed the guards' lamp, then waited a moment, her elvensight taking over. The walking dead were cold—she would see them as faint, dark shapes in the chill of the catacombs, unlike the warm red forms of the living. Drawing her dagger, she eased down the tunnel.

Cobwebs, dust, cloth-wrapped skeletons in niches: she noted them all, as well as the scuttling forms of beetles on the floor. The passage went on for what had to have been a quarter of a mile, the ceiling so low that she had to stoop to walk. Cobwebs hung in sheets and covered ancient runes cut into the rock, crusted at their edges with flecks of long-gone paint. Men had built this place, in some ancient age, though they had been smaller, then. And she was taller than most men.

The catacombs had to be trapped, as well. She knew this from experience. The old people, long lost to those histories that had survived the Destruction, had used all manner of tricks to safeguard their tunnels. She moved slowly in the dark, testing every step, waiting for the tile that shifted beneath her weight or the tug of a tripwire. She watched for tiny cracks in the walls and holes in the ceiling. Arrows, spears, swinging blades, spiked pits—all of these might be ahead. Gently she made her way along the passage. . . .

And *there*: the slightest depression in the floor, as if some part of the stone had settled crookedly. She wouldn't have even seen it if she hadn't been looking. She reached for a burial niche beside her, brushed away a large, hairy spider, and yanked a bone from the remains that lay there. The ancient muslin wrappings crumbled like chalk, and she came away with a femur, long and smooth and mantled with dust. She shook her head. Bending down, Shedara extended the bone and brought it down sharply against the floor.

She heard a sound, the faintest puff of wind, and felt something move through the air above the place she had touched. She saw nothing. There was a clack and a rattle as something hit the wall and fell to the floor. Shedara looked closely, trying to make out what it was: a small chain of bronze links, lined with tiny hooks of obsidian, each one sharp and barbed. She grimaced at the sight, at the wickedness that had designed such a trap. The chain had flown through the air, spinning as it went. Had she stepped on the trigger, it would have ripped into her eyes or her throat and stuck there, wrapped around her face. She would have been blinded, most likely. She would have had to turn back, had to try to feel her way out of the catacombs . . . back into Coldhope Keep, with no way out without being caught. If she didn't die from a cut jugular first.

Glaring at the chain, she stepped over the depression—some traps could be triggered twice, to fool thieves who thought they were safe—and went on down the tunnel, the bone still gripped tight in her hand. The catacombs began to branch out, weaving this way and that, spliting and merging again. It was a maze, perhaps following some long-forgotten pattern, or perhaps dug at random, according to whim and the vagaries of the rock. She had no map to tell, and kept to the widest of the paths—some of which were so narrow that she couldn't fit unless she squeezed through sideways. The thought of the statue, always before her, hidden in its vault, guided her on. She could sense it; could almost physically feel its presence, like heat radiating through the cold and dust-choked air.

She was nearly there. She could feel the Hooded One, close, calling to her. A gate of carved stone stood in her way. It was locked and the keyhole was old and rusted. She took out her picks, eyed the lock to make sure it wasn't trapped, then set to work.

It was easy. A twist, and another, and then a third, and *snap*. With the scraping rumble of hinges unoiled since the gods knew when, she pushed the door inward. On the other side was a cavern, naturally made, with fluted walls and a ceiling abristle with stalactites. Water dripped from the great stone needles and ran in rivulets down to a pool on her right—a milky pond that rippled in the dark. Metal gleamed within the cave—gold, silver, and even some platinum. Coins, mostly, but also a few cups and necklaces and other artifacts bejeweled with sapphires, emeralds, and topaz. A small fortune was piled in heaps on the dry patches of the floor. It had the look of old wealth that had belonged for many generations to whatever family owned Coldhope. Shedara gave it a quick glance, but no more. Gold wasn't why she was there.

She'd come for the statue. And there it was, on the vault's far side, perched atop the stub of what had once been a great stalagmite. It stood taller than a man, black stone carved into the likeness she had seen in Thalaniya's seeing-pool. Ruskal Eight-Fingers had died because of this artifact, as had Harlad the Gray and the nameless dwarves of Uld. Died, never knowing why. The murderous shadows were seeking the Hooded One even now. Maladar an-Desh. The Faceless Emperor.

Hers to claim.

She stepped forward, and knew even before she felt the rumble under her feet she'd made a mistake. Something clicked beneath her step and a slab of stone was dropping behind her, blocking the doorway, her escape. She turned to lunge for the stone slab, realized she couldn't get underneath it without being crushed, and watched it fall, helpless. It thudded to the floor, sealing her in. She didn't need to look around to know there was no other way out.

Stupid, she thought, her lip curling. Careless fool. Even an apprentice burglar should know better. Never be so dazzled by the prize that you forget yourself.

Then there was hissing, somewhere in the dark. Not the sound of a serpent, but of breath blown between pursed lips. She knew what it was even before the sweet scent hit her. She caught her breath and held it, knowing it was already too late. She looked up. There, clinging to the rock above the doorway, was the flower: a gigantic bloom the color of ashes, its petals drooping and its stamens heavy with white pollen. Motes of dust showered down from it, falling like rain around her. The gray lotus was a magical plant, so rare many thought it was only myth. It could grow in darkness and lived almost forever. It often guarded the tombs of kings, according to legend. The ancient vaults of the old empires. Vaults like this one. Dust from the gray lotus was rare and prized—though not so much as that of its black-blooming cousin. *That* lotus killed. The gray one only brought sleep.

Careless *fool*. . . .

Weariness weighed on her like a coat of armor, making it harder and harder to keep her eyes open. The bone she'd been carrying fell from a hand gone nerveless. She collapsed a moment later, her body no longer listening to the strident voice in her head saying: don't give in, don't let it work, find a way out.

The voice went away, and the world followed. With monumental effort Shedara turned her head and stared at the statue, shivering as unconsciousness crept over her. For a strange moment, she thought it was smiling at her. Then her sight failed, and there was only darkness.

Chapter 15

THE MALTON FRONTIER, THE IMPERIAL COLONIES

Bounds-duty was not a favorite thing among the Malton Guard. There were certainly better jobs. Keeping watch over the booming trade-town's marketplaces was far more comfortable. Escorting merchants' caravans as they rumbled along the coast was more lucrative. By comparison, riding along the edge of the colony—built north of the Tiderun two hundred years ago as the first step of a larger imperial expansion that had never happened—was tedious, unrewarding, and unpleasant. Most guardsmen considered it a punishment.

The storm made it worse. It was the most violent summer tempest anyone on that side of the Run could remember, lashing Malton and the surrounding countryside with raindrops the size of acorns. The winds had long since torn away every banner and awning in town—not to mention anything not battened down in the harbor—and the thunder was ceaseless. The din robbed the townsfolk of sleep and was beginning to strip away their sanity. The accompanying lightning had blown apart two watchtowers, set fire to the masts of four great ships at the wharf, and turned the town's central monument—an eighty-foot-high granite statue of the minotaur hero Orrek the Stout—into smoldering shards, scattered across the courtyard where it had stood.

The strangest thing, though, was how *long* the storm was lasting. Malton was accustomed to hard weather in the warm months, and had suffered through some terrible storms since the Godless Night ended, but their power was always tempered by brevity. One would rise, batter the land for half a day, then move on or dwindle. This one was different. This one had gone on for three days. Long enough that the merchant lords who ruled the town grew worried it might destroy the season's trade. Both the clerics and the wizards who dwelt in Malton were busy seeking answers and blaming each other for the weather. It was a curse from the gods; it was a spell gone awry. Whatever the answer, half the city was flooded and the sewers were overflowing, making noisome rivers in the streets. Folk moved to higher ground, or higher floors. Smaller ships, broken free of their moorings, drifted down inundated streets and smashed up against houses as much as half a mile inland. The storm was proving a disaster with no end in sight.

Lorreth Accal, riding patrol alone along the storm's edge, was caked in mud, head to toe, as was his horse. The rain had long since soaked through his oilcloth cloak, and every other piece of clothing he wore, and he shivered constantly, unable to light even the smallest fire for warmth. And he wasn't doing a damn bit of good out there, anyway. With the storm-dark and the lashing rain, he couldn't see anything beyond about ten paces away: just mud, puddles, and grasses beaten flat.

He swore vigorously. A week ago, Lorreth had been comfortable in the town barracks, drinking beer and playing at dice. That had been the start of his problem. He'd actually won the last throw, and a tidy sum of gold, but another guardsman—gods, he'd been too drunk to remember *who*—had accused him of cheating. That led to shouting, which led to fighting, which led to a broken arm—one that wouldn't swing a sword for a month, even with Mislaxan healing. Lorreth's commander had offered him a choice: being locked in the pillory as a target for the folk of Malton's rotten vegetables, or a shift on the frontier. He'd seriously considered the pillory, and now was coming to regret his choice.

It had been six days since he'd seen another soul. Summer had come with a vengeance, sweltering and making him sweat beneath his helm and mail. Then the storm came, which would probably give him an ague that would last till winter. He'd finished the last of his beer the day before, and now had to make do with rainwater, collected in his upturned helm. The only thing that could make matters worse was a case of the trots. He signed the horns of Jolith at the thought.

"This is foolish," he said. He'd taken to talking to his horse, which he knew was not a good sign. "We patrol the frontier, day after week after month, and for what? It's been years since there's been more than a cattle-raid along the bounds. The barbarians don't bother with us any more. They know it's easier to kill each other."

The horse offered no reply. Lorreth snorted and went on.

"Waste of time, is what it is. I could ride back and forth to no good end for a fortnight! I've half a mind to ride to Estagon to spend the rest of the time at their brothels. They'd never know the difference, back home. At least I'd be *dry*."

He slogged on at a pace little more than a crawl. Ahead, through the mess, he could see the next Horn-tower atop a low hill: a spire of stone, a winding stair running round it, and a huge horn, longer than a man's height—and once belonging to a red dragon—set into it, pointing south. It was one of many built along the frontier. If he sighted trouble, his duty was to ride to the nearest tower and wind its horn. The sound would carry back to patrols nearer to Malton, who would alert the town. That was the plan, anyway. In his twenty-three years, Lorreth had not once heard the tower-call.

"Not that they'll be able to hear the blasted thing anyway," he muttered, glowering at the tower. "Not in this muck."

Lightning flared, sun-bright, and struck a copse of bentwoods maybe a furlong away. One of the trees blew apart, splinters flying, and left a jagged finger of a blackened stump behind. Larreth saw fire for a moment, but the rain promptly doused the flames. Then the thunder crashed, loud enough that it felt like someone had struck him, leaving him momentarily deaf *and* blind. His horse reared, whinnying in panic, and he clung to the animal, hauling on the reins to keep it from bolting. He shouted blasphemies at the sky, cursing every god he could name—Jolith and Mislaxa, Sargas and Hith, and a half-dozen more.

Then, in the space of a breath, the storm abated. One instant there was nothing in the world but gale-whipped rain and the bellow of thunder; the next, all that was gone, leaving only the terrible black clouds roiling overhead. Lorreth blinked and cast about in terror. Then he saw something that made his heart feel like a shard of ice, lodged in his breast. There was a rise to the north, not far from where his horse stood—just a swell of the land, with a few exposed rocks along its crown. He'd been following its length as he rode his patrol, for it marked the edge of the colony, the end of League lands and the beginning of the Tamire proper, where the Uigan barbarians ruled.

Now it was covered with those same barbarians—hundreds of them, maybe thousands, mounted on horses and arrayed in a long row for as far as the eye could see. He couldn't make out much about them, particularly with the green ghost of lightning hovering before his eyes, but he could tell they were arrayed for battle. He saw the horsetail helmets, the thickets of raised spears, and the banners and standards and staked heads.

Warmth spread at Lorreth's crotch as he wet himself. He neither noticed, nor cared. He stared at the Uigan—gods, it had to be every tribe on the damned Tamire! The Horn-tower is close, said some dim part of his mind. You might be able to get to it before they kill you. You can warn the town. They might not hear you, with the storm, but you can try. It's your *duty*.

But he did not move. Couldn't even reach for his sword. He could only stare, drenched in rain and his own piss, with his mouth so wide open a sparrow could have built a nest there.

The arrow seemed to dive out of nowhere, punching through the armor below his collarbone and going in deep. Pain exploded in his chest. Lorreth stared at the shaft, blinking stupidly. He opened his mouth to shout, but coughed instead. Blood misted the air. With a groan, he slumped sideways and fell from the saddle.

"Well shot, *tenach*," said Chovuk. He peered at the sentry's body, lying motionless in the grass, then turned to the rider on his right. "Go take his head, Nabal. Bring the horse back with you."

Nabal, the youngest son of Sugai Tegin, grinned and clucked his tongue. His mount sprang forward and galloped down toward the dead soldier, leaving the ranks of the horde. He raised his spear as he went, and the assembled Uigan responded with a lusty roar.

Hult lowered his bow and shook his head. "This was too easy. One arrow, and their defenses have a hole large enough for all of us to ride through?"

"These are soft folk, *tenach*," Chovuk replied, and spat. "They think they are safe behind their walls of stone. We have not troubled them since the time before Krogan was Boyla." He nodded at the dragon-horn on its spire, not far from where the dead man lay. "Yon tower will stay silent—their war-horns will not sound until we are close to the city. Too close for them to stop us."

A victorious shout from Nabal drew their attention away. The youth was holding something high: the soldier's head, gripped by the short-cropped hair, his *shuk* bloody in his other hand. The riders cheered again, clashing their weapons against their shields. Hult glanced at the tower. The dragon-horn at its top gleamed in the storm-light. It would remain silent, as Chovuk had said. The bull-men would think themselves safe until the Boyla's horde was at their doorstep.

It had been a long ride, south from the feet of the Ring Mountains. Chovuk had sent messengers wide across the Tamire, gathering the last clans of his people, sending the heads of Kazar lords as trophies to prove his might. The lands of their enemies lay burnt and blighted behind them, swarming with crows and jackals who fought for the bodies that lay among the ashes. Between them, the Uigan and the Wretched Ones had crushed the Kazar, destroyed every town, slaughtered those who fought, and hunted down those who tried to flee. Some had doubtless escaped, or hidden, but not many. It would be generations before the Kazar recovered—if they ever did.

Krogan Boyla had been avenged. Now it was the minotaurs' turn.

The earth had shaken beneath the men on horseback and goblins riding wolves as they streamed across the plains crying for blood and gold. For three weeks, they had poured ever southward, the mountains a blue line on their left and the plains rising and falling in grassy waves as they made their way toward the Tiderun. Toward Malton, the first and largest of the League's colonies.

Chovuk had a map, taken from a trade caravan they'd killed along the way. He and the Tegins—and Gharmu of the Wretched Ones—had discussed their plans around it long into the night, drinking *kumiss* and boasting of who would take the most heads, or the most gold, when they came to their goal. Malton was a trade-town, and rich. Its fall would be a great blow to the bull-men, and would leave their other major town, Rudil, exposed. There were other villages along the coast, but Rudil and Malton were the poles that held up the yurt. If they took both—*when* they took both—the colonies would collapse. The Tamire would belong to the tribes once more.

Hult should have been reveling in the bloodlust that had swept over the men. Part of him was. Certainly he'd felt a stirring when Nabal spitted the soldier's head on the end of his spear and held it aloft. But he was also troubled. He had seen the green light in Chovuk's tent. He had heard the strange voices, late at night. He had felt the presence, however briefly, of the *other* who had been in the yurt, unseen, with the Boyla. And he could see changes in Chovuk, too. The man was leaner, his face drawn, and there was white in his braid and beard. He seemed to have aged ten summers since the start of the season. Understandable, perhaps, since he had worked so tirelessly to bring the horde together, but the changes ran deeper than just what had happened to his body. Hult knew his master. He could tell. The Boyla's spirit had aged as well.

The Tegins had proclaimed the wild storm over Malton good fortune, a sign Jijin smiled upon them, softening up the target before the killing stroke. Hult, however, knew there was something at work besides divine providence, and the way the storm broke before them . . . how it had lifted enough so that he could shoot this tone outrider . . . no, that was magic. Magic from the same source that gave Chovuk the power to shift his skin and become a steppe-tiger in the heat of battle.

If he had been a free rider, he might have spoken of this magic, might have wondered aloud about the Boyla's new powers. But he was *tenach*, so he said nothing. Only followed, and protected his master. It was his place.

Nabal shouted with glee as he rode back, leading the dead soldier's horse. He left the man's body for the crows.

"He was still breathing when I found him!" the young rider cried. A boy's glee, trying to please his father. "It was *my* sword that killed him!"

Chovuk laughed—not warmly, as he had before, but with cruel humor. "Too bad, *tenach*. The head is his to claim."

"No matter," Hult said, not much wanting the head anyway. The man hadn't seen his death coming. It was not a noble kill. "Let it fall to him."

Nabal whooped with joy. Nearby, Sugai Tegin smiled.

"Aye, no matter," the Boyla said. "There will be enough heads for everyone tonight." He turned to the Tegins, who gathered near. "This is only the first blood to be spilled today. Sound the horns. We ride to Malton, and glory!"

The riders' cheers were louder than the thunder.

When Sammek Thale first heard the shouting, he thought nothing of it. It was an hour before midday and he was already drunk and working on his fifth flagon of wine—cheap, sour stuff, rather than the southern vintages he was accustomed to—in the Broken Keel. The Keel was a dingy waterfront tavern, one of the few that weren't flooded out, though the roof leaked constantly beneath the storm. He couldn't afford to drink in the parlors of the rich Hilltop Ward anymore. When he had returned from his last journey with an empty hold, his partners had thrown him out and seized his ship. They had *ruined* him. He'd spent the past week drinking away the last of his gold and thinking about Harlad the Gray. He hoped the pirate was enjoying his booty.

He wasn't the only one in the Keel that day. The storm had driven many captains to their cups. They certainly wouldn't venture out on the Run during the storm. Most of the sailors paid little mind to the yelling that drifted in from the streets: maybe it was a brawl, or maybe the imperial guard had caught someone looting abandoned warehouses in the storm. Things happened at the wharf. You didn't look up from your mug at every cry of alarm. You drank more, and waited for the din to die down.

But, the din grew louder and more insistent. It sounded like half the town was in the streets, running this way and that, bellowing and screaming. That was odd, with the rains as bad as they were. The Keel's patrons began to take notice and moved to the windows and doors. Then they started to leave and join the panic outside.

Sammek raised an eyebrow and got to his feet. The room swayed like he was back on the deck of the *White Worm*, plying the high seas. He weaved toward the crowd at the entrance.

"What is it?" he asked, catching the arm of a bare-chested minotaur, a stevedore he'd employed in the past to load his ship. "Lightning strike somewhere? Is there a fire?"

"Lightning?" the stevedore repeated, then laughed. "Haven't you been listening? The storm's let up, Thale."

Sammek scowled, cocking an ear. He could have sworn he still heard thunder, though it sounded far off. And the noise had a strange rhythm to it, now that he thought of it. A constant low rumbling. "What's that?" he cried.

"Barbarians!" the minotaur snapped. "Uigan riders. They're attacking the city. Goblins too!"

Nonsense, Sammek thought as the stevedore shoved out the door and bolted for the waterlogged docks. There were sails unfurling all along the waterfront—people fleeing despite the rough winds and lashing rain. The sky was like slate, seeming to hang so low the Hilltop spires might scratch it. The storm hadn't departed. It had simply paused, as if it had more to say but was waiting for the right moment. People streamed south under the rain, packing the streets, while armored guards tried to force their way north toward the walls.

Barbarians and goblins, together? An army at Malton's gates? No, the minotaur had to be mistaken. Sammek knew the signals. The Horn-towers would have sounded. But then, with the storm, who would have heard them?

He began to fight through the frightened mobs, ignoring the shouts that he was going the wrong way and the hands that caught at his sleeves and tried to turn him around. He ducked down an alley, found another lane that was less crowded, and climbed slopes and steps to the higher ground, up the shoulder of the hill around which the city's black-roofed buildings clustered. Here people gathered on balconies and rooftops, pointing and staring north. Women wept, men cursed and went to find swords or knives, and servants ran for their lives.

There was a house with a high turret belonging to one of Sammek's former wives, bought with his gold, years ago. She wasn't there, gods be praised. He had glimpsed her in the throng moving toward the docks. The door was slightly ajar, so he slipped in and quickly climbed the circular steps to the roof. Out of breath, he shoved open the door, walked out onto the widow's walk, and felt his blood go cold.

The sound, the rumble he'd taken for thunder, had been the pounding of thousands of hooves across the plains to the north. The fields beyond Malton looked like a kicked-over anthill, swarming with tiny figures of horses and men . . . and goblins and wolves, their shapes unmistakable even from a mile away. It was a horde like the ones that had once fought the League, decades ago. Nothing its size had been seen since the days when Malton was a little trading outpost—well before Sammek's grandfather was born.

"Gods' grief," he murmured, panic burning in his breast. "Where in the Abyss did they come from?"

Run. The thought flashed through his brain like an arrow, put new energy into his tired limbs, and cleared his wine-muddled mind. Run and run and don't stop until you can't see Malton any more.

Malton's walls were high and its gates were strong. The guardsmen on the battlements had bows and many arrows. There were supplies to last out months of siege— surely more than a rabble of barbarians would have the discipline to mount. The town could send for help by sea, if necessary. There looked to be ten thousand blades out there, all yearning for League blood, but it would take more than numbers to overwhelm Malton. Unless they were betrayed, they were safe—and no one in Malton was fool enough to sell themselves to the Uigan.

Still, that voice. *Run.*

"Something terrible is going to happen," Sammek whispered, not knowing where that sudden thought came from. The gods, perhaps, or intuition, or just luck. Later, he would spend long nights remembering those words, glad that—whatever their source—he had listened.

He turned and ran back down the stairs, to the street, and on toward the docks.

Arrows thudded to the ground, barely ten yards in front of the horde. The Uigan laughed, brandishing their sabers at the distant archers, whose helms appeared now and then among the merlons atop the wall. Bodies littered the ground before them—men and goblins who had gotten too close, and had been felled by lucky shots. They could smell the minotaurs within the walls, and their fury was unspeakable.

But they did not charge, as much as the bloodlust urged them on. Even the Wretched Ones held back, though the twisted creatures were half-mad with the call of battle, their riding-wolves snapping and snarling, tense as bowstrings and ready to leap forward the moment Gharmu gave the word.

Still they didn't charge. There was a problem.

"That wall is strong," said Hoch Tegin, waving his arm toward Malton. He glowered at the town, disgusted. "We cannot knock it down. How do we get in, Tiger?"

Chovuk Boyla didn't answer. He stood apart from his chiefs, Hult at his side. Unlike the Tegins, who were either anxious or angry—even Sugai looked concerned at what they faced—Chovuk was calm, and his brow was smooth. He held his fingers steepled before his mouth, and his eyes might have been shards of iron, so fierce was their gaze. They seemed to gleam with their own inner light, like the storm clouds had, moments before. The rain and the lightning over Malton had stopped, leaving only the pall of black, hovering like dragon-wings above the city.

"Boyla," Sugai pressed. "We have not the craft to topple those battlements. We cannot even get close, with so many archers waiting. This place was not so fortified in the old days. If we attack, we will surely be defeated."

Chovuk only smiled. "You are wise, Sugai Tegin," he said. "But you do not know everything."

"What does that mean?" blustered Hoch. "You have led us all this way on promises of glory, and now it lies beyond our grasp. And all you do is mock our worries?"

Hult glared at the young lord, though inside he had to admit the words had the ring of truth. Getting into Malton would be like beating down a mountainside. Nothing short of a dragon's breath could do such a thing—and there hadn't been any dragons in that part of the world since the ancient days. He looked at Chovuk, unable to keep the fear from his eyes.

"And even you doubt," said the Boyla. He sighed. "I had hoped for more faith from my own *tenach*. Very well . . . let it begin."

He raised his hands, shut his eyes, and spoke words that made Hult's skin feel like razor-beetles were crawling all over him. The Tegins shied back, glancing at one another in alarm and biting their hands to ward off evil spirits. Hult fought the urge to do the same. He must remain at his master's side, watching for danger. He had to, no matter how unsettling the Boyla's behavior. There was no doubt what he was doing now—it was sorcery, not the will of Jijin. He was calling down the moons' power, as no Uigan had done in nearly half a century.

Above, the storm started to shift. It was barely perceptible at first, the dark clouds beginning to spin slowly above the citadel. But the Uigan noticed, pointing and shouting to one another as Chovuk's hands danced through the air. Hult held his breath, only realizing what he was doing when his lungs began to burn. He forced himself to draw in air. Was there a green light around Chovuk now? A flicker the same color as the glow he had seen in the Boyla's yurt?

Yes, there was. In spite of himself, Hult shivered. "Master. . . ." he began, reaching out.

Chovuk's voice rose from a murmur to a shout. The spell was cast; it was done. He pointed at the sky, at the place where the clouds were revolving, and they started moving faster and faster . . . reshaping themselves and becoming a maelstrom above Malton. A hole opened in their midst, a wide, staring eye that was improbably blue. There was movement within the clouds, too—sinuous shapes of pearl and charcoal that slid through the wisps, one moment out of sight, visible the next, just long enough for a glimpse. Hult couldn't say what they were, but the quicksilver shapes had faces, and they were cruel, sharp-featured and long-fanged. Something dwelt in the storm and was shaping it at the Boyla's command, spinning it faster and faster. . . .

The finger grew in an instant, starting as a ragged stub extending down from the storm's eye, then extending, reaching down, down. . . .

The Uigan fell silent, their shouts and whoops giving way to speechless awe. The goblins screeched in panic, for they had never seen a storm-finger before. This was kin to the great columns of murderous wind that ripped across the Tamire in the summertime, but it was also something more: larger, darker . . . hungrier, if that could be said of clouds. The shapes Hult had glimpsed around the eye ran up and down its length . . . *dragons*, but of no kind ever seen before. They were dragons made of storm, there but not there, creatures born of air and wind. They fell upon Malton with a roar a hundred times louder than any thunderclap.

And they swallowed the wall.

There was a bright flash, like an exploding star. The explosion blinded Hult and left him wincing and gritting his teeth in pain. For a breath, there was silence. Then a sound like nothing Hult had ever heard before, like the earth's bones breaking: a *boom* that made his ears ring for days after. The ground shook, and his horse reared, nearly throwing him. He heard voices around him, yelling in the Uigan tongue, riders trying to keep their own mounts under control. Some failed and fell. A few were trampled. The goblins milled about in utter terror, their wolves howling as the vast storm-finger ripped through the town. And there was something else, too. A patter, like rain falling, but . . . solid.

An avalanche. Stones.

The wall.

Men were cheering now, thousands of ululating voices. Hult still couldn't see. He rubbed his eyes, willing them to work. Slowly, the world returned, and it was in ruins.

Later, men would speak around the fires of the great storm-finger, called from the heavens by the Boyla's voice. It had struck Malton's wall in the very center, where the mighty gates stood. The moment it had touched the battlements, lightning had coursed through it, dozens of forked bolts, and they ripped the mighty edifice apart. An instant later, the storm-finger broke apart into shreds of sparking cloud, leaving behind a hole wide enough for the Boyla's hordes. Corpses of the town's defenders lay in mangled pieces among chunks of wall the size of houses, and the stone rained down as far as a mile away. On the wall's broken top, nothing stirred.

Hult stared in awe at the ruins, then looked at Chovuk. His master was laughing, his eyes wild. The green light blazed in them, terrible to behold. The Boyla raised his *shuk*, and in that moment the rain came pouring down again.

"Blood!" he raged.

His men answered, sabers and lances thrust up at the sky. With Chovuk laughing in the lead, they charged toward the shattered wall.

Sammek Thale wept as he looked back from the stern of the *White Worm*, his tears mingling with the rain. Despite the storm, fires were raging all across Malton. The wharf was ablaze, the markets boiled with smoke, and the wealthy manors of Hilltop were pillars of flame. His home and all he had known would be ashes by morning. His instincts had been right: the town was not safe. The horde had breached the wall somehow, and was putting those foolish enough to stay behind to the sword . . . or worse. The barbarians had their cruel, bloody games. He realized his former partners were either dead or soon to be and felt an unexpected twinge of regret.

The waves beyond the breakwater were thick with ships, though only half had made it out of the harbor before the riders reached it. Sammek had been one of the last. There had been wolf-riders on the pier when he cast off and made for open water. One goblin had actually leaped for the *Worm*, and would have crawled aboard had he and his men not beaten it into the sea with belaying pins. He thanked the gods he'd escaped, and swore he would be a better man from then on—or at least try.

He would make a start, anyway. He had to tell someone what had happened to Malton. Someone who could warn the League and tell them of the nightmare that had destroyed his home.

Wiping his eyes, he turned away from the rail and shouted for his men to make for the far side of the Tiderun, and Coldhope Keep.

Chapter 16

THE TEMPLE OF HITH, THENOL

Barreth Forlo was not a fearless man. No sane warrior was. There was always that spark of dread, going into battle, because that battle could always be your last. Even minotaurs felt that fear—Grath had confessed it to him once, after one too many cups of wine. The key wasn't in snuffing the spark, but in keeping it from growing into a flame. Feeling fear was one thing. Showing it was something else.

He knew he was showing it now, but couldn't help himself. He had never been anywhere that frightened him like the church at Hawkbluff. Bishop Ondelos's fane was *built* to cause fear. Its tunnels were barely lit and filled with niches and alcoves drenched in shadow, where anything might lurk. The walls were carved with images of death and torment, with reliefs of rotting corpses and flayed men. Human skulls—some with scraps of flesh and hair clinging to them—rested in dark nooks, baring their teeth in rictus grins. A few of these were not totally dead, for they shouted or shrieked as he and his men passed, making all of them jump. Alarms against intruders, empowered by Thenol's dark god. Grath and Forlo put an end to each of them, smashing the skulls with sword and axe to silence them forever.

"No need to be quiet, at least," the minotaur said after shattering yet another yowling skull. He grinned to hide his own gathering fear. "It's not like they don't know we're coming."

There were thirty in their party, besides Forlo and Grath. It had been a hundred when they first passed through the gates at the foot of Hawkbluff, with their portcullis of bone. The tunnels branched, however, and they had been obliged to split up. Elsewhere, Forlo's men were combing other parts of the church, hunting for the high priest and hoping to collect the bounty on Ondelos's head. Ahead, Forlo could already see that the passage divided yet again, splitting into two identical forks. He and Grath exchanged glances.

"You want left or right?" Forlo asked.

Grath shrugged. "You're the commander. But left's always been lucky for me."

"Take half, then," Forlo said. "I'll see you when this is done."

"Aye," the minotaur replied, clapping his arm. "When it's done. Watch yourself, my friend."

With that, the party split up again, Grath and Forlo each taking fifteen soldiers. The light of their torches grew dimmer as Forlo moved on along the path, always sloping up and curving deeper into the rock of Hawkbluff. To Forlo's right, another leathery skull screeched. He put his blade through its face, caving it in.

They hadn't fought anyone yet, and hadn't seen a single fanatic or walking corpse. Ordinarily, Forlo was sure, this place thrived with priests and their undead servants, but right then it was . . . well, like a tomb. He guessed why. The war and the last battle before the Bluff had left the church of Hith weak. They had expended most of the temple guardians out there, in the mud. The rest probably waited in some inner sanctum, guarding the Bishop and poised for the final battle.

No sooner had he thought that than something appeared

in the passageway before him: a shape, human enough, but small—no more than three and a half feet tall. A kender, was his first thought, but that made no sense. Then what? The small form was moving toward him with the lurching, unsteady gait of the dead. A lone guardian, still wandering the temple halls . . . but what was it?

This is where it always ends, some part of him thought. He'd dreamed this many times over the past several weeks. It was the last part of the dream that had been tormenting him since the battle. But he never got any further, never made it to Ondelos's lair. He couldn't even remember what had happened there, anymore. It always ended with this lone shadow, staggering toward him down the tunnel passage. The next night, the cycle began again. Always the same, and never coming to the end.

He swallowed, gripping his sword tighter. *This* time, the dream would continue. This time, he would see what happened next.

"Show yourself," he muttered, trying to keep his voice low. It sounded foolishly loud, making him wince. He raised his torch with his other hand, shining its light ahead.

I will not wake up, he thought. I will see what this thing is. He gritted his teeth, stepped forward . . .

. . . and saw.

It was a boy, a child of maybe five summers. He was dark-haired, dark eyed . . . and beautiful—or had been. Death lent a bloodless pallor to his cheeks, and his flesh was shriveled just a little. A ragged wound gaped over his heart, crusted with dried blood. He'd been killed with an expert thrust of a knife or sword. Not long ago, either—no signs of rot yet, not like the festering things his men had been fighting through the entire war. The boy didn't stink like the dead, either.

Freshly killed.

His sword drooped in his hand. There was something about the boy, something familiar. . . .

The child stopped and looked up at him, the memory of pain still glimmering behind his glassy eyes. Then it hit him. The child was familiar because it looked just like him—or rather, just as he had looked when he was a boy. He was staring at himself, only with nearly forty years stripped away—and dead. Something cold slithered in his belly. This is not right, he thought. It isn't possible....

The boy spoke. His voice was strange, raspy and distant, as if it came from the bottom of a well.

"Why did you do this?" he groaned. "Why did you do this to me, Papa?"

Forlo screamed and jerked awake. His heart thundered so hard it sent spikes of pain down his left arm. For a moment, he was sure it would burst and he would die right there, camped in the woods by the road, still two days' ride from Coldhope. For a long time—it felt like hours—all he could do was sit there, his skin as cold as death, shivering as the last image of the dream hung before his eyes. His son, his yet-unborn son . . . dead. A knife-wound in his heart. He knew the apparition hadn't been at Hawkbluff. It was something new.

A premonition? Was something terrible going to happen?

Had it already happened?

By the time he got his senses back, he was a mess. Tears covered his face. His throat burned and his eyes stung. He couldn't keep his hands from shaking. But finally, he had the strength to move again, to stand, his legs pinging and prickling as the blood flowed back. Moving almost like one of the Thenolite corpse-warriors, he doused the embers of his campfire and gathered his things. His horse stood nearby, eyeing him with puzzlement. Dawn was several hours away, yet he was breaking camp. But he knew he wouldn't sleep again that night. Wouldn't sleep again at all, probably, until he saw Coldhope again, and Essana. Essana, with her belly swollen and filled with life. Not death.

Stifling a sob, he went to saddle his horse.

Forlo rode through the night. Solis was high and full, lighting his way and gleaming on the occasional glimpses of water visible through the trees. Worry gnawed at him, unfounded and foolish. But this time, it felt more like certainty.

Something had happened at Coldhope.

His throat was tight as he rode up the last fold of land before reaching the keep. He reached across and loosened his sword in its scabbard. He nearly drew it, and held himself back only through will. Something told him it would be a bad idea. He spurred his horse, already tired from hours of riding, to go faster. Forlo's heart kept time with his horse's speeding hooves.

Coldhope wasn't in ruins and was not ablaze. There was no blood on its flagstones. But light blazed from its windows, and torches danced on its battlements. The whole keep looked to be awake, and the guards on the walls were alert enough to have their crossbows ready. It was three hours past midnight. There should have been few signs of life save the watch-fires. Indeed, something was afoot in the keep.

He nearly didn't make it to the gates. The guards saw him and sighted down their weapons. He was a lone rider moving fast in the dark at an hour when only villains were on the roads. If he'd had his sword out, they would have shot him. As it was, he had to slow his pace and shout up to them before they stayed their hands. Someone inside barked orders, and with a thud and creak the gates swung open. He galloped through, reined in—an armored guard took hold of his horse's bridle—and leaped down from the saddle.

Voss was there, the chamberlain looking old and sallow. Maybe it was the hour of the morning, or maybe something worse. "My lord," he began, "we had not looked for your return—"

"Essana," Forlo interrupted, waving him off. "Where is she?"

"The mistress is unharmed," Voss said, and the tightness in Forlo's chest relaxed a little. "She is in the keep, watching over the catacombs. We aren't sure what to do about the elf."

Forlo blinked. "Elf? Catacombs? What are you talking about? What's happened here, man!"

"Barreth!"

Essana. She stood in the doorway of the keep at the top of the steps. Her hair was uncombed and her eyes were frightened. One of her hands lay over her belly, as if protecting the child growing there. He took the stairs three at a time.

"Starlight," he began, taking her hand. He touched her, felt the life inside. His throat filled with tears.

"I didn't know when to expect you," she said. "I roused the household and posted extra guards. She's still in there, Barreth. Down below."

"Who?" he asked. "What in the blue Abyss is going on?"

She was barely in control of herself. He tried to remember seeing her afraid like that before, but couldn't. It hurt to meet her gaze. "A thief," she said. "An elf, by what the men say. She came to the keep earlier tonight. Broke in, and went to the catacombs. It was the damned statue, Barreth. She came for the statue."

Forlo's brow furrowed. An elf, here? There hadn't been an elf seen in the Holding since . . . had there *ever* been an elf seen in the Holding? It made no sense. What did the woods-folk have to do with the statue?

Another thought came to him then, filling him with cold fury. Whoever this elf was, she had violated his home. With his wife here, defenseless. She could have killed Essana as she slept, had she been an assassin rather than a simple burglar. Killed her and the child.

Making an animal noise, he stormed into the keep's great hall. Lamps glowed up and down its length and there was a larger pool of torchlight by the way down to the cellar. He heard men's voices and saw shadows stretching long across the floor. He hurried to them, Essana hastening behind.

"Stay back," he snapped, holding out a hand. There were guards at the top of the stairs. One was tall and had an ugly, purple bruise on his jaw. One of his more trusted sentries, he'd set the man to watch the catacombs. "Iver, what's going on here? Where is this elf?"

"My lord!" The guardsman looked up, surprised, and clasped his wrist in salute. "We hadn't looked for your return—"

"Yes, yes. The elf, Iver."

The man flushed and looked down, unable to meet Forlo's eyes. He'd been drinking on duty, from the guilt on his face . . . or gambling . . . or both. Forlo put that aside for the moment.

"Speak, man."

"I—I don't know where she came from," Iver said. "Poor Davin didn't even see her. He got the worst of it— he's still out cold. I got a look, but there wasn't much to see. She was wearing a mask, but I saw the ears. One o' them Silvan elves, I'd bet my balls on it. Pardon, milady."

Essana had come up, but was unfazed by the guard's language. She'd heard worse—she'd married a soldier, hadn't she?

"Where is she now?" Forlo asked.

"In the vault," Essana said. "I was going to tell you, but you ran off. She's down there still, with the statue. Sealed in."

He raised his eyebrows. "The lotus got her?"

"So it seems."

He nearly laughed. The gray lotus had been there when Coldhope was built. Generations of lords had tried to get rid of it, but to no avail. No blade could cut its stems and no fire could burn it. Whoever had built the catacombs had wanted that particular room well watched, and so it remained. It made for a good guardian over the keep's riches, anyway.

And after all that time, the lotus had finally proven useful. He couldn't help but be amused.

"How long ago?" he asked.

"Three hours, or about," Iver replied. "Davin and I were halfway done our watch."

And drinking, definitely. Forlo could smell the beer on the man's breath. Discipline later: there were things to do.

"She'll be coming out of it soon," he said. "Maybe already is. Essana, listen to me this time—*stay here*. Iver, you watch her. The rest of you, with me. We're going to find out just who we've caught down there."

※━━━※━━━※

She dreamed of *him*. Faceless, wicked, and blue-robed in a city of gold. He held her captive, shackled to the roof of the highest tower in his palace. The tower didn't belong in Aurim, and it had not been in the vision Thalaniya had shared with her. It was a creation of her mind, of the dream-world. Wind whipped around her, cold because they were so high. Maladar looked down upon her, amused. Shedara had seen terrible things and had faced evil men. Some had died on the blades of her knives. But this man, this wicked creature, was entirely different. There was no humanity there, no trace of compassion or care in the way he looked at her. No passion at all, not even hate. Just cold, staring.

"You thought you could thwart me," he said, his voice grating, toneless. She thought of his tongueless mouth and shuddered. "You came close to doing it, too. That impresses me. But you failed, in the end—as all who work against me will fail. My triumph is foreseen and my victory is as sure as the coming of dusk. No mere thief can stop it."

"I will," she snarled through clenched teeth. "I will see it done."

The hood shifted as the head cocked sideways. She saw beneath for an instant, just the faintest hint of the ruin hidden there, and shuddered again.

"Oh?" asked the Hooded One. "And how will you do that, with no legs to pursue me . . . no arms to wield your blades?"

The pain was instantaneous, rising from a dull ache to searing agony in an eyeblink. The shackles moved, impossibly, for they were bolted to the stone floor beneath her. Still, there was no doubting it, for they pulled *apart* in all four directions at once. Her joints burned, straining as the shackles began to rip her to pieces. Ligaments stretched and bones ground. Men had been making torture devices like that for thousands of years—but it was no ordinary rack. Just the shackles, following the bidding of the sorcerer above her.

Oh, gods, the *pain*. A shoulder dislocated. A hip popped out. She tried to scream, swallowed her tongue, and began to choke . . . the world slipped away, and all that remained in her sight was *him*, staring down, pleased to watch her die. . . .

She woke to the sound of voices nearby, muffled by stone. It took her a moment to remember where she was. The floor was hard beneath her and the air was cold—underground—the smell of decay was in the air. The catacombs. She opened her eyes: it was dark, the shape of the Hooded One was looming over her, just as Maladar had in her mind, moments ago. She shivered, tried to rise. . . .

Her arms and legs wouldn't move.

Then the scent, heady and floral, hit her. She glanced to her left and saw the lotus, bowed low over her, its petals bunched like lips preparing for a kiss. It still had her, and it wouldn't release her from its grip, no matter how hard she struggled.

Come on, she thought. Move. There were people outside, talking. They would come in soon. She couldn't escape now, but maybe, if she could use her hands, at least, she might be able to cast a spell . . . to make herself invisible again . . . *something*. The thought of being captured without a fight sickened her. There was too much at stake . . . and to be caught by some petty *humans*. . . .

Try as she might, though, she couldn't break the paralysis. She fought for nearly a minute to force some part of her to move—even a finger!—but the fight was useless. Tears squeezed from her eyes and slid down her cheeks.

The voices outside stopped. Somewhere, ancient gears turned. The floor trembled as the door slid open. Torchlight spilled in, stinging her eyes and blinding her elvensight. She groaned and fought to see through the dark. There were shapes, moving. Several men. All but one had swords. They gathered around her, looking down. The lotus craned, as if glancing at them, then turned back to Shedara again. It knew them, somehow. Knew they belonged.

Slowly, her vision became clear. She saw guardsmen, fully armed, with an unarmored man in their midst. He wore rich traveling clothes and a blue cloak spattered with dried mud. His eyes were dark and grim, and his mouth was a lipless gash. He was handsome, as humans went, with a short, dark beard and a slightly crooked nose that looked as though it had been broken several times in the past. His hair was graying at the temples and thinning on the top, as happened to many of his race. He was the lord of the keep, newly returned from abroad. Bad timing, there.

He bent down beside her. "I am Barreth Forlo, once marshal of the Sixth Imperial Legion. My wife is the Countess Essana. You are a thief, who meant to rob us of our riches. I would have your name."

A bee had stung her on the lip once, when she was a child. The way her mouth felt reminded her of that. Still, she forced her sluggish tongue to move and formed words that were thick in her mouth. "Shedara of . . . Armach-nesti."

"Welcome to Coldhope, Shedara," said Forlo, with the hint of a smile on his lips. "The lotus is making things difficult for you, I see. Ramal, you drink wine. Give me your flask."

Grudgingly, one of the guards stepped forward and offered a clay bottle. Forlo removed the cork, smelled it, winced, then bent down and set the neck to her lips. Burning fire poured into her mouth, sour and awful. It could barely be called wine. Shedara took a swallow and nearly choked, then lay back, tired.

A tingling filled her body as the wine went down her throat—the thorns-and-brambles feeling coming back. The numbness was going away, as was the paralysis. She could move her fingers first, then her hands. As the strength coursed through her arms and legs, Forlo nodded to two of his men, who carefully searched her and removed her blades. They found them all, even the little stiletto sewn into the hem of her tunic, which she rarely used, and the pearl medallion, her contact with the Voice. She winced as they pulled the amulet off her and took it away.

They also found her pouch of spell components. Forlo opened it, peered inside, then returned his gaze to the elf, more intent than before. "You're a mage? Then know this: if you speak one word of sorcery, it will be your last."

"I . . . am not stupid," she said.

"That remains to be seen. Why are you here, Shedara? Why did you seek to take the statue?"

She blinked and tried to look confused. "St-statue?"

"Don't be coy," Forlo said. "I've ridden hard the night through to find my keep in an uproar, my wife frightened, and a thief in my treasury. I haven't the patience. Do you think I would believe a random burglar by chance sought to rob me, right after I came by our hooded friend, there? I'm not stupid either."

Shedara closed her eyes. It was over, then. She had failed. "You're right," she said. "I came for the . . . Hooded One, at the behest . . . of Thalaniya, Voice of the Silvanaes. As to why . . . I am sworn not to say."

"Shall I cut off her fingers, my lord?" asked the guard named Ramal, lifting his sword. "That'll make her think about oaths."

Forlo looked tempted, then shook his head. "Elves think we're all savages. I won't give this one the satisfaction of proving her right. As to you, lady . . . you should count yourself lucky that I was the one who caught you, and not the statue's previous owner."

"You mean Harlad the Gray? He is dead."

That caught his attention. She saw him pale, just slightly, in the torchlight. "Dead?"

"And the dwarves, who had it before him. And Ruskal Eight-Fingers, who sold it to *them*."

Several of the guardsmen looked up at the statue, their eyes wide. Ramal even sidled away. Forlo kept his eyes on her, biting his lower lip. Trying to figure out if she was lying. Trying to hold back his fear. He opened his mouth to speak.

"My lord!" called a voice from behind him. The sound of boots on stone echoed up the hall. "Lord Forlo, you must come at once!"

He straightened and looked back. It was the tall guard, the one she had taken down when she broke in. He glared venom at her as he stepped into the vault.

"What is it, Iver?" Forlo asked. "I told you to stay with your mistress."

"I am sorry, milord," panted Iver, out of breath. "She sent me. Told me to fetch you at once."

Forlo put a hand on his sword. "What is it? More trouble?" He glanced at Shedara. "Did you have help?"

She shook her head. "I am alone."

He held her gaze to see if she was lying.

"It's not another thief, Lord," Iver said. "It's a visitor. Bearing ill news." He leaned in close to whisper in his master's ear.

Forlo's swarthy skin went white. He looked at the guardsman, who nodded. Both men looked as though they were about to be ill. Shedara had to bite her tongue to keep from asking what Iver had just said. She glanced from one to the other, trying to glean some clue.

But Barreth Forlo's attention was no longer on her. "Go. Tell the mistress I'll be there at once," he said. When Iver ran out of the room, he turned back to his other men and nodded down at Shedara. "Take this one to the tower. I'll question her more later. Gag her, so she can cast no spells. If she does anything suspicious, kill her."

The guards nodded and Forlo left her to them, hurrying after Iver. Shedara neither struggled nor spoke when they closed in, swords bared, and hauled her to her feet. As they dragged her away through the catacombs, though, she dared a glance back at the Hooded One, standing in the shadows, forbidding and cold. In her mind, she heard the distant laughter of Maladar the Faceless.

※━━━※━━━※

There were nights, Forlo reflected, when a man's life turned. Moments that divided time into *before* and *after*. A warrior came to accept this. He'd had many such moments in his life: joining the legions, meeting Essana, winning his first battle as a marshal, and quitting the army. That night, he sensed, would be another pivotal moment.

He looked across the table at Sammek Thale. The fat

merchant looked alarmingly gaunt as he picked at a bowl of chicken-and-longroot stew. He was smudged with soot, and a cut on his cheek was rimmed with dried blood. Sweat stood out on his forehead. But the worst thing was the look in his eyes. Forlo had seen that look before, on the faces of women after he told them their husbands' bones were buried on some faraway battlefield. He'd hoped never to see it again.

Essana slipped her hand into Forlo's and squeezed it. She was strong and wouldn't show weakness before Thale, but Forlo knew her. He could feel the clamminess of her palm and see the shadows behind her eyes. He knew she could see the fear in him, too. Dread hung thick in the air at Coldhope.

"Sacked?" he asked. "Are you sure?"

Sammek nodded, dropped his spoon with a clatter, and jumped at the noise. He hadn't eaten a bite. "I saw it burn. They say the chief of the barbarians summoned the storm to fight for him and brought down the wall with a word. They razed it to the ground. Only a few of us got out."

"Malton," murmured Essana. "I can't believe it."

"This Uigan horde . . . how large?" Forlo pressed.

"Many thousands. It was hard to tell." Sammek put a hand to his brow and rubbed the cut there. Fresh blood appeared. "They had goblins, too. Wolf-riders." He buried his face in his hands.

They sat in silence for nearly a minute, the merchant weeping helplessly. Forlo didn't blame him. The man was spent. He had just lost his home. Forlo turned to Voss, who hovered nearby, his own face deeply troubled. "Have the servants make guest quarters for Master Thale. See that he has rest."

Voss nodded and led Sammek out. Forlo sat quietly for a time with his wife. The trouble with the elf and the statue was gone from his mind. What Sammek had told them was far worse. Essana met his gaze, and together they rose and walked out of the great hall and onto the spur overlooking the Tiderun. The water was still high, but receding. They stared out across it and into the darkness where the far shore lay. Men and minotaurs had died there. A town had fallen and barbarians were prowling its ruins.

"I thought I saw something last night," Essana said. "A red glow . . . I thought it was beautiful." She bowed her head and her shoulders began to shake.

Forlo put an arm around her shoulders, drew her close, and kissed her forehead. Thale's tidings bored deep, like a worm in his gut. The world had changed. Rudil will be next to fall, he thought. We can't save it. Can't get the men there in time. He would have to send a messenger in the morning, warning the colony of what was coming. Maybe a few would get out.

At least they're on the other side of the water, he thought. At least the Run divides us—

Then it struck him, like a hammer blow to the middle of his chest. He moaned and stepped away from Essana to lean hard against the balustrade. "*Khot*," he swore.

"What?" she asked. "Forlo—"

"The Run," he said. "The Run . . . they mean to cross it."

"Cross it? How could—oh, gods." She looked up at the night sky.

The moons. There were concordances, sometimes, when the Run ran dry. When all three were in phase, it stayed that way long enough for a man to traverse it on horseback, if he knew where to cross, if he knew where the bottom was rocky and the silt shallow. The closest such crossing was to the west of Coldhope, three days' ride away. And the next concordance was at Reaping, only two months away.

"If they do," Essana whispered. "If they come here. . . ."

"Yes," he said.

There was something he had to do. They both knew it, though neither said a word of it.

"What about the elf?" she asked. "And the statue?"

He shook his head. "That'll have to wait. Make sure the guards don't slack. I'll deal with them when I'm back again."

She nodded, then stepped in and kissed him on the lips. He pulled her to him and held her, their mouths together. Then he released her, and she turned away to look out across the water. He touched her belly, felt the warmth beneath, and swallowed what felt like shards of glass. Then he turned and walked away.

A few minutes later, the front gates of Coldhope swung open, and Forlo rode out again, a fresh horse beneath him. He hoped the Sixth Legion hadn't traveled too far south yet.

Chapter 17

THE RUINS OF MALTON, THE IMPERIAL LEAGUE

The smell was the hardest part.

On the third day, the fires were still burning. It wasn't happening everywhere. On the hilltop and by the wharf the worst of the blazes had come and gone, leaving ashes and charred stones and bodies. Many bodies. Some were blackened and others lay in pools of congealing blood, covered with flies and picked over by rats, crows, and small scavenging lizards. These were harsh sights, but none were new to anyone in the horde. They had seen similar sights, though in lesser numbers, all through the Kazar lands, as they wrought vengeance for Krogan. There was one moment that burned in Hult's mind, however, one sight that would stay with him forever—a mangy dog, its fur matted with filth and soot, limping down the street with a severed hand in its mouth. It had shied away, then dropped the hand when he approached it. That grisly trophy—the gods alone knew what had become of the rest of the body—had belonged to a wealthy man, from the looks of the gold and emerald rings upon its fingers. Hult had kicked it into the gutter and left it.

No matter how gruesome the sights, the smells were worse, and would haunt Hult's sleep until he died. He knew the stink of death, just as he knew how it looked.

He recognized the various scents that wafted through the air after the sacking of a village: the thickness of smoke, the cooking-fire smell of burnt buildings, the tang of blood, and the sickly sweet stench of scorched flesh. Here there was no wind, and there had been no rain since the storm that destroyed Malton's wall. The smells stayed, accumulated, and worsened with the odor of rot under the blazing sun. Thousands of people had lived in Malton, and most had died beneath the hooves and blades of Chovuk Boyla's horde. That much death put a reek in the air that was horrible.

Three days, and the fires still burned. Especially the eastern quarter, where the homes had been packed together so closely that the Uigan wondered how the townsfolk had lived there without going mad. The rubble still smoldered and ropes of black smoke writhed up into the sky. There were clouds above, gray and unhappy, and the sun burned sickly yellow behind them. A pall of brownish haze hung over the town, probably visible from many miles away. To those with eyes, it would be clear that something awful had happened to Malton. Soon word would spread that the Tiger's blades had started taking their ancestral lands back from the bull-men.

It was like spending three days in the Abyss, Hult thought as he walked through the wreckage, his *shuk* in hand. He was searching for the wounded and the dying. If he found them, he was to give them a quick, clean ending—orders of the Boyla. Other warriors were doing the same, all through the town. Tormenting the enemy would earn Chovuk's wrath. Anyone well enough to walk was not to be mistreated, but was to be brought before him—unless they tried to flee. "If they do," the lord of the Uigan had said, "feather their backs and move on."

Hardly any survivors had been brought, and none since the previous morning. The horde was almost finished with Malton. Hult squinted through the smoke at the westering sun. It would be night soon. In the morning, they would move on. There were more places to loot farther along the coast, and the hunger was in the Uigan and the Wretched Ones alike, a yearning for glory, blood, and riches. It would take more than this one town to sate that hunger.

He stopped for a moment, listening. There was something going on farther along; there were sounds coming down the street. He peered through the haze and saw the shards of a fountain. It had been smashed with hammers, like all the stone art in Malton, and the water had drained away. The centerpiece, a rendition of some bare-chested minotaur wielding a trident, was broken into more than a dozen pieces. The face had been pulverized and the rest had been smeared with filth. That last touch got his skin prickling. The goblins had been there and had claimed that part of the town for themselves.

The Wretched Ones had been hard to control, once the sacking began. Savage creatures, cruel and brutal, they had done things to the people of Malton that Hult didn't care to think about. They liked to play vicious games with their captives and enjoyed killing them in painful ways involving hooks and ropes and large cleaving knives. They were the reason Chovuk had forbidden torture in the aftermath.

But just because the Boyla had banned torture, that didn't mean they had stopped altogether. And sometimes, if they caught a lone Uigan among the ruins, they played their games with him. Hult held his breath, his saber rising as he heard nasty, taunting laughter amid the debris. *I should turn back now*, he thought. *This place is only trouble. I could end my life here.*

Then he heard another sound, and all thoughts of leaving left him. Amid the goblins' jeering, almost inaudible, someone was crying. A child's terrified voice. Hult's lips skinned back from his teeth. He couldn't bring himself to abandon a youngling to the Wretched Ones. *Shuk* at the ready, he stole forward, past the despoiled fountain.

There were seven of them, foul little creatures with spears, in a small plaza off a narrow laneway, where the charred buildings loomed overhead like the cave walls beneath Mount Xagal. The goblins stood in a tight circle around a small, ash-caked boy, goading him with the points of their weapons, laughing as they jabbed at him, making him yelp. Even from twenty paces away, Hult could tell much about the child. He looked about nine or ten summers old, stronger than most city lads—they were near what looked like the remains of a forge, so maybe he'd been a smith's son or apprentice—and he was hurt. His left arm was bent at an awkward angle and he held it gingerly. Blood was caked on his side. The soot on his face had been nearly washed away by tears.

The goblins cackled at the boy, thrusting their spears at his feet to make him dance and swinging their weapons' butts to strike him hard across the rump. They mocked his weeping, moaning at him and rubbing their eyes with their free hands. Their leader, a taller, snaggle-toothed beast with skin the color of red clay, had a grisly necklace around his neck: hanging on it were human fingers, freshly severed.

It was then Hult noticed the boy's hand was bleeding.

After, he found he couldn't remember the next few moments. A red mist settled before his eyes, and the next thing he knew, he was standing by the boy's side, black blood dripping from his blade and two of the goblins sprawling where he'd cut his way into the circle. Neither would be getting up again, he was sure. He swung his *shuk* in broad, snapping arcs, forcing the other Wretched Ones back, lopping the heads off their spears when they got too close. They dropped the useless weapons, drawing hooked swords and baring their fangs.

Five were left. That made a hard fight. Better if he got it down to four before they regained their courage. He feinted left, knowing it would make the goblin to his right come forward, and quickly reversed his saber to stab behind him. He felt it slide in, a precise thrust that caught the creature under its left eye. The creature went limp and dropped to the ground.

Four.

The boy was staring at him, half-afraid, half-hopeful. A quick glance told Hult the lad still had all his fingers, but one was badly cut. He saw that the goblins had thought him dead and had tried to take their grisly trophy, and been surprised when he leaped away. They had been playing with him, just then, but they would have killed him shortly, if Hult hadn't come along. The same scene was surely playing out all over Malton.

It wasn't right. It had to stop. He must tell the Boyla.

"Stay with me," he said, though he was sure the boy spoke no Uigan. "Don't run, or they'll chase you down."

There was no chance to see if the boy understood. At a shout from their leader, the other three Wretched Ones charged at him, from three different directions. He caught the boy's arm, swung him out of the way, then lashed out with his *shuk*, opening a gash in one goblin's gut. It fell to its knees with a groan, then onto its side, not dead yet . . . but certainly soon to be, the way guts were spilling out of it. Hult kicked in the opposite direction and felt a satisfying crunch as his boot slammed a second goblin in the mouth. It stumbled back, howling in pain, half its teeth broken. Out of the fight; he would finish it later.

He whipped around, ducked a swinging sword from the third creature, parried a second blow, missed a third and took a nick to the shoulder, then went low and split the creature's knee. It stumbled and dropped its weapon, and he brought his *shuk* up, then down, hard. A head rolled in the dirt.

"One," he grunted, turning to face the goblins' leader.

The horrid creature stared at him, brow beetled above bloodshot eyes and fear written plain on its face. Then, with a snarl, it turned to flee into the rubble. Hult had a knife at his belt. He drew it, threw it, and caught the coward between the shoulders. It went down without another sound.

Battle-rage burned in Hult's blood. He stood seething for a moment, then went to the two goblins who still lived, the ones he'd gutted and kicked. Two swift stabs ended them. As he was pulling his knife out of the last goblin, a hand caught the leg of his trousers, tugging. He whirled, *shuk* rising—and stopped when he saw the boy through the red mist.

The child stared at him, afraid. He held out his hands, his eyes large and beseeching. He spoke a frightened word in the tongue of the League. Hult didn't understand, but he could guess the meaning.

Help.

Where is your father, child? he thought. Your mother? All you once loved? We have burned it all, and pillaged the ashes.

Strange, how even a *tenach* could feel shame. It was a new sensation for him, and confusing. Not just doubt—he'd had that before, starting with Krogan's death—but shame.

He stood staring at the boy, who repeated his single, plaintive word. Then, striding forward, he caught the child up with his wounded arm and carried him away through the smoke.

※————◆————※

The Boyla's throne sat atop the high hill in Malton's western quarter, in a wide square where cherry trees had once bloomed. The trees were gone now, cut down by horsemen with hatchets. In their place, a new forest had arisen composed of stakes driven into the ground between the cobblestones, each mounted with a severed head. These heads were all that remained of the town's wealthy, the fools who hadn't fled aboard ships when the wall came down: merchants, nobles, and a few high clerics. Men and minotaurs alike. Crows perched on some, fighting over the best bits; others were already stripped. The buzzing of insects filled the air.

There was more than just slaughter there, though: there were pearls and silver and fine-woven rugs, spices and ivory and silk. It stood in heaps among the carnage, plundered from the mansions on the hilltop. Even Chovuk's seat, a fine chair of mahogany and gold inlay, lined with red satin, had been pulled from a noble's manor. He sat on that chair now, surrounded by the Tegins. Sugai perched at his right hand on a plain stool also dragged from the wreckage.

Hult looked up at his master, still clutching the boy, who had long since passed out from the pain of his broken arm. Chovuk stared back, his face a mask of fury and his *shuk* across his knees.

"Goblins, you say?" he rumbled.

"Yes, master," Hult replied, bowing his head. "They were making sport of this child. They would have killed him, had I not intervened."

Chovuk's lip curled. He made an ominous sound, then turned to bark at a nearby cluster of warriors. "Find Gharmu! Tell him to bring ten of his best warriors at once!"

The Boyla was breathing hard, nostrils flared wide with rage. The warriors scrambled to obey. No one said anything until they returned with the goblin shaman and ten strong clan-chiefs. All the leaders of the Wretched Ones were draped in gold and jewels, proud of the loot they had taken. Hult thought they looked ludicrous, like ugly harlots.

"You call, great king," said Gharmu, kneeling. "We come. Why you want?"

Chovuk glared at him. Then he looked up at his men. "Shoot them," he said, and pointed at Gharmu. "All but that one."

The goblins yelped, startled. Some reached for weapons. Then bowstrings thrummed and they sprawled on the ground, arrows quivering in their corpses. Gharmu gaped, leaning on his staff. They had died all around him, but he remained untouched. He looked up at Chovuk, fear in his eyes.

"What you do?" he cried. "We friends . . . why you kill?"

"I gave orders, slime," Chovuk replied, his voice low and steady. "All kills were to be clean. Yet Hult caught your people torturing this boy."

Gharmu turned to stare at Hult. Hult knew the furious look on the shaman's face: it was the look of one caught doing wrong, feigning anger at his accuser. "He lies!" Gharmu wailed, waving his withered arm. "He evil man, king. You not listen to him."

"He is my *tenach*," the Boyla said. "He will always be true. No more of this, Gharmu. Tell your people—the next time I hear of the Wretched Ones doing such things, I will shoot one hundred of them. The third time, a thousand. Now go."

Hateful and terrified, the goblin scurried out of the plaza, leaving his dead fellows behind. The Uigan warriors gathered the bodies and dragged them away. Chovuk looked back at Hult with a slight twist to his lips.

"And what of the child?" he asked. "You saved his life. So he is yours, if you want him."

Hult gazed at the lad, a strange feeling coming over him. As *tenach*, he was forbidden by custom from marrying and bearing sons of his own. The thought of having a boy he could raise, teach to ride, and show how to use a bow and a blade roused emotions he'd never experienced before. But they were at war, and far from home. None of the tribes in the horde had brought boys younger than fourteen summers. The child would be a burden. He would only get in the way.

"Master, I cannot," he said, bowing his head. "Not in

this time of blood and swords. I ask that he be sent back with the crippled, to our grazing lands in the north. When we return victorious . . . *then* I will claim him."

Chovuk regarded him, his eyes gleaming with pride. Beside him, Sugai nodded, his old face crinkling as he smiled. "You are wise, *tenach*," the Boyla said. "We will do as you ask."

At his gesture, several women came forward and pulled the boy from Hult. The child tried to hold on and began to cry. Hult listened to his wails, sick at heart, as the women carried him away. They would splint his arm, wash him, feed him . . . then put him on a horse and send him north with the warriors who were too badly wounded to raid any further.

In time, the boy's cries faded away.

"This was an ill day," Chovuk said. "It shall be our last in this forsaken place. Let the word go out . . . tomorrow morning, we leave it to the crows and ghosts."

※

Hult didn't see the child again. By the time Chovuk dismissed him, the boy had already gone, along with the wounded and the larger pieces of plunder. The horde spent the rest of the day, and into the evening, preparing to leave. They would sleep beneath the stars that night, and be in the saddle before the morning broke.

He wondered, as the night passed, how the boy would fare among the Uigan. He was not one of them and never would be. Pale skinned and blue-eyed, he would always be an outsider on the Tamire. But he might yet have a good life—horses and cattle, wives, even children of his own one day. Perhaps he could become a *tenach*, serving a lord. He might even protect a Boyla, years from now. The riders would accept him and give him a home on the plains. Hult doubted the minotaurs would do the same for a Uigan child, were the sword in the other hand.

BLADES OF THE TIGER

The silver moon was waning and sinking in the west. A good omen. If they rode swiftly, the horde could be at Rudil when Solis was new, and attack in darkness. When that was done, they would need only to sweep along the coast, burning whatever villages remained, and the League would be purged from Northern Hosk, for the first time since even old Sugai Tegin could remember.

Chovuk's yurt was not taken down, alone among the riders. The Boyla slept within and there was darkness behind the flap. It was the sleep of victory. Already, his great deeds had won him a place in tales told around campfires. The elders sang of Chovuk Boyla, the Tiger, Storm-caller, who could make cities fall with a word.

Maybe there will be a verse for me as well one day, Hult thought, staring out across the dark ruins of Malton. Here and there, dull orange glimmers showed where fires still burned among the toppled stones. Beyond, the ruddy light of Lunis danced on the waters of the Tiderun. On the far shore, more lights gleamed. The cities of the League lay there, jewels waiting to be plucked. The riches of Malton were nothing beside fabled Kristophan, and Thera, and Vinlans. All that lay between the horde and those targets, all that thwarted their path, were a few miles of water.

"It will go away," said Chovuk.

Hult started, glancing over his shoulder. He hadn't heard movement within the yurt and hadn't sensed the flap spreading open. He struggled to push himself up, and knelt before the Boyla, bowing his head.

"Master," he murmured. "Forgive me. I have been inattentive."

Chovuk shrugged, gesturing with an open hand. "Sit, *tenach*. You do not need my pardon. You have had a long day, and you wonder what the boy's fate will be."

"Yes," Hult said.

"Jijin will provide for him," Chovuk declared. "The god must watch over him, since his ancestors do not. You did a brave thing, rescuing him from the Wretched Ones."

233

"Yes," Hult repeated, then licked his lips. "What harm did I do to the horde, though? I have driven a wedge between us and the goblins."

The Boyla smiled. "No mind. The Wretched Ones will not speak against me again and will follow my commands. Of course, they may still cause trouble, even then. Gharmu knows his skull will decorate my yurt if he crosses me again—but the other chiefs will be harder to control, if he fails. We may need to be rid of them in that case, for they will be of no further use."

Hult looked out across the water again, at the lights so invitingly close, yet far away. "You said it will go away," he said at length. "I do not understand."

"That is because you know nothing about tides," Chovuk replied. "They vary with the moons. When the moons are high in the sky, so is the sea; when they are not, the tides are low. And when all three moons are together . . . then the waters of the Tiderun disappear completely."

"Disappear?" Hult echoed, wondering: how can that be? But he knew about the moons and the magic of them. Men went mad when they were full, it was said. Why not the seas as well? "If such a thing happened . . . could we then cross to the far side?"

"We could. And such a thing *will* happen, *tenach*. Very soon. On that day, the bright cities of the south will be ours to raid. Let the bull-men and their thralls tremble in their houses of stone. The Uigan will indeed come, with fire and sword."

Hult trembled, thinking about it: the hordes of Chovuk Boyla, riding across the sea to destroy their foes. The elders would sing of *that* until the world's ending. He felt a surge of joy at being there, alive, to see the events happen. The joy must have shown on his face, for Chovuk laughed, throwing back his head to shout his mirth at the stars.

"Ah, *tenach*! You look like a boy who has just been

given his first bow," the Boyla said. "I am glad to see you so eager. The rest of the horde will feel the same, I am sure, when they ride out tomorrow."

"They?" Hult asked. "You mean we."

Chovuk shook his head. "Do not tell me what I mean, *tenach*. The horde leaves without us tomorrow. Sugai and Hoch will take them to Rudil, to attack it as well. That place's walls are weaker than Malton's—even without my power, they will crumble. You and I, though . . . we must ride north again. North, to seek a new ally for the coming fight."

Hult thought about that a moment, puzzling out the meaning of the Boyla's words. The north belonged to the Uigan. But all the horse-clans were accounted for. It must be something else the Boyla meant, something in the valleys beyond the plains. Something like . . .

"Jijin's horse," he breathed. "You would go there? You would seek *their* help?"

"We will." Chovuk's eyes gleamed as he stared out into the night. "We must, as fell as it may sound to your ears. On the morrow, we two ride out to ask the Elf Clans for aid."

Chapter 18

THE TWIN WATCHERS, THE IMPERIAL LEAGUE

The history of Southern Hosk was a recent one, for neither the minotaurs nor the humans of the League and Thenol had lived there longer than a few centuries. The humans had come from Styrllia, one of the outlying provinces of Old Aurim, as survivors of the First Destruction, fleeing the doom of their homeland. They had found the woods and valleys south of the Tiderun friendly and more or less free of the poisons and monsters that had ravaged the lands to the east after the rain of fire. They proclaimed several kingdoms, subjugated the peaceful tribes that already lived there, and built the great cities of Kristophan and Vinlans. They felt that the gods had smiled on them again, after turning their backs on Aurim.

Then came the Uigan, sweeping down from the steppes across the Tiderun. The Run had been drier in those days, the waters receding for weeks sometimes, when the moons were aligned. When that happened, the horsemen poured across in droves, burning, slaughtering, and carrying gold and women back across the straits. For nearly a hundred years it went on: the men of the new kingdoms would rebuild, refortify, regain the riches they had lost—then the Tiderun would empty and the barbarians would return, scattering ashes and blood in their wake.

The raids were why the men of New Styrllia and the other kingdoms welcomed the minotaurs when they came. The bull-men had expected to be met with sword and spear when they made landfall in Taladas—for where had anyone met them with anything else? But while there were some clashes at the beginning, they soon found themselves greeted with open arms. The minotaurs were at least civilized, unlike the riders, and they were brilliant warriors. So the kings of men made a pact with them: they could settle in Southern Hosk, and even rule it as an empire, as long as the humans of those lands remained free. And they would have to fight the Uigan.

Thus was the Minotaur League born. When the barbarians crossed the Run again the next summer, they found the land much changed. The fiefs they had raided with impunity were guarded by horned giants who were each the match for three ordinary men. For the first time, the Uigan were beaten back across the Run. They returned in greater numbers the next year, but while they claimed some victories, even these were costly. The minotaurs would not be moved. At the same time, the dry times on the Run were growing shorter and less frequent. In the end, the Uigan gave up and returned to slaughtering the Kazar and their other rival tribes. No barbarians had crossed the Run in over two hundred and fifty years—not even during the dark times of the Godless Night. They stayed up in their grasslands and dusty hills, barely even troubling the colonies of Rudil and Malton on the strait's far shore.

Things change, though; things end.

Malton was a burning ruin. Rudil, Forlo knew, would soon follow. And soon, too, the moons would align. The Run would be dry again. It wouldn't last as long as it had in the old times, when the land was still settling after the Destruction, but the two halves of Hosk would be one for six days. Plenty of time for the Uigan who had sacked Malton to cause widespread ruin across the League's northern provinces. Plenty of time to destroy all he held dear.

When he finally caught up to the Sixth again, fifty leagues south of where the army had been previously camped, he was dazed in the saddle. He'd barely slept and hardly eaten since leaving Coldhope three days before. When he did try to rest, he kept having the same dream—always the same now— no more battles against fanatics and the Thenolites' buried army. Only the tunnels beneath Hith's temple, the darkness, the stink of decay . . . and the sight of his unborn son, shambling toward him with mindless, sorrowing hunger in his eyes.

He didn't want to close his eyes, so he rode day and night, trusting his horse and his instincts to keep him from getting caught in a thicket or plunging off a cliff in the dark. He was battered and bleeding from the branches and bushes that whipped by him as he rode. He could barely think, let alone speak. Still, he did find them again, his former legion, camped in a valley between the Twin Watchers.

The Watchers were older than any histories told— more crumbling reminders that there had been realms there in the ancient days. They were once statues of white-stone, perched on hilltops of brown, wind-bared rock. No one knew who the statues signified, for they had fallen to rubble from the waist up, leaving only their armor-kilted legs standing on adjacent hilltops. Even these were barely recognizable, worn away by centuries of wind and rain, their features gone. Some scholars said the statues weren't intended to be human, claiming the legs bore signs of having been covered in scales. Other sages called those scholars fools. There had been duels fought in the Kristophan Arena over this debate. Forlo didn't care about scales or the Watchers. In his mind, he saw the horror in Sammek Thale's eyes as he told of Malton's fall. He saw the Tiderun dry and the waves of riders thundering across, their curved swords raised high, their horsetail banners streaming, and their voices yelling for blood. He saw Coldhope in ruins, Essana dead, and himself and many others too. The keep would barely slow the horde as it thundered on toward the richer cities. They had destroyed Malton in hours. In six days' time, they could lay waste to Thera and Trilloman . . . maybe even the shards of the capital that remained after Ambeoutin's death. The minotaurs, divided and distracted with the fighting over the throne, would not be ready. The Uigan would bring ruin to the League, then carry its gold and women away as in the old days. The days of peace were at an end.

The Uigan had to be stopped. Any reasonable fool would know this. Duke Rekhaz was undoubtedly a fool. Forlo prayed he was reasonable as well.

Crossbowmen nearly shot him out of his saddle as he galloped down into the camp in the dark, only hesitating when he raised his hands to show they were empty, then pulled off his helm to show who he was. Through the cuts and bruises, they recognized their old marshal, took his horse's reins when he slowed, and caught him as he slumped and toppled from the saddle. They called for Grath, gave him watered wine and fried bannocks, and tried to clean his wounds. They were good men and loved him still. It made him glad.

Then Grath was there, his face swimming into the firelight, creased with worry as he took Forlo's hand. He knew something was terribly wrong. After bellowing for a healer, he turned his troubled gaze back to Forlo.

"*Khot*," he swore. "You look like you rode through the Abyss to get here."

"No Abyss," Forlo panted, smiling. He'd bitten his tongue as he fell; there was blood on his teeth. "Just . . . forest."

Grath grinned a moment, then the smile faded. "Tell me," he said. "Why would you come back here? What brought you these many miles, my friend?"

Forlo took a deep breath and let it out. He and Grath had been shield-brothers, had killed together, and had watched comrades die. Thank the gods for such true friends, he thought.

The healer came—not a Mislaxan, but an older soldier adept in herbs and leechcraft. He was a gray bearded human with a surcoat emblazoned with the knife-and-leaf sign of a physic. Wyndan, his name was. He'd tended Forlo's wounds before, had been with the Sixth through the whole of the Thenol campaign. He shoved other warriors aside, making room for himself.

"Wait," Forlo told him, raising a hand. All his knuckles were bloody and raw. He'd never ridden so hard in his life.

Wyndan stopped, looking to Grath, who nodded. "Speak, Forlo," the minotaur said. "Tell me your tale."

Forlo let out another breath—a sigh—and began.

In the morning, when Wyndan had treated him, they brought him to Rekhaz and he told the tale again. The Duke listened, eyes narrowed, as Forlo spoke of Malton's fall and of the enemy gathered across the Run. Rekhaz stroked his chin as Forlo repeated what Sammek Thale had seen, of the Uigan lord who could call down the storm with a word, and of the allies he had gathered on his bloody mission: goblins as well as riders, many thousands strong. Then, when Forlo was done, Rekhaz sat quietly for a long moment, his brow furrowed.

"Barbarians and Wretched Ones," he said at length. "A savage who brings down walls with whirlwinds and lightning. And they are coming here, just as I'm about to do away with Count Akan?"

Forlo nodded, aching. He'd barely slept—his son's staring, lifeless eyes still haunted him, no matter how tired he was. He'd woken in pain. The ride had cost him . . . might have killed a lesser man, one who'd spent fewer years in the saddle.

"I've told you all I know, Your Honor," he said.

A lie. He hadn't mentioned the statue or the elf who'd been caught trying to steal it. It would complicate things, and he didn't know if it was part of everything. Rekhaz would understand, he'd told himself over and over as he rode. Despite their differences—despite their hatred for each other—he would recognize the great threat. That hope had been a candle for him as his horse's hooves devoured the land. That horse would never run like that again.

Rekhaz looked down on him, and the candle flames in his tent began to waver. There was no belief in the Duke's eyes, only disdain. Folding his massive arms across his chest, he stared at Forlo in silence for a long moment, then spat in his face.

"*Khot*," he said.

It was Grath who responded first. Forlo was too shocked to speak. "Your Honor," he said, stepping forward, "that was not well done. If there is a threat in the north—"

"*If*," Rekhaz interrupted, stopping Grath with a glare. "Yes, if. What proof have we? What evidence that what he says is true?"

"You have my word," Forlo said tersely, wiping his face. "The word of a lifelong defender of the League. It should be enough."

"Should it? I see no defender here," sneered the Duke. "All that stands before me is a weak man who turned away from his duties before they were done. Who refused the call to glory when it was sent to him, not a week since! Now you come crawling back—"

Forlo shook his head. "I bring you warning, Your Honor."

"Warning of barbarians who haven't threatened us since our grandfathers' *grandfathers'* time!"

"Perhaps," Forlo allowed, "but they gather now."

"*Khot*," Rekhaz said again.

Grath stepped in again. "Lord Forlo has never been aught but a friend of the realm. I will stake my own honor upon his word. If this invasion—"

"Keep your tongue!" the Duke roared. "You overstep your bounds, Lord Grath!"

Grath's eyes burned with fury. Forlo saw it, held up a hand to stay him, and gave him a look that said *not now*. The Duke would kill them both if they joined against him—it would only take a word to bring the guards waiting outside his tent.

"Is there anything I can do, Your Honor"—Forlo could no longer speak to the minotaur without his mouth twisting contemptuously—"to convince you this is no trick? That I tell the truth?"

Rekhaz regarded him slowly, evenly. Cunning sparked in his eyes. He smiled, and not in a friendly way. "There is one thing. Return to the army, Forlo. Serve the League, as you swore to do. Vouch for my claim to the throne and fight on my side. Then I will give you a cohort to settle this little invasion you speak of."

"A cohort?" Forlo asked incredulously. "Only six hundred men? The Uigan and their allies number twenty times that many. We'd need the entire legion—"

"A soldier of the imperial army is *worth* twenty savages," Rekhaz shot back, "and a hundred goblin scum. You have my offer—and humans only, none of the true warriors. I will keep the minotaurs in my company. Now, will you give me your answer, or shall I have you flogged and sent away?"

Forlo ground his teeth, cursing himself. He saw his future clearly. If he survived the coming battle—and with only a cohort, the chances of that were slim—he would be called south immediately to help affirm Rekhaz's hold on the throne. He would spend the rest of his life in Kristophan, or leading its armies until he was old, his son was grown, and Essana, probably dead. It was exactly what he had not wanted, what he had struggled to avoid.

But if he didn't accept . . . what then? All he had believed in and fought for would be lost anyway. And the League's glory, which he had striven to keep bright, would dim—perhaps for good. If history remembered him at all, people would say that Barreth Forlo had possessed the chance to stem the invasion from the Tamire, and had refused it out of pride.

He bowed his head, tears in his eyes. Essana, he thought, this is the only way I can save you. Us. I'm sorry.

"Very well," he said. "I am yours to command, Duke Rekhaz. I will rejoin the army."

"This is not right!" Grath snapped.

Rekhaz turned and punched Grath in the jaw, sending him staggering. "You will *kindly* stop telling me what is right and wrong!" he shouted. Then he saw Grath put a hand on his axe and smiled. "Oh, do try it, Marshal. Give me the opportunity to gut you like a pig."

Grath tensed, blood on his lips, and for a long moment he stared at the Duke. Rekhaz regarded him with disdain, his arms at his sides, not even touching his own blade. Then, finally, Grath relaxed, though hate obviously simmered in his eyes.

"You're lucky I still have need for you, Marshal," Rekhaz snapped. "Now get out. Both of you."

Once they were outside, Grath finally drew his axe, whirled, and brought it down on a map table outside Rekhaz's tent. The board shattered, splinters flying. Parchment flew everywhere, drawing stares from all around.

"Be easy," Forlo said, guiding his friend away. "It is done, and nothing can change it now."

"You were right about him. I should never have sworn

my men to that scum," Grath snarled. "You earned all you had, and he made you give it up as if it were *nothing*. I ought to go back in there and put steel in his gullet!"

Forlo rested a hand on his arm. "I won't let you throw yourself on his sword for my benefit, my friend."

Grath seethed for a moment before slowly getting control of himself. "All right," he growled, "all right. I'm sorry, Forlo. I'd hoped for better. You're right, by the way—if this horde is as large as you say, a cohort will barely slow them down. Especially a cohort with no minotaurs! I'll send word to the other legions—maybe they'll send some men, too."

"No," Forlo said, "they're too far south, from what you've told me. Even if they did send reinforcements, they'd be too late. No, my friend . . . it does seem a lost cause. But at least what I swore in there won't matter, in the end—because in a few weeks I'll be dead, and then it will be very hard for me to serve the Duke."

Grath thought for a moment, rubbing his bruised jaw. He met Forlo's eyes, and soon both were chuckling grimly. "Not you alone, Forlo," Grath said, his voice hard. "*Both* of us."

"What?"

"I'm going with you," Grath said. He raised a finger. "Don't say it. I still command the Sixth, not you, and certainly not Rekhaz. Let him name a new marshal for the legion. He'll be more than happy to see my back for a while. I'd rather fight and die beside you than ride to glory with that one."

Forlo stood silently beside Grath, staring out into the night. Campfires glimmered in the gloom, lighting the featureless Watchers from below. The dancing shadows made them look eerily alive. What Grath intended was foolish, almost to the point of madness. But Forlo knew his friend wouldn't be the only one. Most of the soldiers in the Sixth would gladly follow him. He wished he could take more. Wished they could just kill Rekhaz and bring the whole legion north. But that wasn't honorable, and the minotaurs would never accept such a move. Nor would half the men. They were bound to their duty. So was he, now.

"It's good to have friends," he said at last.

"Yes," Grath said. "Come, Forlo. Let's go choose who will die with us."

Essana gazed down from the wall of Coldhope, tears in her eyes. Below her, the tents of the cohort spread out, covering the fields. Blue and red banners snapped in the wind. Men moved to secure the camp, shouting and cursing. There was no laughter, though: the soldiers had an idea of what they would face once the moons aligned. They had no room in their hearts for mirth.

"So few," she said. "You gave Rekhaz your whole life, and he gave so little back!"

Forlo reached out and took her hand. He saw Grath down below, barking orders and urging the men on. They had arrived just two hours earlier, Forlo riding ahead to prepare the way, the rest marching behind. Essana had been elated to see them, but that hadn't lasted long. She'd been expecting a legion—and a husband who would stay when all was done. Now, she looked out at the cohort and saw death. Never mind that the death would be glorious and in battle—the soldiers' wives would be widows anyway. And so would she.

"I tried, Starlight," he said. "Rekhaz . . . he shamed me and put me in a place where he knew I could not live. He's ready to sacrifice the northern provinces for the throne if it comes to it. He's betting he'll have beaten Akan and united the armies again by the time the Uigan turn their attention south."

"You make it sound like a *shivis* game. Pieces moving on a board," she said. Her voice was dull and empty.

He sighed. War *was* a game, if seen from above. You

needed to think of it that way sometimes, when you were in command. The key was never to forget that for the soldiers doing the fighting—and the dying—it was far from play. Rekhaz had forgotten that, and now Forlo looked back on his years in command, during the Thenol campaign, and wondered if he had too.

"Coldhope may fall," he said. "Everything along the coast is in danger. Grath's already sent riders to the east and west, warning the other lords to start their people moving south. It probably won't help, but it's worth trying."

She looked at him, hurt. "You want me to leave too."

"Yes."

Essana shut her eyes, put a hand to them, and pinched. She was trying not to cry, to be strong for him. The wind blew around her, tangling her hair. Gods, it hurt Forlo to see her like that.

"Starlight," he said, "please."

"I can't!" she snapped, her voice breaking. Down in the camp, some of the soldiers glanced up and looked away again when Forlo glowered their way. "This is my home, Barreth. My family has lived here as long as there are records. Since New Styrllia was settled. We weathered the hordes before, in the old days. We can do it again."

"It's not just you I'm trying to protect, Essana. Think of the life inside you. I don't want it endangered."

A mistake. Her eyes turned cold. "You think *I* do? I want this child to live too, Barreth. I want an heir—but I don't want to give him birth in exile from his home. I want our son's first days to be here, where he belongs—not so far away that he only hears of Coldhope from tales."

He felt his own anger rising, venomous words on his tongue. He gritted his teeth, saying nothing. Essana turned and stormed away, back toward the keep. He heard her sobbing, took two steps to follow, then stopped himself. Anything he said now would only make things worse.

He went down to the camp instead and walked among the tents and campfires, the training grounds where the soldiers sparred, and the archery range where they practiced with crossbows. He was proud of them—six hundred men, all ready to die at his command. But Forlo wasn't ready any more.

"Trouble?" Grath called out. He was carrying a keg of ale from the supply wagons, the big barrel perched easily on his shoulder. "Anything I can do?"

Forlo walked toward him. "Never marry. It complicates things."

"Why do you think I haven't done it yet?" the minotaur replied, grinning. "Let me guess—she refused to leave?"

Forlo nodded.

"I could get a couple big lads to *make* her. Abduct her, take her down to Trilloman. She'll hate us forever, but at least she'll live to do the hating."

It was tempting, but Forlo waved the suggestion off. "No, we need to do something else."

"And that is?"

"Fight and win."

Grath laughed aloud—then stopped, seeing the gravity in Forlo's eyes. "How do we do that, with these numbers?"

"Send men around to the villages. Organize the commoners and make an army of the people."

The minotaur chuckled again, this time without much humor. "How many will that get us? A few hundred more? Rabble armed with scythes and rusty spears their grandfathers gave them? That'll put the fear of Sargas in the Uigan, aye."

"At least it's something," Forlo shot back.

"Doubling the watch on Aurim's walls the night of the Destruction would have been *something*, but it wouldn't have stopped the burning rain." Grath looked around, rubbing his snout with a callused hand. "We need disciplined troops, someone who knows which end of a sword goes in the other fellow." Grath threw up his hands. "If you can think of any place to find *that*, I'll gladly kiss the first dwarf I see."

Forlo caught his breath, a thought occurring. He turned it over in his mind. Grath saw him thinking and tilted his head curiously.

"What?" the minotaur asked.

"I don't have any dwarves handy," Forlo said. "How about an elf?"

Chapter 19

THE DREAMING GREEN, NORTHERN HOSK

Hult dreaded little in the world. He mistrusted much—every Uigan did—even feared a few things, though he kept such feelings hidden. Only the mad didn't feel the hot flash of terror in the moments before riding into battle, or when the ghost-fingers descended from summer storms to tear great furrows in the plains ... or the walls of cities. But true dread, the coldness of the soul, was not something he'd felt often.

Only once before had he experienced anything that made his knees weak and his sword arm heavy. It had been on his name-quest, a dragonhunt on the frozen Panak in the bleak winter. He and five others: boys out seeking the cold-drakes that dwelt there, to prove themselves men. Every Uigan warrior had to hunt some great beast and make a necklace of its remains, thus proving himself a man in the eyes of the tribe. He and his friends had decided to hunt the small, white dragonlings that stalked the snowy plains. The elders still told tales of Chovuk's quest to slay the same monster—and there wasn't a young warrior in the White Sky clan who didn't want to grow up to be Chovuk.

The idea turned out to be a bad one. Of the six who had gone north, only three returned, and Hult alone carried the skull and talons of a dragon to show for it. There, in the freezing wind, they had disturbed something other than the drakes. Something older and angrier. He still didn't know what it was. He had only ever seen it as a hulking shape through the snow, with eyes that burned a soulless blue. It had hunted them for three days and nights, silent and patient, until a violent winter storm descended upon them. They made camp in a cave to wait out the blizzard. Then the deaths began. Each night it took one of his friends away, with no warning at all. It left nothing of its victims for them to bury—not even blood. Only screams, soon swallowed by the wind. On the fourth day they abandoned the cave and made south through the storm, the wintry wraith in silent pursuit. When the weather finally broke, it was nowhere to be found. They had found no sign of it since.

But Hult still saw it, sometimes, in his dreams.

Not since that time had he felt true horror, not even in the caverns beneath Mount Xagal, when he and Chovuk fought the goblins' serpentine king. That night, though . . . it was back, a dull glimmer in the back of his mind, a shadow beginning to move. They had crossed the borders into the elf-lands.

The *hosk'i imou merkitsa*, the elves of the Tamire, were creatures spoken of only in hushed tones around the campfires, long after sensible folk had gone to sleep. Few men claimed to have seen them, and most of those were liars. The tales of the elves' powers varied with the telling. They were shapeshifters, some said, or they stole Uigan children to sacrifice to their gods. Their songs could cause a man to forget all he had ever known—even his own name—and leave him in a dreamless sleep that lasted centuries. To kiss one of their unspeakably beautiful women was death. And they were fiercely protective of their lands, the river-rich woods and lush, green lands where they had dwelt since long before humans came to the plains. No matter who told the tale, that was the common thread: those who entered elvish lands seldom came out again.

And there they were, he and Chovuk alone, two weeks' hard riding north of the Tiderun. The horde would be at Rudil by now, driving the minotaurs before their horses with spear and bow, leaving their stone halls smashed and burnt and spattered with blood. Other villages would be ashes behind them, destroyed as they swept west along the coast. It was where he and Chovuk should have been, it was their place—not in elf lands, in the night, surrounded by evergreens and eerie sounds.

The Dreaming Green was a strange land, a long, deep valley among the foothills of the Ring Mountains, north of the Kazar Lands, where winter snows blanketed the land for much of the year. During the short summers—as now—the land became a riot of greenery, all swaying firs and bristling spruce, cut through by white-foaming streams of meltwater that ran down from the mountains. The scents of sap and wildflowers filled the air, which danced with clots of pollen that gleamed crimson-gold in the moonlight. It was so strong that it made the eyes burn and breath come shallow and hoarse. There was noise everywhere, the melody of nature—the groan of the trees as the wind shifted them, the twitter and croak of birds, the splash of water over stones. And something deeper, something that made the hairs on Hult's arms stand tall—music, so distant and muted it seemed to disappear when he concentrated on it. Drums, and flutes, and a strange, skirling wail, playing in a scale alien to Uigan ears. This was the song of the *merkitsa*, and its message was clear: the elves knew they were there. Were watching, waiting. Perhaps laughing at them, making a game of it, not striking until they tired of the chase.

He hadn't seen the elves yet, though now and then he caught a glimpse of *something*—movement in the undergrowth, a shadow where there shouldn't have been one, a shimmering like warm air on the steppes—always out of the corner of his eye. When he looked directly, the shadow was gone. In a way, he was glad the *merkitsa* hadn't revealed themselves yet. He was half-certain the sight of one would drive him mad.

The worst part of it, though, was not knowing why they had come. Chovuk had spoken of making a bond with the elves, but hadn't said why or how, or much else on the matter. Hult had asked several times, always wary of arousing the Boyla's ire, but he received no answer. Finally, he'd given up, riding in silence beside Chovuk to the crest of the great ridge that made the south edge of the Green, then down a narrow, wending path into the woods. There had been totems at the forest edge, strings of feathers, stones, and bones tied from one gnarl-branched oak to the next, red whorls and handprints painted on the bark. Warnings all, and all ignored. They had ridden on, with the woods closing around them, swallowing the sunlight so that only slanting rays found their way between the overhanging boughs.

Night came. Chovuk had taken first watch, and Hult took the second. They had no fire to warm them and the bloody gleam of Lunis was the only light. Hult sat on a tall boulder draped in moss, sticking at an angle out of the vine-tangled ground above their camp. He kept his *shuk* unsheathed and across his knees. He didn't bother with his bow. The things that stalked him were much better archers than he could ever hope to be.

"Harm nothing here," the Boyla had warned before dozing off. "Even if wolves drag off our horses, do not draw blood. The *merkitsa* will be insulted."

Hult thought of the elves and of what they did to those who displeased them. They did not feel pain as men did, the elders claimed, so pain fascinated them. They would slit an intruder open and study his face as his entrails spilled out upon the ground. They would slice the flesh off a man's hands in tiny slivers and bet on how many cuts he could stand before he passed out. They would seal a man in a clay jug with a nest of fire-wasps, just to hear the music of his screams.

In the dark, he imagined *merkitsa* all around. They were out there, watching him, just out of sight. He could feel their arrows trained on him, aiming to cripple but not kill. If they loosed their shafts, he would never see them coming; only feel the contact as they flashed out of nowhere and buried themselves in his breast. That was what made dread rime his heart: the knowledge that something was watching him, stalking him and marking his every move.

Foolish, he told himself. These are just woods. You only think they're a threat because that's what the elders told you when you were a boy. You are like a soft southerner, fearing things you can't see. Afraid of strange songs and shapes in the dark.

A twig snapped. It was a near thing, but he kept from yelling at the noise. He scowled, shaking his head at himself. "Stupid," he muttered, reaching for a flask at his side.

The *kumiss* was sour and burned his throat, but it warmed him and made the fear recede a little. He wished they had brought more. If they were in these woods too long, they would run out, and he would have to get his courage elsewhere. Putting the stopper back in the flask's neck, he glanced down at the foot of the rock, at the hollow where they had camped, and sucked in a startled breath.

The camp was empty, Chovuk's blanket a bundled heap among the bushes. The Boyla was gone.

"Master?" Hult hissed, twisting to his feet. Raising his *shuk*, he looked one way, then the other, seeking some sign of Chovuk. He was alone here, as near as he could tell. Nothing but him and the shadows. "Boyla?"

No answer came. Hult clambered down from the rock, landed in a crouch, and stayed there as he checked the ground. There was no blood and no sign of struggle. Had the *merkitsa* been there while his head had been turned? Had they taken Chovuk without waking him? Could they be so quick? No—the Boyla was a light sleeper, and Hult felt certain there had been no magic. That meant Chovuk had left of his own accord.

Luckily, it was easy to find his trail: the earth of the Green was soft and moist. Chovuk had left footprints, a faint path through the brush. It wove away into the dark and at once Hult knew where it led. They'd stopped at a pool shortly before making camp, to water their horses before seeking shelter for the night. He hesitated a moment to check on the animals; they were quiet. His was sleeping and Chovuk's was watching him calmly from where it was tethered.

He followed the trail, feeling eyes on his every move. The path wound among the trees, then over the rim of an embankment and down toward the pool's edge. He stopped atop the bluff, his scalp prickling. There was something down there: voices speaking spidery words and an eldritch green light. He recognized the light, and the voices as well. They were the same as he'd seen and heard through the flap of the Boyla's yurt, all those nights on the Tamire while the horde was gathering. One of the voices, indeed, was Chovuk. The other was strange. Together they were like two voices coming from the same mouth, one low and sonorous, the other raspy and thin. He froze, listening as the other voice spoke words in a tongue he didn't know, and the Boyla answered.

He felt a presence he'd encountered once before, on the eve of the attack on Khal. There was the same chill in the air, the same disquiet. Whatever was down there with Chovuk, it didn't sound friendly. Taking a deep breath, he offered a prayer to Jijin, asking for bravery and strength. Then, blade clasped tight in his right hand, he peered over the bank's edge, down toward the pool.

The water was broad, glistening like blood in Lunis's light. Blue-white motes danced above its surface: glow-flies mating. On the far side, a series of low cataracts babbled over stones. To his left, a narrow creek led away, carrying the water on into the Green. Three tall rocks stood in the pool's midst, columns of pink granite asparkle with embedded crystals. Bands of black and white paint ran round them, some straight, some in waves, some in jagged lightning bolt shapes. His skin prickled at the sight of the stones, as it had when they first saw them the day before. There was power pent up in them, some magic as old as the elves themselves. It was a sacred place, and the spirits who dwelt there were not welcoming. He could feel the *merkitsa*, all around.

But that wasn't the horrifying part.

Chovuk knelt by the side of the water, naked to the waist, the long scars upon his tattoo-covered body glistening like fresh wounds in the red moonlight. Beyond him, green flames danced and raced across the pond's surface, rising into pillars that coiled and writhed more like serpents than like flames. The fire made no sound and gave off no smoke—nor heat, it seemed. If anything, the breeze blowing off the water was cool.

And there, in its midst, stood the presence.

It was difficult to make the figure out, through the fire. Hult was aware of darkness in the form of a robed man, standing on the pool's surface as though it were solid stone. He saw neither its face nor hands, for the darkness that cloaked the presence hid them from view. The robed figure did not look up at him, keeping its attention on Chovuk, but Hult knew it had seen him. A thought formed in his mind that did not seem his own: *STAY WHERE YOU ARE.*

The dread in Hult's bowels gnawed deeper. There was sorcery in the glade, strong, rich, and dark. Like all Uigan, down through the centuries, he had learned to despise magic at an early age. He still had uncomfortable thoughts about the spells Chovuk had cast at the Mourning-stone, at Xagal, in the Kazar lands, and before the walls of Malton.

It wasn't right, relying on the demons that dwelt within the moons for power. A warrior should live by the strength of his sword arm, the pull of his bow, and the speed of the horse beneath him. That was the way of the Tamire clans.

But Chovuk was Boyla, and Hult—along with most of his fellow riders—told himself that if the Boyla used magic, it must be for a noble purpose. The blood of the hated Kazar and the plunder of the minotaurs had helped persuade them.

This, however . . . *this* was different. Chovuk wasn't the one with the power here, obviously. It was the shadow upon the water that held the magic, and the Boyla was helpless before it, half-naked and unarmed. Years of training, of life as a *tenach*, took hold. Hult was sworn to protect his master even if it meant his death. For a long moment, that instinct warred with the alien voice in his head, the one that compelled his body not to move.

Warred, and won. With a shout, he leaped up and vaulted over the embankment, throwing himself down a slope slick with fallen needles, his sword held high. The shadow looked up and away from Chovuk. Toward him. The Boyla turned too, and Hult knew he had been right to move: Chovuk's eyes showed nothing but white. They were rolled back in their sockets like a dead man's. His mouth hung slack and a rope of drool dangled from his lower lip. There was no recognition in that face, none of the familiar fierceness. It was a dead man's visage, and the shock of it spurred Hult downhill even faster.

He skidded to the bottom, dashing out into the pool without hesitation, and into the fire. He expected to burn and gritted his teeth against it, but the flames were like ice instead, chilling him as they licked over his flesh. He barely noticed. His rage, his need to protect his master, was too great. He bellowed, letting loose an ululating warcry the Uigan used to frighten steppe-wolves from their goats and horses. His saber whipped around and above

BLADES OF THE TIGER

his head as he splashed out, knee-deep, then waist-deep, on toward the shadow.

The presence looked down upon him, not seeming to care. It was tall, perhaps two heads taller than he was, and it stood on the water, not in it. A notion formed in Hult's mind: this thing wasn't paying him any mind because he was no kind of threat. The elders' tales abounded with spirits who were invulnerable to good steel, who could take a sword through the neck and not die. Was this such a phantom?

If I die here, he thought, at least it will not be said that Hult, son of Holar, failed as the Boyla's *tenach*.

The presence loomed before him, and the voice in his mind began to laugh. Not a happy sound. The strange laughter made his heart blossom with hate. "Begone, fiend!" he cried. "Leave my master forever!"

He raised his *shuk* high with both hands. Then something heavy hit him from behind, knocking him down. He went under the water, swallowed, and began to choke. He lost his sword, somewhere. The weight bore down on him, hands catching around his wrists as he fought. He kicked and struck something, which fell back. With a roar he pushed himself up out of the water, spat and gagged, black spots whirling before his eyes.

The flames were gone. There was mist on the pool now, ruddy in Lunis's glow. It was a warm late summer night, and the chill that had blown off the water was gone. Hult turned, looking this way and that. The shadow was gone. As for his attacker ... when he saw the Boyla standing in the water a few paces away, doubled over and breathing hard, he knew.

"Master?" he asked.

Chovuk looked up, pale, in pain. He grinned. "You fight like a lion, boy," he said. "A lion with the strength of a dragon."

Hult stared. "Why did you stop me?" he demanded. "Why did you protect that ... thing?"

257

The Boyla raised a hand, straightening up slowly, pain in his eyes. "Be still, *tenach*. There is much you don't understand. Nor need you. Only trust me when I say that what you saw is not as it seemed."

"No?" Hult shot back, his voice quavering. "It looked to me that you were under a spell of darkness and evil."

"It may seem so," Chovuk replied, calm in the face of his *tenach*'s anger. "It seemed so to me, the first time it happened. It was not long before Krogan Boyla died and I was afraid as never before. But the Teacher has shown me many things . . . the shape of the tiger, the way to control the goblins, how to call the storm to wreck strong, stone walls. All that I have done for our people, I would never have accomplished without *his* help."

Hult remained silent, thinking about this. He had *felt* the evil of the thing, as sure as he felt the beating of his own heart. But if it had helped Chovuk, helped his people . . . was that not good? In the end, weren't the Uigan stronger for it?

"*Tenach*," said Chovuk, the word full of weight. He held out a hand. "You are sworn to trust me, whatever that may be. Will you not abide by your oath?"

Hult hesitated, staring at the proffered hand. All his training told him to accept it, to clasp his master's arm, but what he'd seen that night made him stand still, trembling.

That was when the first arrow hit the water in front of Chovuk, barely a pace away. It dived out of the darkness and plunged into the water, its black-fletched end sticking out above the pool's surface. Both men stared in surprise. The nock was meticulously carved to resemble a dragon's mouth.

Elven work.

Instinct and training took over again. Hult threw himself at Chovuk, hoping to knock him down and to shield him with his own body. As he took his first step, however, two more arrows darted out of nowhere and hit him in the chest and thigh. They bit deep, bright blooms of pain erupting within him. He didn't scream, but instead made a growling sound deep in his throat. Then he splashed down into the pool again. The water went red with moonlight and blood, then all was dark.

Chapter 20

COLDHOPE KEEP,
THE IMPERIAL LEAGUE

She could feel it, and that was the worst part. Down, down, far below her—for the room where the people of Coldhope had imprisoned her was at the top of one of the keep's slender towers, well above the ageless catacombs—the statue waited. No, bided—for it *was* biding. The mind (could it be called a soul?) within the statue was marking the time until . . . what? Something terrible was going to happen, Shedara knew. Something to do with the shadows. The only comfort of knowing the Hooded One was down there was that it meant its dark pursuers, the twisted shadow-kender and the cloaked killer who sought the statue, hadn't found it yet. Probably didn't yet know where it was. But they would find out. Of that she was sure. They would close in and they would take it, and the lord and lady of Coldhope and all their soldiers and servants would die hideous, bloodless deaths.

And so will I, she thought grimly. Unless I get out of this place. Unless I find a way.

Lord Forlo had done a good job of imprisoning her. It wasn't the first time men had caught Shedara. Dungeons, slave-mines, city jails . . . she'd spent her share of time in many such places. It went with being a moon-thief.

So, however, did escaping. She knew many spells for escaping—spells to open a hole in a solid stone wall, or to make a cell door burst its hinges, or to charm a guard into leaving a door unlocked, or to freeze iron bars so that a good, solid kick could shatter them. But spells didn't do any good if you couldn't cast them, and Forlo's guards had made sure she wasn't able to do that. Her hands were bound with bowstrings and a silk gag stifled her voice. They had taken her spellbooks, too. Shedara could still sense the magic of the moons—growing tantalizingly stronger as they waxed, then easing back when they waned—but she couldn't do anything about it. Even when they fed her, they kept two loaded crossbows trained on her, ready to shoot if she spoke or moved oddly. When she was done, the gag went back on.

The days trickled by. Enough time to get to know every rock in the bare fieldstone walls and floor of her cell, a round room fifteen feet across, with two high, barred windows that let in spears of sunlight and the scent of the sea. There was a locked trapdoor near the middle of the floor, leading down a circular staircase to the storeys below. A simple cot. A chamberpot. And that was all.

Thalaniya would be wondering about her and worrying that something had gone wrong. Her brother, too. She had no way of telling them she was in trouble, for the warriors of Coldhope had taken the pearl amulet, the charm of speaking. Without it, the Voice remained silent to her ears. Perhaps her people would send a party to rescue her. Perhaps the Silvanaes were on their way to break her free.

As the days pooled into weeks, then on toward a month, however, that hope began to fade. If the elves wanted to break her out, where were they? Why were they taking so long? She could think of no answer.

One evening when she was dozing on her cot, as close to real rest as she'd gotten since her capture—the cold prickling of the Hooded One, so close to her and yet so far beyond her reach, kept her mind from absolute rest—she heard muffled voices outside and the scrape of a key in a lock. She sat up quickly and got to her feet like an uncoiling serpent. She'd had her dinner an hour before—chicken broth and unrisen bread, the same as every day. Her minders never disturbed her between then and breakfast. Her flesh tingled as the latch slid back and the door moaned open, grinding inward a little, letting in lamplight. Shedara tensed, sidling slowly toward the door . . .

A man came through. At first, she didn't see who it was. Nor did she care. In an instant, she decided this was it: she would escape now or not at all. Biting down on her gag, she spun herself around, lashing her foot toward the tall figure's head . . .

A hand caught her ankle and shoved it away. Off center, with no arms to balance her, Shedara crashed sideways into the wall. She let out a grunt of pain as her forehead scraped the stone. She felt the warmth of blood on her face, then a sharper pain as her knee hit the floor. Nausea welled up her throat.

"That was stupid," said the man in the doorway. "Did you really think I wouldn't be ready for you?"

Forlo.

Shedara glanced up, tears of pain and frustration welling in her eyes. He looked down at her, a smug smile on his face. The two guards who always watched her cell came up behind him, crossbows ready. She glared poison at all of them, then collapsed onto her back with a groan.

He bent down beside her, a rag in his hand, and pressed it on her forehead. It hurt, but helped with the bleeding. "We need to talk," he said. "If I take your gag off, you'll be good, yes? I don't want Iver or Ramal here to have to shoot you."

Shedara stared up at him, eyes narrowed. What trickery was this? Slowly, she nodded: yes. Forlo reached down and untied the gag. The knot came loose and air poured into her lungs, cool as mountain water. For a moment, the world seemed to glow around her, then it subsided. Forlo stepped back, eyeing her.

"Y—" Shedara began, then her voice caught and she spent the next several breaths coughing. Forlo produced a wineskin, and tossed it to her. Whatever the stuff inside was, it burned like gnomish fire—but it brought her voice back, too. "You have waited a long time to . . . question me."

"I have been occupied," Forlo replied, and he shrugged. "I could have just had you killed. Some lords would have done that and not lost a night's sleep."

"I know." With a struggle Shedara sat up, propped her back against the wall. "So it makes me wonder, why didn't you?"

Forlo shrugged. "I wanted to know more about you. Why you're here. What the statue means to you."

"Too bad."

The other men, Iver and Ramal, grumbled at this, but Forlo held up a hand to silence them, grinning. "Really? And here I thought you might be willing to make a bargain. Ah, well." He rose again, turned his back, started toward the door and held out the gag to the guards. "Give her another month, then we'll see how she feels."

"Wait!" Shedara yelped. She got to her feet, somehow. Forlo stopped, then turned.

"Yes?" he asked. A ghost of a smile quirked his lips.

She sighed, liking this man and hating him all at once. Another time, another place, and she'd gladly have shared a bottle with him. Now, though, his cleverness grated.

"Fine," Shedara said. "Let's talk."

Neither of them told the whole truth, and they both knew it. They sat at the broad table in Coldhope's great hall, Forlo with a big, battle-scarred minotaur beside him,

Shedara backed by Iver and Ramal. He let her eat real food, roast boar and turnips and some kind of greens, with more awful wine to wash it down. She told him the tale of the Hooded One, or most of it. She left out the part about Maladar's spirit being bound within the statue, nor did she mention that the Voice wished to destroy the statue. She did tell him about the shadows, though, and how they had slaughtered Harlad's crew, the dwarves of Uld, and Ruskal. His mouth hardened at this.

"I'd heard Ruskal was murdered by thieves," said the minotaur.

Shedara raised her eyebrows. "You heard wrong."

The bull-man snarled, but Forlo touched his arm. "Never mind, Grath."

The minotaur sat back, looking furious.

"As for us," Forlo went on, "war is coming to these lands, and soon. A Uigan horde masses across the Run. They will cross when the moons align."

Shedara caught her breath. She could sense the moons, their places in the sky, and where they would head next. "A month from now," she breathed.

"Twenty-nine days," Forlo corrected. "I don't have enough men to stop them, and no more are coming. So I'm willing to offer you a deal."

"The statue," Shedara said. "You'll give it to me? For what in return?"

Smiling without humor, Forlo reached beneath the table and pulled out the amulet. Thalaniya's pearl of seeing. It glimmered with enchantment as he set it on the table. "I think I can figure out what this is," he said. "It lets you speak with your queen. Right?"

Shedara nodded. "You want me to contact her."

"Yes."

"And what, ask for reinforcements against this horde?" she asked, scoffing.

"Yes."

Shedara closed her mouth and regarded the man carefully, trying to read him. He seemed honest, but blood of Solis, he was deluded. "My people will be reluctant to help," she said.

Forlo spread his hands. "And I'll be reluctant to give up the Hooded One. But I think we can both manage something, given the circumstances. Do we have a deal?"

The medallion gleamed. Shedara stared at it hungrily. The statue for a few hundred elven bowmen. It seemed a fair trade to her. She hoped Thalaniya would think so, too.

"I will try," she said. "But there is a problem. The magic is weak now. The moons are waning. I can't use the amulet's power for another week."

"A week," Grath muttered. "We don't have a week to spare!"

"Is there no way you can work this spell now?" Forlo asked."

Shedara frowned, her eyes on the medallion. She stroked her chin for a long moment. Then she raised her eyebrows. "Well, there may be *one* way."

The standing stones rose high around them, disappearing into the evening fog, their pinnacles lost in the sky. A fine rain, slightly too heavy to be mist, left the rocks glistening and made the torches gutter. Shedara shivered in the growing dark, cold to the bone: the weather here was strange for summer, as if time followed different rules in the hulderfolk's circle.

The ring stood near Coldhope, a little less than two leagues to the southeast on a bald hilltop that rose above the woods. The Witch-fangs, the local folk called it when they had to call it anything. Mostly they bared their teeth at the tall, white plinths—seventeen in all, six of them fallen over and three leaning precariously—to ward off whatever evil they contained. Cattle that strayed too near the Witch-fangs never gave milk again, or so the stories went. Children sometimes disappeared, though none in living memory. Magic was strong there.

At least that last part's right, Shedara thought, taking a deep breath as she stood in the circle's midst. She could feel the power in them, floating all around her like the air after a lightning strike. She marveled at what the hulder had done with these rings: storing enchantment in them like water in a cistern, to draw from when the moons were weak. She shut her eyes, drinking the power in, her nostrils flared. Sensing.

"Well?" asked Lord Forlo. "Is it enough?"

Shedara ignored Forlo and ignored the surly minotaur with him when he growled and reached for his axe. They needed her. They could learn to be patient. At last she opened her eyes again, looking toward them, faded shapes in the gloom.

"It will do," she said. "Though the damage done to the circle weakens it. I may need your help."

"How, help?" snorted Grath, the bull-man. "We are not wizards."

"But you *can* give me strength," Shedara replied. "I may need your aid, to hold the spell. Will you give it, if the amulet's power isn't enough?"

Forlo nodded. "I will. But no tricks, if you want to keep your head."

Shedara rolled her eyes.

"I don't like this," Grath grumbled.

"You'd like our odds facing the Uigan alone even less, I think," Forlo said. The bull-man didn't answer.

"All right," Shedara declared. "Give me the amulet and cut my bonds. The sooner we start, the better. And stay near me through the spell, lord. If I have need of you, it will happen quickly."

Forlo and Grath exchanged glances. There was a lot of history in that look. Then the Lord of Coldhope strode forward into the circle, moving swiftly through the wet, knee-deep grass. When he reached Shedara he drew a dagger from his belt, reached for her wrists, and cut the bowstrings. They fell away, and a moment later a thousand tiny knives began to prick her palms. She rubbed them together, getting the blood moving again and willing the feeling away. She reached out and he drew the amulet from a pouch. It was quiet, the pearl dark and inert. He let it unspool between his fingers, dropping it down on its chain, then let it fall into Shedara's hand. It felt heavy and cold, like something dead. She shivered again, staving off a question that was growing in her mind.

Begin, she thought. Do it now, before someone loses their nerve.

The gestures were different here. Rather than drawing the magic down from the moons, she adjusted them to focus on the stones instead. Somewhere up there in the fog were orbs of red, silver, and black. These were the hulderfolk's means of collecting sorcery, substituting for Solis and Lunis and—alone of the three in being close to full—Nuvis. They opened to her mind without hesitation, giving up a measure of their power to one who could work it. Just as one did with the moons, except *their* potency was limitless.

The words came without much bidding, though her tongue struggled at first, after so long, to form the complicated sounds. The magic flowed strangely, sluggishly—it had been pent up in the stones for a very long time. The medallion grew warmer, but only slightly. After a few moments she knew she'd been right. She would need help, the strength of another to help knit the spell together. She looked to Forlo, still speaking the spidery words, and nodded.

To his credit, the man didn't hesitate. He stepped forward, hands outstretched. She made one last, grand gesture—gathering in as much power as she could—then thrust her own hands out, clapping them to his. Their fingers locked around each other.

She felt something then, and nearly pulled away at the

shock of it. She'd used common folk to help her with difficult spells before, knew the feeling of them—the strange emptiness where the Art ought to be. But Barreth Forlo was not empty; there was something there. Not much, just a glimmering down deep, but something out of the ordinary. She frowned, studying his face as she drew on his strength and brought the incantation to its climax. The stones' magic surged through her, burning in her veins. The man had no idea he was ensorcelled.

Something to use there, she thought. Something to look into later. Then she put it from her mind.

At last, the medallion was glowing, silvery light pooling on the pearl's surface and beginning to leak out. It had gone from warm to hot in her grasp. She extended her will, forcing it to become stronger, to form images . . . sounds. *Show me*, she thought. *Show me Armach-nesti. Show me the Voice.*

The moment the picture began to waver into view, she knew something was wrong. It was instinct that told her, nothing more, for all she could see was Thalaniya's glade, at the rim of the seeing-pool where she had first glimpsed Maladar the Faceless, high atop his golden palace. It was dark in the elf-home, the last vestiges of twilight fading violet in the west. Stars burned above in a cloud-dotted sky. The trees rustled and murmured in the warm night wind. She felt like she was there, in Armach-nesti, rather than on the rain-soaked hilltop among the hulderstones. Gritting her teeth, she willed the image to form itself clearer, sharper, and stronger.

"Where are we?" murmured Forlo. His face was slack, like a sleepwalker's. He blinked, peering around blearily. "What is this place?"

"Armach-nesti," Shedara replied. "My people's homeland. No *heerikil*—no outsider—has ever come here and lived."

He nodded, taking that in. Tears sheeted his eyes, and she knew it was the beauty of the place that overwhelmed him. The perfect blend of tree, rock, and water, that simply did not exist in the wider world. Certainly not in the lands of man and minotaur. The starlight danced on the pool's surface, disturbed by ripples from the waterfall on the far end. Astarin's fingers, she missed this—all the more so after so long in Coldhope's tower!

Yet something wasn't right. It was like the smell of some pest that had died within a house's walls . . . had died, and was rotting. Just the faintest whiff of decay. Grimacing, she looked this way and that.

"Highness?" she asked. "Thalaniya? Where are—"

The shadow struck her from behind. She felt its blade rake across her back and only reflex kept it from cutting her open. Twisting and sucking in a breath at the hot pain the creature's knife left behind, she spun to face the threat. It was one of the little ones, the shriveled fiends that once had been kender, before they became something else. She heard Forlo cry out at the sight of it and saw him draw his sword. She wondered, briefly, what Grath might do . . . on the hilltop . . . the man would have unsheathed his weapon there as well. If the minotaur tried to defend Forlo, he would surely disrupt the spell. She prayed to all three moons that Grath would stay put.

Apparently, the moons listened.

She stared at the little shadow and heard a second one creeping up, just out of sight. "Another behind us," she said. "Kill them. Now, or we're dead."

Forlo needed no more prompting. He lunged, his sword lashing out. He was good with the blade, for the swing knocked the kender-thing's dagger away, then bit deep into the creature's side. It shrieked, and a breath later it unraveled, turning to smoky shadowstuff before her eyes. Even as that was happening, its mate leaped at Shedara. She raised her hands, wishing she still had her knives . . . Abyss, *anything* to defend herself with. A tree branch, even. She stumbled back, trying to give ground, and fell at the seeing-pool's edge. Her hand dipped into the water: cold. The kender-thing was on her in a blink, its blade darting toward her throat . . .

Then it, too, screamed and tore asunder into charcoal wisps that vanished on the night breeze. Forlo stood over her, bits of shadow dripping off his sword like blood. He looked down at her. She looked back. He was confused, she could tell, but he held out his free hand and helped her to rise.

"What in Hith's Cauldron were *those*?" he asked.

She shook her head. "I have no idea. But they seek the statue."

He turned pale and grimaced. "What of your people? Where are they?"

Shedara didn't answer. To put words to her thoughts might make them real. She looked around again, for any sign of the Silvanaes. Her brother . . . Nalaran . . . Thalaniya. Anyone. But there was no one in the grove, and there were no lights among the trees. The elves were gone. She swore under her breath.

"Shedara," Forlo pressed. "What—"

A horrendous noise from above cut him off and made them both start and look up. It was the shriek of a gnomish steamwhistle, the roar of a tylor, and the bellow of a madman, all at once. Forlo was bewildered, but Shedara knew it at once, the recognition sliding a cold spear into her stomach.

She had seen dragons before. She knew what they sounded like.

And there it was . . . yes, winging high above, black against the night sky, its passage blocking out the stars. The wyrm was enormous, with eyes that burned like dying coals and scales that glistened like obsidian. Its batlike wings seemed to cloak half the firmament as they spread wide and the dragon wheeled in a circle above the glade.

Softly, Forlo wept. The fear had taken him, and Shedara felt her own will begin to falter. A voice in her head told her to run, to hide, for the gods' sake to get away from that place. She fought it back and stayed rooted to the spot, trembling and pale. The effort nearly broke her.

There was something on the dragon's back. The wyrm had a rider, clad in black fluttering robes. She could barely make the figure out, but she knew it was the same one she'd seen coming aboard Harlad's ship. All at once, she knew what had happened. It had seen her and marked her as Silvanaes. It thought she had taken the statue and had gone to Armach to seek it . . . and to take vengeance.

She thought of the dwarves of Uld, lying broken and scattered around their village. She pictured the elves the same way, bloodless and dead. Rage exploded in her, and a bloodthirsty scream burst from her mouth, aimed up at the dragon and the one who rode it.

I will find you next, said a voice. It sounded like it came from within her own head. *I will do to you what I did to her.*

And with that, the cloaked form let something drop. It was small, white, round, and trailing a silver streamer. Moving slowly, Shedara reached out, stepped forward, and caught it. She looked down at the thing in her arms and groaned in horror.

It was Thalaniya's head, the eyes rolled over white and the mouth pinched with agony. The torn flesh where her neck had been was gray. Bloodless.

Shedara stared at the head, bile surging up her throat. Then sensation fled her, and she dropped to her knees, then onto her side. The world drained away.

The world came flowing back, cold, misty. She opened her eyes. She was back on the bald hill, near the feet of the Witch-fangs. Forlo and Grath stood over her. They had dragged her out of the circle. The amulet was cold in her hand once more. She opened her fingers, and wasn't at all surprised to see the pearl had broken, a long jagged crack running through its heart. Its magic was gone and would never return. She let it fall to the ground.

For a long time, no one spoke. Then Forlo shifted, turning his sword in his hand.

"That was the Voice," he said. "Wasn't it? They killed her."

Shedara nodded slowly. Thalaniya's severed head wasn't there with her, but she could still see it in her mind. She could see the fear and agony on her face. She took a deep, shuddering breath and let it out.

"I don't think," she said, her voice seeming to come from far away, "that my people will be able to help you."

Chapter 21

UNKNOWN, THE DREAMING GREEN

It seemed, when the world came swimming back, that a thousand bees were buzzing inside Hult's skull. He groaned, lifting a hand to place on his forehead. His body responded sluggishly, aching. His mouth was dry and his tongue was thick and swollen. Where am I? he wondered. What happened?

Then he remembered the arrows. Remembered them entering his body. Not killing shots, but enough to bring him down. Elf-shot arrows. The pain had been incredible. Now, though, he felt nothing. No lancing agony that flared with every breath. No strange sensation of something *in* his body, of wood rubbing against his muscles, or of steel grinding on his bones. Biting his lip, he reached to where the second arrow had gone in, just below his collarbone. His fingers found bare skin and a hard knot where the shaft had been. A scar. Someone had healed him.

"Who—" he mumbled, trying to sit up.

"Be still!"

He froze, recognizing Chovuk's voice. The voice, and the feeling in it. The Boyla sounded tense and troubled. Afraid? Not a thought Hult would dare speak aloud . . . but yes, there was something fearful in how his master spoke.

"Do not move!" Chovuk called out again. "Listen to me. It will take you if you get up now."

Hult could hear something else now—the low, gurgling hiss of something very large. It was no animal he knew, no beast of the plains. It was, he thought, almost like a dragon . . . but not quite. Reptile, definitely. He heard the leathery scrape of scales against . . . sand? Yes, he was lying on sand. Strange. He could still smell the trees and flowers of the Dreaming Green.

It took a moment for him to find the courage to look. Finally he managed it. He was lying on his back on a floor of fine white sand . . . on the floor of a pit? Yes, that was it. A deep pit—five men on each other's shoulders couldn't reach its top. It had stone walls, and the shadows of pines encircled it above. The elves had built it, he was sure . . . and a breath later, he saw the proof. There, dimly lit by the stars, were the *merkitsa*—dozens of elves, ringing the upper lip of the pit. They were strange looking creatures, with long, braided hair dyed bright colors, red, green, and gold. Their tunics and breeches were just as vibrant and were embroidered with scenes of animals and hunters. Their limbs were long and slender, their chins and noses pointed, and their eyes slanted and pale. Large silver plugs were set in their earlobes, and their cheeks and foreheads were daubed with paint, making whorls and jagged lines and tiger-stripes. They stood utterly silent and expressionless, watching like the ancient stone statues that dotted the Tamire.

Hult had never been so frightened in his life.

He saw Chovuk a moment later . . . not down on the sand as he'd expected, but up on the rim with the elves! The Boyla stood between two of the most gaudily arrayed of the *merkitsa*, an older and a younger elf who looked too alike to be anything but father and son. Even in his dazed, confused state, Hult recognized them as the heads of whatever clan had captured them. But why was Chovuk with them? Wasn't he their prisoner, too?

Another low, hissing growl startled him and brought him back to the immediate danger. Holding his breath, he glanced up and over his shoulder, taking care not to move too quickly. When he saw what was there, he had to bite his tongue to keep from crying out.

The first thing he made out in the dim light was teeth. A great many of them, in fact, long and sharp as spearheads and curving wickedly back along a long, blunt-tipped snout. It had scales, too—the colors of rust and sun-bleached bone, mottled in uneven patches. It had a short neck and a thick body with a long, whiplike tail. All of the creature was knobby and uneven, more like rock than flesh to the eye. The creature had squinting, stupid, hungry eyes set high on its reptilian head. And in place of legs, where they might be found on a lizard, it had flippers tipped with spurs of glistening horn. The thing had to be more than seven paces long . . . maybe as many as ten, snout to tail-tip. The stink of its breath, hot metal and rancid blood, made his nose burn and his eyes water.

Hatori, the creature was called. Hult had heard tales of it on his youthful journey into the deserts of Panak. Such creatures dwelt in the sands, lying half-submerged, pretending to be outcroppings of stone, then snatching up prey that strayed too close. The beasts grew huge in the wild wastes, as much as sixty paces in length, large enough to swallow whole caravans. This one was young, probably only a few years out of the egg—still large enough to bite him in half, though. The *merkitsa* must have caught it as a hatchling and brought it here to use for . . . public amusement. Throwing outsiders into its pit to enjoy the slaughter. There were the cracked bones of previous victims strewn on the floor of the pit.

Hult stared at the monster and realized he was going to die there. Part of him wished he hadn't woken, that while he'd been unconscious those fangs had ripped him apart. He thrust such thoughts aside, ashamed. He was Uigan. He would fight. He would not let the hatori slay him without a struggle. He looked around, seeking a weapon. He was unsurprised to see that he was completely naked, without even a breechcloth to cover his manhood. He would have been amazed to see anything like a sword in the pit with him. No, there was nothing useful . . . even his dragon-claw necklace, which he'd never taken off since becoming a man, was gone.

The hatori hissed, inching forward. Hult had to do something soon.

"Be careful," cautioned Chovuk from above. "No sudden moves, *tenach*, if you value your life."

Sound advice, Hult thought wryly—as close as he'd come to sarcasm in his life. Slowly, he sat up, tucked his legs under himself, and twisted smoothly to his feet. His braid, unbound, spilled down over his shoulders as he faced the beast. It was two paces away, the countless sharp teeth glistening.

Great Jijin, Hult prayed. Let me survive this and I will burn the fat of twenty goats in your name. I will take the heads of a hundred enemies. I only wish to keep my life.

He took a step back. The hatori hissed and wriggled toward him, its flippers pushing it along. Its tail lashed behind it, throwing up sprays of sand. He had nowhere to go, but kept moving away, never once taking his eyes off the creature. Its gaze was malevolent in a dull-witted way: the beast craved meat and reveled in the kill. The elves probably kept their pet hungry, to make sure it was always ready for prey.

"What do I do?" he called, as loudly as he dared. "Master?"

"Just keep moving. But don't run. They have promised to give you your *shuk* if you survive a hundred-count."

"Ah," Hult said. "And what is the count now?"

"Twenty-three."

Hult swore inwardly. The hatori kept pace with him, always a breath away from charging forward. He backed up and started to turn to his right when he sensed a wall behind him. If the beast cornered him and pinned him against the stone, if he tripped over anything, it was over. If he spooked it, if he let it get too close, if it simply got the urge to strike....

He shook his head, clearing such thoughts. Just keep moving, he told himself. Don't think of anything else.

"Forty," said the Boyla.

Hult kept moving and turned enough to see the tunnel on the pit's far side, which no doubt led to the hatori's lair. A grate of fire-hardened wood was raised on cords of sinew. Gnawed skulls—some of men, others of larger beings, with sloped foreheads—rested in niches to either side. The *merkitsa* had been feeding their pet well and the sight made him shiver. If it had killed the First People, the Abaqua ogres who lived in the mountains to the east, he was in a lot of trouble.

"Sixty," Chovuk intoned, as Hult too counted silently.

At seventy-one, it happened: a cracked bone, half-buried in the sand. He stepped on it and felt it dig into the sole of his left foot, felt it break the skin. He stumbled, nearly fell, and caught himself—but there was blood on the sand, and its scent was in the air. The hatori tensed, a row of scales on the back of its neck standing up. Its jaws parted, ropes of green spittle hanging from its teeth. A roar, a noise like tearing metal, burst from its mouth.

"*Run!*" the Boyla yelled.

But Hult couldn't run very well. His foot was hurt and bleeding, the bone still stuck in his flesh. Even if it hadn't been, fear would have slowed him. It stiffened every joint in his body. He could only stare, his mouth gaping in a voiceless scream, as the hatori threw itself at him.

Sheer luck kept his next breath from being his last. The monster's jaws snapped shut an eyeblink too soon. The front fangs grazed his leg, drawing yet more blood from a long gash. A moment later, the monster's full weight smashed into him, bearing him to the pit's floor. The breath exploded from his lungs as it slammed him to the ground. Its scales scratched his body, opening more small cuts. It bellowed, mad with the stink of blood. Its maw opened and snapped shut on the air, then turned toward Hult again, hovering over his face.

Hult groped to both sides, clawing at the sands. The hatori was too heavy to heave off of himself and too strong to wrestle. He had to find something . . . *anything* that might help. "Eighty-five," he heard. He would have his sword soon . . . if he could keep the thing from ripping his head off first.

At last, after what seemed like hours, his groping fingers found a long, thick bone: the upper arm of an ogre. He seized it, brought it around, and clouted the hatori on the side of the head. Not hard enough to do any real harm—but it still surprised the creature. The hatori made a hacking sound, then its eyes narrowed and its jaws spread wide again.

Hult moved quickly, jamming the bone between the creature's fangs and lower jaw. Let the monster's bite do the rest, he thought desperately, as the hatori clamped down.

The bone bent and splintered a little, but didn't break. The hatori bellowed, its jaws wedged open, tossing its head back and forth. Wildly, Hult punched and kicked at the monster . . . found another bone and pounded away. The weight lifted off him, enough for him to squirm away. He was covered in blood and cut in a dozen places. He limped away, his injured foot blazing, as the hatori thrashed behind him. There was a cracking sound as the bone finally gave way.

"One hundred!" Chovuk cried. *"Tenach!"*

Something flew down from above, hit the sand point-first, and stuck there, quivering. His *shuk*. Hult dived for it. He heard the hatori wriggling after him, snarling in rage at having been outmaneuvered thus far. Hult hit the ground flat out and reached for the blade—then, in a moment of agony like he'd never felt before, the hatori's maw snapped shut on his leg.

He grabbed his sword, screaming, and whipped around. He didn't look at his leg. He couldn't bear the sight that went with the awful, sawing pain. In another instant the beast's fangs would grind through his shin, then tear the limb from his body. Bellowing, he thrust his *shuk* at its face, directly in its eye.

The hatori shrieked, nearly yanking the sword from his grip, then almost broke his wrist when he held on. It jerked its head this way and that until the sword came free, leaving a ruined, gelatinous hole where its eye had been. In its agony it released his leg and Hult pulled away, rolling across the sand to get away from the beast. It squealed a while longer and he took the time to stand up again. He couldn't put any weight on his injured leg. He could feel that it was held together only by a ravaged bone and a few strips of flesh. He ignored the crippling wound, brought his *shuk* up, and leaped forward, swinging it with all his strength.

The blow caught the monster directly in the middle of its snout. Steel sheared through scales, flesh . . . bone. Half the monster's mouth fell away and black blood sprayed everywhere, darkening the sand. He stabbed the hatori again, this time in the other eye. Blind and mutilated, the creature wailed piteously. Above, Hult heard the creak of bowstrings: several elven archers had pulled their weapons out, ready to put the beast out of its misery.

Hult held up a hand. "He is mine!" he called angrily.

Wondering, the *merkitsa* bowmen relaxed again. Hult hopped forward—not using his half-severed leg—then reversed his grip on his *shuk* and brought it down on the spot where the hatori's skull met its spine. Its cries stopped and it fell limp. It let out its final breath as a whimper.

All was silent. He looked up. The elves remained still, their painted faces devoid of emotion. The archers held their arrows upon their strings and for an instant he thought they might now aim at him instead. But that moment passed and they did nothing, and his eyes moved on to where Chovuk stood. The Boyla was smiling, his face aglow with pride. Hult found he couldn't return the smile. He thought of the Wretched Ones' hideous king, deep beneath Mount Xagal, and how the two of them had fought that monster together. This time, though, Chovuk had left him to fight the hatori alone, unarmed and naked. And he had nearly died.

The *shuk* fell from his hand onto the sands. He looked down at the ruin of his leg. There was blood everywhere, and more pouring from the wound. He felt the strength draining from his body. He sat down heavily, the world blurring, and leaned back. He rested against the hatori's scaly hide, bowed his head, and shut his eyes.

When he woke again, he lay in a shaded bower on a bed of bearskins over pine boughs. Sunshine and blue sky peeked between the branches overhead. Birds sang and a brook babbled nearby, out of sight. The scent of lavender hung in the air.

My leg, he thought, remembering what had happened. He tried to sit up and looked down. Woolen blankets covered his body. He could feel his foot, but he'd known warriors who'd lost limbs in raids. There were a few in every tribe, and often they spoke of ghost-pains, the sense that a missing part was still there. He reached out and tried to pull back the blankets, but couldn't find the strength to lift his arms. Gods, he ached. . . .

"Here, *tenach*," said a voice to his right. "Let me."

Chovuk Boyla sat at his side. Gently, he reached out and pulled back the blankets. Hult caught his breath, anticipating the sourness of bile . . . then his gorge receded again when he saw his leg. It was still there, intact, the flesh white and ridged where the hatori had nearly ripped it off. Like the arrow wounds, it was miraculously healed.

"The *merkitsa*," said Chovuk. "They themselves healed your wounds. You did well, Hult. Won honor for yourself and for me. The elves would have killed me if you failed. I staked my life on you, and you did not let me down."

Hult felt a flush of pride, which quickly abated. "You could have killed the hatori easily, had you fought for yourself," he said. "If you'd changed into the tiger. Why me?"

"Because I could not!" Chovuk snapped, then looked away. His face turned dark. "Because you interrupted before the Teacher could give me the power to change my skin again. Because you meddled, you nearly died—and I with you. So do not try to lay blame on me, *tenach*. I let you fight because I had to, and to teach you a lesson—never interrupt again when the Teacher and I are communing."

Hult sat silently, ashamed. Ashamed of himself, for having doubted Chovuk's courage—but of Chovuk as well. He had no doubt the robed figure he'd attacked in the pool the night the elves captured them was a servant of darkness. No uncertainty that it was evil. And his master was in league with this evil, had used the powers it granted to him all these months to become Boyla, to win the alliance with the goblins, to defeat the Kazar, and to throw down the walls of Malton. And he would use the evil again when the time came to cross the Tiderun. He looked away, hoping the disappointment and dismay in his face didn't show.

"There, *tenach*, do not hate yourself," the Boyla said, misunderstanding. "You did not know about the Teacher. I should have told you myself, but . . . I did not know how. It must seem strange to you, to see me consorting with such a man. But I ask you to trust me. This is the way to victory and glory for our people. Look at what we have already gained by it!"

"Yes, master," Hult said, nodding dully. "What happens to us now?"

"Now we are free to go, when you are mended—and to take with us what we came for," said Chovuk, smiling.

He turned, looking behind him. Two figures emerged from the shadows beneath the trees: the two elves he'd been standing beside at the fighting-pit, elder and younger, kin. They looked even stranger up close: feral, like wild cats. They were taut as bowstrings, but their faces—both painted with crimson stripes—showed no emotion at all, even when they bobbed their heads before them.

"This is Tho-ket, chieftain of the Singing Rain clan," said Chovuk, nodding at the elder, who steepled his fingers before him and said something in a language that sounded like the twittering of birds. "And his son, Eldako."

The younger elf stepped forward, also saying something unintelligible. His hair was the color of flame, and it hung in braids to his waist. He wore a breastplate made from some giant insect's shell, iridescent and shimmering in the daylight, with a longbow and a quiver of arrows slung across his back. Solemnly the younger elf pressed his fingers against his throat, then reached out to touch Hult's. Hult smiled, understanding it was a show of respect. He had impressed the *merkitsa* by slaying their dangerous beast in the pit.

"Eldako will be riding with us, back south," Chovuk explained. "Tho-ket has granted him leave to join the horde."

Hult blinked, staring at his master in shock. "Just him?" he exclaimed. "We rode all this way and nearly died in these accursed lands . . . all for *one* elf?"

Eldako said something, and Tho-ket bristled too. "This *one elf* is best archer in all Tamire," said the chieftain in halting Uigan. "Is my son I give. You should be glad, and not asking more."

Hult flushed, lowering his eyes: he hadn't realized the elves could understand him. "I am sorry."

"It is all right, *tenach*," Chovuk said. "You do not understand, and that is well. But know that we will need

Eldako's bow when we cross the Run. And perhaps before then, as well."

The Boyla turned to Tho-ket and spoke a few words in the *merkitsa* language. Hult supposed he should have been surprised by this ability, but he wasn't. Nothing about his master surprised him any more.

"We will leave you now," said Chovuk, turning back to Hult. "Rest. You will need your strength again soon. We ride south on the morrow, we three. And from there, to the League and victory."

They left then, his master and the two elves, disappearing into the woods. Hult lay back on the pine-bough bed, the peace of the woods all around him, and shuddered. He had never felt so unsettled. His master was a thrall of evil. He knew that now. He was not the man he'd once been.

But what of it? He was *tenach*, sworn on his life to protect Chovuk. Hult lay there a long time, thinking.

Chapter 22

COLDHOPE KEEP, THE IMPERIAL LEAGUE

Smoke and screams filled the air: the dying, the wounded, and men, women, and children fleeing for their lives. Everywhere there was movement—soldiers charging one way, their spears and swords reflecting the glare of burning buildings; bellowing figures on horses and hunched shapes on wolfback galloping the other way; and common folk scattering in all directions, trying to escape. The riders ran them down when they could, trampling them under their hooves or running them through with long lances. Bodies and parts of bodies lay everywhere, islands in the rivers of blood that poured down the cobbled streets.

Rudil was burning, and Forlo watched.

It was so real, so . . . *there*. Like Armach-nesti had been on the night they found the shadows had slaughtered the Silvanaes. Forlo knew he was sitting in the great hall of Coldhope, surrounded by stone walls and tapestries and banners, but to his eyes he was in the League's second great colony north of the Run. It was dusk and the red and silver moons swelled above the eastern horizon, the reason the spell worked in the great hall now, when ten days ago they had been forced to use the hulder-ring to aid Shedara's magic. He could hear the sounds and smell the fear of battle and the stink of burning buildings. He was even half-convinced that, if he tried, he could reach out and *touch* the Uigan and goblins who charged all around him, unaware he was there.

But he stood still instead, a lump in his throat as he watched the barbarian horde tear the town apart. Rudil, a peaceful port that had never seen war and sported little in the way of fortification. In the dying afternoon light, wave upon wave of horsemen descended upon it from the north. He'd watched the flash of their sabers, seen their helmet-plumes streaming in the wind, and knew for a certainty the town would fall. And he'd known, in that same moment, what he'd suspected since Sammek Thale told him of Malton's fall: he could not stop the horde. Not alone. Coldhope was doomed.

He heard a sound and glanced to his right. Essana. She had refused to leave, even when Thale offered her a well-appointed cabin aboard his ship. Forlo had begged her to go with the merchant, but the next morning the *White Worm* set sail for southern waters without her aboard. Now with him and Grath she stared at the destruction all around and watched as a pack of goblins chased down several young priestesses of Sinar . . . hacked them to death with cleavers and axes . . . and fed the pieces to their wolves. She saw a minotaur stagger out of a blazing house, the whole upper half of his body on fire, then collapse in a heap across the broken-necked corpse of a young boy. She looked on as a gang of Uigan riders, led by an armored chief, dragged the torn and battered corpses of the town's elder council on ropes behind their horses. One broke away and tumbled end over end to finish sitting up, its head dangling backward from its neck. She watched all of it and wept.

Forlo felt bad for her, but he also felt a new kinship with his wife. *This* is battle, he wanted to tell her. This was my life, all those years. This is what I want to spare you. But he said nothing. None of them did. They only gazed numbly around them as Rudil fell to flame and sword.

There would be no prisoners. A few would flee, mostly by water, though Rudil's harbor had fallen much faster than Malton's. A handful might survive, somehow, hidden amid the rubble. The rest would die that night and in the days to come. Then . . . then the League's time in Northern Hosk would be done. The waters of the Tiderun would lower, then run dry, and the riders would come flooding across.

He turned to Shedara and saw the strain on the elf's face, the pallor caused by holding together the magic. He nodded to her, sweeping his hand in an arc before him. "Enough," he said. "We don't need to see any more."

Gratefully, she let the magic go. The images came apart like a crumbling mosaic, pieces falling away to reveal the great hall in their place. The sounds and smells faded as well. It was disorienting, and for a breath Forlo thought he might vomit. Essana put a hand to her mouth, then buried her face in her hands. Grath, leaning against the table across from Forlo, made a sour face.

"Cowards," the minotaur spat. "They cannot live like civilized men, so they fight like animals, without honor. My axe hungers for them already."

"You and your cohort won't last an *hour*!" Shedara shot back. She staggered to sit down on a chair, but nearly missed and had to catch herself. She shook all over.

The minotaur glowered at her, eyes burning and sharp teeth bared. He drew a sharp breath, but Forlo spoke before he could reply. "You're not a prisoner here any more," he told Shedara. "You're free to leave."

"And where would I go?" she answered, not for the first time. "Armach-nesti is overrun and my queen is dead. Shall I make for Thenol, or the Marak Valleys? Or Kristophan, perhaps? The statue isn't safe in any of those places, and you know it."

"It's not safe here, either," Forlo noted—again, not for the first time. This was already a familiar argument.

She shrugged. "Safer than most places. The shadows haven't come here yet."

"Enough about the bloody statue!" snapped Essana, looking up. Forlo flinched at what he saw in her eyes, surrounded by swollen, red skin. Her lips quivered as she spoke, stretching her mouth into an ugly shape. "We've got to do something. We've got to find a way to stop them."

"There *is* no way," Forlo said. "Starlight, you have to leave. Find someplace safe to protect our son."

She shook her head, laying a hand on her belly—the swelling just visible now. Her eyes shone in the lamplight. She didn't say a word. Forlo felt, for a flickering instant, the urge to reach across and strike her, to grab her and *shake* some sense into her. Instead he turned and walked away, moving quickly out the door to the Northwatch. It was hot out. Summer was wearing on and the air was close and still. He walked to the railing and stared past the shimmering water at the ominously dark far shore. Nothing was left there, across the Run. Nothing stood between the horde and Coldhope any more—once the moons aligned.

With an inarticulate snarl, he punched the balustrade. His fist came away bloody, and he sucked at his cut knuckles in silence.

Heavy, booted feet broke the silence. Grath. He didn't turn as the minotaur approached and came to stand beside him. Neither of them spoke for some time.

"This is hard," Forlo said at last. "I've faced my own death enough times to be used to it. But her . . . and the child. . . ." He trailed off, waving his hand helplessly.

Grath nodded. "If somehow Sargas lets me live through this, I swear I'll cut out Rekhaz's black heart for not sending more men. If the whole Sixth were here—"

"Then they'd all die with us. You know that." Forlo's lip curled. "You saw how many there are. It'd take half the imperial army to stop them. No, Rekhaz made the right call. Let us slow them down. We expendable humans will . . . soften them up, and once he has the crown he can fight them properly."

Silence. Grath didn't argue. Waves broke against the rocks below.

"They'll come over at the Lost Road," Forlo added, nodding to the west. The Tiderun narrowed that way, down to a neck where the sea floor was rocky and the crossing was easy. Two days' ride, or about. "We'll have to face them there."

"Good a place as any," Grath agreed. "And better than most. We'll have the terrain on our side. Hold them longer and do some real damage. You could make her leave, you know. We can spare a couple soldiers to take her out of here."

"Abduct her, you mean."

The minotaur shrugged. Forlo thought about it. The idea was tempting . . . but he couldn't bring himself to do it. Essana had lived here longer than him, and that counted for something. She was the lady of Coldhope. He sighed.

"I'm going to bed," he said, turning away from the water.

Grath nodded, still staring out at the Run. "Try not to dream."

Forlo let out a mirthless laugh and walked away, back into the keep and up to his bedchamber. Essana was already there, asleep or pretending. He watched her for a time from the doorway, the curve of her back lit by Solis through a window, then sighed and started undressing. Naked, he lay down beside her. He fell asleep holding her, his hand touching her belly.

When the nightmares came, he prayed they would be about Rudil. But they were not.

He woke with a pain in his chest. His heart was beating so fast he thought it was going to burst. He lay blanket-tangled on the edge of the bed, far from Essana.

She slept on, moaning quietly with bad dreams of her own.

A face floated in the dark before Forlo's eyes: the same cold, dead face he saw every night. The dream didn't change. Every time he closed his eyes, every time he tried to sleep, he found himself back in the temple, in the tunnel under Hawkbluff. And there, standing before him with feral eyes and fingers hooked into talons, was his dead son. A son who didn't even have a name yet.

He got up, as he always did. He threw on a long-skirted tunic, enough for modesty, and walked barefooted to the door. He went down the steps to the darkened great hall. Maybe get some wine, he thought, or some cold chicken and potatoes. The cook would have left some for him in the kitchen; the servants were used to his nightly wanderings. After that, some air on the Northwatch. The moons were much higher now. Grath would have gone down to the cohort's encampment to be with the men.

"More nightmares?" asked a voice from the shadows.

Forlo nearly jumped out of his skin. He reached for a sword he wasn't wearing and made fists instead.

"Who—" he began.

Shedara stepped forward, into a pool of light. She might have been smiling; it was hard to tell. The color had returned to her face, strength flowing through her veins again after the spell.

"I couldn't sleep, either," she said. "Not after what we saw."

He nodded. "They'll be rounding up captives now. Executing them."

"They'll use knives, or trample them with their horses. Won't want to waste the arrows." She steepled her fingers and glanced away. "I'll take her, if you want. Just promise me I can have the statue too, and I'll make sure your wife's far from here when the Uigan come."

"That's a kind offer," he said. "But it's not my choice to make."

"It can be."

"No."

Shedara rolled her eyes. "At least let me help you with your dreams, then. You're not going to be much good to anyone if you haven't slept for weeks when they cross the Run."

He scowled and looked away. "I don't need any help."

"Of course not," she said. "You *like* dreaming of your unborn son as a walking corpse."

Forlo caught his breath and stumbled back as though she'd punched him in the chest. He stared at her a moment, then fury boiled inside him. "How do you know so much?"

"I'm talented," she replied. "I hear you yelling in your sleep, every night. Half the *keep* can hear. I've no idea how Essana sleeps through it. After the first few days, I cast a spell to look into your mind. I needed to know what could make a man like you make a noise like that. Now I know."

He glared at her for a breath longer, then looked away, ashamed. His face grew warm. He shut his eyes. Gods, he just wanted the dreams to *stop*.

"I can help you," she said. "Let me share your dream. I know magic to keep it from breaking. There's sorcery in you, Forlo—a spell, working deep in your mind. I think it has something to do with these dreams of yours. This nightmare about your son . . . it's not real, but it's hiding something else. Something you don't want to remember. Or can't."

He looked at her, his eyes wide. "Something in the temple?"

Shedara nodded.

"All right," he said wearily. "Not tonight. Tomorrow. Then, will you please leave with the statue?"

Chapter 23

THE TEMPLE OF HITH, THENOL

"I know this place," Shedara said, looking up and down the dark tunnel in Forlo's dream, with its carvings of demons and skeletons leering redly in the soldiers' torchlight.

Forlo looked at her, eyebrows raised. He was dressed as a warrior, in his plate armor and the red and blue surcoat of the Sixth, emblazoned with golden horns to mark him as a marshal. He was spattered with mud and bits of gristle—leavings of the walking corpses he and his men had fought on the marshy ground outside. A cut above his left eye leaked blood that dripped down to his bearded jaw in a shocking crimson line. His sword flashed fire-glow orange.

Shedara wore the same simple leathers she'd had on when she cast the spell, back in the lightless shadows of Forlo's bedchamber. She was still in that room—some part of her remembered she sat in a chair at this man's bedside, her right hand laid upon his forehead as he slept, his wife and the minotaur, Grath, close by, observing. The other two were not inside the dream and would see nothing of what passed, although they might hear some of the words she spoke, mumbled through white-clenched lips as the moons' power coursed through her.

She was not a part of the dream—his dream. But she

could walk beside him, talk to him, and watch. This was not real, she reminded herself again and again—it was only memory, clouded by time and whatever magic had been cast on Forlo, the mystery she was determined to solve. She walked not the halls of Hawkbluff, but of Barreth Forlo's mind.

"I have been here before," she said. "I was sent to steal something from the Thenolites at the start of the Godless Night. I came this very way, I think."

"What did you steal?" he whispered, though his voice sounded strangely loud in the stillness.

She thought a moment, then shook her head. "I don't remember. Some Hithian relic, I'm sure. It was forty years ago—I've had a lot of jobs, since then. Even elven memories fade."

Forlo considered this and seemed to decide she wasn't lying. "This is where the worst part begins," he said. "I've just sent Grath down a passage back there, with half my men."

He nodded behind them, into the shadows. There were soldiers with him, men and minotaurs alike, about a dozen strong. The humans were all afraid. With the bull-men it was harder to tell. Shedara stared back down the tunnel, her brow furrowing, then turned to peer ahead again.

"This is the right way," she said. "I recall that much. It leads to the Great Fane."

"And Ondelos," Forlo said.

"Do you remember that?"

He thought about it and shook his head. "Nothing. There's something—it's like a wall of fog, covering my memories."

"I know," she said. She could *feel* the obscuring magic, just ahead. Certainly it lay before the Fane, where the bishop was probably praying to his dark god. Where he hid, awaiting his doom. "We should keep moving. The dream pulls us."

And it did—a subtle tug, like a breeze blowing them from behind. *This way.* Forlo seemed to feel the pull too, for he nodded and held out his free hand, motioning them both forward. They walked, the soldiers following behind. The others didn't seem to think it was strange she was there—but then, they weren't real people. It was all in Forlo's mind.

She saw the little shape even before he did, and stiffened, the hairs on the back of her neck standing straight. The torches made her elvensight hazy, but the shape was so cold. That was what made Forlo shout in his sleep, what woke him every night and sent him out onto the Northwatch, gasping for air. It was his unborn son, a child of maybe four or five summers, as humans reckoned it. A boy who would never see six.

"Hold," Shedara breathed, stretching her arm out to block Forlo's path. "If you get too close, the dream will break."

He obeyed, suddenly pale, his eyes wide, like black pools. He was shaking a little and the tip of his sword quivered before him.

"What now?" he asked, his voice almost inaudible.

She studied the dead boy, standing still in the dim before them and watching them with eyes rolled back in their sockets. His mouth hung slack and a rubbery rope of drool hung from his lower lip. The boy wasn't real . . . he was a dream, not a memory. Probably brought on and given his form by the dark crevices of Forlo's own deepest thoughts, when he learned Essana was with child. The human mind possessed a strangeness Shedara would never fully fathom.

Staring at the little corpse, she saw the threads of magic, winding and tangling around the boy, binding it to something—whatever spell was blocking Forlo's memory. The magic threads drifted like strands of spidersilk, black, writhing, and leading back down the tunnel. She knew then what she had to do.

"Leave it to me," she said. "Whatever happens, don't move from where you stand."

Forlo said nothing, only grimaced as the dead child in the tunnel lolled its head, making rasping sounds in the back of its throat. Shedara stepped forward and the dream-boy snapped back to itself, tensing with a snarl. It sniffed the air, its long-nailed fingers twisting into hooks. She ignored it and did not fear it. It was not real. It could only harm her if she believed in it.

She reached out, focusing her mind on its binding-spell, calling on the magic that coursed through her veins. The air seemed to ripple and quiver, making a shimmering wake behind her hand as it darted toward the child—then deliberately missed him, grabbing hold of the black threads instead.

They were cold to the touch, as cold as anything she'd ever felt. Cold enough to burn, and she caught her breath and nearly let them go. But she didn't. She fought through the jolt of dark power that surged out of them, tightened her grip . . . and, with a violent wrench, ripped them away from Forlo's dead son. The apparition screamed, its face bunching into wrinkles around a huge, blackened mouth . . . then dissolved like sand, vanishing in the time it took for her to draw her next breath.

The spell was almost broken. But she still held the threads. They had to be destroyed. Shedara focused her mind on them, and sent a single thought into each and every fiber. *Break.*

And they broke. One by one, like a harp with a blade drawn across it. She even imagined they made sounds—a faint, glasslike ringing as they gave way. Behind her Forlo shuddered, and the walls of the tunnel shifted, swelling and contracting like a living thing. Shedara held her breath, worried he might wake and end the dream before her work was finished. Instead he groaned, and the walls grew still again. She exhaled, slowly.

"Is it gone?" he asked, his voice shaking.

She glanced back at him. His face was as white as marble and there were deep shadows under his eyes. Breaking the spell had hurt him, but he would recover. He would be better for having gone through this, for knowing what had happened in the Thenolites' high church. She hoped so, anyway.

"Gone," she repeated. "We need to go on."

He nodded, trembling. Not wanting to move, he took a step anyway, then another. She fell in beside him, resting a comforting hand on his shield arm, and they walked on down the tunnel together.

They walked in silence and darkness for a long time. Nothing came to thwart them and nothing appeared out of the gloom, until finally, a door faded into view at the edge of the torchlight. The door was tall, fifteen feet high, and made of black stone. Chunks of red crystal—garnets, by Shedara's guess, worth a small fortune on their own— were set into it, forming the shape of a skeletal hand. Yes, she had been here before. Had gone through these very doors, to steal . . . a holy text, that was it. A book printed on pages of human skin, sacred to Hith. She'd taken it from the Thenolites' altar and brought it back to Armachnesti. Thalaniya had ordered the book burned.

On the other side of the door lay the fane, and the bishop. And . . . what?

"Only one way to find out," murmured Forlo. The tip of his sword came up. Around him, the other soldiers tensed as well.

Shedara nodded. "Let's go."

The doors opened easily, soundless, offering no resistance. Ghostly blue light spilled out, turning everything gray and killing the last vestiges of Shedara's elvensight. Within, the fane was a vast cavern, lit by braziers where flames the color of glaciers danced in silence. Bones were piled everywhere, arranged to form benches, columns, and tall pyramids of skulls that stared at them from a thousand dark eye sockets. Flayed bodies hung from hooked chains, many still clad in the regalia of the Imperial League, all too badly mutilated to tell whether they had been man or minotaur in life. All were sacrifices, lives taken in the name of the Thenolites' horrible god.

There, on the far side, stood the altar. It, too, was made of bones: pelvises, femurs, and spines, arranged to form a great block ringed round with the curving arcs of ribs. The whole thing was stained dark with blood, shining wet and black in the ghost-light. Fresh kills, made just moments ago.

Ondelos was stooped over the altar, his robes soaked through, working at something with a knife. He glanced up as Forlo and his men entered—he wouldn't be able to see Shedara, for she hadn't been there when this happened—the madness in his eyes glaring like a beacon. Something fell from his grasp, to lie in a bundle on the floor. Scores of other bundles lay there too.

Only they weren't bundles at all. They had arms and legs. Little arms and legs. They were children.

"Oh, gods," Shedara groaned. Behind her, one of the soldiers retched. Forlo stayed silent, standing perfectly still.

Ondelos grinned, raised his bloody, sickle-bladed dagger, and spoke a single word with such force the brazier-flames billowed away from him. A wave of power—not magic, but divine, and as foul as anything Shedara had ever felt—swept over them. It brought with it a charnel stink, strong enough to make their eyes water. Then, one by one, the children's bodies began to move.

First their limbs twitched, then they started to fumble at the floor, trying to find purchase. A few breaths later they sat up. Some fell over again as they tried to push themselves up further. But bit by bit, they managed to make their flailing, mindless way to their feet. When they were all up—there had to be seventy of them, dressed in robes all covered in blood—they turned, as one, to face Forlo and his men.

Shedara knew exactly what had happened. This was Ondelos's last defense. He had expended all the adults under his command, had sent them all to their deaths against the League. Now he had spent the children as well. He had murdered them, Hith's name on his lips, all so he could raise them and send them into battle against his enemies. Each and every child had an identical red slash across his or her throat. Each had felt the kiss of the bishop's knife.

Shedara looked back at Forlo. Tears sheeted down his cheeks. His sword wavered in his hand. His resolve was faltering and so was his men's: Shedara didn't blame them.

"They aren't children any more, Barreth," she said. "Look at me. These are monsters. They must be destroyed . . . and so must he."

She drew a dagger and pointed it across the cave at Ondelos. The bishop was still grinning like a maniac. There was blood on his *lips*. Seeing him, Forlo scowled and shook himself, throwing off his doubts. Then he looked to his left and right, at his men, nodding. He raised his sword high.

And they charged at the lurching abominations that had been the youngfolk of Hawkbluff.

―――――※―――――

It was some time after Forlo woke before he would say anything. The others didn't try to make him speak, only sat and waited in the dark, their faces troubled, while he shivered and beat his fists against his temples. Finally, after nearly half an hour, he slumped and looked up at them. The hurt in his eyes made Shedara have to look away for a moment. He'd been the only one of his men to survive the fight, had fought his way to Ondelos and cut the mad bishop's head off with one vicious stroke. But even that moment of righteousness didn't make up for what came before. Could anything?

Essana put her arms around him and drew him close. He clung to her like a man afraid of drowning. He buried his face in her hair and breathed in. Then he looked up at Grath.

"You *knew*," he growled. The words were like stones dropped from a great height.

The minotaur nodded, sighing heavily. "You were out of your mind when I found you. I had to do something. So I had one of the mages cast a spell on you. I thought that if you were able to forget the horror . . . you would be better."

Forlo stared at him with venom, then he looked away. "Get out, Grath. Go back to Rekhaz. I don't want you here."

"My friend—"

"*Go!*"

The shout's echoes snapped around the room. Grath flinched as though he'd just been whipped. Then, head bowed, he turned and left the room.

"Forlo, I'm sorry," Shedara said.

He turned to look at her, his eyes empty and his mouth a crooked hole. She'd seen that look once, on the face of a man who'd just taken a spear through his stomach. He didn't seem to recognize her at first—and then he did, and composed himself. He became very calm. Somehow, that was worse.

"The statue is yours," he told her. "Now leave me alone with my wife."

She thought for an instant of protesting, of telling him what she'd said in the dream—that he hadn't slain dozens of children, there in the fane. That the things that perished on his sword were unholy abominations. But he himself knew that . . . she could see it in his eyes. Knew it, and still couldn't forgive himself. There was nothing she could do.

So she left him. The door, when it shut behind her, made a sound like a stone rolling to seal a tomb.

Chapter 24

THE LOST ROAD, TIDERUN COAST

The wind had teeth and a chill that hadn't been there a few days before. It was autumn, the change of the seasons a week past. The raiding season would end soon. In a little over a month, the women, children and elders of the Uigan tribes would begin their annual migration southward, taking the herds and flocks with them. The White Sky would return to Undermouth, there to graze for the fallow months while the snows blanketed the Tamire. The women, children, and elders would remain there until the thaws came, then they would ride north for the summer. It was the way of things, the way it had always been.

It would not be the same ever again. Hult knew this in his bones. Once the horde crossed the Tiderun, their world would change. How could it not? From then on, every time the moons aligned the tribes would unite and drive south, bound for the Run and the rich lands beyond. The bull-men's time in Taladas would wane. Chovuk had seen it happen in his dreams. He had seen it even before he became Boyla: a vision that never left him, through all they had faced.

Hult asked Chovuk, the second night of their ride back south, if Krogan's death truly had been a mischance.

He'd known the answer even as he spoke the question.

"Of course not," the Boyla said, taking a pull from a flask of elfwine—sweet, thin stuff compared with *kumiss*. "Do you really think the Kazar just happened to be there?"

"You told them where he would be?"

Chovuk nodded. "An anonymous message sent in the night. I worried they might not believe it, that I'd need to try something else—but the Kazar are stupid and easily beguiled." He laughed. "Though even then, they couldn't get it right and didn't kill them all."

So he had shot the Boyla there in the canyon, before Hult's eyes. A cold-blooded murder. The Teacher's magic had taken care of the rest until that night among the elves, when Hult's sword brought the fey folk to his side.

Hult shuddered at the memory, turning away from Eldako. He could not look at the elf, his expressionless face beneath the war paint he wore. He had not spoken a word since they left the Green, to either him or Chovuk—only listened, watched, and rode in silence. He often traveled ahead, to scout and hunt the evening's meal. What the Boyla had said about his skill with a bow seemed true: he brought down game from over a hundred paces away, always with a single shot and never losing or breaking an arrow.

Even uncannier, though, was the fact that he never seemed to sleep. When Hult lay down at night beneath his blankets, the elf was always awake, sitting just outside the light of their campfire, gazing out across the wind-blown grasses of the Tamire. When he woke again in the cold light before dawn, Eldako was still there and still looking north, back toward his home. Hult had asked him, once, if he worried he might not see the Green again. Eldako had looked at him for a long time, unblinking. Then he had turned away.

The wind grew colder every day.

On the ninth morning, they smelled the sea. Chovuk

reined in, and Hult came to a halt beside him. Eldako, halfway up the hill before them, stopped his own gray, long-legged horse and turned to look back, his piercing eyes like two chips of ice. He stood still and silent in the shadow of a tall cliff, atop which leathery-winged skyfishers nested among a ring of ancient, toothlike pillars. Hult reached for his *shuk*, but the Boyla waved him off.

"Not yet," he said.

Hult raised his eyebrows. Would there be fighting soon? What did the Boyla know? He had spoken again last night, in the dark, and a deep voice had answered from the shadows: the cloaked figure he had seen at the pool the night the *merkitsa* captured them. The Teacher. What had the voice said?

Eldako rode back, a tall, proud figure in a headdress of golden feathers. They looked to have come from a griffin—a beast he had hunted and slain himself, from what little Hult knew of elven tradition. He had his bow—a white, gently curving arc of ghostwood—in hand, and a delicately carved arrow already fitted on the string.

"Trouble?" Eldako asked. The first word he'd said in weeks.

"No," Chovuk said. "Not yet, anyway. But you must not ride any further with me."

Hult looked at Chovuk in surprise, but Eldako only nodded, a thin smile on his lips. He and the Boyla shared a silent moment, staring hard at each other.

"What you want?" the elf asked.

Chovuk nodded up the bluff, at the ruins. Atop one of the columns, a big, batlike creature spread its wings and took flight with a squeal. "Will you come with me?"

Eldako glanced at the columns, baring his teeth. Hult shivered at the sight of that grin: the elf's teeth had been filed down to points, and there was something predatory in the way he smiled, the way he turned and rode away toward the ruins

"Stay here, *tenach*," said Chovuk, wheeling to follow.

Hult blinked. He had just gathered his reins, ready to follow. "Master?"

"Remain here, for now," Chovuk explained. "We will be safe in the ruins without you. If I have need of you, my horn will call."

Hult bobbed his head, then watched as the Boyla and Eldako made their way up to the shattered shell on the cliff—a castle, maybe, or a church of old, too worn and overgrown to tell exactly. A younger ruin than most on the plains, of minotaur make: some earlier colony, destroyed by raiders centuries before the coming of the Tiger-horde. Hult shivered as the cold wind blew beneath his vest. The Boyla and Eldako vanished among the tumbled stones, and he sat alone, watching the skyfishers—unpleasant, carrion-loving birds that sometimes hunted Uigan flocks—wheel in weaving circles above.

Finally, after a quarter of an hour, Chovuk came back down again. He was alone now. Shading his eyes, Hult gazed at the ruins, trying to see where the elf had gone, then turned a questioning eye on Chovuk. The Boyla said nothing, only shook his head slightly.

"*Tenach*, you and I must go on alone. Our companion will join us, later."

"Yes, master."

The ruins stood on a prominence atop a tall ridge, whose crest was scoured clean by wind to reveal jags of red rock that stuck up like a dragon's spines. It was the last such rise north of the Run. Beyond, gulls wheeled against the clouds like white shadows, less ominous than the 'fishers. The tang of salt hung strong in the air. The Run was very close now. Chovuk and Hult rode up together, side by side.

When they crested the rise, Hult had to shake his head in wonder at what lay beyond. The grassy hills ran down, more than a league, to the sea. Only white fog and steel-gray water were visible past that. The other shore, so tantalizingly close, lay hidden from view. Upon the Run's near side, the ground was dark with yurts, horses, campfires, and men, sharpening swords and gambling with dice made from goat bones. The horde had returned from Rudil with all its treasures.

Scouts saw them and ran to alert the Tegins. By the time Chovuk and Hult reached the bottom of the ridge, a party of twenty horsemen had broken away from the mass and was galloping to meet them. Hult picked out the standards of Sugai and Hoch and saw that a dozen of the riders had bows ready. He glanced at the Boyla, whose mouth was a grim line.

"Halt where you are, Chovuk!" cried Hoch when they were still fifty paces away. "Any closer, and we will loose!"

Hult caught his breath, hauling on his reins to stop his horse. Chovuk did the same, then walked his mount forward several steps. Twelve bows creaked and twelve arrows pulled back. The Boyla stopped.

"So it *has* happened," he said. "You have turned against me, Hoch Tegin, as I feared you would."

"I, turned against you?" asked the young lord. He threw back his head, laughing. "I am not the one who deserted our people to speak with elves, Chovuk. I rode with the Uigan, fought with them, and put sword and torch to the last of the bull-men! And did you even return with the allies you sought? No. From now on, you must call me Hoch *Boyla*, for I am the new king of our people."

"You are no Boyla, Hoch," shot back Chovuk. "You are dog-filth, the dirt on a snake's belly! But I expected this of you." He looked past the lord, to the older man beside him, and took off his helm. "You, though . . . this saddens me, Sugai. I had hoped you might have more faith."

Sugai Tegin bowed his head, but said nothing.

"Lord Sugai is wise, Chovuk Elf-lover," taunted Hoch. "He knows what hand holds the *shuk* now."

"Does he?" Chovuk asked.

Something dived out of the sky then, almost straight down. Hult saw it and recognized the fletching. An identical arrow had nearly killed him, back in the Dreaming Green—nearly, but not. That shot had been aimed to wound—not to kill. This one was well aimed, too: fired high, from cover in the ruins behind them, to come down sharply, unseen by Hoch and his men until it was too late. It struck the rebellious Tegin on the top of his helmet and punched through steel, skin, and skull to bury itself deep in his brain. Hoch went rigid and blinked once—the arrow sticking straight out of the crown of his head—then he toppled sideways in a lifeless heap.

Eldako, son of Tho-ket, was a very good shot.

The archers could have loosed, then—could have killed Chovuk and Hult with a twitch of their fingers. But they didn't. Frightened, they lowered their weapons and let their arrows drop. Sugai Tegin edged his horse forward.

"Forgive me, Boyla," the old man said, drawing up before Chovuk. "I was a fool."

Chovuk looked at Sugai fondly, shaking his head. "I'm sorry, my friend," he said.

Sugai saw the second arrow coming and had just enough time to sigh before it pierced his left eye. His head snapped back, and he crumpled to the ground as well.

"You are a fool no more, Sugai Tegin," Chovuk said. "Come, *tenach*."

Stunned, Hult stared at the old man's body. After a long moment, he came back to himself. Gritting his teeth, he dug in his spurs and hurried after the Boyla, galloping down toward the waiting horde.

✦━━✦━━✦

They are out there, Forlo thought, staring across the Run. The far shore was just barely visible in the light of dawn, edging out of the morning haze. It was warm, not like the day before. It was summer's last gasp. The next day, the cold would return and stay till well into the next year. Fitting, in a way, that it would be the day he was leaving Coldhope.

For the last time.

Leaving to join his cohort at the end of the Lost Road. He'd already walked the halls of the keep, marking every room and drawing memories of the place to himself. Even if he *did* return, he sensed, he would no longer be the same man. What he'd learned abut his dream, what had happened in Ondelos's temple, gnawed at him. He alone had slain the last of the dead children and put steel in the mad bishop of Thenol. Even the sight of Ondelos's headless corpse hadn't calmed him or stilled his grief. Grath had found him huddled beside the bishop's body . . . had carried him away and arranged things so he would forget.

Now the minotaur was gone, west with the soldiers to prepare the defenses. They hadn't spoken again before he left. Forlo wondered if their friendship was over. He hadn't had a dream he could remember in the week since Shedara had lifted the spell. He'd slept through every night, and soundly. He'd needed the sleep, to be at his prime for the coming fight.

He turned away and walked back into the keep. He was clad in mail, ready to ride out with the last fighting men left in Coldhope. Its weight and the rattling sound it made soothed him. The sword that hung at his side felt like a part of his body. This was what he was born to be. Duke Rekhaz had seen it, but he'd ignored it and sought to become something he wasn't.

They were waiting for him in the great hall, sitting at the long table, the remains of a morning meal spread out between them—cold chicken, eggs, and the first good apples of the season. Essana and Shedara both looked up when he came in, but only the elf rose. His wife, who was showing her pregnancy more, chose not to stand. He went to Essana first, sitting down beside her and taking her hand. They'd parted before, many times, but this was different, for so many reasons.

"Starlight," he said, softly.

She looked up at him, her eyes shining with fear and love. Her mouth was red and her lips trembled.

Shedara edged back and out of the room.

When they were alone, he bent forward and kissed her, then lowered his head to place his lips against her swollen belly. I wish I could know you, he told the life within her, silently. I wish there were time.

He looked back up at her again. She was so beautiful, even torn apart by grief as she was. She drew a shuddering breath and squeezed his hand tighter.

"Fight well," she said. "I will be with you."

"Starlight...." he began.

But she had turned away. "Go. I do not wish to watch you leave."

Putting a hand to his forehead, he turned and left, heading out into the entry hall. Voss, the chamberlain, stood there with his old, gray head bowed and tears on his face. He would not leave Coldhope either. He would remain as long as his lady did. Many of the other servants were gone, set loose to flee into the hills and woods. Voss's family had supervised Coldhope as long as Essana's had ruled it, though, and he would not abandon it, or her. Forlo gave him a nod as he passed, and the old man saluted in return, hand on fist.

Forlo walked out the tall wooden doors and down the steps to the dusty courtyard. His horse stood ready and waiting. The guardsmen—Iver, Ramal, and a dozen others—were gathering the last of their gear. Only two men would remain to watch over the keep, and even that seemed an extravagance. He needed every warm body he could find out at the Lost Road. The men watched him solemnly as he strode across the bailey.

Shedara stood by his horse, waiting, a hand on her hip. Her face might have been carved of stone. "What do you want of me?" she asked as he approached.

"A favor," he said. "Not a debt."

"Your lady-wife?"

"Yes." He opened his mouth to go on, then shut it again, ashamed.

"Perhaps," Shedara murmured. "Tell me."

He took a deep breath. "She won't leave, though I've begged her. She thinks there's still hope, that this fight can be won."

"A stubborn woman," the elf said. "I've known a few."

He caught her eyes and chuckled in spite of himself. She smiled in return. A moment later, though, the humor drained from his face again. "I will wait," he said, "until the battle's end is certain. Then I'll send a rider with a banner. If the banner is blue, we have lost. If it is red, it will mean victory. I do not think I will need to bring a red flag with me."

She nodded. "And when I see the blue flag . . ."

"You must forcibly take her away. Don't harm her, but get her out of this place and protect her as far as you can ride."

"She'll hate you for it," Shedara said.

"But she'll be alive, and the baby too. That is all I want to know. And when you go, take the Hooded One with you. This will get you to it."

He held out a key made of bronze and set with white stones that shone with inner light. She stared at it.

"If you unlock the door with it," he said, "its magic will make the lotus sleep. The statue is yours, as I promised. I don't know what you should do with it, now that the Voice is slain . . . but you'll think of something. I know you will."

Shedara bit her lip and took the key, her fingers wrapping around the glowing gems. Then she leaned forward and lay her right palm, gently, on his cheek. "Do good, Barreth Forlo."

"Just save her," he said, blinking back tears. "Save *them*."

He turned and walked up the steps, already tired, already defeated. She watched him go, the key held tight in her hand. A thought began to form in her head.

Chapter 25

COLDHOPE KEEP, THE IMPERIAL LEAGUE

The great hall was quiet and dark that night, almost eerily so. Hardly anyone remained at Coldhope. The air was thick with magic. Shedara didn't need to look skyward to know the convergence was coming. The next day, all three moons would align, and the air would fairly sing with enchantment. For the moment, only Solis was still waxing; Lunis and Nuvis already ran full. Good enough.

Seeing the tapestries, the animal heads, and the swords hung upon its walls, she felt a prickle of *alinsa quar*, the sense that her life was fated to that place. It was not the first time she had lived that moment, nor would it be the last. Things changed and the world moved on—how much was different from the night when she first came to Coldhope?—but while the river of time was ever-flowing, sometimes it seemed to loop back on itself.

The door to the cellar was locked, but unguarded. The only two fighting men left in the keep were out on one of the watchtowers, huddled tiredly around one lonely lantern.

Shedara didn't need to pick the lock. The key Forlo had given her opened the door, which swung wide on yawning darkness. The stairway was unlit. No matter—she let her elvensight take over to guide her downward and shut the door behind. The stones were cool and the air was slightly colder. It was enough to find her way in the black. She hoped, idly, that there weren't any more traps. She couldn't let herself be caught again. Too much was at stake.

She walked down the hall, past the niches where crumbled bones had lain for millennia, past the funeral urns where dead men's organs had long since turned to dust, and past the markings in strange alphabets that no man could read any more. She saw warmth, here and there: a rat, spiders, and a centipede as thick as her wrist that hissed at her, then died on the quivering tip of a thrown knife. Nothing else. She wiped her blade clean and moved on.

The vault's door was sealed. She heard a faint sound beyond, a raspy noise, like breathing but not quite. The bloom, she realized: it could sense her—*smell her?*—and was tensing to unfurl, to cover her with its paralyzing pollen again. She smiled grimly, holding up the key. Not this time, she thought.

The key's white stones had shed the slightest glow when she came down the steps. Now that she stood near the door, however, they shone like little stars, casting flickering shadows all around. In that pale light, everything seemed gray and lifeless. Even her own skin had a deadish cast. She bit her lip, feeling the enchantment that spilled from the key to the door like wine flowing from ewer to cup. There was a lock in the stone, silver and gold with more white stones on it. They gleamed as well, brighter and brighter as she stepped near, until it stabbed at her eyes and she had to turn her head to keep from looking at it directly. The key shook in her hand as she reached out . . .

There was a *click*, then a louder grinding sound of stone and stone together. She started and stepped back: she hadn't even reached the lock yet. Evidently, that didn't matter. The magic was strong enough on that night that the key didn't even need to be in the lock to turn it. The white light blared sun-bright, then dimmed again as the door shuddered and ground its way open. Musky perfume spilled out of the vault beyond.

In she went to stand on the spot where she had fallen before, to the lotus dust. She flicked her thumb at that place, a gesture against bad luck. She heard a noise behind her, a great inhalation, like someone working a giant bellows. Steeling herself, she turned to face the lotus. It hung above her, huge and ashen, its petals bunched together in an obscene pucker. White powder fell from the gaps in sifting streams, and at once she felt light-headed, as if her thoughts were slipping down beneath the surface of a pool. She bit her tongue, willing herself to keep conscious. The bloom would open any moment, filling the air with its sleep-bringing dust. It seemed to watch her, waiting, and swelling a little larger with every moment.

"Cut it out," she said, and held up the key.

The stones flared bright, casting their pallid light upon the huge, ugly flower. It drew back with a hiss, then made a strange sound, like a man choking. It began to shudder. Then, writhing a little, it wilted. Its leaves and petals drooped, and streams of pollen leaked out, hanging in the air a while before slowly settling. The key's magic had somehow put the lotus to sleep.

Shedara took another breath. Already she felt less giddy and more like herself. She let the key fall to the floor, then put a hand to her head. She'd come close to succumbing again, but the bloom hadn't taken her. The vault was unguarded at last—nothing but her . . . and the other *presence*, the feeling that someone was standing right behind her. Biting back the urge to whirl around, she turned slowly to face the statue.

There it stood, before her, as she had seen it in vision and dream, black and stooped, hands folded, and face hidden. The Hooded One seemed to watch her from the depths of its obsidian cowl, its gaze far from friendly. She felt the urge to shy back, but resisted with a stubborn glare. It was a statue, cold stone, no different to her elf-eyes than the worn dais it stood upon. But other senses, long attuned to magic and heightened by the moons' coming concordance, told her otherwise. Something stirred in the room. The statue had been waiting.

Shedara stood before the Hooded One, lost in thought, for what felt like an hour. It was dangerous business. She didn't even know if what she planned was possible. She had to try, though. She had to take the risk, if the horde was to be stopped. *Merciful Solis*, she prayed, *watch over me now*.

The words came to her, to the spell, full of power. The incantation burned brightly in her memory and flowed from her tongue like quicksilver. Her hands danced and her fingers weaved as she gathered the moons' energy into the room. Solis, for wisdom. Lunis, for control. Even Nuvis, for power. Around her, the air began to shimmer, motes of rosy light flaring and fading. She felt the Art burn in her, stronger with each syllable and every breath. It felt good, exhilarating. The magic swelled and suffused her flesh and bones. There was nothing like it in all the world.

"*Moitak larshat ku talathom,*" she spoke, the walls around her humming with the sound of her voice. "*Ikuno gangarog te apun do.*"

Hear me, you who are dead. Hear my voice and answer.

The air grew cold, as if a winter wind had blown through. The dust and the cobwebs did not move, though. She forced the magic out of her, through the darkness and to the statue. The spell of communing fit together in her whirling mind, like a child's puzzle-game. She felt the presence within the Hooded One, knew who it was and could scarcely believe it. The tales were true. Maladar an-Desh, the Faceless Emperor, was in the room with her, trapped within the prison of his own statue.

Then the last pieces of the spell fell into place, and he stepped forth.

He was pale, a wraithlike smoke, powerless and wretched. His hood hung low, covering the ruin of his face. A feeling of loss and rage rose off him, like heat off hard desert, and it took Shedara's breath away. She had never felt hate so strong before. Hate for her, for compelling him . . . at Forlo for imprisoning him . . . at all who hunted him . . . at himself, for living so long in his prison. Nausea rose in Shedara's throat, and it was all she could do to maintain the spell. He reached for her, misty, gloved hands clawing the air, but she held firm. She did not back away. His fingertips couldn't quite reach her.

What will you have of me? asked the phantom, in a voice like the grinding of a sarcophagus's lid. *I do not belong here. It is not yet the time, and you are not the one who will free me.*

"Perhaps not," she replied. "But you will hear me, nonetheless. And you *will* obey."

Shedara thrust out with her power, made shackles of it, and bound the spirit with them. Maladar snarled as dark cords of magic, violet-black ropes that sparked and sizzled, appeared and coiled around him, tight. He struggled against the magic, but Shedara spoke another word and the spell held him fast. The magic was too strong for him to resist—at least, in his weakened state. She trembled as she watched him, sweat beading on her brow. The ghost gave one last, great push, trying to get past her defenses, to no avail. She held him fast, despite all his protests, and after a long moment he subsided.

She had worried he might be too powerful to command. The Faceless Emperor had been strong in life, one of the greatest archmages ever to walk the face of Taladas. But centuries of imprisonment in the Hooded One had left him a shadow of what he once had been. The hate in him burned bright still, but he lacked the strength to fight. The enchantment that bound his spirit to the statue, bolstered by her own power, was too strong.

You will rue this day, the voice scratched. *You will regret forcing me to work against my will. I will collect the debt.*

"Perhaps," she allowed. "But first, you will do as I say."

Maladar's specter glowered at her. *Speak, then. What will you have of me?*

She nodded, smiling to herself. It was working. There was some hope, after all. "No great thing," she said. "It's quite simple, really...."

There was a thin rain along the coast, a cold presage of the coming winter, when the country along the Run would become damp, miserable, and gray. Forlo and his men rode in silence along a thin trail of mud, the drizzle drumming on their helms. They sang no martial songs. Each was lost to his own dark thoughts. When they made camp, they drank their ale by banked fires and slept early. Beyond them, past the cliffs that overlooked the Run, the waters rose and fell, rose and fell, higher each evening and lower each morning than the last. New islands jutted from the sea, growing taller and broader day by day. There were no ships on the Tiderun—the loss of Malton and Rudil had put a stop to trading, and the fisherfolk had fled south and away from the coming threat. The company's outriders reported no sight of anything on the far shore, but the mist and rain hid much from view.

At last, as the third day was nearing its end, the ground began to slope down, into a deep ravine where a stream trickled into the sea. Dark pines lined the hills to either side, and the broken and charred stub of a tower rose like a skeletal finger from a pinnacle of stone at the gorge's edge, giving a commanding view of the land around. About its base spread a mass of tents, flags, horses and men. Forlo eyed the banners, some part of him hoping to see the colors of other legions, but there were only the red and blue of the

Sixth, and precious few of those. The last defense against the Uigan. Nine hundred humans.

And one minotaur.

"So you decided to show up," were Grath's first words to him, coming down from the wrecked tower to greet him. He wore a massive hammer on his belt, an even larger axe across his back, and a grim gleam in his eye. "Damned fool. Bring any help?"

Forlo made a sour face, and said nothing.

"Ah, well." The minotaur shrugged, asking no more. "We should be fine with what we've got, eh?"

"Oh, yes," Forlo said after a moment. "No trouble at all."

Grath nodded to the tower. "Come on up to the eagle's nest. Damn fine view up there."

Forlo nodded to his men and signaled for them to join the rest of the camp. They did so with scarcely a word, and he and Grath went up a flight of steps to the tower. The stones of the spire's upper floors were scattered around its base, moss-bearded and half-buried in the earth. It looked as if the tower had been blown apart. Forlo had been out there before, explored the rubble, and wondered what had destroyed it. Magic, probably, or dragonfire: no siege weapon could have done that. He had the feeling, though, that whatever had shattered the tower had done so from within.

Through the vine-draped archway at the spire's entrance was a great, wide expanse of charred stone. A crumbling staircase wound around its middle up to the point, thirty feet above, where the whole thing ended in broken shards festooned with nests and bird droppings. The two of them climbed to that point, and Grath hoisted himself up and sat upon a cracked finger of rock, swinging his legs out and gazing down upon the ravine far below. It was a precarious perch, but that didn't seem to bother the minotaur. He patted a spot next to him.

"Come on. It's really something to see."

"Thanks, but no," grumbled Forlo, his stomach dropping. He stayed on the stairs, finding a chink to peer through.

It *was* an astonishing view, as close to a bird's vantage as he'd seen on any battlefield. Miles of land stretched out on all sides, save the north, where the sea lay. It was mostly drained, though not shallow enough to cross, not yet. That would happen the next day, the day after that at the latest. From the tower, he could see the far shore....

His blood went cold. The northern side of the Run was dark—it seemed to be covered with ants, thousands of them.

"*Khot*," he swore.

Grath grunted. "They showed up the day before yesterday. More coming every day. I sent a scout out in a punt the first night for a closer look and to get an idea of numbers."

"And?"

"Haven't seen him since."

Forlo grimaced, feeling sorry for the poor bastard who'd had to sail a one-man boat out toward that multitude. What did exact numbers matter, anyway? Two thousand riders would be too many to withstand, and they clearly had far more than that. Five, maybe six times as many. He shook his head.

"They'll come across there," Grath went on, pointing. The ground beyond the ravine's mouth was rocky, with few pockets of silt: a natural bridge, when it was dry. There wasn't another like it, the whole length of the Run. Twenty horses could cross it abreast. "I've got men making pickets across the gap and some sappers digging trenches up the slope. Should slow them down."

"Back them up with pikes," Forlo agreed. "The Uigan are good horsemen, but they don't know formation fighting. The first waves will break on that, at least."

Grath nodded, grunting.

"Archers on the high ground to either side will pick off any who get through. The main body of swords should be in the ravine. Find a spot where the slope's hard to climb and put them on top. If we pen them in, we can hold them."

"All good ideas," Grath agreed. "There's a ledge halfway along where we could get some skirmishers hidden, too. Hit 'em from behind and cut them off."

Forlo shook his head. "Those men would last about a minute in the press, two if they were lucky. I'd rather have the extra blades on the line. If we had more men, or they had fewer...."

He fell silent, looking out, then clenched his fist. Gods' spit, this would have been a winnable fight, if he'd had all of the Sixth! Or if the Silvanaes had come. They had plenty of terrain advantage, they had superior tactics, and they had discipline that would hold. All they lacked were numbers!

"It won't work," Grath said, echoing the thoughts in his mind. "We knew it wouldn't. This could be a damned good fight, if things were different, but it'll turn into a rout. A slaughter."

"I know," Forlo said, and nothing more.

"You should go," said Grath after a moment. "Take your lady-wife and ride."

"And leave you to die alone?"

"You think I'll be happier knowing you died beside me?"

Forlo shot him a look. "You won't know any better. I'll outlast you."

"I'll take that bet," the minotaur said.

Forlo laughed, a grim sound that died quickly. He turned to look down at the camp and at the men there. They were working hard, readying for the fight. He felt a swell of pride. They were brave men. Yet they must be afraid . . . only madmen wouldn't be, knowing what lay across the receding water.

Grath pulled out a flask, drank from it and handed it to Forlo. He took a sip. Wine. Good stuff; not the sour sludge the army normally carried. A Theran vintage, if he wasn't mistaken.

"You stole this from Coldhope's cellars," he said, "didn't you?"

The minotaur grinned. "I prefer 'purloined.' More poetic."

Forlo took another drink, then handed it back.

"I'm sorry about the spell," Grath said after a time. "I didn't know what else to do. It broke my heart to see you like you were."

"Yeah, I'm a heartbreaker," Forlo replied, with a sour grin. "That I am."

Grath nodded. "Ondelos has a special place in the Abyss for what he did, I'm sure."

"He'd better," Forlo said, "or what's the point?"

They were silent a while longer, finishing the wine. Grath took the last pull, upended the flask sadly, and tossed it over the edge. It sailed, spinning, down into the ravine.

"Someone will probably write a ballad about this stand," Forlo said, swinging around and hopping back onto the stairs. "The sheer desperate hopelessness of it."

"I had a thought," Grath said, hurrying to follow.

"Not unusual," Forlo replied.

"The married men."

Forlo stopped, eyeing the minotaur. "What about them?"

"I want to make the same offer. Let them leave if they want to, to go back to their wives and their children. I don't expect them all to do it, but some might. They deserve the choice."

Forlo looked hard at Grath, before nodding. "Damn. Now you're breaking *my* heart. Fair enough. Make the offer."

He turned and looked out to the west. The sun was going down. Soon, the moons would rise, all three of them full. The Run was filling in again. It would be high soon, swamping the mouth of the ravine. Some of the pickets would wash away and need replacing come morning. When dawn came, the sea would disappear entirely. And the Uigan would come.

"I'm glad you're staying, Grath," Forlo said.

The minotaur clapped him on the shoulder. "I was never the marrying kind . . . Sir."

They stood silent a moment, looking at each other, then went down the steps together. Nothing more needed saying.

Chapter 26

THE LOST ROAD, THE TAMIRE

In the end, when all the questions were asked, three other Tegins were found to have plotted with Hoch and Sugai to usurp the Boyla. They died begging for mercy, killed by their own *tenachai* at Chovuk's order—*tenachai* who then ran their sabers through their own breasts, a final duty they were sworn to carry out. The horsemen honored the *tenachai* with a proper burning, but dragged the rebellious Tegins' bodies out of the camp to the place where Sugai and Hoch still lay. There, the lords who remained loyal to Chovuk took turns riding over the bodies, their horses' hooves trampling them into the ground. After riding over the traitors three times, the lords spat upon the remains and galloped back to camp, leaving the carrion for the vultures.

Only then, when justice was done, did Eldako appear. At a signal from the Boyla, he came down from where he had been concealed, among the ruined pillars on the cliff. The Uigan stared in amazement and fear as he came, tall and wild, his long braids dyed bright red, his face painted with woad and moss and berry juice, and his longbow—nearly seven feet from tip to tip—cradled in the crook of his arm. Only when Chovuk stepped forward and embraced him—and was embraced in turn—did the horsemen relax. Even then, when the Boyla wasn't looking, some bit the heels of their hands, to ward against evil.

Hult didn't blame them. He wasn't the only one who had been raised to dread the *hosk'i imou merkitsa*. And children's stories aside, the two great nations of the Tamire had never been friendly. For all Eldako's cool diffidence, he showed signs of unease, as well. He shifted nervously and bared his teeth when the Uigan came too close, like a cat ready to pounce. Hult knew, instinctively, that the alliance would not last long. If they were lucky, Eldako would remain until the end of the great raid across the Tiderun. No longer.

"Why did we need him?" he asked Chovuk on the third night after their return—the eve of the coming battle. "What does he give us that we do not have already?"

"It is already given," the Boyla replied. He finished a horn of *kumiss* and tossed it away. "Hoch and Sugai had been plotting from the start, from the very day I became Boyla. They were patient, waited for their chance, and took it when it came. If I had not left the horde, they would have killed me in the fighting when we crossed the Run. Because I did go north, they chose to act sooner . . . to their folly.

"The elf does not matter. He will help in the coming fight—he will shoot the commander of our enemies, as he did those two faithless dogs. But even if he leaves today, he has served his purpose. Eldako was a chance for me to force Hoch's hand, and nothing more."

"And you knew all this?" Hult asked, amazed. "How?"

"It was shown to me."

Hult opened his mouth and closed it again, his lips pursing.

"You are discontented," Chovuk noted. "I do not blame you. This has been a strange time, and I have kept much hidden from you. Tell me what you fear, *tenach*."

"Evil," Hult said. He glanced around, making sure

no one was near. "I fear that you have cast your lot with darkness, master."

Just like that, it was said. He could hardly believe he'd spoken the words—they'd come out of him almost unbidden, like a river overrunning its banks at floodtime. He knew a *tenach* who accused his lord of evil merited only death. Chovuk was silent for a moment, leaving Hult to wonder if he would soon join Hoch and Sugai and the other traitors. It would have been just, by Uigan law, for Chovuk to put his *shuk* through him.

Instead, though, the Boyla stared at him with a face that might have been carved of stone. "Evil? I have led our people to glory we have never known. We have united the tribes, crushed the Kazar, and driven the bull-men from our shores! Tomorrow, we will cross the Run and bring woe upon our enemies in their own homes! No Boyla has done this, not even the great princes of old."

"Pardon, lord," Hult said, bowing his head. "What I speak, it is out of love for you. I fear the designs of he who aids you. The good of our people may cloak some greater darkness, one you do not see."

Chovuk stood very still, his eyes hooded in the dusk. Behind him, the moons hung fat above the horizon. Beyond the camp, the waters were rising to swamp the lowest parts of the plain. The men were shouting in the camp, boasts and curses and laughter. Farther away, strange music, windpipes that sounded like a widow's keening, rose from the ruins, where Eldako had gone to rest. Hult raised his gaze to meet the Boyla's.

Chovuk struck him.

Fast as a scorpion's tail, the punch caught him unprepared, right in the middle of his chest. The wind went out of him with a roar, and he sagged first to his knees, then onto his side, where he lay trying to draw a breath that wouldn't come. Chovuk towered over him, his face white with rage, as he writhed and vomited on the grass.

"Disloyalty I expected from Hoch," the Boyla said.

"Even from Sugai, though it pained me greatly, for the old crow had gone soft. But you, *tenach*? I have brought you through dangers and victories that would make the talespeakers know your name until the world's ending! And you repay me by telling me I am guided by evil?"

Spittle flecked his lips. His eyes showed white all around. It was the visage of a rabid animal. Hult turned his head away, so he wouldn't have to look at him. With effort, he got some air into his burning lungs. Sourness filled his mouth.

"I'm . . . sorry," he wheezed.

He lay still, waiting for the ring of the Boyla's saber leaving its scabbard and the hot kiss of steel, oblivion. But it did not come. Instead there was silence, then a hand grabbed his ankle and pulled. He opened his eyes and saw that Chovuk had a hold of him and was dragging him toward his yurt. His master thrust the flap aside with a broad sweep of his arm.

"I will show you, then," Chovuk said. "You will see with your eyes, this thing you call evil."

Then they were inside the tent which was dark save for the dull red glow of a brazier. The smells of leather and sweat and oiled steel were close and thick. War smells. Chovuk let him go, moved away into the shadows, got a lamp going, and set it on a table laden with maps. The inside of the yurt was a mess: furniture overturned, empty flasks and gnawed bones scattered on the floor, and flies buzzing over the refuse. It was like an animal's lair, not the dwelling of a prince. Hult lay upon a woven rug that had once been fine, looted from the Kazar. Now it was stained, frayed, and burned in places by fallen embers. It stank. Hult had never seen the Boyla's dwelling like this.

"Master?" he wheezed. "What . . . happened here?"

Chovuk said nothing, only knelt on the floor before a wide-open space. He reached beneath his vest and pulled out something Hult had never seen before: a talisman, hung on a leather thong. It was made of bones, some still sheathed in dry, gristly flesh, with teeth as well. Hult didn't need to look closely to know they came from no beast or goblin. They were human. He shuddered.

"Come to me," murmured the Boyla, pressing the horrid charm to his lips. "Come, and be heard."

He began to sway back and forth, chanting words Hult didn't understand, that skittered over his mind like dung beetles. A look of rapture came into Chovuk's face, ruddy in the lamp's dim light. His eyes seemed to gleam, like a wolf's at night—or a tiger's. Indeed, his whole body rippled, as if he might change into the great steppe-cat, as he'd done at the Mourning-stone, Xagal, and the Kazar lands. His teeth lengthened to feline points . . . then clamped down on the talisman and tore away a strip of desiccated flesh. With a satisfied growl, Chovuk gulped down the man-flesh, shuddered, then threw back his head and roared at the yurt's ceiling.

Jijin help me, Hult thought, it is worse than I thought. He is mad.

The next thing he knew, the air began to change. It grew warm and damp, as if the tent stood in the middle of a marsh at midsummer. A fetid smell came with it, like something recently buried but unearthed again by a rainstorm. Even the light changed, turning from Abyssal red to noxious brown-green. The color of rot and putrescence. Bile rose again in Hult's throat and his breath came in short, shallow gasps; he felt as if a great, invisible hand were pressing down on him, pushing him into the filthy rugs.

Chovuk stood smiling, swaying and intoning the same words over and over. He was caught between forms, half-man, half-tiger. There were even stripes on his skin, faint but unmistakable. A musky stink hung around him, strong and thick. Far off, almost too far to be heard, the camp dogs had begun to bay and howl. The bone charm dangled from his fingers, spinning slowly, a ghastly sight. For a long moment, Hult couldn't take his eyes off it. Then something else appeared and drew his gaze away.

It began as a flickering, a new-kindled flame rising to life between him and Chovuk. It was the same rancid hue as the lamplight, throwing wild shadows on the yurt's walls as it rose and took form. Before long it became a sinuous column of olive flame, twisting and writhing like a serpent. Hult shied back from it with tears in his eyes, his heart thundering. Sorcery, gods-cursed sorcery . . . and his master was the conjurer! Had it been any other Uigan, the punishment for magery would have been quick and final. It involved ropes, four horses, and a great deal of screaming. But the Boyla made the rules for others, not for himself.

Chovuk's voice rose to a shout and his hands lifted in exultation. Hult stared in amazement. Then the fire flared bright, and the presence, the one Chovuk called the Teacher, was in the tent: dark and cloaked, stepping from the flames as they guttered and died. Hult could see nothing except black cloth, folded and gathered and draped to hide what was beneath. He wondered if the thing were even a man, or if it were something worse.

Its voice, raspy as a rusty blade scraping against stone, gave him no clue. "I have come, Chovuk Boyla, tiger of the plains," it said. "What tidings do—why is *he* here?"

The cowled head turned toward Hult, its gaze boring into him, unseen eyes driving through his flesh like lances.

"All is well, Teacher," said Chovuk, smiling. "There is nothing to fear."

"Fear?" The cloaked thing reached out a gloved hand, a bony finger, pointing. Chovuk dropped to his knees as though he'd been struck with an axe. "I fear nothing, horseman. Others fear *me*. I told you, none must be present when you summon me."

"Hult is my *tenach*," Chovuk replied. "He doubted me, thinking I had fallen to evil. I wanted to show him he was wrong."

The dark being paused, then made a sound that was all razors and glass. It took Hult a moment to realize the noise was the thing's idea of laughter. "Oh, he is very wrong, isn't he?" it asked. "Evil. Such a quaint idea."

"What are you, then?" Hult dared to ask in a quavering voice.

"I *am*," said the being. "Just as you are. Good and evil have no meaning. I serve something greater than either—time, history, and memory. So does your master, boy—as do you, if you are faithful. Are you faithful, Hult son of Holar?"

Hult stared at the stranger, catching no glimpse of what lay within the shadows. But in his heart, he knew the Teacher was no beast, no fiend from the Abyss. The Teacher was a man, just a man, no different from him . . . save for the power to flay the flesh from his bones by moving a finger.

"I ought to kill this wretch, Chovuk," said the Teacher. "No—I ought to make *you* do it. Another time, I might have done just that. But not today, not on the eve of battle. Perhaps, when the fighting is done . . . if he still lives . . . I will ask for his blood."

The Boyla bowed his head. "If that is your wish."

The words hit Hult hard, despair now mingling with terror.

"Now, boy," the Teacher said, "you will sleep, and forget. When you wake, it will be time for battle."

He waved his hand.

Hult bit his lip and clenched his fists so his nails dug into his palms, determined to resist the spell. It did him no good. Drowsiness settled over him like midwinter snow. His vision began to swim, the stranger and his master blurring in the green light. Sounds came from the bottom of a yawning, deep chasm.

"That is done," said the Teacher. "Now let us speak of the morrow. . . ."

Hult heard no more, only the rushing of wind through the grasses in his dreams.

He woke outside the yurt, rested and alert. His head snapped up with a start, and he glanced around, getting his bearings. He was sitting in his usual spot, outside the tent, his *shuk* across his knees. The red and silver moons peered full over the western hills as they sank into day. The stars had dimmed, and the sky was the color of a bruise, brightening in the east. There were no clouds. It was a beautiful autumn morning.

The camp was already springing awake, though dawn was an hour off. Half the warriors hadn't slept at all, kept awake by the anticipation of battle. They had stayed by the fires, drinking and dicing and boasting of how many minotaur heads they would cleave, and of how much gold they would bring back across the Tiderun. Now they were dousing fires, sharpening blades, and saddling horses. Farther off, the goblins burned offerings to their primitive gods. Eldako stood nearby, silent and unreadable, his bow at the ready.

The Tegins gathered before long, and Gharmu of the Wretched Ones as well. They came to the Boyla's tent and waited, the sky brightening to scarlet above them.

Hult glanced over his shoulder. The yurt stood dark and quiet. A strange feeling came over him—a prickling at his mind, like there was something he should remember, but didn't. Strange images flashed through his mind: green flame, a man in a black cloak, and his master grinning like a lunatic. . . .

He shook his head. Bad dreams, he told himself. It happened sometimes, the night before battle. He spat to ward off evil spirits.

Behind him, the flap opened.

The Tegins gasped. Gharmu cried out, throwing himself prostrate. Even Eldako raised his eyebrows, though the rest of his painted face remained emotionless. Hult turned, his blood running cold, and saw Chovuk Boyla.

The man appeared to have aged thirty years overnight. His hair and beard, once as black as a raven's wing, were snowy white. Deep wrinkles creased his face. One eye had gone milky-blind. His teeth and nails were long and yellow.

"Master . . ." Hult blurted, horrified.

"Be still, *tenach*," Chovuk snapped. "I am stronger now!"

With that, he strode out of the tent, to stand before the lords of his army. Reaching across, he yanked his *shuk* from its sheath.

"Let the crows gather," he declared. "We will give them a feast ere the night comes. We attack when the water falls!"

Chapter 27

TIDERUN SHORE, THE IMPERIAL LEAGUE

Everything was quiet as the sun rose. Even the birds ceased their songs. The men of the Sixth, of Coldhope, of the fishing villages, and of Malton's ruins—all stood speechless. The only sounds were the creak of leather and the rattle of mail. All were in place and all had prayed to their gods, if they had any. They held their weapons and waited.

From the top of the ruined tower, among the tangled bird's nests, Forlo saw it all. His men, standing ready, resigned to their fate, but not to go to the hereafter unaccompanied by their enemies. The shadows of the horde, gathered on the yonder shore, biding. He wondered if he would see the one who led them, the chief who had gathered so many savages together, before he fell. It seemed a faint hope.

And between the two armies, the Run. Already the tides were low, the waters dotted with land where there had been none an hour before. It churned and foamed in places and formed whirlpools in others. The dark shores glistened, spangled with tidal pools and gasping sea creatures. Ordinarily, commoners would be swarming over the rocks, scavenging for the bounty the tides had left behind—crabs and clams, urchins and sea turtles, and thousands of flopping fish. There would have been feasting that night, in the nearby towns. That day, though, the only ones gathering to feast were the skyfishers and crows, who circled above, squalling. They always sensed when a bloodbath was near.

"Not long now," said Grath. He stood at Forlo's side, following his friend's gaze. "I should get down to the men."

Forlo grunted, but said nothing, so Grath tarried.

Fortunately, a few of the married men had possessed the sense to leave when Grath dismissed them. There had been about sixty in the cohort who had families. Some two dozen rode away last night, going back to their wives and their children. No shame, Forlo had said, no recriminations—but they had left with eyes lowered, disappearing up the rocky slopes into the mist like ghosts. The rest of his mismatched army had stayed, stubborn as dwarves. He was still there only because he had to be. He was their commander, and it was his duty. If he were an ordinary soldier, he would be riding like mad to put as much ground as he could between himself and the coming battle.

Grath looked at his friend. Forlo appeared lost once again in the darkness of his memories. Thinking of the little, bloodstained ghouls that had defended Ondelos in that fell temple.

Grath coughed, breaking into Forlo's reverie. He saluted, hand over fist. "Fight well, Barreth."

"And you," Forlo replied, returning the gesture. "It's been an honor to command you."

"If we get out of this," Grath replied with a grin, "the beer's on me."

Forlo clapped him on the arm. "Go."

Grath went. When the sound of his feet on the steps faded away, Forlo bowed his head and blew out a long breath. He pinched the bridge of his nose, and waited for his head to clear. The morning wind tugged at his cloak, cool and soothing. He turned his face into the wind and let it wash over him. Was Essana standing somewhere in the same wind?

He heard footsteps again and looked over his shoulder. It was Iver. The soldier's face was pale as he came up the stairs. Looped through his belt were two banners: one red and one blue. A fast horse waited at the tower's base, ready for the ride to Coldhope.

"I wish you'd pick someone else for this duty, sir," he said.

Forlo snorted. "Don't lie, lad. Any of the others would gladly take your place."

"Is there any hope?"

Forlo shrugged. "There's always hope. The Third Destruction could come. A god could ride down from the clouds. Their prince could fall from his horse and break his neck. Whatever, it's out of my hands."

Iver nodded, his face grim, staring out at the Run. Forlo did too. It had dropped more, maybe twenty feet in the last three minutes. There were more pools, the islands were bigger and the eddies were stronger. The sun had climbed all the way above the horizon and was moving higher, unstoppable. The moons were sinking together on the far side of Krynn, pulling the seas down.

I wish they had never come back, Forlo thought. I wish we still had the one, pale moon. Then we would be safe. He chuckled at the irony of it: the end of the Godless Night, a glorious day in Taladas, had sealed his doom.

"Look," said Iver. "They're moving."

The shapes across the Run were shifting: moving forward and massing at the water's edge. He imagined the Uigan, gripping their reins and their bows and their curved swords, tensed in their saddles like coiled springs, ready to thunder across the strait. So damned many. . . .

He drew his sword and raised it to his lips. The metal was cold, but he pictured *her* as he kissed it, and felt her mouth against his. Then he lowered the blade and thoughts of Essana left his mind. There was only the enemy, inching closer along what had been sea floor just hours before.

The water kept draining away.

"Wretched Ones, to the front!" roared Chovuk Boyla, waving with his *shuk*. "Gharmu, get your men up there!"

The shaman of Xagal bowed, loping away and screaming to his men. A chorus of guttural, bestial cries arose in response, and crude weapons were thrust into the air. The goblins swarmed forward, on foot and wolfback, pushing gleefully past the horsemen. It was a glorious day for the Wretched Ones: they would be the first across, the first to spill their enemies' blood.

They would also be the first to feel their enemies' steel, so the men let them go. The goblins massed at the head of the horde, a sea of ruddy flesh and moldering furs, dotted here and there by poles sporting the rotting remains of those they'd conquered in the campaign. Stupid creatures, they hungered for battle, for blood, and nothing more. They didn't know why Chovuk had chosen them. But the Uigan understood: the goblins were expendable, good for wearing down the defenders across the Run, testing them.

If there *were* any defenders. Hult had yet to see any signs of life among the trees and rubble on the strait's far side.

"They lie hidden," said Chovuk, sensing his misgivings. "Cowards, they fight to trap, to ambush. But they are not enough. We are ten thousand and more—they might stop half our number, with the luck of the gods beside them, but they cannot stand against this many."

"Not with *hosk'i imou merkitsa* by your side," agreed Eldako, fingering his bow. The elf stared across the water, his painted face a gruesome mask.

Chovuk nodded. "Remember your place. Don't waste your arrows on the bull-men. Find their commanders, the officers and the marshal, if you can. Feather their skulls."

Eldako looked grim. He didn't need to be reminded. He wheeled his slender gray horse and rode away from the Boyla. Chovuk stood nearly alone. The Tegins were with their clans, where they belonged. Only Hult remained by his master's side, and he did not speak. Neither man had said a word to the other since morning. They sat their horses atop a rocky crag, worn by surf and crusted with drying salt—and, below, barnacles. From here, they could see the retreating hither shore, and the far side as well. The Wretched Ones crept forward as the waters retreated, gnashing and gibbering and howling for the slaughter. Soon.

And then, so suddenly it seemed a miracle, the waters vanished altogether.

The islands became mounds, and the mounds became hills. Sea yielded to dry land studded with lakes and ponds, and thousands of dying fish, lobsters, and stranger beasts lay stranded and suffocating in the strangeness of the air. A few dozen yards from the road, a gigantic serpent with blood-red scales and flippers tipped with massive claws lay writhing and thrashing, wheezing pitifully as its gills fought against the air. The thing had to be eighty feet long, and could have sunk a small ship without much trouble. The failing tide had betrayed it and left it as vulnerable as the day it hatched from its egg. Its yellow eyes bulged without comprehension as it slowly died.

The Lost Road lay bare and gleaming in the sunlight: rock of white and deep gray, buckled and spotted with colorful coral, and dotted with creatures both spiny and shelled. Here, before the First Destruction, folk of the old kingdoms, the lost, long-dead kingdoms, had traveled north and south. The Tiderun lay empty, the halves of Hosk united again as they had been in those olden days, before the rain of fire ravaged Taladas.

It was a miraculous sight, one clerics and scholars often invoked as a worldly wonder. The horde was already a quarter of the way across, having followed the retreating waterline. Now that the Run had emptied altogether, leaving the way open, they broke loose and charged.

Or, rather, some did. In fact, to Forlo's surprise, only the foremost ranks of the throng picked up their pace, racing across the damp and broken rocks. The rest stayed behind, stopping to watch what would happen. Forlo frowned, looking to Iver, who held up a hand to shade his eyes.

"Goblins," the young man said. "A thousand."

Forlo nodded, understanding. The goblins were crowbait, nothing more. They would die beneath the blades of the Sixth, stupidly believing they held a hope of winning through. He'd fought goblins before, in the eastern provinces abutting the Steamwalls. A thousand weren't enough to overwhelm his lines. Weren't even close.

But that wasn't the point, and he knew what the Uigan chieftain was about. The goblins would try his defenses, and give the horde some sign of what it faced. Forlo saw several horses break away from the main mass, following the goblins toward the battle, keeping at a distance all the time. Scouts, they would stay out of bowshot and ride back to the main body when the fighting was done, to report what they had seen.

"Whoever this Boyla is, he's smart," Forlo said. "Iver, go down to Grath and tell him to lighten our archers' fire. Make it look like we only have half as many bows as we do. Leave the rest as a surprise for the main force."

The guardsman saluted and sprinted away, down the steps. Forlo looked back at the charging goblins, now less than a mile from the southern shore. He could hear them baying and barking like mad dogs, waving spears and cudgels in the air. Occasionally one would lose his footing on the Road and vanish beneath his fellows' flapping feet, only to emerge again behind the mass as a trampled smear upon the stones. Forlo's lip curled: he hated goblins. He had never seen fighters so mindless and undisciplined. His boys would have no trouble with them. He only wished there was a way to do it without giving away all the traps and pits his men had laid upon the shore.

Ah, well.

As he'd suspected, the riders following the goblins reined in a few hundred yards from shore, not far from the writhing, suffocating sea serpent. The horsemen halted, watching as the goblins swarmed up the slick slopes toward dry land. More goblins fell and died, their bodies tumbling back downhill.

Iver came bounding up again, taking the stairs two at a time and breathing hard. He answered Forlo's look with a nod: already the archers on the canyon's edges were pulling back, some lowering their bows altogether to hide from view. The rest waited, watching as the goblins came closer . . . closer. . . .

The traps took almost two hundred of the creatures, the ground opening up to swallow the horrid beasts, who died shrieking on sharpened stakes below. Their cries of agony and alarm filled the air. Many more of the Wretched Ones made it through, though, and kept coming. The bowmen fired down at them, cutting them down in waves—but still not enough died. With the shafts raining down in half the numbers they could have, nearly half of the goblins survived to reach the spot where the main body of soldiers stood.

The line buckled a little when the mad little creatures crashed into it, and some men perished in the initial shock. The ones who didn't fall locked shields and pushed back, stabbing with spear and sword—the kind of precision and cooperation the Uigan and the Wretched Ones would never have. The goblins' onslaught crumbled, falling into ruin beneath the blades. Screeches and whimpering filled the air.

Forlo winced at the slaughter and spat, trying to clear the bitter taste from his mouth. There was no glory in this kind of fighting, and while goblins were the most reviled of all the races he couldn't help but feel a measure of pity for them and their single-minded need to catch, crush, and destroy. It was their undoing. Soon the ground was slick with black goblin blood, and the corpses were piled high upon the ravine's floor.

Brave in numbers, goblins were cowards once outfought. They were also thick-witted, and didn't realize at first their predicament. Finally, panic set in and the remaining mass—less than a hundred strong—broke up, running back down the gauntlet they had just passed through, fleeing toward the Tiderun. Forlo's archers picked off most of them, and a few more were actually dumb enough to fall into the pits. The rout dwindled, as the rest managed to flee back down to the stones of the Road. Back toward the horde.

"Never make it," muttered Forlo.

Iver glanced at him. "Sir?"

Forlo said nothing, only nodded for him to watch.

The scouting party still sat their horses by the sea serpent, whose throes had weakened as its strength gave out. The serpent lay still, its gills fluttering, its needle-fanged mouth working feebly. As Forlo expected, the riders had bows. They fitted arrows on their strings and pulled them back. The goblins, foolish creatures that they were, never saw the arrows coming. They were cut down like summer barley. Then, when the last of the Wretched Ones lay dead, bloody and riddled on the rocks, the riders wheeled and galloped back the way they'd come.

There was some cheering down in the valley, mostly from the villagers and the youngest soldiers. Forlo felt a scornful laugh rise within him and fought it back. Bit by bit, the celebration died down as the veteran warriors explained the strategy to the rest. Grim silence followed. Some of the soldiers moved to clear away the goblin bodies, or to bear their fallen fellows away from the line. By his crude tally, Forlo guessed he'd lost about three dozen men to the goblins. Not a great loss, but more than he'd hoped.

The soldiers gazed beyond the battlefield again, pointing with swords slick with black blood. Forlo looked out toward the Run. The scouts were back with the main body of the horde, no doubt describing all they had seen. The Boyla would know much of what he faced.

Forlo and his men watched the riders, a dark mass that stretched almost halfway across the dry strait, moving to form a broad line, across the full width of the Lost Road. They would come, soon enough.

"It's started."

Shedara glanced sideways along the length of Coldhope's western wall. Lady Essana stood alone, her long, dark hair streaming in the wind. She stared beyond the forests and the hills, as if she could see far enough to know what was happening on the battlefront. Her cheeks were wet and her eyes were filled with a hurt that made Shedara's mouth run dry.

"The fighting's begun," she murmured.

She was right, Shedara knew. She'd marked the moons last night, all of them full—even Nuvis, invisible to all but those who knew its power. To her right, beyond the cliffs, the Tiderun stood dry. A kelp-covered shipwreck lay naked in the silt, canted at an odd angle and surrounded by dead and dying sharks. She bowed her head a moment, thinking of Forlo and his men.

Essana turned to look at her. "I will die here," she said. "In my home, as is right. But I will not be a plaything for these barbarians. Will you help me?"

"Help . . . ?" Shedara asked, then stopped, understanding what the woman was asking.

"You know how to use those," Essana said, pointing.

Shedara looked down at her knives, then shook her head.

"Please," Essana insisted. "You know what they'll do to me. And to you. Take my life and run as fast and as far from here as you can."

"I'm sorry, milady. I cannot."

Essana looked at her, hurt, her eyes shining. After a moment, she shrugged, letting out a long, trailing sigh. Unsteadily, for she was great with child, She climbed up onto the battlements and perched on a merlon, looking to the west. She steadied herself, then began to lean forward.

Shedara caught up to her in three steps, yelling meaningless words as she grabbed the woman by the neck of her gown and dragged her off the stone, back to the catwalk. Essana struggled, her face pale and her eyes wild. It took a spell to calm her, a quick burst of the silver moon's power, pulled into Shedara's body with one breath, then flowing into the grief-crazed woman with the next.

"*Ast tasarak sinularan krynawi*," she spoke.

The magic went to work, easing the fear and despair in Essana's face as her eyes closed. She fell into a deep slumber. The spell would last for hours. Nothing could break it, short of drawing the Lady of Coldhope's blood. Shedara stared at her, at the peace in her sleeping face, so strange after the desolation that had been there before: not terror, but emptiness and hopelessness. She smoothed away an errant lock of Essana's hair, then rose and turned to face the two remaining guards, men barely old enough to shave, who ran toward her with fear in their faces and weapons drawn.

"What happened?" asked one, kneeling down beside Essana.

Shedara shook her head. "Do not worry over that,"

she said. "The lady is well. Take her to her chambers and lay her in her bed. See that her rest is not disturbed." She turned to go.

The second guard reached for her arm and nearly grabbed it before she pulled it away. "What are you doing?" he asked.

She gave him a long, hard look. "The only thing I can do, now."

If they had tried to stop her, then, she would have killed them. They must have seen that in her eyes, because neither made another move toward her. They turned instead to their mistress. Shedara didn't give Essana another glance. Later, if she saw the blue banner, the elf would take the woman from here. Until then, she hardly needed to pay the sleeping noblewoman any mind.

Down the stairs to the courtyard she went and on toward the keep. She had much to do and little time left to do it.

Chapter 28

COLDHOPE HOLDING, THE IMPERIAL LEAGUE

It was different this time, though nothing looked strange. The great hall, the stairs, and the catacombs were all as they had been the last time she had been down there. Even the vault was undisturbed, the statue looming there in the dark. All of it, unchanged—and yet, something was not the same. It was as if the air itself had soured, dampened, and chilled. There was decay in it, too subtle to call a smell. Her skin prickled, and she had a strange feeling, like she might begin to rot if she stayed too long. Everything seemed tainted, blurred, as if she were regarding the world through discolored glass. Cold sweat beaded on her forehead.

Then she knew, even before she looked up: the bloom. The gray lotus, which had stood guard over the room for uncounted centuries, had died. It drooped pathetically where it had grown, its petals hanging limp and blotched with black and rusty brown. Mold, already growing on them, and white ants swarming in its center, a moving carpet dragging away the few bits of the thing they could eat. It was a husk and nothing more. She wondered if it had been the last of its kind—and if so, if she should feel sorrow at its passing? She couldn't quite manage that.

Another thought, even worse, drove that from her

mind. The gray lotus could not be killed! Forlo had told her that much: the key could put it to sleep, but nothing could slay it. That was what made it so useful as a ward against thieves. And yet here it was, rotting before her eyes. She wondered who could have caused its death—but only for a moment. There was only one answer.

A sound, soft and grating, like a distant hinge many years unoiled, drew her attention back to the statue. It took her a moment to recognize the sound as laughter, and her skin grew crawling-cold. He had slain the lotus, and now he was waiting for her, watching and listening. He was waiting for her, watching and listening. Maladar the Faceless was awake for the first time in centuries. Two ages had passed since his death, a long time to endure. Now he lurked in grayness, just beyond the veil of the world, crouched like a panther ready to spring. It would be difficult to keep him imprisoned, a balance as delicate as Silvanaes crystal. Thalaniya would have called her a fool for even trying it. Any mage might.

I *am* a fool, Shedara thought, staring up at the blankness within the statue's cowl.

She cleared her mind and willed herself to relax—no small feat, with the closeness of the air and the hungry anticipation that swirled around her. Her hands hung loose at her sides, beside her sheathed daggers. Her blades would not protect her if the spell went awry. Even the fabled swords of the old elf-kings wouldn't have had the power save her. Only her own will could do that. She closed her eyes.

Dear gods, the magic was strong. Like a river of red and silver and inky black, surging all around her.

"*Moitak larshat ku xalathom,*" she spoke, moving her fingers and gathering the spell's threads together. There was nothing in the world but her, the statue, and the power she wielded. "*Ikuno gangarog te apun do.*"

Sorcery surged through her and filled her. It was almost too much, like trying to drink from a bursting dam.

With all her strength she bore down, shaped it, and forced it out through her reaching fingers. It swirled and gushed, an invisible wave that swallowed the Hooded One. She felt the presence react, stirring, vengeful. It tried to break free, furious, battering at the edges of the spell. She thrust aside her misgivings and focused on binding the unfriendly spirit that lurked within the idol.

He stepped forth, much different from the last time. Then, he had been a wraith; now he looked as solid as her own flesh, a being of regal bearing, grim aspect, and might beyond imagining. It had taken a dozen archmages to bind him to the statue. Their ancient wards crumbled now, like rusted chains, leaving only the threaded strand of Shedara's magic. She gritted her teeth, grunting out one spidery word at a time to keep him under her control.

"Stubborn," said Maladar with a chuckle—an unpleasant bubbling sound from his tongueless mouth. "Submit. It will be easier."

Shedara felt him push at the edges of her mind, and she pushed back, her face ashen from the effort. "I . . . am not the one . . . who . . . must . . . submit," she grunted, trembling.

"Oh?" the dead emperor asked. His voice was light, almost pleasant—but foul all the same. "You don't seem to understand who I am. I ruled the greatest empire Taladas has ever known. I cast spells no man had dreamt of before—or since, I am certain. I bound demons to my will, and would have done the same with the gods, in time. I could crack this world in half, were it my whim. And you would claim dominion over *me*?"

He laughed his rusty laugh, folding his hands within his sleeves.

"You were . . . vulnerable," Shedara said. "They . . . imprisoned you. You are not free . . . unless I . . . will it."

"Then will it," said Maladar.

And suddenly she wanted to—that was the worst part. It would only take a gesture, a word, a moment. The mind that strove against hers pushed its tendrils in, trying to convince her that its release was necessary, even a good thing. With Maladar back in the world, there would be order. She saw herself at his right hand, going to war, and ruling Taladas again. Armach-nesti would be hers to govern, at his whim—she would be the new Voice of the elves. The hordes of the Tamire would be swept away by fire and wind. The Imperial League would fall to rubble. Under the faceless emperor's tutelage, she would learn new magic, spells she couldn't control by herself even with a hundred years of study. It all was hers, if she only willed it.

Will you? asked his voice, deep within her mind. *Dare you will it?*

"Nnnnnnnnnnnn," she grunted. "Nnnnnnngh."

"You cannot say it," mocked Maladar. "You, who would deny me—and you cannot even say the word!"

"NNNNNNNNNNNNNN . . ."

"Go on, Shedara—free me. Unleash me upon your foes."

"NNNN*NNNNO!*"

Something gave. For an awful moment she was certain she had failed. She staggered, fell to her knees, felt her leggings and her skin tear on sharp stones. Tears poured down her cheeks, and she bowed her head, waiting for the emperor's homunculus—or whatever it was—to take its vengeance upon her, to snuff out her life like a candle in the gloom.

Nothing happened.

She took a slow, shuddering breath, then another.

She looked up.

Maladar stood frozen before her, shaking with fury, still bound. She could *see* the magic holding him fast, silver cords of energy leading from his body back to the statue that was its prison. The old spells still held, if only barely. He was hers to command.

"Tell me your bidding," he said, his voice dark and flat with hatred.

Shedara's heart leaped. This proud specter, this great

BLADES OF THE TIGER

evil, none more powerful in Taladas's long and death-strewn history—and her magic had held against it! The statue would do her will. She rose, bleeding, and steepled her fingers.

"You know what I wish," she said.

Once in Aurim there had been a city, a beautiful place called Am Durn, whose walls were sheathed in silver and whose towers gleamed blue with lapis. It had been a city of song, and art, and peace. But when it rebelled against him, Maladar's wrath had wiped Am Durn from the face of Krynn.

He had not used fire or wind to destroy it. Nor the earth.

"I understand," he growled. "Where shall I strike?"

Shedara smiled. Her plan had succeeded. There was a chance now.

"Near here," she said, opening her mind to him. "I will show you."

She did, and a moment later Maladar nodded. "*Elas,*" he said in the old tongue that had perished in flame with his realm, long ago.

It shall be done.

Again, the magic began to gather—but this time the threads of it were dark, fed by Nuvis alone. Maladar drew down the black moon's power, shaping the spell and speaking words that burned Shedara's ears. He held his hands high, forcing the power out in a great, blossoming fountain, that streamed across the walls of the vault and rained down all around them.

Shedara watched, unable to take her eyes off him. This was why she didn't see the shadows behind her begin to move.

※————¤¤————※

The suffocating sea serpent was dead, its thrashings stilled, and lay in a limp coil of ruby scales. Most of the creatures laid bare by the Tiderun's retreat had perished before it, though a few scuttling crabs still moved through the muck. Gulls had begun to settle and to feast on the carrion. A few skyfishers joined them, though their eyes stayed on the Road, where the horsemen had gathered and the soldiers of the League waited to resist them. To those large and foul birds, no meat was as sweet as battle-dead manflesh. They ignored the dead goblins, for the taste of *those* was foul and rancid.

At the head of the column of horsemen, halfway across the bed of the strait, Chovuk Boyla sat his horse, flanked by Hult and Eldako. He watched as the scouts he'd sent to watch the Wretched Ones' attack rode back to him, leaving Gharmu and the last of his warriors arrow-riddled and ruined on the shore. "Speak," he bade when they got close. "What do we face?"

"They are few," scoffed the lead scout, keeping a tight rein on his nervous horse. It sidled to the right two steps, tossing its head, and he stopped it with a yank. "A few hundred, mostly swords and spears, at the mouth of the ravine."

Chovuk nodded, his strangely aged face grim. He stared out at the southern shore, the wind blowing the white, wispy hairs of his beard. The sun's light glinted off his dragon-scale armor. "Archers?"

"A few, on the surround," the scout replied, grinning. His teeth were yellow, and his breath was foul. "They didn't do much to stop the Wretched Ones."

"Of course not," the Boyla replied. "They knew that was a test. They knew they could handle Gharmu's lot, and held back their bows—one in three, maybe half."

Hult and Eldako both nodded, though the scout looked confused. Not a brilliant man, but he didn't need to be. All that was required of him were good eyes and a fast horse. The other two understood, though—so far the enemy followed good tactics, and whoever led them was a cunning warrior.

"Anything else?" Chovuk asked.

"Snares," replied the scout. "Pits. Goblins found most of those, though."

The Boyla never took his eyes off the far shore, where Gharmu's body sprawled over a rock. He had been one of the last to die. "Well done," he said after a pause. "Go back to your clan and arm for the charge."

Clapping his open hand against his chest, the rider wheeled and rode away, his fellows galloping after him. With the scouts gone, nothing else stood between Chovuk and the cliffs and trees to the south. Looking at the stunted, twisted bodies of the Wretched Ones, Hult thought of Mount Xagal. How close they had come to dying there, at the mountain-folk's hands! Now the goblins were dead, slaughtered in a battle they were too stupid to know they couldn't win. The look in his master's eyes told him he would use the Uigan just as callously, if it came to it. Not White Sky, not if he could sacrifice the other clans first, but still. His own people.

Chovuk pointed. High above the ravine, the broken finger of a tower stuck up from the clifftops. Figures moved atop it. "That is our goal, *tenach*," he said. "The one who leads them is watching from there. We will break through their ranks, you and I, even before we have the victory. We will break through and face their marshal sword to sword."

Hult nodded. An at earlier time, he might have reveled at the prospect of such a glorious fight. Now that he had seen the madness in the Boyla, though, he wondered. Didn't the horde need them on the line of battle, not stalking one man in a tower?

"Yes, master," he said.

"What of my arrows?" asked Eldako. "Where shall I spend them?"

"On the one who commands them below," Chovuk replied. "The marshal will have dispatched an officer to be his voice on the line. Bring him down, and the battle will crumble."

The elf bobbed his head. "As you command."

Chovuk grinned, a little too wide. A tiger's smile, a maniac's. Merciful Jijin, Hult thought, resting a hand on his *shuk*.

A horn from an *ajagh* hung on a baldric over the Boyla's shoulder. He raised it, licked his cracked lips, and blew a long, loud note. It rang up and down the valley of the Run, echoing off cliffs both behind and ahead. Glancing back, Hult saw the mass of the horde raise their swords and spears in response. A great bellowing rose from ten thousand throats. Beside him, Chovuk brought his horse about and rose in his saddle, standing on his stirrups and shouting in a voice like thunder. He seemed to grow as he spoke, his body swelling and his eyes flashing with fire. His magic at work.

"Men of the plains, warriors of the steppes!" he roared. "Today we stand on the edge of legend. For hundreds of summers, the lands before us were as unreachable as the moons. Long have the waters stood in our way, long have they kept the minotaur realm beyond our reach . . . but today, today the waters have fled, and the lands of the bull-men lie naked before us, like a virgin in her bridal bed!

"Great will be the feasting of the crows tonight, on the ground that lies before us. Great it shall be in the villages and towns, the temples and cities where the bull-men hide, rich with gold and jewels. We have already avenged our people against them, driving the foul beasts from our shores. Now let us strike like an arrow through the heart of this fat, lazy empire! Let the League tremble before the sound of our hooves!

"For the Tamire!" he shouted, thrusting his *shuk* high. "For the Uigan!"

"*For the Boyla!*" came the bellowed reply.

Blades stabbed the air above the riders' heads. More horns sounded, from all the clans. Horses reared and spears lowered. Chovuk Boyla turned, slamming his helmet down on his head. It was the kind of moment the elders sang about . . . would sing about, even generations after. Maybe longer. Hult drew his sword, feeling the battle-rage rise within him.

"*Hai!*" barked his master, and his horse leaped forward.

Hult dug in his spurs, and the two of them bolted north, rising swiftly to a full charge, their helmets' crests streaming behind them. Eldako followed, silent. Then, with a roar like a storm, the Uigan thundered after them, a raging flood of men, horses and steel.

When the Uigan spurred their horses and surged across the Run, all the strength seemed to drain from Forlo's body. His knees weakened, and he had to lean against the ruined stones of the tower to keep his footing. If Iver noticed, the young guardsman never said—probably, he was too busy fighting off his own crushing panic to care.

"You are soldiers of the League!" Grath was raging down below. "You will hold the line, no matter what happens! Even if the maw of the Abyss opens and all of Hith's demons come flooding out, you will not budge!"

It was a heartening speech, but a few of the troops still turned and bolted from the charging horsemen. The sight angered Forlo, but he couldn't completely blame them. It was one thing to boast about meeting a valiant death against impossible odds when you were sitting in camp with a flask of beer in your hand. It was another thing entirely to watch it bear down on you in lunging, roaring fury.

There were three riders at the head of the horde, Forlo saw, outstripping the main mass of barbarians. One was, incredibly, an elf with a painted face and brightly colored hair. The second was Uigan, dressed like a common warrior. The third wore armor of bronze scales, polished so they burned like molten gold. Forlo knew this was the riders' prince, their Boyla. He offered a silent prayer, to whatever gods might be listening, for the chance to confront the man before his time was done. Just a chance to slay their prince . . . it might not pay back for all the lives that would be lost that day, and in the days to come across the northern provinces, but it would be a start. He couldn't hope for more.

He turned to Iver. The man's face was white and his eyes were staring. His mouth hung open when Forlo touched his arm.

"You'd better ride now, lad," Forlo said. It surprised him, how calm his voice sounded. "Take this and go."

He pulled the blue banner from the young guardsman's belt and held it out.

Iver stared at the flag and took it without seeming to understand. He twisted the cloth in his hands, then all at once seemed to come back to himself. This was it—the chance to leave the field alive, and with honor. He turned to go, then remembered to salute.

"The gods watch over you, sir," he said.

"We'd better hope they do," Forlo said, hand clasping over fist. "There's not much else left."

Then Iver was gone, running down the stairs so fast it was a wonder he didn't fall and break his neck. Forlo heard his horse whicker, then the clap of hooves above the thunder from the Run, as the guardsman streaked away, bearing his token of doom. He didn't turn to watch. His eyes stayed fast on the horde. The throng was a hundred yards from the shore now, seventy, forty . . . Grath howled curses as more men bolted from the line. The archers took their positions and nocked their arrows. The footmen lowered their pikes.

"*Khot*," Forlo whispered as the horde started up the slope.

※━━━━※━━━━※

Far away, at the eastern edge of the Tiderun, where it runs into the Boiling Sea beyond the Steamwalls, something happened.

No one was there to see it save a lone brass dragon, a young wyrm whose scales still shone bright, without any of the patina of age. The creature soared high on the thermals, above the clouds of yellow, noxious gas that rose from the water, watching—not for prey or foes, but out of pure curiosity. He was safe up high, and he could watch the dwarves and the other bent and twisted denizens of the land below, scratching out meager lives from brimstone-crusted rocks. Nothing fascinated dragons, who could fly wherever they chose, more than those who dwelt in such lethal places. Taladas was full of them.

Then, suddenly, it wasn't safe any more.

There were volcanoes down deep, and not just among the fuming peaks. There were rents in the sea floor—clefts in the stone that ran right down to glowing magma at the world's heart. It was why the sea boiled: scars in the sea floor that mirrored the blazing wound of Hitehkel to the east, where the land still burned from the Destruction.

That morning, seven such faults erupted at once, right at the Run's dry mouth. This caused a great bubble to well up from the depths, filled with venomous vapors. The dragon saw this and tried to pull away, tried to bank north to escape, already knowing it was too late. The bubble reached the surface, bulged for a moment like some awful blister, then burst. A billow of noxious steam blew out from it, rising a mile into the air.

The dragon never had a chance. The geyser roasted its flesh in midair. Shrieking in agony, the dragon spun across the sky, tried to catch itself, and failed. The skin of its wings was charred, and peeling away. Fluttering uselessly, it plunged down toward the sea like a spent arrow. It hit the water with the snap of shattering bones, then was gone, sunk beneath the roiling surface.

No one was there to bear witness as the water swelled in the geyser's wake . . . and the waves began to rise.

Chapter 29

THE LOST ROAD, THE IMPERIAL LEAGUE

Grath stared down the ravine, through the trees and over the drifts of goblin corpses, to the sea floor below. The Uigan were coming, a wall of death moving up toward him, toward the Sixth. There was no surviving it, not for long. The men knew, which was why some had fled and more were getting ready to follow. He could smell their fear. Let them go, he thought, bracing himself as the ground beneath him shook with the rumble of hooves. The cowards wouldn't be any use in the line anyway. They'd only get in the way, and he didn't want any complications.

It wasn't every minotaur, after all, who got to choose the day and manner of his dying.

"Spears!" he bellowed, and a signal-standard arose to echo the command, fluttering in the breeze. It wasn't needed: Grath's voice boomed from one end of the ravine to the other. "Shields!"

The soldiers who weren't already armed bent now to pick up their long-hafted pikes, each twice as tall as the largest man in the cohort. Great oblong shields locked together, rim over rim, to form a wall in the front rank, and they and two more ranks behind lowered their spears to present a thicket of steel. Centuries of military strategy had led to this: the perfect formation against a cavalry charge, short of a phalanx of wizards hurling fireballs. Grath didn't care for sorcery: it took all the fun out of fighting.

He glanced up at the tower. Forlo was still there, watching. Grinning, the minotaur raised his axe toward the figure atop the ruin. He was sure they would be seeing each other again soon, in the gods' feasting halls. Then he turned back and watched the riders come.

The pickets slowed them down, though not as much as he'd hoped: their scouts had spied them during the first sortie, and had warned their chief. There were some goblin corpses impaled on the sharpened stakes, which made their purpose quite clear. Some horses still got skewered, and some riders died screaming, run through on the fire-hardened stakes . . . but only a scattering. The same went for the pits and snares. As the bulk of the horde picked its way past his men's hard-made traps, Grath muttered curses against the damned goblins and whatever gods made them.

Now came the archers, their arrows hailing down on the Uigan like swarms of deadly wasps. They had more effect, for the barbarians carried no shields, and had nothing to protect themselves but their armor—which was made of leather and stopped only one shaft in three. The front ranks of the horde collapsed, falling by the score, and their fellows began to pile up behind them, howling curses and battlecries as they tried to leap over the bodies of the dead and dying. The bowmen kept bombarding them, twice as many of them as they'd shown to the goblins, and a cheer went up from the spearmen, for it looked for a time as if the horde had stopped.

Grath did not cheer. He knew better. The enemy was still advancing, though more slowly, and the archers couldn't keep it up forever. There simply weren't enough arrows. Already the volleys were beginning to thin—and the horsemen were returning fire, letting loose with small bows of wood and horn at the cliffs above. They were good marksmen, and even in concealment some of the archers fell, the songs of their bowstrings stilled. Bit by bit, the horde gained back their momentum. The soldiers' cheers died.

Amid it all, Grath picked out the bronze-mailed figure with the horsetail helm, the one who had led the charge. The man was shouting in the Uigan tongue, furious and wild-eyed, exhorting his men to move on. He seemed impervious. Arrows glanced off the plates of his armor. There were a couple stuck in his horse, but even the animal seemed battle-mad, and didn't appear to notice. It had to be their prince, their Boyla. Grath's eyes narrowed, his nostrils flared. He pointed with his axe, raising his voice for all to hear.

"That one is mine!" he barked. "Let him come to me! Let him feel the kiss of my steel!"

All that remained was glory, and he would have his share. His men shouted back, acknowledging the order, and Grath smiled, his eyes never leaving the armored chief.

"Come on, whore's son," he growled. "Bring yourself to me."

※———※———※

Chovuk pointed up toward the mass of spears at the ravine's mouth. Hult followed his gaze, twisting sideways as an arrow hissed past. Beside him, a man caught a second shaft in the side of his neck and pitched over his saddle horn with a gurgle, bright blood fanning the air. A third struck the Boyla's shoulder and shattered against the bronze plate protecting it, the pieces spinning away.

There stood a bull-man, right in the center of the front line, taller than the rest and more finely clad. His shield bore an emblem, crossed golden axes over the red and blue all the soldiers bore. He appeared to be the only minotaur among the enemy.

"That captain!" Chovuk roared. "He is mine! The man who touches him will die by my blade!"

The Uigan didn't all hear, but the ones close by did, anyway. That was enough: the word would spread from man to man, on down the gully to the sea, where the bulk of the horde still waited. The riders would obey.

Hult raised his bow, pulled an arrow back to his cheek, aimed high, and loosed—all in one motion without pause. He lost track of his arrow's flight, but saw it strike. A crouched figure on the ridge above jerked, his head snapping back as the shaft struck him in the roof of his mouth. Then he slumped over, one arm hanging over the cliff's edge, his bow dropping to shatter on the rocks below. Many of the League's archers were dying that way, the riders claiming one for every two the hidden bowmen brought down. A bad trade, but there were many more riders than bowmen. The horde inched on up the ravine, threading among rocks and trees, trampling the remains of goblins and crawling up toward the line.

"On! On!" cried the Uigan, needing no urging from Boyla or Tegin. The scent of battle was upon them. "Forward the riders! Blood for the Tiger's blades!"

They plunged on toward the shield wall, abristle with spears, knowing they would have to hew their way through, with sword and sweat and blood. Chovuk led the advance, untouched yet—not even scratched. That was rare among the front ranks: even Hult had cuts on his arm and cheek, where arrows had grazed him. But he was the Boyla, and a sorcerer besides. Hult guessed he'd cast a spell on himself the previous night, to protect him from harm: there seemed to be the faintest shimmer around him, as if it weren't Chovuk, but his image in a still pool. They closed the last stretch of open ground.

Then they were to the spears, the waves of horsemen slamming hard into the bristling weapons. Scores of riders died, gored by the long weapons. Horses screamed, thrashing as they crumpled to the ground. Chovuk didn't fall, though: he laid about with his *shuk*, lopping the heads off pikes, armor and spell alike turning them aside when they sought to pierce him. Hult followed his lead, chopping the pikes into pieces. His horse died under him, and he leaped clear, still hewing and cleaving. Chovuk's steed collapsed too, blood flowing from its torn throat. Boyla and *tenach* kept fighting, side by side, their sabers blurring as they chewed through the wall of spears. Up and down the line, the Uigan followed their lead, and though the riders continued to fall like scythed millet, the League's formation was beginning to weaken.

Chovuk drove straight for the soldiers' commander, roaring like an animal. The minotaur saw him and grinned nastily. Hult spun to his left, avoiding a stabbing spear, and cleaved it in half with his *shuk*. All of a sudden, Hult thought he felt something strange: a trembling of the earth beneath his feet, almost imperceptible amid the clash of battle. Then it was gone again, and he put it from his mind. All he could focus on were the spears, the men who wielded them, and his master, slashing and bellowing as he drove closer and closer to the bull-man in the midst of their foes.

Forlo watched his men beat back the press of the horde. It wouldn't last, *couldn't* last: for every rider they brought down, thirty more waited to fill the ravine from end to end. More than half the barbarians still remained down on the floor of the Run, waiting for the horde to advance so they could return to dry land. There was no hurry. Midday hadn't yet come and it would be many hours before the tides would return.

He cursed Rekhaz for giving him so few reinforcements, himself for being so stubborn, and the moons for stealing away the sea. He wished he were down there with Grath, who was casting aside his spear—the weapon cut apart by the Uigan's whirling sabers—and drawing his greataxe. Other soldiers did the same, for the riders had weakened the pike wall too much for it to hold.

The battle's end was beginning.

Ride, Iver, he thought. Ride as fast as you can, and don't look back.

"Swords! Swords!" Grath boomed below. "Hold the line! Don't let the horse-lovers through!"

So it began, the fight in earnest: up till now, the goblins, the archers, and the spears, had been only the opening moves of the endgame. Now true warriors fought, blade to blade. The barbarians' numbers against the cohort's discipline, and no trickery between. The riders, many unhorsed by the pikes, climbed over the bodies of their fellows, curved sabers slashing, and slammed into the wall of shields. The soldiers' ranks buckled, and for a moment it seemed from Forlo's vantage that it would end there, that the line could *not* hold and the Uigan would breach it immediately and sweep it away like driftwood in a storm. But then, with a shout the men of the Sixth shoved back, slashing and battering with their straight swords, their axes, their iron-headed maces. The riders had no armor and no shields: nearly every blow the soldiers struck was lethal, four barbarians falling for every one of Forlo's men.

There were thousands more coming, and only a couple hundred soldiers in reserve. Watching the battle play out, Forlo knew he'd been right: with twice as many men—or the help of the Silvanaes—the line might have held, might have driven back the enemy. But the defenses were dwindling. The men in the rear of the cohort tried to spread out, to make sure there was someone at every point to replace those who fell in the front, but it was getting harder. The wall was crumbling, soon to be washed away.

The din from below was horrible: sword against sword, sword against shield, sword piercing flesh, men hurt, men dying, battlecries, cursing, horses shrieking, and Grath and the Uigan prince bellowing for their men to fight on. It all melded into a din that echoed off the cliffs and carried across the Run.

Then, all at once, there was a new sound: a rumbling deep below the rest, so low it made the stones of the tower tremble beneath his feet. It came from the east, far away. Forlo half-expected to see an army of stone giants charging along the sea floor. But there was nothing there.

And then there was.

Forlo's eyes widened, his mouth went dry, and his breath stole away. It wasn't possible, was it? It made no sense. But he ran to the other side of the ruined tower anyway, leaning out over the merlons, and could only stare in amazement at what he saw in the distance, still far away but coming fast.

Eldako climbed, moving unseen up the cliff face across from the ruined tower, making no sound as he went. This would have been hard going for most—all sea-worn stones, crusted white with bird droppings, and nests and tufts of weeds that grew out of clefts. The elves of the Tamire learned to climb at a young age, though, and Eldako had been scaling cliffs sheerer than that since he was a child. He wasn't even breathing hard when he reached the purchase he'd chosen: a narrow ledge fifty feet above the ravine floor, with fifty more to the top. Below him, the horsemen choked the valley. If he fell, they would trample his body to mush. He would not fall, though.

His sharp ears heard Chovuk yelling, heard him singling out the minotaur, the lone one of his kind among the paltry few human soldiers who'd shown up for the fight. Eldako frowned, wondering where the other bull-men were. He cared nothing about the humans who dwelt in the League, but the minotaurs were another matter. His people hated them more than anything. He'd hoped he could pick them off from this perch, one by one. He would settle for the one captain, but later . . . after the battle he and the Boyla would have words.

Though the outcrop where he stood was only half an arm's length from cliff to edge, he strung his longbow easily, bending it around his leg, then drawing a long, green-fletched shaft from his quiver. Just then an arrow struck the stone near his head, making him wince and turn away. Looking across the ravine, he immediately spied the one who'd shot: one of the archers their enemies had placed along the clifftops had spied him and was already drawing a second shaft. He never got the chance: Eldako pulled and loosed, almost without looking. The man was pulling his own string back when the elf's shot took him cleanly in the left eye, sending him sprawling over backward.

Eldako paused for a moment, pulling out another arrow as he did so to make sure no one else was aiming at him. There wasn't, and he nodded to himself. Later, he would curse himself for not seeing that one bowman, but now was not the time.

His bow creaked, old familiar music as he drew the arrow back. He turned, sighting down the shaft, and saw the bull-man, the captain bellowing to his men to let Chovuk come to him. That was foolhardy and brash— Eldako felt a flash of admiration for the minotaur. That was all he allowed himself, though. He grew very still, holding his breath and preparing for the shot. He prayed to Astar, his people's god, to guide his aim. He envisioned, as he always did, the arrow flashing through the air, striking home, killing in an instant.

That was when the tremor struck. The whole cliff began to shake beneath him. His shot flew, but went wild, well over the bull-man's head and off into the trees. Eldako had a moment to be surprised—he couldn't remember the last time he'd missed a shot like that—then the stone began to tremble so violently that he nearly dropped his bow and had to cling to the cliff to keep from getting shaken loose. What in the Abyss was going on?

Then he knew. He had lived his whole life in the Dreaming Green, save for occasional ventures into the Ring Mountains, the snow-fields of Panak, and the steppes of the Uigan. Like many of the riders, the Run had been his first glimpse of the sea. But Eldako was an elf. He understood all the movements of the earth. He'd stood on the edges of raging rivers, foaming white as they poured down from the highlands above his home. He knew how the stones around those torrents thrummed. This was like that . . . and not. It was greater.

Much greater.

Fear took hold of Eldako, son of Tho-ket. He forgot his quarry, forgot the battle beneath him—forgot everything but the shuddering of the cliff. His heart in his throat, he began to climb.

Grath heard the noise and wondered what it was, that rumbling in the distance. He might not have believed it was real, but he could feel it, too: the ground trembling, like a prelude to the kind of quake that had swallowed Kristophan. He hacked with his axe, splitting the skull of a rider, showering gore all around, then glanced up at the tower, at Forlo. His friend was looking the other way, back east. Something was happening.

Too late, Grath thought. They were doomed: the line could not hold much longer. Any moment now, it would break.

A shout drew his attention. The bronze-armored warrior, the barbarian prince, was very close. He'd been waiting for this, fighting harder than ever in his life just to make sure he didn't fall before he faced the Boyla. Looking closer, he was surprised to see the man's face: he was *old*, wrinkled and snow-bearded, although he fought like a man still in the summer of his life. His eyes were young, too, and full of fury and shadowy madness. Only a few Uigan remained between the two of them now, and Grath laid about with his axe, working to clear them away, thinking of a glorious death all the while.

"Come on, worm!" he shouted, brandishing his blood-streaked blade. "Come find your fate!"

The Boyla saw him. He had been watching him all along. The ground between them lay open, and a smile spread across the chieftain's face. A smile beneath eyes as red as heart's blood. And his teeth were pointed!

What in Sargas's name? Grath thought.

Then the man began to change, the armor falling away as its straps strained and burst, revealing a shape beneath that grew less mannish with every heartbeat—the body elongated, the arms and legs became paws, the face twisted, and the sharp teeth turned into fangs like daggers. Fur grew out of the man's hide, white striped with black. Only the eyes remained as they were, as insane as ever. The rest had become a huge, feline form, a steppe-tiger.

Grath's mouth dropped open. He had a moment to blink, then the great beast crouched and sprang.

There was no time to swing his axe. The great beast hit him like a charging war-chariot, hammering him back and pinning him to the ground. He felt claws pierce his shoulders and rip open his flesh. His weapon fell from a hand gone nerveless, from fingers he couldn't feel any more. The tiger's weight on top of him was incredible, crushing the wind from his lungs. Its rear legs came up, dug into his stomach, and raked. Pain exploded within him as his innards shredded, and began to spill out. He screamed into the great cat's face, at the jaws opening above him. Then he butted his head against that horrible maw and felt a moment's satisfaction as one of his horns pierced the animal's cheek. He'd blooded the bastard, at least.

The tiger screeched and pulled back—only for a

moment. Then the mouth opened again, fangs bared. The hot stink of its breath beat down as they clamped around Grath's head, driving through flesh and bone. A good death, Grath thought, as his world burst into roaring flames of agony.

The tiger shook him hard, and something snapped.

Hult stared at the hulking form of his master, the wild animal Chovuk had become, as the bull-man's shredded remains dropped to the ground. The minotaur was dead, of that there was no doubt. There wasn't enough left of him to be alive. The tiger turned, blood dripping from its maw as it glared back at him. All around, the fighting seemed to slow, as rider and soldier alike paused to stare at what had become of Grath Horuth-Bok, and at the monstrous man-beast in their midst. They hesitated and shied back. Hult didn't blame them: seeing the wild gleam in the animal's eyes, he too felt like dropping his *shuk* and fleeing.

A moment later, though, something drew their attention away: the rumbling, which had been building as they fought, grew very loud. Screams rose from the horde's rear, and when Hult looked he saw bedlam down on the floor of the Run. The riders who still hadn't come up into the ravine were scattering, seeking desperately to escape something.

His skin felt cold. He had never seen warriors of the Tamire flee like that.

"Master . . ." he said.

But Chovuk wasn't listening, was barely even Chovuk any more. The tiger had moved on, raging deeper into the ranks of the League's soldiers, swatting them with its massive paws, seizing them, and crushing the life out of them with its powerful jaws. Some swung their swords at it, but its flesh was as hard as stone, turning their blades aside or shattering them to the hilt. The rest just scrambled away, letting the cat push deeper and deeper into their midst.

Hult had to follow. He was bound to by his oath to the Boyla. But before he did, he risked another glance over his shoulder at the insanity that had consumed the riders behind. What was making them run? What could possibly—

The roaring got so loud then that all the fighting seemed to stop and everyone turned to stare back down the ravine. A dark, looming shadow fell over the Run and the men there. Then, with a ferocity and suddenness that drove every thought from Hult's mind, a wall of water swept down the strait.

Chapter 30

The Run

With incredulous eyes, Barreth Forlo watched it come.

The wave was enormous. There were tales of such phenomena, from long ago. In the First Destruction, swells like it had rushed across the face of Taladas, wiping out entire kingdoms and drowning millions. In the years before, when Aurim held sway, wizards and emperors—and emperor-wizards—had summoned giant waves to punish their enemies. Once, according to a tale Forlo had heard at court in Kristophan, a tyrant had called on the sea to destroy an entire city—Forlo couldn't remember its name, or the emperor's. One day, the citadel had stood proud and silver-walled on Aurim's western shore. The next, nothing had remained but rubble and floating bodies, in brine frothed red by sharks.

This was like that.

The wave came on like a mountain, three hundred feet high and capped with white foam that gnashed like giant, ever-hungry fangs. It wasn't the blue of summer water, or the greens of the shallows in the south. No, it was angry water, storm water, winter water: gray as steel with a heart that was almost black. It roared down the chasm of the Run, the world's largest flash flood, swallowing the dead sea serpents and smashing the bared shipwrecks to flinders. Used to the gentle ebb and flow of the tides, the debris dotting the strait's floor could not stand against the weight of the swiftly moving torrent. Cliffs crumbled on either shore and great stones and avalanches of earth cracked and slid into the maelstrom below. Vast, billowing clouds of spray rose high into the air and drifted south on the wind. The noise the wave made was the voice of a thousand angry dragons, all roaring and breathing death. The tower shook so violently underfoot that, for a wild moment, Forlo feared it would collapse beneath him. He gripped the battlements.

Most of the Uigan were still in the Tiderun, waiting for the forefront of the horde to advance so they could come ashore. Now they panicked like spooked birds, scattering this way and that, doomed but trying whatever they could to escape. Some bolted headlong down the strait, mindlessly trying to outrun what was coming. Others turned north, in the wild hope of getting back to the far shore. A scattering gave up their treasured horses and dashed for the cliffs, trying to climb to safety.

None of them made it.

The wave came on, merciless and unstoppable. Time seemed to slow as it towered above the barbarians, casting a horrible shadow over them. From above, Forlo saw the riders look up at the wall of water, eyes wide and mouths slack with terror. He felt sick, pitying them though they were his enemies. It was no way for a warrior to die. There was no glory in it. And there were so *many*—thousands, entire clans' worth. The Tamire would be a nation of widows and orphans.

The wave slammed into the horde, and in an instant it simply disappeared. Days from then, many miles to the west, the fisherfolk would find hundreds of bodies—men and horses alike—scattered like driftwood along the Run—bloated, broken, and swarming with scuttling crabs. For the moment, though, they simply vanished as if they had never existed, the fighting men of the Uigan obliterated by the sea's fury.

As the wave roared past, carrying on in its thundering journey, a lesser hammer of water rose up the ravine, clawing up and snatching away the rear ranks of those who thought themselves safe on dry land. Many horsemen flew from their saddles, knocked through the air by the force of the blow. Others went under, dragged away by the undertow. Trees groaned as they tore from their roots, then swept along, smashing into barbarians. Rocks tumbled from the canyon's walls, crushing those beneath. Men tried to ride forward, hacking with curved sabers and thrusting with spears, killing their fellows in the mad crush to escape the devouring flood.

Then, finally, the deluge stopped. The water slowed, the swell lessened . . . stopped . . . and started to roll back, leaving corpses shattered on the stones and dangling motionless from branches. Most were gone, snatched away into the roaring flow.

It grew very quiet. The din of battle was gone and the cries of the dying were faint. Both sides stood still, the survivors of the Sixth Legion—Forlo felt a twist in his gut to see no sign of Grath among them—staring warily at the Uigan. Some of the surviving barbarians stared back, but most had turned to look at where their sword-brothers had been only a hundred-count before. Gone, now, like they had never been born, the sea raging in their place. Ten thousand Uigan, now reduced to barely eight hundred. Probably much less.

A miracle, the clerics would call it. Forlo knew it was no such thing, though: no god had intervened here. He had never called on them to do so. No, there was something else at work. Magic, mightier than any he had ever known, than any seen since the time of Aurim, and the city—Am Durn, it came to him now—drowned by Maladar the Faceless.

Maladar.

The Hooded One.

He understood now, and it knocked the wind out of him. He stood stunned, realizing what must have happened, leagues away in Coldhope. He saw clearly in his mind's eye the statue, saw Shedara standing before it, magic seething in the air. He heard her command the spirit within the stone, felt it reply, and felt the oceans hear its call and begin to rise.

He felt the urge to laugh and held it back. The statue, the Sargas-be-damned statue, had done this! If he'd given it up, if he'd given it to the Silvanaes, the horde would have run rampant across the League. Now the Ulgan were shattered down to a handful, and the riders' spirit was broken by the shock of it all. Their people were destroyed. The plains and steppes would be different places, now. Emptier places.

The fighting began again, uncertain at first, then with growing ferocity. But everything had changed. The Uigan were not as fierce any more, their blades slowed by horror—both at what had just happened and at their new position. They were no longer the tip of a great spear poised to drive through their foes, but a scrap of a slaughtered army, trapped between steel and the sea. The soldiers were still outnumbered—some three hundred had lived this long, by Forlo's guess—but the horde's destruction awoke something new in them, something none had dared to feel when the battle began.

Hope. They could win the fight.

So the line reformed, thin but strong, and held firm against the disheartened riders. In fact, before long, the defenders started pushing forward, driving the Uigan back toward the rushing water. The barbarians did not run, for there was nowhere to go. They stood and fought, backing up slowly, stumbling over jetsam and burst corpses as they gave ground back down the slope. On the cliffs, the remaining archers loosed their last shots into the throng, then drew their shortswords and charged back along the ridges to the canyon's mouth, to bolster the rest of the soldiers in the fight.

Forlo scanned the battleground, searching for one figure. But of the prince in bronze mail there was no sign: like Grath, the enemy chieftain seemed to have fallen in the fighting. His body must be lying somewhere—now drawing crows. A pity, that. Forlo had wanted to face the Boyla, to see the despair in his eyes at the horrible way he'd lost. To put a sword through him for what he'd done to Malton and the other colonies, and again for what he'd nearly done to Coldhope and Essana.

Another thought came to him then, making him shake his head. Iver. I should have waited, he said to himself. The lad has the wrong banner. No matter, though: at worst, he would have to send riders out to intercept Shedara and his wife. It might take a while, but they would be found and kept safe.

Smiling, he drew his sword and turned to descend the steps. One more blade on the line would bring the battle to a quicker close. He wasn't needed in the tower any more. Victory was coming to them. It was time to go join his men.

Forlo started down the stairs—then stopped. He'd descended only three steps, and froze, listening to sounds from below. Someone was coming up. No—*something*. And it sounded very large.

His grip tightening around his sword, he climbed back up to the top of the steps, set his back to the crumbling wall, and waited.

※

Soaked with spray, Hult stared at the drenched earth behind him. Cliffs crumbled, trees toppled and the earth was reduced to slogging muck. That and a few bodies were all that remained. The hammer of water retreated down the gully, taking with it the greatest horde the Tamire had ever seen. Gone, all gone, the Lost Road become the Road of the Lost.

He felt numb, sick, and cold. Thousands of his people had died in a horrible instant, devoured by a sea that had appeared out of nowhere. Even if they survived the day, the Uigan could not raid any deeper into the League. And if the water remained, they were trapped there. The riders of the plains were no boat-builders. The bull-men would hunt them down and put them to the sword, day by day. They would have to be lucky indeed to return home alive. It was over.

Jijin, he wondered as he gazed upon the drenched destruction, why have you forsaken us?

A roar of inarticulate fury caught his attention and made him turn back toward the front. There, surrounded by soldiers who stood as shocked and still as the surviving Uigan, stood the Boyla—or rather, the white tiger he had become. The great cat was gazing down the slope, his red eyes flashing. Madness in them, but beneath the beastly form he understood as well as anyone what had just happened to his horde. To him. Hult watched as the last strands of Chovuk's sanity frayed, then snapped. The tiger crouched to spring.

"Master, wait!" he cried.

But Chovuk was beyond caring now. He leaped upon the nearest soldier, ripping the unfortunate man to red ribbons with his claws. Fangs tore and a gurgling voice screamed, then stopped, blood misting the air. Dripping crimson, the tiger hurtled into the defenders. He caught a grazing spear wound across his flank and ignored it, then caught another warrior in his jaws, dragged him shrieking for several paces, then let go and trampled him into the ground.

Some of the riders rallied, but most fell back, desperate and anguished. A few dropped their weapons and surrendered, and took blades in the heart for it. The League's defenders were in no mind to take prisoners, particularly ones they couldn't ransom. Chovuk continued to shred his way through the ranks, alone, pushing madly ahead.

Hult understood why, glancing up at the tower. In his berserk rage, his master was leaving his men to die so he could face the soldiers' commander. It was the only triumph he might salvage, the one victory he might extract from his defeat.

Hult bit his lip. He was *tenach*. He had sworn an oath always to be at the Boyla's side, unto death. Raising his *shuk*, he plunged forward, into the fast-closing gap the tiger left behind.

He almost didn't see a sword whistling toward his face, and ducked so late that he felt the wind of the blade against his shaven head. He lashed out at the weapon's owner with his *shuk*, rammed the blade halfway to the hilt in the man's stomach, jerked it free, and shoved onward as the soldier dropped to his knees. A moment later, another soldier loomed up before him, a heavy mace held high. Hult twisted aside as the weapon came crashing down, spun, and struck off the man's hands at the wrists. Screaming, his maimed opponent stumbled back and fell. Hult didn't bother to finish him, but pushed on to the next soldier, the next, and the next. He killed three more, wounded seven, and did not look back at all.

Then the battle was behind him—already it was a rout, the soldiers pushing his fellow riders back and back toward the sea. Hult plunged into the pine woods, saber flashing to hack branches out of his way. Some of the trees were snapped in half and others were broken and sagging: marks of the white tiger's passing, curving to the left and uphill, toward the tower. Hult followed the trail, bleeding and tired, legs and lungs burning, until he finally caught sight of white and black, flashing through the trees.

"Master!" he cried.

The tiger spun and leaped. It hit him hard, bore him to the ground, and knocked the *shuk* from his hand. The breath was crushed out of him. He could only lie still as claws pierced his leather armor and gore-dripping fangs opened above his ashen face. A single twitch would kill him.

"No," he begged. "I am your *tenach*, Chovuk Boyla. I am your friend."

The great cat snarled, the carrion stink of its breath gagging him. Warm blood dripped on him, some of it his own. He waited, eyes open, pleading.

After what seemed like hours, recognition dawned amid the howling turmoil in the tiger's eyes. It drew back, blinking, then climbed off him and slunk away through the undergrowth. Aching and limping, Hult got back to his feet, found his sword, and stumbled after.

The ground grew rocky and the trees thinned. Then there was the tower: moss-bearded and ivy-strangled, with fallen shards of its missing upper reaches scattered about its base. Chovuk slipped through a gap in its crumbled wall, and Hult edged in after. It was dim inside, on the bracken-wracked flagstones of its floor. The air was close and warm. The tiger was already climbing the stairs, growling deep in its throat. It had the scent of its prey, atop the ruined spire. Hult followed, sword ready.

He'd expected to find several men, but there was only one: weary and defiant, a veteran with a gray-frosted beard showing beneath his helm. He had good armor, a long, straight sword, and a round shield with a gilded boss. He had a red surcoat and a blue cloak, with a gold commander's blazon on both of them.

The soldier said something, but it was in the tongue of the League, guttural and harsh to Hult's ears. The words meant nothing to him. When he was done, he raised his sword in salute. Hult did the same, a courtesy between warriors.

The tiger growled, tensing to leap—

—and stopped, letting out a startled whimper. All at once, the air shimmered and the skin-prickling feeling of magic swirled about the tower's top. Their foe must have felt it too, for he drew back another step, and the furrows of his brow deepened. Hult glanced about, sure he would see the cloaked figure of the Teacher nearby, watching. But there was no one.

A howl pulled his attention back to the scene before him. The sound of abject despair came from Chovuk's mouth. It was so terrible that Hult felt the sudden, wild urge to turn and flee.

He stayed, though, and a moment later understood his master's anguish. The magic he'd felt wasn't some new spell arising; it was an old one departing. As Hult watched, the tiger's form rippled and shrank, bones crackling and fur falling out. Teeth shortened and lost their points. Red eyes turned back to shining black. Bit by bit, the skin-change wore off.

When it was done, the great cat was gone and Chovuk Boyla stood hunched in its place, naked, unarmed, ancient looking—and utterly broken. As Hult watched, the Tiger of the Tamire, the prince of all the Uigan, sank to his knees and wept.

Chapter 31

COLDHOPE KEEP, THE IMPERIAL LEAGUE

Shedara hadn't breathed for minutes. Black spots danced before her eyes and roaring filled her ears. She stood rigid, back arched, every muscle tensed—balanced on her toes, as if any moment the power coursing through her body might lift her off the ground. Her fingers curled into claws. Magic seethed in the air of the vault, making it glow like a thundercloud at night—more power than she'd ever felt before. Intoxicating.

Maladar's ghost hovered before her, gloved hands outstretched, almost touching her face. He, too, was afire with the moons' power, not just Nuvis but its red and silver cousins as well.

Together, they watched it happen. The quake, far away, beneath the Boiling Sea; the rising swells that swept out from it, making towering waves that battered the seaward edges of the Steamwalls and the burning lands to the east; and the column of water that broke high over the edge of the Tiderun, then thundered along its length, mile after mile, without mercy. She caught sight of the distant figures of the Uigan horde, spread out across the Run, panicking. She watched them die, thousands of men drowned and crushed by the watery hammer.

The wave carried on. There were many leagues yet to

go before it spent itself, washing on to the distant western ocean. She didn't need to see that happen, though. The deed was done and there was no use dwelling on it. She prayed to whatever gods might be listening that it was enough—that it had bought victory, or at least the chance of victory, for Forlo and his men. She hoped they weren't already dead. She wished she would be forgiven for her terrible act, for her collusion with darkness to slaughter so many men.

"Enough," she spoke through gritted teeth . . . and released the spell.

The magic boiled away and flashed through the air like crimson lightning before fading into motes that fell around her like snow. She exhaled, lungs burning. Bowing her head, she stood trembling in the dark.

"That was a fell thing we did," said the spirit. Not an accusation—simply a statement of fact. Perhaps a note of approval in his voice, even amusement. It was hard to tell, with no face to read.

"It was . . . for the good," Shedara gasped. "It . . . had to be . . . done."

Maladar laughed. "Oh? Where is it written that all things necessary are good? I know better, lady of the Silvanaes. Sometimes the things that must happen are terrible and foul. If you learn nothing else from this day, know that. Triumph has its cost."

Shedara looked at him, at the wretched mad king. Disgust rose in her throat, bitter.

"It is finished," she said. "Go back to your rest."

"My prison, you mean," the faceless specter said, the voice thick with derision. It folded its hands in its sleeves. "And if I do not wish to?"

Shedara shivered at the arrogance in the voice—not groundless pride, to be sure. Maladar was powerful. But the spell still bound him; the threads of silver light held him fast to the Hooded One. "Not your choice to make," she said. "I compel you. I control you. I hold the power here."

"Then release me!" cried the ghost. "Free me from this captivity! You have that power too."

He left it unspoken, but his tone promised rewards. Riches, power, and knowledge. The bonds holding him were frail; it would be so easy to sever them, to set him loose in the world again. She felt his ancient evil, poised to spring. She smelled it in the air, the attar of night-blooming flowers—not very different from the gray lotus. She had tasted his might: the same power that had slain armies and brought entire provinces to ruin, centuries ago. It had taken a company of archmages to stop him and to imprison him in the stone. It would only take a word to let him go.

"Please, Shedara," he said.

Her mouth opened, tongue set to form the first sound. Maladar had been imprisoned in the statue for ten human lifetimes. His grandchildren's grandchildren, if any of his progeny had even survived, were long since moldering bones. His name and all his deeds were all but forgotten—only sages still knew of him.

"Have I not suffered enough?" he asked.

She stared at him, long and hard. There was no real penitence there, no sorrow for the evils he had wrought. Beneath the false humility she saw the beast he was, and had always been. It was spiteful, vengeful, and cruel: a twisted, pale thing with claws. She thought of the Voice, and her fear at the thought that this wicked man might one day enter the world of the living once more. *The statue must be destroyed,* Thalaniya had said.

And Thalaniya had died for it, at the hands of the shadows.

Shedara bit her tongue hard and tasted the iron tang of blood. She shook herself, throwing off the specter's allure. He writhed, knowing she would not do his bidding. His form swelled, growing taller than her—seven feet, eight, nine. The room grew painfully cold. She spat red on the floor.

"Go back now," she said thickly, past the swelling in her mouth. "Return to the darkness of stone."

Silence. The spirit glared at her from the depths of its hood. Then, with swift violence, the silver bonds that held it grew taut. Maladar screamed with rage.

"*I am awakened!*" he cried, his voice shrill, shaking the stones. "*I will not sleep again! My time will come, and you will suffer for denying me!*"

"Maybe," Shedara said. "But not today."

With a final push of willpower, she flung her arm out in a sweeping, dismissive gesture. The bonds pulled back at him, yanking him back toward the Hooded One. He fought, snarling, but the spell's power was too great for him to resist. With a final, wrathful howl, Maladar vanished into the statue once more.

Shedara sucked air into her lungs, then bowed her head and began to shake. How close had she come? What had she nearly done? Tears spilled down her cheeks. For several minutes, she did not move. Finally, wiping her eyes, she looked up.

And screamed.

The statue had changed.

The hood had fallen back to reveal the face beneath—a face no sculptor could ever carve—a horror that had haunted her nightmares, ever since she had first glimpsed Maladar in the pool. Its eyes and nose were staring sockets, its mouth lipless, and its upper teeth were bared above a jawless hole. Flesh ran like candle wax down from the hairless scalp to hang in glistening loops from the ruined cheeks. Here and there the flesh had bubbled away—particularly on the hairless scalp—to bare the smoothness of the skull beneath. Behind that ghastly visage, she felt a presence, and knew at once that what Maladar had said was no empty threat. He *was* awake, and watching her from within the stone. Watching and hating.

Cringing, she turned away, and cried out again.

The darkness behind her came alive, small shriveled forms breaking free of the gloom to surround her, push her down, and overwhelm her: the broken shadow-things that once had been kender, that had followed the statue's trail across the breadth of Hosk. Shedara's cries choked off into a strangled pitiful moan. She had failed, she realized as the world slipped away from her, spinning off into dark.

The shadows had found the Hooded One at last.

———※———

An old man, Forlo thought, staring at the stooped, sobbing figure who knelt on the stone before him. The Boyla's white hair had spilled free from his braid and strands were plastered to his scalp with sweat. He bled from numerous small wounds, though only a gouge in his cheek seemed very deep. He looked feeble and spent—Forlo felt a surge of pity for this wreck of a man and had to fight it back. This man was responsible for the ruins of Malton and Rudil, and for the deaths of many of his men—including Grath—and nearly his own. It was hard to reconcile that with what he saw before him, though.

His eyes rose to the young Uigan who stood nearby. A protector. The riders had a name for his role, but Forlo couldn't remember what it was. He looked tired too, and though he held a bloody saber in his hand Forlo knew he wasn't about to use it. Their eyes met, and all he saw in the youth's gaze was loss. The battle was over for him.

There had been magic in the air. He'd felt it. Now it was gone, and he wondered why. Had the Boyla's power simply run out? Had some ally abandoned him? Yes, that had to be it. The lines of betrayal were furrowed like canyons on the old man's face.

The ruler of the Uigan looked up. His eyes were wrathful, bloodshot pits—but a man's eyes now, not a tiger's.

Slowly he rose, his legs shaking a little. He was tall for a horseman, but still shorter than Forlo. He bared his teeth and spat, then turned to his young companion.

"*Tenach*," he said in his strange tongue. "*Shuk yani cha.*"

The youth paled, bit his lip. "*Ardang*—"

"*Yani shuk!*"

The Boyla held out an age-spotted hand, anger breaking his voice. The youth looked at Forlo, looked at his master, and bowed his head. Then, with resignation, he handed the old man his sword.

Forlo raised his blade, instinct taking over. It saved his life: no sooner did the Boyla have the saber in his hand than he leaped forward, shouting a fierce warcry while shoving the tip of the blade at Forlo's face. Even on his guard, Forlo barely turned the weapon aside, swiping with his own blade to knock it wide. The *shuk* scraped the tower's battlements as the Boyla leaped back down the steps. He was naked, but he did not care. Forlo launched three rapid swings—a high cut, a low thrust, and a feint to the man's shoulder that turned toward his hip. The old man blocked them all with ease, his lip curling. The song of steel on steel echoed across the canyon, where the clash between horde and cohort was dying.

There was no point to the fight, no real victory the Boyla could gain. Even if he killed Forlo, he wouldn't survive much longer in lands overrun with his foes. But the Boyla wanted revenge, and he came on shrieking. He was strong and quick—too much so, for one who looked so ancient. Forlo caught his first strike with his shield, but the follow-through was blindingly quick, and his parry came clumsily. The slash was stomach-high, and Forlo deflected it, partly. The saber found a chink between his armor and cut his shoulder—not deep, but painful. Yelling, Forlo pounded the man with his shield, sent him staggering back again. The Boyla lost his balance, dropping to one knee but coming back up again.

Warm blood ran down Forlo's arm. The Boyla grinned when he saw it, and hurled himself forward.

Forlo's sword was already moving to meet him, and the old man had to duck and twist to dodge the blow. He spun as he did so, his foot coming around in a wheeling kick that struck Forlo in the knee. More pain exploded, and Forlo dropped onto the stairs with a crash of mail. He struggled to rise, but the Boyla was on him, his saber pressing toward Forlo's throat.

Khot, he was strong! He bore down with a madman's might, barking curses in his language, and spittle flecking his lips. Forlo couldn't do anything with his left arm, weighted by his shield and pinned by the Boyla's knee. With his right he let go of his sword and got his arm up to block the *shuk*—the blade's edge rasped against his metal vambraces. Forlo kicked and shoved, trying to throw the old man off him.

The Boyla's face bore down, close to his, his teeth bared to bite. His breath reeked of blood. The wild fury in his eyes was terrifying. Looking into them Forlo knew the man wouldn't hesitate. Those teeth would clamp down on his face, grind through flesh and gristle, and gnaw all the way down to his skull if he got the chance. With a grunt, he thrust his own head forward, felt the brow of his helm pound into the Boyla's nose and heard bone snap, followed by a howling.

There was blood everywhere. The old man fell back, clawing his face and yelling. Forlo heaved himself back to his feet, grabbed his sword, then came on as hard and fast as he could.

Even then, with his broken nose smeared across his left cheek, the Boyla was ready for him. He moved like a dancer, spinning, dodging, leaping forward, and drawing back. Blade caught blade again and again. In all his years at war, Forlo had never faced someone so skilled. Not even Duke Rekhaz could handle a sword as well.

The *shuk* won past his defenses again: another grazing

blow, this time across his thigh. It slowed him and made his footing less sure. To his left the central shaft of the ruined tower yawned: one bad step that way, and it would be over. He leaned the other direction instinctively, just as the Boyla's foot came around again and struck him in the side.

His armor saved his ribs from breaking, and probably hurt the old man worse than the kick had hurt him, but it still knocked the wind from Forlo's lungs and sent him staggering. The old man hurled himself forward again, but this time Forlo was ready, turning to swipe the rim of his shield in a whistling arc. It struck the Boyla's sword arm and again there was the snap of bone—louder this time, a nauseating sound Forlo knew well from the battlefield. The saber clattered down on the stairs and the Boyla screamed, clutching an arm that hung limp and useless above the elbow. A jagged white spur of bone poked through the flesh, bringing blood with it in pulsing bursts.

Forlo shoved off the wall and got his balance back. Time to end this, he thought, bringing his sword down.

The old man twisted aside from the killing blow, grabbed the fallen saber with his left hand and came up again. His broken arm flapped horribly, blood bathing it from elbow to wrist. He swung the blade around nimbly, though, and Forlo had to jerk his head back to avoid a mouthful of steel. Pain razored across his lower lip, splitting it open. He spat blood.

He glared at the Boyla: crippled, disfigured, and unclothed—but somehow still alive and still intent on this last kill. The old man snarled something unintelligible in a mocking tone. He swung the saber in long, swooping arcs, faster with each loop, until it became a gray blur around him. Forlo stopped trying to track the blade, focusing on the old man's eyes instead. Death hung in the air, filling the space between them.

He raised his sword. "Come on, then," he said.

The old man charged. They slammed into each other.

Steel pierced flesh. When they parted, Forlo's sword was no longer in his hand.

He'd left it in the Boyla's belly.

The old man sank to his knees, staring at the weapon lodged in his flesh, halfway to the quillons. Dark blood poured from the wound—a vein severed. It was a killing blow. He opened his mouth to speak, but more blood came out that way, too, so he smiled instead, ghastly. Forlo turned away, unable to look at the mad delight on that ruined face, and stumbled up the steps.

It was only when he heard running feet behind him that he realized his mistake, and cold horror washed over him. He'd forgotten about the other rider.

Hult watched his master fall, the tip of their enemy's sword sticking out the small of his back. Dark blood ran out of the wound, promising death. He grieved, and yet also felt a certain relief. Chovuk would not have to live long with the shame of his defeat.

He hurried to his master's side, knelt, and eased him down onto his side. The aged face was white and his eyes were cloudy with pain. He tried to speak, but couldn't. There would be no last words for Chovuk Boyla, no repentance for his misdeeds.

Somehow, he still held the *shuk*. Now he glanced at it and raised it feebly. Hult obeyed. He nearly had to break his master's fingers to pry the blade loose. When he did, Chovuk relaxed and tilted his head back to bare his throat.

There were three duties left to a *tenach* when his master lay dying, three lives he must take. His master's. The killer's. His own.

Hult laid the saber against Chovuk's throat. He saw tears in his master's eyes: it should not have ended this way. No one could have foreseen the horde smashed, the

Boyla's defeat, perhaps the end of the Uigan nation. The world was a cruel place, sometimes.

"Jijin welcome you," Hult said, and cut.

Chovuk thrashed once, then lay still.

Drenched in his master's blood, Hult rose and ran a few steps towards the way the southerner had gone. The man turned and stood facing him, his eyes on the saber in Hult's hand. He had no sword of his own; it was still in Chovuk's body. He shrugged off his shield and let it fall with a clang onto the flagstones. An unarmed opponent: it would be a quick kill, easy to end this one, then put the *shuk* through his own heart. It was the way of things, it was what he was trained to do. *Tenachai* had been doing it for as long as the Uigan had been around.

Hult stared at the man who had slain his master. The man nodded, understanding. His eyes were full of grief. Hult raised the saber, catching the sunlight on its blade.

And flung it away.

Chapter 32

TIDERUN SHORE, THE IMPERIAL LEAGUE

The sword seemed to fly forever, flashing as it spun end over end. Forlo watched it go, over the edge of the tower, over the cliffside and into the space above the ravine. It dropped out of sight, down through the trees onto the rocks below. He heard it hit, the faint, musical clang.

They stood there facing each other, him and the young barbarian, with the Boyla's body sprawled on the steps. Forlo knew little of Uigan custom, but he knew what had just happened was not their way. The riders were hard people, vengeful, and merciless—and yet this young man, who could have cut him to pieces with little trouble, had spared him.

What now?

The man said something he didn't understand. He clapped his chest and repeated it. *"Ajan tu Hult chana. Chana Hult."*

Forlo stared, perplexed. Then it came to him: the man was telling him his name. He pointed. "Chana?"

The barbarian shook his head. *"Hult! Hult chana."*

"Hult," repeated Forlo. He touched his own breastplate. "Forlo."

"Furro."

He nodded—close enough. Tried smiling, but the Uigan didn't mimic him, so he gave up. Again, he wondered what to do, and again the man answered for him. Nodding his head, Hult turned and walked down the stairs alone. Forlo watched him go, then descended to where the Boyla lay. His sword was still there, the wound bloodless around it. The flesh had sunk and shriveled—magic, it had to be. It had mostly fled him when his tiger-shape had failed, and the rest had gone when he died.

Forlo stared at the body. It would be burned that night. They would dispose of all the Uigan that way, in a heap. Forlo bent down, took the hilt of his blade in hand, put a foot on the Boyla's shoulder and yanked the sword free. He wiped it clean on the hem of his cloak and slid it back in its sheath. He bent down, closed the dead man's eyes, and went down the stairs.

The young barbarian was waiting at the bottom. Again, as he had after the duel, Forlo was afraid he'd made a mistake. The Uigan had rid himself of his saber, but surely he still had a knife. He might have been poised to spring, to ambush him, and to cut his throat. But Hult had no weapon in hand. He stood calmly, watching, his face blank.

But not his eyes.

There was a world of pain in Hult's gaze. Sighing, Forlo turned to walk down to the ravine and to his men. He didn't have to look to see the boy was following.

The fighting was over by the time they got there. The Uigan were all dead, except for a few who had managed to flee into the woods. The cohort's surviving commander, a gray haired soldier named Culos, shouted for his men to spread out into the wild, to hunt down the barbarians before they caused more trouble. Elsewhere, the soldiers stacked the dead upon dry wood, hungry for the torch.

There would be a good blaze that night. Their own they laid on their shields, to carry away. Only the defeated were burned on the battlefield.

Of the eight hundred and fifty-six men who had stood against the horde that morning, five hundred and fourteen lay dead. Another hundred and twenty-two were wounded; perhaps half of them would die before they found help. Grath lay in a place of honor among the corpses, his torn and ravaged form obscured by a cloak. He held his greataxe, laid upon his breast. The men joked that the promise of another fight might be enough to bring him back to life. Forlo knew better, and knelt at his friend's side for a long time, speaking gently, words no one else could hear. Or should. Then he rose and walked on, among the heroic dead.

There would be songs of that day, about the men who had fallen. They would be triumphant ballads on the near side of the Run. On the other, dirges. That was war.

The young barbarian following him received either suspicious or baleful glances from the soldiers. Forlo waved away their concern.

When he followed Forlo down from the tower, Hult was almost certain he was walking to his death. The soldiers wanted revenge, and he didn't fault them for it. They had all lost comrades, and nearly their own lives, because of his people and his master. A few spat while others made lewd gestures. Discipline kept their swords sheathed.

The Uigan would have killed him on the spot, would have cut off his hands, his feet, and other parts, and would have ridden their horses over his mutilated body, as they had done to Hoch and Sugai. They would have left what remained for the jackals and skyfishers.

He expected a victory speech from Forlo, some sort of rallying call. But the man who had killed his master said nothing to the soldiers—all of them human, only the one dead minotaur Chovuk had killed. The man's shoulders shook as he surveyed the battle-leavings and waded through mud and blood down to the edge of the water. The deluge had receded, back down the slope. The Run was half-empty again, the water dropping anew. Soon it would be dry once more, the Lost Road exposed again.

Hult kept several paces away from Forlo, wondering why he was following the enemy commander. Chovuk was awaiting him, in Jijin's halls. Death was all that remained for him—and yet, deep down, he didn't want to die. Some part of him wanted to keep living, perhaps to make amends. Perhaps to kill this man later. He truly didn't know.

At the water's edge, Forlo turned and met his gaze. He raised a hand to gesture across the water and said something. Hult didn't know the words, but he understood somehow, and it made his breath falter. The man was offering to let him go. If he wanted, once the waters ran out he could walk back across, to the steppes and prairies. Home. By winter, he would be back among his people, camped at Undermouth beneath the Hill of Lost Voices. He could almost hear the wind in the grasses.

But Hult shook his head. That part of his life was over. He would never find peace on the plains now.

They stood together at the edge of the dwindling sea, the sun westering above. Then Forlo glanced to his right, narrowed his eyes, and walked over to pick something up. He turned and held it out to Hult.

His *shuk*.

Hult hesitated, his eyes locking with Forlo's. The strangeness of the moment unnerved him. Warily he came forward, reached out, and took the saber's hilt in his hand. Forlo smiled, then turned and started back up the slope again. Hult watched him go. Then, sheathing his blade, he followed.

Hult could have run. The men of the cohort left him alone, busy as they were attending to the dead. Forlo paid him only enough heed to make sure he wasn't coming at him with steel bared. Yet he remained, and this said something to Forlo. There was an honor to this Hult that he couldn't help but admire. Killing the Boyla had linked their lives.

Which left the question: what to do with him? Forlo couldn't exactly ride into Kristophan accompanied by a warrior of the enemy. Now wasn't the time to decide, though. It was better to finish things at Coldhope first, before worrying about such matters. There were more immediate considerations.

Essana, for one.

Iver had the blue banner. Even now, he was galloping to the keep like half the Abyss was chasing him. He had much of a day's head start, and there was no way to make that up. Forlo would have to go to Coldhope first, then find Shedara's trail and chase the elf down. Best to get started.

Culos wasn't Grath, but he was a capable commander and deserved some recognition for leading the final victorious push against the Uigan, so Forlo put him in charge of cleaning up after the battle. The cohort would hunt down the last of the horsemen, hold the necessary funerals, and head east in two days. By that time Forlo hoped to have caught up with Shedara and his wife. When he returned with them, the soldiers would be rested and ready to rejoin the rest of the Sixth. He and Culos shared a laugh at the thought of Rekhaz's surprise to see them alive. Then, his wounds bound, his wineflask and food-pouch full, he took the reins of a fresh horse and led it up out of the ravine.

Hult came after. Of course.

Forlo looked back at the young Uigan, walking behind him. He would run all the way to Coldhope, if it came to it—would follow his trail even after Forlo had well outstripped the lad. He thought of that and shrugged.

"Well," he told Hult, knowing full well the young man couldn't understand a word, "you'd better get mounted up, I suppose."

There were a number of Uigan horses left alive: marvelous, proud beasts that would fetch a good price at market. The soldiers were loath to give up their spoils, but acquiesced when Forlo insisted. Hult picked a fine chestnut stallion with black fetlocks and a speckled muzzle. It was ornery in the soldiers' care, but the barbarian calmed it with a word, and it became as tame as a plough-horse when he climbed into the saddle. He gathered the reins in one hand, laid the other on the hilt of his saber, and gave Forlo a firm nod.

They rode, the dusk deepening behind them.

It was two days from the ravine to Coldhope. Forlo hoped to make it in a day and a half—about what Iver could manage. He watched for signs of the young guardsman's passage as he and Hult galloped along the road, through forest and over hills, slowing only to ford shallow, rocky streams along the way. Iver's trail was clear, the ground freshly trampled: a blind ogre could have followed it.

Hult said nothing the whole time, lost in his own thoughts. The Uigan had no idea where they were going, or why—how could he?—but he didn't seem curious, either. Born to follow, Forlo thought, studying his blank face askance. If he grieved for his former master, he showed no sign. If he grew weary from fighting and riding with no pause to rest... well, perhaps he could sleep in the saddle. The Uigan were rumored to do that.

Forlo's thoughts kept straying ahead, across the miles, to the castle clinging to its crag above the Run. He thought of Essana, standing on the battlements, waiting for some sign of what had become of her husband. He thought of Shedara, abducting his wife when the blue banner appeared. By the second sunset after the battle they would be moving, on toward the uplands. They would think him dead. It would tear Essana in two, though they both had been certain when they parted that they would never meet again in this world. He wept to think of her mourning him, then cheered himself with thoughts of the joy in her face when he found her again.

The night moved on and the leagues passed with it. He ran a hand over his eyes, burning and heavy-lidded. It had been long since he'd slept. Hult remained passive and untroubled. The moons rose, drawing the tides back high and hard. By the time Lunis and Solis hung fat overhead, he knew Iver must have reached Coldhope. It would lay dark and quiet when Forlo and Hult got there. Abandoned.

Then he crested a ridge and hauled on his reins to bring his mount to a halt. The horse whinnied and reared, nearly throwing him. Alongside, Hult stopped his steed with ease, and together they sat atop the rise, looking down into a hollow below, where reeds crowded the banks of a shallow creek. There was something down there among the cattails.

Even in double moonlight, it was hard to make out what it was. It seemed as if the darkness itself had thickened, gathering into pools beside the brook. Amid the blackness, something lay upon the ground—no, *two* somethings. Forlo squinted, but couldn't see what they were.

A wave of cold washed over him. Beside him, Hult stiffened, the color draining from his face. Reaching across his body, he drew his *shuk*. The blade made no sound as it cleared its scabbard. Shivering, Forlo did the same, his sword gleaming in the moons' light. It felt heavy in his hand. Gods, he was tired!

The movement was enough. Below, the shadow-pools shifted, held still for a long, breathless moment—then seemed to dissolve, flowing away to meld with the night. As they did, the shapes on the ground became clear, and Forlo caught his breath, nearly choking at what he saw there.

They had been a horse and a man, once, but only the size gave them away. Of the bodies, little remained but shreds of flesh, drained bloodless gray. And lying close by, in a forgotten heap not far away, were the ragged remains of a banner. It was impossible to tell colors in the silver-red glow, but Forlo knew the cloth was blue.

He shivered again.

Hult jumped down from his horse, as nimble as a man newly rested. He glanced around, his sword ready. Watching him, Forlo had a thought: *he knows what has happened here. He knows what those shadows were. And I don't know his tongue to ask!*

He dismounted as well, calming his nervous horse with a word and a touch. The air felt bitter cold. His breath frosted before him, and he knew it wasn't just fear. Something was there. He glanced around, looking for some sign of the things that had murdered poor Iver. There was nothing, though—only the dark, swaying forms of trees, blocking out the stars.

Hult muttered something in his language and kissed the knuckles of his left hand. An invocation to his people's gods, probably. Standing in the darkness, waiting for something to kill him, Forlo wished he believed in any god enough to pray for his life.

The night came alive.

It was so swift, he barely had time to react. Only two paces to his right, the darkness thickened, coalescing into something with the shape of a very short man. The black form slid toward him without a sound and struck his sword arm, latching on with what felt like shards of jagged ice. He yelled and tried to shake it off, but it held him fast. His arm went numb, as if it had frozen on the spot. His fingers locked around the hilt of his sword, as stiff as if they were carven rock. Acting on instinct, he balled his left hand into a fist and tried to punch the thing.

His swing found nothing; it was like fighting smoke. His fist lost all sensation as it passed through the shadow, then felt as if a thousand pins were sticking it as the feeling returned.

The shadow shook him, and he felt flesh tear—but no pain. He was too numb for that. Its weight—*how could it have weight when there was nothing there?*—bore him down and forced him to his knees, then let go. The darkness gathered before his face. He knew that when it struck again its cold would flow down his throat, find his heart, and kill him. Clutching his injured arm, he searched around for some way to stop it.

A curved blade came down and cut through the shadow's midst. There was a distant wail, as of something trapped deep beneath the earth, and the darkness ripped apart, turning to twisting wisps. Then, nothing: it was gone. Hult stood in its place, pale and grim, his *shuk*'s blade rimed with frost. He reached out and offered his hand to help Forlo rise.

The other shadow hit Hult from behind, and he screamed as its dark talons sank deep around his calves. It yanked him back, and the violence of it made him drop his saber. Forlo watched the darkness drag the barbarian toward the dark line of the woods. Hult grabbed hold of a pale trunk and held on as his attacker pulled and pulled, struggling to haul him away. Forlo understood, just as he'd known when he faced his own death a moment ago, that if Hult's grip loosened, if the shadows got him into the trees, he would be lost.

Run, some part of his mind begged. He was your enemy two days ago and you owe him nothing. Only Essana matters—leave him and go.

Hult did not cry out. Veins stood out in his neck as he strove against the shadows. The tree began to bend and to crack. Forlo ran to him.

He nearly died for it. His arm was still tingling, and his sword felt as though it were made of lead. His first feeble swing missed the shadow entirely—came closer, in fact, to hitting Hult. The young barbarian swore in Uigan and jabbered something else.

"I know, I know," Forlo said, recovering his balance from the wide slash. He drew the blade back, held it poised, then thrust hard, right at the heart of the shadow.

Again the scream, the howl of a damned soul. Again, the shadows tore apart. Hult fell to the ground, his legs pierced and gouged, and he lay still, groaning. After a moment he looked up. Forlo nodded, offering his hand—as the Uigan had done, just before the shadows attacked him. Hult took it and struggled back to his feet. Together, they turned and saw the third shadow.

It had come up, silent as death, and killed both their horses while they weren't looking. It hovered over the animals' bodies—pale and torn, but no blood to be seen—glaring at them. Its face was a horrid visage, the merry grin of a kender turned wasted, gray, and terrible. Its eyes were pools of lightless black and its teeth were long, cruel needles. The two men exchanged glances, then strode forward, swords brandished. The shadow-kender leaped—and perished on their blades, ripping away to nothing with a despairing groan.

Hult went over to the horses and paused a moment, his lips moving in silent prayer. Then he bent down and grabbed their supply pouches from the saddles. He threw one to Forlo and kept the other. They looked at each other again. They had saved each other's lives now. Whatever strange bond had formed between them had deepened.

There wasn't much left of Iver, and no more story for his body to tell. The shadows had killed him, then paused to feed on his body, or something. He'd never made it to Coldhope—which meant Shedara had never seen the signal of defeat. She would still be there, and Essana too. That thought gladdened Forlo for a moment, before another hammered it down.

There must be more out there.

His heart pounding, he turned and started up the far side of the hollow, striding briskly on toward his home. Hult followed.

Chapter 33

COLDHOPE HOLDING, THE IMPERIAL LEAGUE

Hult wanted to tell Forlo, wanted to explain the danger. The shadows they'd killed by the dead soldier—he tried not to think of what the creatures had done to the man, or to their horses—they were kindred to the cloaked figure who had taken control of his master. Like goblins were to men, maybe. There was dark power at work, and he couldn't help but wonder that the creatures were there, so close to where the Uigan horde had fought the imperial soldiers. It seemed too great a coincidence.

A thought began to form in his mind.

He left it alone and concentrated on keeping up. Forlo was moving very fast, keeping a remarkable speed for a man in mail—much less one as weary as he must be. Hult was barely able to keep pace, and he was clad in leather, not steel. But then, Forlo had more at stake. Hult had long since guessed where they were bound. No one moved with such urgency or such wildness in his eyes unless he were heading home.

Neither of them sheathed their swords. It didn't seem wise. More shadow-things lay ahead, surely—maybe even the cloaked man, the Teacher. He wished he knew how to speak the southern tongue, so he could tell Forlo these things. He wished he hadn't been so blind in following

Chovuk. As the elders said, though—if wishes were water, no man would die of thirst.

The woods thinned again and moonlight made rosy-gray patches where it leaked through the branches. He could smell the ocean. The salty tang was strong with the great tides at their full extent, covering over the bodies of his people—the ones they hadn't left to burn upon the shore.

On they ran, for miles, neither speaking, neither breaking stride. Up over hills and down into valleys, the moons westering above. Somewhere along the way, Hult forgot his fatigue and fell into that strange state beyond exhaustion, where a man believes he can run forever. The land flowed past, rocks, bushes, and trees. The briny smell grew stronger. He could hear the surf.

The thoughts in his head grew and took shape. If the shadows belonged to the cloaked man . . . if they had come to this place . . . had the Teacher only sent the horde as a feint? Had their charge across the Run been meant merely to draw the soldiers away, to distract them from some other target? Did it really matter if Chovuk and his tribesmen lived or died? The killing flood, the one that had come from this direction . . . ?

No. It was too much. Shaking with rage, Hult ran on.

Then they crested a ridge and Forlo stopped, staring. A castle lay before them: a dark, cliff-perching shape amid sea-mist that glowed silver in Solis's light. Surf exploded against rocks beyond it. There was no movement, no light, and no sound save the roaring waves. The place was silent as a tomb.

The darkness moved. Hult saw something, spun, and drove his *shuk* into its heart. The shadow-devil shrieked—that ungodly noise, the sound of damnation—and tore apart. He let his momentum carry him through its dissolving wisps, then turned slowly, watching around. He expected more, but there was nothing, no other danger nearby.

He heard a sound, the rattle of steel, and turned to look at Forlo. Their eyes met. Together they were ready.

All the times he'd come home. All the times he'd felt that fear, that moment when he was sure the place would be in ruins, or burned. All the times he'd been certain Essana was dead. He'd thought it foolish then and hoped it was foolish now.

Coldhope wasn't toppled. There had been no fire. As far as Forlo could tell, its walls were intact and as strong as when he'd left. But looking down on the keep from atop the ridge, he knew it was a dead place. The watchfires were out and there was no lamp-glow in the windows. The silence made his skin cold.

"Isn't it enough?" he railed, looking up at the wheeling stars, the gods' signs blazoned across the sky. "We won the battle and defeated the enemy. Isn't that enough for your bloodthirst?"

The heavens did not answer.

He understood, then. The Uigan had been a part of it. They had drawn him away, pulled away all the good warriors and left Coldhope vulnerable. The shadows had come and had met no resistance. Gods. Had the flood been part of the grand scheme, too? Had Shedara, willingly or no?

He wished again that he knew the Uigan tongue. He had questions upon questions, and only Hult to answer them. Half of him just wanted to run the barbarian through and be done with it, to satisfy himself with petty revenge. But common sense stayed his hand. There would be time for vengeance later, if needed. For now, the young Uigan seemed a useful extra sword.

More shadows sprang at them, swarming out of the dark. Forlo twisted around and leaped at them recklessly, leading with his blade. It worked well enough, cutting two of the creatures to ribbons and giving the others pause.

Hult moved in alongside, his *shuk* weaving through the air. Hopeless, distant voices cried out as the two of them cut through the living night.

Then it was over, the slain shadows no more tangible than smoke, fading in the air. There were some left, but they drew back, melting into the blackness once more. The short, stubbly hairs on Forlo's scalp stood erect as he wondered how many more lurked out there. He leaned on his sword, breathing hard, fear gnawing his heart. He looked down at Coldhope, for once befitting its name. In his heart, he knew it was his home no more.

And Essana?

That was the question. Had the elf escaped with her? Had they taken the Hooded One? Blue banner or no blue banner, he knew Shedara would have had the wits to flee if it seemed the keep might be overwhelmed. But had she had time?

There was only one way to know. So, trying to swallow the fear that clogged his throat, Forlo set out down the road toward the keep. Home from battle, for the last time.

So quiet. So still.

The two guards he'd left lay at their posts, torn open and drained bloodless. The one who still had eyes—the crows had been busy with the other—stared in glassy horror, or total shock. The eyeless man had drawn steel and died with it in hand; his partner had not. The shadows had struck by surprise and killed them swiftly. Perhaps Coldhope's defenders had slain some of their enemy; perhaps not. There was no way to tell, for the shadows left no corpses.

Spray rose from the bursting surf, beyond the northern wall. The waves were like voices, speaking words Forlo couldn't recognize. His own blood, pounding in his ears, almost drowned them out. Hult glanced around, wary, saber ready as they stood over the bodies. Forlo knew the men's names. Davin and Ramal. Both had been family men and had stayed behind to guard the keep because of it.

The doors of the manor stood slightly ajar and the crack between them was dark. No light burned within, so he found a torch that had fallen in the fighting. It was still good; he struck sword against stone, made a spark, and got it lit. When the flame was bright enough to see by, he climbed the steps, his heart hammering. It was very dark inside: all the lanterns were out. He nudged the doors open, making room, and went in. Hult followed, always two steps behind him, blade ready.

He almost stepped on Voss, who was sprawled just inside the house, facedown, his hand reaching toward the doors. Whatever killed him had ripped his back open—it looked like claw marks, running deep enough to crack ribs and cleave his heart in two. The master of Coldhope's servants had perished trying to shut the doors. Forlo's eyes darted back and forth, across the great hall. The windows were dim, letting only pale, milky light through. The whole building was riddled with welling pools of blackness.

Starlight, he thought. He did not call. *Be gone, my love. Tell me you had the sense to flee this. . . .*

They went from room to room, covering the lowest floor of the keep first. Bodies were everywhere: servants killed as they worked, or tried to flee. Forlo saw it vividly in his mind: the darkness roiling through his home, utterly silent, murdering without mercy, draining the blood from its victims. Hult was very pale beside him, his lips moving, invoking his people's gods. Death on the battlefield or in a raid was one thing, an expected sight. This was entirely different. This was slaughter.

Still no Essana. He went back to the main hall, to the curving stair that led to the upper floors. He paused and glanced sideways at the cellar door. It stood open, yawning blackness beyond. The sight made him shiver, and for a moment he thought of going in—but just then he heard something from above: a faint clank and what sounded like a muffled curse. A woman's voice.

He looked at Hult. The young barbarian was staring up the steps, like a hound that had just found a scent. He'd heard it too.

"Star—" he began to call. His voice caught in his throat, and he coughed to clear it. "Essana? Are you there?"

For a moment, no answer. Then, from above, a cry.

"Forlo?"

It wasn't his wife. It was the elf.

He ran up the steps, two at a time, Hult scrambling beside him. His throat was tight, his brow cold with sweat. There was light up here—orange glimmered, beneath the door of the main bedchamber. He ran at it and kicked it open. The latch splintered and the frame cracked, leaving the door hanging from one hinge as he stormed inside.

Shedara stood there, back flat against the wall, a dagger in each hand. Her clothing was torn, and there were bloodless scratches on her face, legs, and arms. Dark circles stood out beneath her eyes. Candles burned around her, half a circle of them, two paces wide. They had melted down to stubs, some guttering, some out, a few still flickering. One had fallen over—the clank of the stick had been the sound he'd heard from below.

Shadows filled the room, too: half a dozen of them at the edge of the light, held back as though by solid stone. They reacted at once to the crash of the door, twisting sinuously to face Forlo and Hult. Swords went to work. Voices screamed. Behind the fell creatures, Shedara leaped forward, plunging her knives into one of the fiends from behind. It shrieked and unraveled. So did two others, cut in half by Forlo's and Hult's blades. The last three moved to take their place.

A talon of darkness got past Forlo's armor and gouged his wrist. The wound burned like ice, with no warmth of blood after. He bit his tongue to keep from crying out and lashed back with his blade. He saw it swipe through the shadow. The shadow screamed. Hult destroyed another a heartbeat later, then leaped at the last. It twisted away from his flashing *shuk*—and right onto the waiting tips of Shedara's knives.

The doomed wailing faded away; the shadows melted to nothing. Forlo dropped his sword and slumped against the wall, clutching his arm. He looked around the room. It was destroyed, everything smashed or torn apart. The shadows had been furious, waiting for the candles to go out, for the elf's wall of light to crumble.

Shedara stumbled to the ravaged bed and sat down on it, head bowed. Hult stared at her, confused.

"What happened?" Forlo asked.

The elf bowed her head, sighing as if every woe in the world was on her shoulders. "I cast the spell that caused the flood," she said. "I invoked the Hooded One to do it. I thought I was clever . . . but it was what they'd been waiting for, the shadows. They took the statue, Forlo . . . it's gone. And now *he's* awake."

Forlo put a hand to his brow and shook his head. Too much. He just wanted to sleep. Hult looked from one to the other, not understanding.

"We have to get it back," Shedara said.

He nodded, looking up at her, all his fear and dread plain on his face.

She looked away. "They took her too."

Forlo's knees gave out. He slid down the wall and hit the floor hard. Hult took a step toward him and Forlo held up a hand. He sat there with his eyes burning and his face in his hands. "Where?" he asked after a time.

"I don't know," she said. "There was a dragon . . . a black dragon. I tried to get to Essana . . . but there were so many. By the time I fought my way up, it was too late. I saw it fly away with her. Barreth, you must believe me."

"I do," he said. It hit him, then—he knew what else

they'd taken. She still carried their child, their unborn son.

Hult went to the window and looked out. A moment later he came back, holding something in his hands. It was a scale, huge and lustrous black, like a platter of obsidian. He turned it over in his hands.

Forlo felt like someone had driven a spear through him. He could barely breathe. "I have to get her back," he groaned.

"I know," Shedara said. "And worse yet, the statue. If Maladar gets free—"

With effort, Forlo pushed himself to his feet. He looked at the other two, feeling helpless. "So what do we do now?"

"Gods," Shedara said, and shook her head. "I don't know."

Epilogue

THE EMERALD SEA, NERON

Steam rose off the jungle, gleaming in the silver moon's light. Solis was waning, and the red moon was just a sliver. Clouds scudded across the sky. Beneath, treetops made a carpet that swayed in the warm night wind—an undulating ocean of leaves that teemed with life beneath. Strange birdcalls filled the air, and somewhere deeper in the wood a tylor shrieked. They all fell silent at the whoosh of wings and the serpentine hiss of the dragon diving down.

It was a huge wyrm, seventy feet from its horned head to the tip of its long, lashing tail. The night made it almost invisible, its scales shimmering black, a shadow across the stars. When the dragon, whose name was Whispershade, held still in a dark place, only its eyes could be seen, gleaming like embers. It swooped low over the treetops, it wingtips touching the highest branches on the downstroke, ripping leaves free to storm in its wake. It gave no call and made no sound other than that of its flight.

The beast was not alone. A lone figure, cloaked in black, sat upon Whispershade's spiny back. It had no saddle and did not grip to stay put. The figure seemed to stay where it was by will alone, even as its fearsome mount banked above the trees. Even its hood stayed in place, drawn low to hide its face.

The dragon carried two other things gripped in its claws.

In the left, it held a statue of black stone, depicting a man resplendent in ancient robes. A deep hood had fallen back to reveal a ruined, pitted face that was the stuff of nightmares. The sculpture throbbed with power and pulsed with the spirit trapped within.

In the right was a human woman. She was unconscious, scraped, and bruised from the long journey south. Her belly was swollen, great with child. She was very far from her home and from all she had known.

Ahead, dark shapes loomed out of the trees: three towering ziggurats of worn brown stone, webbed with vines and creepers that bloomed crimson in the moonlight. Atop the one in the center, the tallest of the three, stood several figures. Like the dragonrider, they were swathed in black cloth, concealing them among night's shadows. They watched the wyrm approach, utterly still, their cloaks flowing in the wind. A flurry of bats billowed up from the ruins and away, fleeing Whispershade's approach.

With a screech, the dragon pulled up and away from the trees. Its wings worked as it rose, then spread wide, guiding it down to the pyramid's top. Gently it set down its freight—first the statue, then the woman. Its rider leaped off its back, landed in a crouch, and rose to face its fellows. Then Whispershade pulled up, shrieked again, and wheeled away, over the trees to the distant caves that were its lair. The cloaked figures watched it go.

"You are late," said the leader of those who had been waiting. Its voice was a harsh rasp, the sound of a strangled man. "We expected you three days since."

The dragonrider nodded. "It was unavoidable. The lands of the League are covered with armies. They fight a civil war, even now. We had to fly around to keep them from seeing us."

"What matter if they had?" asked the other. "They could not have stopped you. The war is part of our design, or we would not have destroyed their capital."

The rider shrugged. "I thought it better to be safe. Anyway, we can afford to lose those days. No one knows where we are."

"But they will find out."

"Yes," the rider said. "They will. And they will follow. The elf has pursued the statue too long to stop now. And the man . . . he will want this one back."

The cloaked figures walked to where Essana of Coldhope lay, crumpled and shivering, upon the stone. They all looked down at her, gathered around, and nodded their heads.

"Good," said the leader. He looked up, his gaze turning toward the statue, and seemed for a moment to sniff the air. The scent of magic hung in the air like orchid attar. "The Hooded One has awoken, I see. As we hoped. And what of the horde?"

"Destroyed. The one led to the other."

The robed ones glanced at one another, murmuring in alarm. The leader raised a hand to stay them. "A pity, but it matters little," he said. "The Uigan were an asset, but far from our greatest. And they did what they were meant to do—they gave a reason for the elf to summon Maladar."

"Yes."

Far away, the dragon skirled. Hooded heads turned to stare in its direction. They watched it fly awhile, across the faces of the moons, then turned to one another again.

The leader nodded. "You have done well, brother. Now things have begun that cannot be undone. The Minotaur League is paralyzed by infighting. The Silvanaes are leaderless, and Thenol and the Tamire besides. The isles to the east we shall deal with at our leisure. Together, they might have stopped us. But that will not happen now."

"It is time," said the others. It was a plaintive sound, almost a sigh.

As one, they cast back their hoods. Their faces were like that of the statue, burned away, cut apart, and ruined. They stared at one another, hideous, barely more than skulls, bloodshot eyes gleaming like fire in their sockets. Marks of self-mutilation, of years of horrid discipline: these were the Faceless Brethren. Now their day was finally at hand.

"Yes," hissed the leader. "It is time. But the road ahead is yet long, and we have much to do. Come, my brothers. The great one belongs to us at last. Let us prepare the way for his return."

As one, the figures bowed. Several went to lift the statue and two more hoisted Essana. Together, they strode across the ruined rooftop and down the stairs into the moist, waiting dark of the jungle below.

GLOSSARY

Geographic terms and place names:

Armach-nesti: A small elven kingdom, home to the Silvanaes elves.

Aurim: A vast empire that once covered much of Taladas, smashed in the First Destruction.

The Dreaming Green: A swath of forest north of the Tamire, home to the merkitsa elves.

Hitehkel: A sea of magma and fire at the center of Taladas, where Aurim stood before the Destruction.

Hosk: The western half of Taladas, divided by the Tiderun into southern and northern parts.

Ilquars: A mountain range running down the middle of Northern Hosk. Divided into northern (Uesi) and southern (Burya) halves.

The Imperial League: An empire of minotaurs and humans that covers much of Southern Hosk. Also called the League.

Marak: Several valleys in the central Steamwalls, home to clans of kender.

Neron: A little-known jungle land in the southeast of Taladas.

Panak: A frozen wasteland in the north of Taladas.

Rainward Isles: A piece of Aurim that survived the Destruction, now home to scattered refugees.

Steamwalls: A range of volcanic mountains in the east of Southern Hosk, forming a barrier against fumes from the burning lands.

Styrllia: Once a human kingdom in Southern Hosk, now a province in the League.

Taladas: A continent on the northern hemisphere of the world of Krynn.

The Tamire: A vast stretch of grasslands and steppes, covering much of Northern Hosk.

Thenol: A human realm in Southern Hosk, ruled by evil priests and necromancers.

Tiderun: A shallow strait running east-west across the middle of Hosk. Also called the Run.

Xagal: The tallest of the Ilquar mountains, home to the Wretched Ones.

People and Cultures:

Arshuk: A two-handed Uigan saber, used by very strong warriors.

Boyla: The prince of the Uigan, the highest lord of all the Tamire.

Fianawar: A hardy race of dwarves who dwell among the Steamwall mountains.

Heerikil: A Silvanaes term for non-elves.

Hosk'i imou merkitsa: A loose alliance of barbaric elven clans native to the Dreaming Green. Also simply known as the merkitsa.

Hulder: A mysterious elfin people once common in Hosk, now almost never seen.

Kazar: A nation of barbarians native to the Tamire. The enemies of the Uigan.

Khot: A minotaur obscenity, often used by soldiers.

Kumiss: A drink of fermented mare's milk popular among the Uigan.

Shivis: A boardgame popular in the Imperial League, also used by the minotaurs as a tactical tool.

Shuk: A curved Uigan saber, used effectively from horseback.

Silvanaes: An elven people of Southern Hosk, descended from the survivors of an ill-fated expedition from Ansalon.

Tegin: A Uigan clan-lord, answerable only to the Boyla.

Tenach: A warrior sworn to protect and serve a Uigan lord.

Uigan: A powerful people of horse-riding nomads, native to the Tamire.

Varun: A cleaving sword favored by the Kazar.

Voice of the Stars: Ruler of the Silvanaes elves.

Wretched Ones: Tribes of goblins dwelling in caves beneath the Uesi Ilquar.

Yarta: A root chewed by the Uigan to give energy.

Yemuna: Old Uigan women who tend the bodies of the dead Boylas. Also known as the Ghost-Widows.

Creatures:

Abaqua: A primitive race of ogres dwelling in the mountains east of the Tamire.

Ajagh: A rare sort of antelope, much prized by Uigan hunters.

Hatori: A giant reptile that swims in the sands of the Panak wastes.

Skyfisher: A large, ugly carrion bird, usually found among ruins and on battlefields.

Steppe-tiger: A huge, man-eating predator, native to the Tamire.

Tylor: A vicious, wingless dragon, prized by the rich as guards and pets.

Gods and Moons:

Astar: The god of the elves, a hunter and bowman. Called Astarin by the Silvanaes.

Hith: A death god, worshipped by the people of Thenol.

Jijin: The god of the Uigan, a warrior and protector.

Jolith: A human war-god, revered in the League.

Lunis: The red moon, called Lunitari in Ansalon.

Mislaxa: A healing goddess known across Taladas.

Nuvis: The black moon, called Nuitari in Ansalon.

Reorx: A god of the forge and the patron of dwarves and gnomes.

Sargas: The warrior god of the minotaurs, a patron of the League.

Sinar: A flame goddess worshipped by some humans in the League.

Solis: The silver moon, called Solinari in Ansalon.

History:

Dread Winter: The troubled times immediately prior to the Second Destruction, when much of Taladas was covered in snow and ice.

First Destruction: Taladan term for the Cataclysm, when the gods rained fire upon Krynn. Also called the *Great Destruction*.

Godless Night: The years after the Second Destruction, during which both gods and magic vanished from the face of Krynn.

Second Destruction: The Second Cataclysm, caused by the Chaos War.